HELL GATE

HELL GATE

Peter Tonkin

HEADLINE
FEATURE

First published in 1998
by HEADLINE BOOK PUBLISHING

A HEADLINE FEATURE hardback

10 9 8 7 6 5 4 3 2 1

British Library Cataloguing in Publication Data

Tonkin, Peter, 1950-
Hell gate
1. Thrillers
I. Title
823.9'14 [F]

ISBN 0-7472-1875-7

Typeset by
CBS, Felixstowe, Suffolk

Printed and bound in Great Britain by
Mackays of Chatham PLC, Chatham, Kent

HEADLINE BOOK PUBLISHING
A division of Hodder Headline PLC
338 Euston Road
London NW1 3BH

For
Cham, Guy and Mark.

And in memory of:

Charles Hodgson
1910–1997

Adventurer, explorer, treasure seeker,
hunter, broadcaster, adviser,
inspiration, friend.

Chapter One

The night was balmy, the moon full and high, the tide sweeping up towards the flood. A warm wind followed the tall seas in from a spangled horizon then continued up over the massive cliffs to whisper among the twisted trees and the soft heather, adding a salt tang to the heady richness of the heather flowers. The wind brought with it a ceaseless, muted thunder to drown the sleepy screaming of the nesting gulls below. High cloudlets meandered eastwards like black holes edged with silver among the stars. Away westward, on the low horizon, the clouds served to distinguish between blotted constellations and the occasional jewel-bright ship's navigation light, but none of them moved across the white face of the moon. All the wild country from Malin Head to Mullaghmore lay still and silver like the throne of ancient kings. It was high summer in Donegal and there had been no rain since St Swithin.

Eamonn O'Hanlon led Mary-Ann Hennessy over the springy heather, too wise to whisper sweet nothings as yet, content to let the Foreland and the Atlantic beyond work their wild magic. He wore his shirt open almost to the waist and its tails outside his jeans. She wore the lightest of summer frocks, a thing of half-transparent cotton with a tight bodice, a swirling skirt and a timeless gingham print. The desolate wilderness of sea-swept land hunched back like the flank of a wolfhound waiting to spring. Under the steady whisper of the wind which flirted with the hem of her skirt and wandered where his fingers wished to follow, the land seemed to be breathing.

The ruins of a castle stood stark atop their pinnacle of rock away to the right, separated from the coast by a cleft, seventy metres sheer and seven or more wide, at whose jagged foot the Atlantic itself served in the office of a moat. Basalt walls, as black as the cliffs themselves, sat lowering over the ocean, full of

1

breathtaking, brooding menace in the soft silver light. Dundark Castle was shut off to the world on this side, its windows blank and empty, its great doors fallen closed, its rotted drawbridge long ago tumbled into the void, but open to the Atlantic on the other, gaping, like a skull that has lost its face. Eerie, exciting.

Eamonn was from Ballymore, the village five miles back along the tiny track at whose near extremity his old Ford Sierra lay parked. Mary-Ann was from New York, a tourist come to sample the romance and to test the tales of her emigrant grandfather. During the last weeks she had travelled by bus and train up from Shannon, exploring the dreams of her childhood. But it was only now, and here, that some of the romance was coming to irresistible life.

In O'Reilley's, the Ballymore local, Eamonn had stood out in Mary-Ann's eyes because of his wild dark hair, green eyes and flashing teeth. She had stood out in his eyes from the half-dozen strangers there that night because of her soft red hair, her Brooklyn drawl and her air of available innocence. It hadn't really needed any blarney to tempt her out with him at all. She had handled the Irish and Italian Lotharios of the mean streets of her home city since childhood. She could take care of herself – even against a man who passed himself off as a junior officer in the Provisional IRA.

Silently under the awesome beauty of the place, Eamonn led Mary-Ann down to the Lovers' Chair, a fold of rock mattressed by a springy covering of heather, protected from prying eyes by a stunted but full-blossoming fuchsia bush. Here, when they sat, the whisper of the wind became less invasive, the rumble of the surf a little more muted but the vista of sea, cliff and castle more beautiful than ever. The ground beneath them seemed to throb to the steady rhythm of the surging tide, as though the wild, magical ocean had insinuated fingers into the black rock bones of the place. And, indeed, it had. As the lovers took their ease in each other's arms and paused to look across the slope they had just negotiated, the first plume of spray soared upward out of the heart of the rock, as though the west coast of Ireland had been transformed into a spouting whale. All around them, there stood chimneys in the rock tumbling to tunnel mouths at the tide line, anything up to two hundred metres in from the edge of the cliff. As the tide reached its flood, these blow holes all began to send up their cloudy, lacy fountains into the air in a timeless water show more wonderful than anything even Coney Island could offer, which he had arranged, especially for her.

With practised calculation, Eamonn had laid her so that she could see the full glory of the scene and he could roll over on top of her with ease. This allowed him to keep an eye on the cliffs and the castle, but put his back to the ocean. And this meant that he remained unaware of the boat which was currently detaching itself from the shadows away out to sea, silently untangling its jewelled running lights from the galaxies above. Eamonn was here as a lover, not a lookout, no matter what he had said in O'Reilley's bar. And, indeed, after the first warm embraces, he moved to action. His fingers slithered beneath the lacy cup of Mary-Ann's underwear and his left hand lay snugly across a warm swell of thigh no longer protected by a summer frock. And Mary-Ann's fingers, by no means passive themselves, were busy at the buckle of his belt.

The last thing she said before he rolled on top of her was, 'I hope you brought protection, buster . . .'

He had. But it was not protection enough.

The bullet took Eamonn under the left shoulder blade and exited through the middle of his chest, entering Mary-Ann's chest immediately between the breasts and exiting through her spine. Neither ever knew what hit them. They didn't feel a thing. They danced, as though in ecstasy, and lay still. The ground beneath them darkened and the darkness began to spread.

The wind whispered. The ocean surge thundered. The heather seemed to heave. The waves roared again and a cloud passed over the face of the moon. As it did so, a wall of spray exploded over the cliff top, making a pale curtain just substantial enough to outline a couple of figures wearing combat gear and camouflage paint as they detached themselves from the cover of a ridge. Both wore bulky belts and light bergens which could have contained arms, but neither was carrying an obvious weapon.

'Who did that?' one asked the other in flat, accentless English, yelling to be heard above the wind and the waves.

'I'll bet it was Pitman.'

'Jesus . . .'

'Look, Captain Dall, the kid said he was PIRA in the pub,'

the second figure countered defensively.

'That was to get off with the Yankee tart, Paul. There's no way he's a dicker. This is supposed to be an old cache. They wouldn't be guarding it now. And anyway—'

'I know. But you know the way they are over here. Sometimes the right hand doesn't know what the left is up to, for all their fucking blarney.'

Two more figures appeared, also in combat gear and dark berets. Neither carried obvious weaponry. One was tall and square, the other slighter. The first figures both rounded on their slight companion. 'For God's sake, Pitman. You've really made this messy!' snarled the captain.

'We have to be at the pick-up point ninety minutes after the top of the tide. Unobserved.' Pitman's voice was light, husky, unfazed by the hostility; the accent flat, nasal. Dutch or South African. 'And there's a lot to do in the meantime, Captain Dall.'

Automatically all four of them looked away beyond the castle to where the silent vessel was just distinguishable pitching in towards the land. As if on their signal, all her running lights went out.

'Right!' snapped Captain Dall. 'Let's go.'

The four figures ran down to the edge of the cliff where the ruins of the drawbridge entrance still stood as bulges beneath the overhanging vegetation. Here the captain and Pitman secured two lines and watched silently as their companions rappelled down the sheer cliff face, bouncing out cautiously as though they might strike their heads on the opposite wall of the deep cleft, and landing with care on the vertical wall as well, hoping not to disturb the razor-billed herring gulls which nested there.

About halfway down, on this side, was a ledge. Normally it was impossible to see and only someone after the gulls' eggs would ever have found it. Behind the full nests, the black basalt opened into a cavern. And here the local command of the Provisional IRA had secreted a large cache of arms and explosives. The two men pushed in past the stirring birds and, crouching in the black-walled confines, using infra-red torches and night-vision glasses, they swiftly made their selection. The chosen boxes were secured together and hauled up to the cliff edge. Pile after pile of boxes was swiftly pulled up and stacked beside the anchor points. After an hour, the cavern was all but

4

empty and the two men made their way back up the cliff. Their passage was complicated by the stabbing beaks and battering wings of the stirring birds. Then the four figures came and went between the ruined drawbridge and the cliff top a hundred yards distant, which overlooked a deep bay where the boat currently picking its way in through the narrows was due to anchor in thirty minutes. At last all four were able to collapse onto the heather beside their ill-gotten gains, gasping for breath, unmolested.

The instant the slight figure hit the ground beside him, the captain said, 'Not you, Pitman. You have a mess to clear up. I don't want any trace of them left near here and I don't want them causing trouble if they're found.'

'Sling them down one of these blow holes,' suggested one of the others.

'Not good enough. Even if you put them in the car and torched it . . . What did you use?'

Pitman held up a customised Smith and Weston nine millimetre automatic, a slim, skeletal weapon, its side open so that the contents of its magazine could be seen. It had been customised by Armament Systems and Procedures of Appleton, Wisconsin, USA. It was loaded with equally customised bullets designed to open into barbs in flight. 'Used the ASP,' she said flatly. 'It's loaded with Talons.'

'You used Black Talons on them?'

'One shot. One Talon.'

'No wonder it was so messy. All right. I want you to get them well away from here and I don't want any authorities asking questions about Special Forces weaponry. Talons are special kit, Pitman. Cover it all up. Here.' Dall reached down into a pile of the arms and pulled out a sawn-off shotgun. 'This should cover a multitude of sins. But well away from here. I don't want the Garda stirred up too soon.'

Pitman took the shotgun. 'Is this really necessary, Captain? I mean we're only trying to fool a hick Mick pathologist.'

The captain's silence said enough.

'Mind if I help?' asked Pitman's partner.

'You have an hour,' said Captain Dall. 'Then we're out of here and you're on your own.'

As the two figures picked their way across the heather, Dall turned to Aves. 'Look at this,' he said quietly. He bent and opened one of the wooden boxes, one whose identification codes had been incompletely scrubbed off its wooden side.

Inside the box there were heavy-duty, moulded composite containers, deep green in colour, a metre and a half long, maybe half a metre wide. Dall hefted one out onto the heather. 'Know what these are?' he asked apparently casually.

'I don't believe it,' said Aves.

Expertly, Dall turned the toggles round the sides until he could lift the whole lid free. 'You'd better believe it,' he said quietly.

Nestling in its protective padding there lay a Stinger anti-aircraft guided missile.

'This changes the whole game,' said Aves, looking nervously around. 'Maybe the kid was a dicker after all. I can't imagine the PIRA leaving kit like this lying around unprotected.'

'Maybe. Maybe not. But I was thinking further ahead than that. This changes things for us. We signed up to this for a price. If there are Stingers involved then I say the price doubles.'

'Is that wise, Captain? If you start screwing around now, the Boys are going to be pissed.'

'What do we care? We got the hardware. We got *Calcutta*. We can get *New England* to Great Egg as agreed and sit there armed to the teeth with Stingers until they stump up the extra. What can they do?'

'Buggered if I know, Captain, but they'll think of something. You know who we're dealing with here.'

'Screw them. They'll be helpless.'

'I don't think so, Captain. And I don't think Pitman and the others'll be too keen either.'

'Screw them all,' spat Captain Dall. 'What I say goes. We double the price and we don't tell the men. We keep this "need to know" until the payoff. What can they do? We hold all the aces, and every one of them's got a Stinger on it.'

Separating the bodies was difficult and messy. The single Black Talon round had opened in flight and the barbs that had sprung out from the body of the bullet had compounded the destruction to both thoraxes, especially the girl's. They heaved the flaccid corpses away to one side, then Pitman used the night glasses to look at the mess on the ground. The head of the bullet, squashed against the basalt, showed clearly. Pitman picked it up and pocketed it.

They carried the bodies to the boy's old Ford. The keys were still in the ignition so it was easy enough to open the boot and pile the pair of them in there. As they stood beside the vehicle, Pitman said, 'You don't have to do this, Sam.'

'Forget it. You driving?'

'Yup.'

'I'll take the shotgun then. Think we should change?'

'Not worth it. No time anyway.'

'Tell you what, though . . .' He pulled his balaclava down over his painted face. Pitman did the same. If the boy really was a player, two figures looking like this in his car would hardly raise an eyebrow among the locals.

They bounced down the pitted track until they gained a metalled road and sped eastwards through Inishowen. They followed the dull headlight beams up twisting mountain roadways with the widening ocean at their backs; then they hopped unhandily between the peaks of the watershed and down deserted byways in the still of the small hours until they had gained another cliff top, this one facing away from the Atlantic coast, and well away from Ballymore.

Here they pulled the corpses from the back of the old Ford and arranged them at the cliff top.

'Hands and feet?' asked Sam quietly.

'Take them off,' said Pitman.

A few minutes later the same flat tones added, 'Put them back in the Ford. But leave the heads. No dental work will survive this . . .' Over each bullet wound Pitman added a blast of shot which hurled the shredded bodies back over the cliff edge. For several hundred feet the battered bodies flailed and fell like a couple of broken dolls down into the wild white water.

'So far so good,' said Pitman as the pair of them climbed back into the old Ford.

Well within the allotted time they were back at the cliffs above Dundark. Sam joined Captain Dall and his right-hand man Paul Aves as they lowered the last of the boxes into the waiting boat below, while Pitman worked on the Ford, rolling it forward, lining it up, putting explosive and a timer into it, priming and preparing it.

7

Then the four figures gathered briefly at the cliff top, talked urgently and prepared to descend. They rappelled down onto the deck below and pulled their lines free. Then the four of them stood on the afterdeck and looked up at the cliff while the boat, crewed by personnel in camouflage kit and freighted with a cargo of illegal arms, motored out of the bay.

After twenty minutes, when the boat was well clear of the coast, Pitman said, 'Now!'

On the flat monosyllable, a distant spark of fire sprang into life and, trailing flame, it began to roll unerringly down the slope. Four pairs of eyes watched its progress with critical concentration. Just at the point where its carefully calculated progress led it down into the blood-soaked hollow of the Lovers' Chair, the Ford exploded into vivid flame, then it hurled itself on down and over the edge of the cliff.

The brightness of its demise spread like the glow of a shooting star across the wild water and illuminated the face of Angela van der Piet, known to the others as Pitman, as she pulled her mask off and ran her long strong fingers through her short golden hair.

Away on the other side of Inishowen, the combination of tidal inflow and outwash of the river swept the bodies of Pitman's victims across the funnel of Lough Foyle, out of the jurisdiction of the Garda, whom she so despised, and into the remit of the RUC whose pathologists are among the most experienced in the world at dealing with gunshot wounds.

Chapter Two

Richard Mariner's thoughts could hardly have been further from death and destruction – except that he could cheerfully have strangled the twins. Wild with excitement, they had been up since four. They were nearly ten now, but showing only variable signs of maturing. Richard loved them without limit or reserve, but this did not blind him to the social shortcomings which they seemed to reserve especially for Robin and himself. In his heart of hearts he suspected William and Mary were subconsciously getting their own back for the times in the last years when they had been dumped with long-suffering grandparents or friends, or shuffled off to boarding school while their errant parents got themselves into adventure and danger all over the world. Robin, for her part, was certain that this was the case.

But the early start, although unwelcome after only four hours' sleep, had at least allowed Richard to finalise their plans for the day. And it was a day which needed planning in the finest detail, for it was his father-in-law's wedding day and for all that someone else was best man, it was Richard who had assumed the best man's duties. And not just those onerous tasks either, for the bride and groom had requested that the reception be held on one of Richard's new super-cats, part of a small fleet preparing to enter the cross-Channel arena but not quite in commission yet.

So, apart from running a sizeable independent shipping company, and smoothing the way for the new cross-Channel venture, and arranging that the wedding be successfully mounted in the exclusive environs of St Clement's, Knightsbridge, that all the bridal party and the assorted international register of guests should arrive, be housed, be supported and guided thither at the required time, Richard was also in charge of getting them down to Dover and onto the super-cat. From Dover, at the better part of 80 knots – nearly 100 mph – they would cross to Calais, a matter of half an hour or so, depending on weather and shipping. Then they would, at an equivalent speed in kph, come back after a small ceremony ashore arranged, again by Richard, for the bride – for his prospective stepmother-in-law was French.

The happy couple, Madame Helen Dufour, Chief Executive of Heritage Mariner, and Sir William Heritage, Chairman of the Board, were, respectively, at the company flat above her office in the Heritage Mariner building on Leadenhall Street and at his usual suite at the Savoy. Sir William was sharing the suite with his oldest friend and best man Sir Justin Bulwer-Lytton, whither they had repaired after an exclusive dinner at the Savoy Grill which had been held instead of a stag night the previous evening. In younger days Bill and Bull would have been game for any sort of high jinks, but both were in their eighties now and much more aware of fleshly weakness than of spiritual strength.

Having overseen the return of several other guests to various suites and hotel rooms all over the West End, Richard had boarded his new Land Rover Freelander and driven home to Ashenden, the big old house overlooking the Channel partway between Beachy and Seaford Heads. He had not driven down alone, for one of the other guests at that exclusive little gathering was bunking down with him. This was Bob Stark, senior captain of the Heritage Mariner Shipping Company, lifelong friend to Richard and Robin and godfather to the twins.

One might have thought that two old friends would have whiled away the drive with commentary on Richard's new top-of-the-range off-roader or with memories. No so these two. They spent the unexpected quiet time in discussion of the future. Richard had sold a small shipping company centred in Hong Kong at a considerable profit less than a year ago and had added to the profit of the deal more than a million pounds sterling of treasure trove. This small fortune had financed the new super-cat venture. Heritage Mariner were all set to take the Channel by storm, and the super-cats were destined to sweep into the American market as well. Richard had asked Bob to put aside his tanker work for a while and train to command the fastest of the ships. But there was more to it than this, and here lay the nub of their discussion.

Richard had also put some of his company's new-found wealth into a new super-freighter, a jet-ship. The new craft, a 10,000-ton freighter called *New England*, was powered by the same propulsion units as the super-cats and so designed that it could rival their speed. As soon as he had finished his course on commanding the super-cats, Bob had started training to command the jet-ship, a course he had completed only days before flying east to attend his old friend and sometime boss's wedding.

Bob, resplendent in dress whites, was between William and Mary in the back of the Freelander as Richard piloted her northward again on the morning of the wedding day. The American, son of the recently retired senior senator for New England, scion of a family whose only rivals in Newport were the Kennedys, found the intensity of the puppy love he inspired in Mary almost as unnerving as William's unashamed hero-worship. With his cow's lick of blond hair forever falling into his dazzling eyes, his lean, straight nose and wide, generous mouth, Bob was so much the filmstar matinee idol that the children melted to supine adoration in the sunlight of his presence. The pair of them were too over-awed even to play I Spy.

An hour later, at ten thirty on the dot, they were pulling into the car park of the King's Head, across the road from the church, and the designated meeting place for the wedding guests.

'Right,' said Richard as they disembarked, taking charge with that calm decisiveness which was his trademark. 'Bob, you and Robin can sort things here. Got the money, darling? Guest list, Bob? Good. I'll just pop across and check that everything is in place in the church. Five minutes, no more.'

Within four minutes, he was back in the lounge bar of the pub, his bright eyes sweeping over the guests as though over stormy waters threatening his command. He glanced down at his trusty old steel Rolex.

Kick-off in half an hour.

He glanced up and his eyes met Robin's. They exchanged one of those achingly intimate, almost invisible smiles. God, she looked beautiful. Had he told her?

The phone in his pocket throbbed and he pulled it out, his face folding into an automatic frown. But it was only his father-in-law checking in. 'Be there in ten minutes, the driver says. All present and correct?'

'All AOK this end, Bill,' said Richard. 'Haven't heard from Helen yet. I'll give her a call now.'

'OK.'

Helen answered on the second ring. 'We're on the way,' she said, her husky voice made more mysterious by the little handset.

'Right, ladies and gentlemen,' began Richard but his voice came out as his famous quarterdeck bellow, loud enough to rattle the windows. He cleared his throat and tried again, more quietly.

Half an hour later, Bill and Bull were safely ensconced in the front pew with Robin, Bob and the twins immediately behind. Relatives filled in on Bill's side and friends in lieu of family on Helen's. For all it was a quiet affair – the formal union of a widower and a maiden lady who had been lovers for more than a decade – the little church was full enough, and the super-cat *Hero* would get a stylish christening. Richard checked the ushers one last time, had a word with the canon and made sure the photographer was on the ball. Then he called Dover and updated the captain, the purser and the chief steward on *Hero*.

'Here she comes,' whispered John Higgins the chief usher urgently, but Asha his wife hissed a negative just in time to stop Richard giving the signal. Late and more than a little flustered, Ann Cable the journalist, another old friend, rushed in and sat at the back. Richard crossed to her and leaned down.

'It wasn't the flight in from New York,' she said, her voice low, 'it was the traffic in from Heathrow.'

'Still, you're here now,' he soothed. 'Deep breath and—'

'Here she comes!' announced John. And this time there was no retraction as Richard straightened, caught the organist's eye and walked swiftly to his place as the Wedding March from *Lohengrin* boomed out.

If Sir Justin Bulwer-Lytton was a trifle unsteady on his feet three hours later, thought Richard, it was nothing to do with his advancing years or with the progress of the super-cat across the millpond Channel, for all she was just coming to full speed and moving forward at velocities undreamed of even five short years ago. The elderly best man could have told stories and to spare of wild days of war service in battleships long broken up, of Bill's early post-war days setting up a shipping line, of his own more secret days in intelligence and counter-terrorism. He could have told how their two worlds, never far apart, had overlapped more than once. But he chose not to. Instead, on the bright, shining, spanking new vessel, with the newly married couple at his side, Bull was looking to the future and keeping his observations short, for Calais was swiftly approaching.

Richard was beginning to relax at last. Captain Andrew Fawley was in charge of seeing them into Calais and handing them over to the specially prepared reception committee there. The French civil ceremony would take an hour at most – the hour they were enjoying now, in fact, given the time difference – then they would be off back to Dover. Home by teatime. It would take them longer to return to London than it would take them to get to Calais and back.

Really, this was a most extraordinary vessel, decided Richard. The big passenger area they were in at the moment was the central elevation between two lower areas that looked for all the world like the cabins of a couple of aeroplanes complete with high-backed, state of the art airline seats. He had seen all over her at every stage of her construction from the agreement to purchase over a year ago; had seen her being built, launched and tested. He knew her propulsion system almost as well as her engineers did, knew every inch of her sleek hull, knew every instrument on her flight deck of a navigation bridge. He had been on one of the courses with Bob Stark – as had Robin. Either one of them could have taken command had Captain Fawley been struck down.

'Excuse me, Captain Mariner,' said a young steward, leaning solicitously in over his shoulder.

'Yes?'

'Captain Fawley would like to see you, at once, please, sir. And Captain Stark . . .'

Richard and Bob walked onto the super-cat's bridge side by side. Captain Fawley was standing just behind the radio telephone, his square body outlined by the bright wide-screen curve of the windows, while the first officer sat at the helm. On either side the sea was speeding past in a breathtaking blur, like a speeded-up film. Calais was rushing at them as though this was the cockpit of a fighter coming in at sea level. The captain

13

was deep in conversation but the instant they entered he completed what he was saying and turned.

'It never rains but it pours,' he observed obscurely, as though talking to himself as he strode across the bridge towards Richard and Bob. 'Gentlemen,' he said, 'I am in receipt of two urgent radio signals. Both have come through by word of mouth and fax.'

'Trouble?' asked Bob sympathetically.

'Perhaps you can tell me – about one of them at least. You are requested to return to Boston at once. Captain Stevenson, it appears, is dead. So is Cohen. And they can't find Newbold.'

'Jesus . . .' Bob swung round to look at Richard. He knew some of these people too. Jet-Ship Inc. was such a small company at the moment – one hull and one small family with many friends who shared their hopes and dreams – it was almost like Heritage Shipping had been in the early days.

Richard was frowning, his face set like granite. 'The other message hardly makes any more sense,' Captain Fawley said. 'It's for Sir Justin. They've found two floaters in Lough Foyle. Man and a woman. No hands or feet. Shot with more than one gun, apparently. They want his thoughts so could he pop across to Lisburn ASAP.'

'Lisburn?' said Richard, the frown deepening.

'That's what they said.'

Richard tried to fathom who would send this much information to a senior if semi-retired intelligence officer with such detail, in clear language. They must want him very badly indeed, he thought. Unless they were playing dangerous games with the IRA.

Only such chilling speculation could have pulled his mind away from the horrific news from Boston.

'Bob, it sounds as though you'd better be ready to go straight out. I'll get the girls at Crewfinders to put you on the first flight west. I'll see if I can free enough time to come with you myself. Sounds bad.'

'Stevenson and Cohen dead . . .'

'And Newbold missing.'

It was suddenly as though the two radio messages, having arrived together, should have something to do with each other. That the bodies found floating in the cold dark waters off Ulster should have something important to do with death and disappearance in New England.

'I'd better get Bull sorted as well,' said Richard, reaching for his phone.

'And what in the name of God,' asked Captain Fawley, scrutinising the scrawl at the bottom of the fax, 'is a Black Talon?'

Chapter Three

At about the same time as Richard, Sir William and the rest were settling down to their stag night dinner at the Savoy Grill, Harry Newbold was bringing the jet-ship *New England* into port in Boston Harbour. Harry was not actually in command of the bridge – Captain Stevenson was out there and the harbour pilot was at his side – but the young computer officer's machines and programmes were in such complete control of every aspect of *New England*'s disposition and progress that there was no doubt in Harry's mind who was really in charge.

Harry's domain extended the old-fashioned chart area at the rear of the bridge into what in traditional ship's architecture would have been the captain's day room. Effectively, this mirrored the radio room on the starboard side of the wide, airy command bridge. In fact, the computer area did more than mirror the radio room. With its fax and modem facilities, E-mail capabilities, satellite connections and Worldwide Website, it usurped the old-fashioned radio equipment altogether. Which was one reason why Sparks hated Harry Newbold.

Radio Officer O'Reilley (Harry, calculatedly, pronounced it 'Oh Really') was not alone in his hatred of the computer officer. Chief Bligh and his engineers also found their expertise challenged by the apparently modest young officer's computers, which they did not trust or fully understand but which they felt they should control. But Harry had the power. Every aspect of the massive water jet and standard jet engines which thrust *New England* forward at such amazing speed was at least monitored by the equipment here, though each of the sixteen engines which made up the propulsion unit had its own computer control system which was under the engineers' purview.

The deck officers, led by First Officer Larry Cohen rather than the scholarly, hesitant, ineffective Captain Herbert

Stevenson, also had Harry on the top of their shit list and again it was largely because of the computers. The tall, slim, forthright young officer would have been a natural butt of their jokes and jibes anyway, but it was the computers that drove them to excess. And Harry could see why. Every observation and measurement, every decision or order that any of them made could be double-checked or double-guessed by this equipment. No matter what any of them was up to at any time, the computers were there, doing it better and quicker. It was as though there was a permanent time and motion man behind each one of them, and that man was Harry Newbold.

Even now, as Captain Stevenson and the Boston Harbour pilot guided *New England* into the North Channel past the Graves, cutting speed as they proceeded, a series of graphics on the screens in front of Harry monitored every aspect of what was going on. A three-dimensional schematic of *New England*'s hull showed all the power sources and stress points. Readings demonstrated that the captain's demand for slow ahead was being fulfilled by the closure of all the standard aero jets and all but two of the eight port and starboard water jets; 10 per cent power on these two water jets brought *New England*'s speed right down to that of a conventional freighter and made it possible for her to proceed safely through the busy harbour. Red lights on the bow and side sections showed the thrusters powering up, ready for the docking manoeuvre.

Beside this central screen, a schematic of the harbour itself, at water level and below, warned of all currents and potential hazards along their proposed route through the North Channel into the Main Channel and thence through the traffic to their designated berth on the Mystic River. The harbour screen was glowing in a range of colours denoting *New England*'s position and progress and the movement of all other traffic nearby. Above this, in white on an old-fashioned black screen, the current notices and directions from the Port Authority were displayed, so current that not even the Massachusetts Port Authority pilot, who had come aboard at the B Lightbuoy a few minutes earlier, was as perfectly up-to-date.

By dusk, *New England* was tied up at one of the empty petroleum berths on the north bank of the Mystic. She had turned quite a few heads on her way here through the harbour.

18

Tomorrow she was destined to move out of her obscure berth and welcome aboard a delegation of local businessmen, a party to be hosted nominally by the captain but actually by that indefatigable representative of the owners, *New England*'s creator, Professor Alan Miles. The professor was due to fly in tomorrow morning from New York. *New England* would take the party for a trip round Massachusetts Bay and drop them back here in twenty-four hours' time.

This was supposed to be the last of the 'glad hand' cruises. After it was finished, *New England* was due to return to Fall River where she had been built for a few final checks, then she would go back to Philadelphia, her home port, where facilities to dock and lade her would be completed soon. Here she would take aboard cargo and also the last of the glad hand visitors, an eye-catching array of celebrities geared to attract the maximum publicity for the elegant jet-ship as she sped across the Atlantic for the first time. Sixty hours after leaving Delaware Bay, she was due to pull into Southampton water. And on her return, she would pick up the blue Riband for the fastest Atlantic crossing ever.

After that, she would settle into her workaday routine, sailing between Philadelphia and Zeebrugge in Belgium, crossing in little more than fifty hours and turning round within the day. It was an enormously expensive undertaking and a very risky show for a company as small as Alan Miles's Jet-Ship Inc. But the Englishman had networked his way from Heriot Watt University in Scotland to the Massachusetts Institute of Technology by way of universities in Australia, Hong Kong and Singapore. He had made a lot of contacts, and all who could afford it, like Richard Mariner, had pitched in a little, buying a slice of the dream. And now it was all due to come true. In only a few days' time—

'Hey, Newbold, did we do it right?' First Officer Cohen's sneering voice broke into Harry's reverie.

'We're tied up all safe and sound, Larry, so I guess you must have.'

Larry Cohen pushed his way into Harry's work area uninvited. His face darkened beyond the normally sour expression and the sarcastic tone became genuinely belligerent. 'Hey! You got a schematic of the lading up.'

'It's the three-d of the whole hull, Larry. I'm not looking at the cargo areas.'

'I thought I told you I was the only one to call up the lading schematic.'

'It's the whole hull, Larry. You've got the lading schematic on your own computer, for God's sake. I don't want to look at the thing. It's not as if we've any cargo aboard yet anyway.'

'Damn right. And you just remember, when we do have a cargo in, you keep your snoopy little eyes out of my area. I don't want any jumped up, button-pushing little anorak—'

'Larry, Larry . . .'

Harry and Larry both swung round. Captain Stevenson was standing nearby, his thin, ascetic face folded into a frown of concern. 'I don't want you two fighting now,' he said, sounding like an exhausted parent chiding two warring children. 'Come on, shake and make up.'

Harry shoved out a hand obediently. Cohen looked from one to the other then turned away. 'What's the point, Herbie? It's not as if Officer Newbold here is really one of us. You know? I mean we're off into town for a drink and a bit of fun, right? Officer Newbold here's off to the Schubert or the Wang, or Symphony Hall, for Christ's sake. If we're off to Quincy Market, Officer Newbold will be down at Harvard Square. Down at the old *alma mater*, eh, Newbold?'

'Well yes, but—'

'See what I mean, Herbie? You're wasting your time!'

The captain lingered after his first officer's exit. 'What do you say, Harry?' he ventured after a while. 'It's our last night ashore in a while. Certainly before the Southampton run next week. It'd help morale if you could mend a few fences here. Cohen and O'Reilley say they know this first-rate place down in Quincy Market. Even Bligh and some of his men will be going down there later. What do you say to a drink with the boys? Just to show willing?'

'Aye aye, Captain,' said Harry, with deep reluctance.

It should have been called the Cat House or the Beaver Bar. It was just the sort of place Cohen would know about, and he and O'Reilley were happy as pigs in filth. While the traffic came and went on Chatham, Clinton and State outside, Harry, Stevenson

20

and the two other senior officers sat back in a booth sinking long jars of Boston Beer. On the floor in front of them a chorus of girls went through an ill-rehearsed but graphic bump and grind. Every now and then one of the more adventurous dancers would come across and the increasingly lively officers would wedge five dollar bills into smaller and smaller sections of her clothing. Harry was positioned at the back of the booth and so kept hold of more money than most. But the girls, either by chance or under the direction of Cohen or O'Reilley, made more and more spirited attempts to get nearer.

Harry was rapidly running out of patience with this. The opposite of Herbie Stevenson's plan was happening as the radio officer and the first officer vied with each other to add insult to injury. Harry had never felt so isolated, so patronised, so threatened.

'Hey!' bellowed Cohen suddenly. 'Hey, I got a great idea!'

In a moment the table was cleared and the most persistent of the dancers summoned. By this stage, the well-curved, sweat-gleaming body was almost totally uncovered. The last remaining thread, a tiny thong, only left room for question in the area of pubic hair because its rudimentary gusset was so tightly packed with money. In an instant she had been helped up onto the table and was cavorting graphically with her wad immediately above Harry's head.

A hand, thrust between the wide-spread thighs, pushed a glass of beer into Harry's face then rose to try and wedge another note into the gyrating bundle. Harry took the beer and looked away. It was not that the woman was ugly or unattractive. It was not that Harry felt nothing at the sight of her admittedly well-designed body. It was the atmosphere. The sub-text. The lack of control. This situation, the whole show was not about sex but about power. It was not about this girl and her body; it was about Harry and the computers. Cohen wanted Harry under his thumb.

The girl crashed to her knees and the whole table shook – but not as much as the glistening breasts. The full, pale orbs were thrust into Harry's face. A spray of salt perspiration hit the young officer's skin. A massive cheer went up and Harry sprang erect.

But the cheer was not for the dancer, it was for the arrival of Bligh and his engineers. In a trice the girl was gone and Harry was thrust out to the edge of the booth as the rest of the party was packed in. Bligh and Cohen exchanged looks. This was clearly prearranged. In spite of a natural antipathy between the deckhouse and the engine room, and between the men themselves, necessity had made them bedfellows. They had united against the greater threat. And that threat had Harry Newbold written all over it.

The arrival of the engineers cranked up the action. The beer was replaced by bourbon. The conversation got louder and lower. The jokes got bluer. And the management of the dive they were in moved to match the floor show to the mood of the clientele.

From the rudimentary wings on one side of the performance area there came a throbbing roar, echoed by the throats of the men who clearly knew what was going on. Slowly, arrogantly, a gleaming black and chrome motorcycle eased into the light. Astride it was a black-helmeted, square-shouldered, black-leathered biker and a short-skirted, tight-topped moll. No sooner had the machine stopped than Meat Loaf started, 'Bat Out Of Hell' first, then a selection of greatest hits. Almost independently of the music, the biker and his moll dismounted and then re-mounted, using the long black-leather saddle as a sofa and a bed.

The blonde girl's tight top was lingeringly removed, then the black skirt, followed by the black fishnet stockings and the red lace underwear. At last, when she was nude, she undertook the revelation of the biker's body. Lingeringly, missing no opportunity to rub herself against the gleaming outfit, the blonde removed the jacket and the waistcoat to reveal a grubby grey T-shirt. The helmet remained tantalisingly in place. The pants were unzipped and peeled away to reveal faded Wranglers which in turn slid away to reveal army-style green shorts clinging to square-sculpted thighs . . .

'Your round, Newbold,' bellowed O'Reilley.

'Oh really?' said Harry, but staggered stiffly erect anyway. Ten strides to the bar obscured the show, but the raucous bellowing of Harry's shipmates revealed that it was still going on. Harry leaned on the bar and waited until the barman noticed.

'Two bottles of bourbon,' Harry bellowed over the combination of Meat Loaf and co-workers.

They came with the same arrogant slowness with which the

22

barman had moved so far. 'Hundred dollars . . .'

'You're joking!' Harry's face burned. 'Fifty dollars a bottle for cheap bourbon?'

'That and the floor show. It's your treat.'

Harry swung round, rage threatening to explode. But just at that moment the moll pulled down the biker's shorts and no one was paying attention to the situation at the bar. Even Cohen who had set it all up was entranced at the vital moment by the all too graphic revelation that the big butch biker was a woman.

Harry turned and left.

'Hey!' yelled the barman, breaking the moment of almost religious silence. 'Hey!'

'What's the matter, Harry?' yelled Cohen.

'Newbold! Come back!' called the captain.

But Harry hit the door and strode out onto Clinton. There was a cab rank at the corner of State, less than one hundred metres away, but even closer was a cruising cab. By the time Cohen erupted onto the street, yelling insults, Harry was in the back and speeding towards Lynn and home.

A grudging whip-round settled things at the bar, but the failure of the trick on Harry left the men a little short. The proposed night of licentiousness with some of the chorus had to be put on hold and Cohen and Stevenson were hard put to it even to find the cab fare back to *New England*'s berth. In the cab, the beer and bourbon really began to hit home, particularly in the aftermath of the adrenalin rush engendered by the strip show. The cabby took a bit of a liberty with the two drunken, loud-mouthed sailors and had taken a firm dislike to Cohen in any case. So he dropped them early, just after they had crossed the bridge, and drove away.

Which is why they were walking, unsteadily, arm in arm down the middle of Revere Parkway when the big Mac truck from Chicago hit them as its tired driver hurried in from Interstate 93 to deliver a load of car spares to a body shop in Chelsea.

Harry, in blessed ignorance, was just crossing the Lynn Harbour Bridge, at the point where North Shore Road became Lynn Way and home. 'Next right,' ordered the young officer wearily.

'You from round here?' inquired the chatty cabby.

'My mother lives out on Nahant.'

'Hey! Some primo properties out there.'

'I guess.'

'You going home on furlough?'

Unlike the others, Harry had remained in uniform.

'I guess.'

The question sparked off all sorts of unwelcome associations. For the fact was that Harry was not really welcome at home. Home to Harry was a mansion out on Nahant Point overlooking Nantasket to the south across the reach of Boston Harbour and Marblehead to the north across Nahant Bay and Swampscott. The house would be Harry's one day and maybe then it would really be home again but at the moment its empty rooms housed only a bitterly disappointed, widowed mother who felt that Harry had betrayed blood and breeding, education and family. Ever since climbing aboard, Harry had been regretting giving the cabby this as a destination. And as the big car pulled to a stop outside the gate and the first swathes of misty rain rolled in over the familiar iron scrolling, Harry came to a new decision.

'I guess not, after all. Here. That's the fare so far. Now take me back to Boston, please. Do you know Harvard Square?'

Harry had found the house behind Harvard Square in late student days. Quite how or why were lost in depths of memory now. It had probably been something to do with loneliness and isolation even then. The cab pulled up beside an all-night cafe on the square and Harry walked stiffly round to the familiar door. 'Shave and a haircut' on the bell signalled a regular client and the black portal opened welcomingly onto a formal, over-ornate hall. When Madame Rose saw who it was, she smiled. 'Hello, Harry,' she said. 'Home from the sea again?'

'Hi, Rose. Yeah. Home again, I guess.'

'Will you be staying the night?'

'Yes. And I don't want to be disturbed.'

'Naturally. Will you take a look at the book?'

Within ten minutes, Harry had made a selection from among the Polaroid portraits in the house book and was following Madame Rose upstairs. Not for the first time, the young officer was struck by how theatrically old-fashioned this place was. They could have been mounting the stairs of a Victorian bordello, not a modern whorehouse. Only in Boston, thought Harry and began to feel a little more at home.

The girl Harry had selected was quiet, willowy, stylish. Everything that the women in the sailor's bar had not been. Rose introduced her as Veronica, and the pair shook hands almost formally.

'Get you anything?' asked Rose on the way out of the little chintzy bedroom.

'Champagne. How much is it?' Once bitten was enough for one evening.

'Domestic. Seven fifty. You won't notice it on your account.'

'Is that to your taste, Veronica?'

'Fine, thank you, Harry. Here, let me make you more comfortable . . .'

By the time the champagne arrived, Veronica was in her modest silken lingerie and Harry's uniform trousers were neatly folded over the back of a chair. They sat on the edge of the bed and sipped the icy liquid from wide-bowled tulip glasses. Between sips they kissed and caressed with increasing urgency.

But it was not until the bottle was almost finished that Harry at last lay back and let Veronica undo the buttons of her white uniform shirt and reach beneath it to the front fastenings of the computer officer's sports brassiere. 'Call me Harriet,' Harry ordered quietly. 'No one's called me Harriet since I left Radcliffe . . .'

Chapter Four

Sir Justin Bulwer-Lytton's flight touched down at Belfast City airport at ten on the morning after Bill and Helen's wedding day while Richard and Bob were on their way west over the Pole. Ulster lay under a blanket of grey cloud and the run out to Lisburn was dull.

'We'd make an excellent target for a terrorist strike,' observed Sir Justin dryly as the introductions were completed. 'Best since Phoenix's chopper went down on Kintyre.'

'D'you think that's what this is really all about? To get us all in one place?' asked Pat Conroy, the Garda liaison man, a little nervously.

'Five and I Corps have nothing,' said George, the Deputy Director of Intelligence's representative, an ex-SAS man. 'Nothing on the big computer, no word from the street. Nothing from the Shed or the Cousins. Nothing from your people, Pat.'

'Not a thing, George, as I've said.'

'Then this doesn't look local at all.'

'Murder must go on, even here,' said Sir Justin. 'Ordinary, non-political crimes of passion. Same as everywhere else.'

'There's the hands and the feet, d'you see,' said Pat. 'That's not the sort of thing we tend to find in our average crime of passion.'

'And the second blast, from the shotgun. That's not right either,' supplemented George.

'Aye, that's a fact. Nor is the dead man's car burned out on the Bloody Foreland. Or under it, at any rate.'

The car, so carefully precipitated into the bay, had been swept by an ironic vagary of ocean humour into a tunnel leading to a blow hole close to the castle. It lay there now, at the bottom of the chimney, on its nose, with its boot in the air and its number plate on clear display. As soon as the tide went out again the

Garda would winch it up. But it wasn't the car that had sparked this, nor the ease with which it had been linked with the male corpse, which had in turn been easily identified because of an unusual tattoo on the left buttock.

'It's the gun that makes the difference, Bull,' said George. 'Well, not the gun so much as the bullet. That's a very exclusive piece of kit.'

'But there's no doubt?'

'You'll see for yourself.'

'Oh, wizard.'

In fact, Bull did not see the corpses. Instead he was briefed by a pathologist from the Musgrave Hospital in Belfast, a renowned expert on gunshot wounds. Dr O'Neill had brought the corpses with him, but they remained in bodybags below while he concentrated on detailed photographs.

A long, artistic finger pointed to a pale fragment on one bright photograph. Without scale, it could almost have been the peak of a distant alp, mused Bull.

'The bone ends here are in the wrong place and pointing the wrong way. Once I'd spotted that it was clear that something odd was going on.'

'I'd have thought that the absence of hands and feet would have given a hint or two,' said George wryly.

The doctor nodded. 'Of course. The hands and feet were the reason I was brought in, and why I was looking so closely. That and the wounds to the jaws, of course. Whoever placed the shotgun did so with practised expertise. That was very worrying. At least, I should imagine it's worrying the hell out of you chaps.'

'That's as may be,' said George, holding a hand up like a fencer acknowledging a hit. 'But meanwhile, the bullet . . .'

'Ah, indeed. The bullet. I've heard of them of course, but I've never seen one used. I saw what it had done to the bone, there.' Another photo. Another pale alp. 'And I was scratching around for an explanation. It's a very particular signature, you see.'

'So Dr O'Neill asked a colleague of mine in the Greenjackets to take a look,' said George.

'Indeed. And the whole thing sort of snowballed from there.'

'I can see that it would have,' agreed Bull. 'Your friend in the Greenjackets?'

'Reading the Official Secrets Act in solitary at Aldershot as we speak.'

'How to dispose of friends and influence people,' said Bull, and George shrugged. 'But I see your point. So, suddenly in our most risk-filled theatre, we have, as you put it, George, a very exclusive piece of kit. Special Forces stuff. It's as worrying as if the Provos had got their hands on those Stingers the Cousins have lost.'

'And who's to say they haven't,' mused George.

'Irrelevant at the moment,' said Bull. 'But the fact is, Provos *don't* have access to kit like this. No one in this theatre does except some of the more specialist SAS teams. And none of them should be using them beyond the Pale. We are sure about that, aren't we, George?'

'One hundred per cent.'

'So, what you've called me in to assess,' continued Bull slowly, 'is do we have a current player with access to dangerous new kit or a new player altogether.'

Bull was uniquely placed to give an overview. His days in Security had given him an unrivalled expertise in the Middle East theatre and in the inter-linking of the terrorist groups that moved through it – and, indeed, with the shipping in which they moved. It had been Bull's men who had watched the meetings between the IRA and the Libyans in Tripoli. It had been his men who had watched the links form with ETA, with elements in Cyprus, with the PLO. It had been his men who had shopped the *Claudia*, who had fingered the team on the Rock. He still had close contacts with Lloyd's intelligence section the International Maritime Organisation, SO13, and MI5.

After Dr O'Neill had left, the discussion continued.

'Either scenario could have given rise to the unluckily botched cover-up,' said Bull.

'Why unluckily?' asked George.

'Well, because it was so thoroughly and professionally done. Who could possibly have known that the bodies would wash up on the Ulster side of Lough Foyle? Who would ever have dreamed that the Atlantic might wash the burned-out car back ashore?'

There was a little silence. Then they looked at each other as the penny began to drop. Bull got there first.

'Local men would,' he said. 'Of course! Local people would

realise there was a possibility that such things might happen.'

Pat nodded. 'There's no Donegal man would throw a body they were trying to conceal into Lough Foyle like that. And the car . . .'

'And the dead boy, O'Hanlon, wasn't he a player in any case?' said George.

'On the edge, maybe. But he was young.'

'The girl?' probed George.

'Irish-American tourist,' answered Pat. 'She could have been sworn to silence and no harm done. Well, less harm than this.'

'Someone playing away, then,' said Bull quietly. 'But who? And why at Dundark?'

'Well now,' said Pat quietly, the slow weight of Garda intelligence on his shoulders, 'there is just a possibility that there was an IRA arms dump there or thereabouts.'

Into the silence that greeted this grudging suggestion came a sharp rap on the door. A signalman entered and saluted. 'Call for Officer Conroy,' he said.

'I'll come at once,' said Pat, glad to get away from the suddenly narrow eyes around the table.

'Anyone in Special Forces with a special grudge against the Provos, George?' asked Bull.

'Thousands. SAS, Paras, plus anyone else in the army, navy, RAF, intelligence—'

'That's not what I meant. Anyone currently operative, out of control?'

'Ah. Now there you have me. Can't think of anyone mad enough. Or desperate enough. Not that I know of. But I'll warn them to go slow on anything unusual for the next couple of weeks. Consult us before they move, that sort of thing. Softly softly, so to speak.'

Pat Conroy came back in. 'I've had a phone call,' he said soberly, 'and a fax. And I think I have three pieces of news.'

'Fire away,' said Bull equably.

'First, they've recovered the car. Four hands and four feet in the boot. Burned and battered, but good enough.'

'So we can at least make the identification official,' said George.

'Secondly, we have confirmation that there was an IRA arms dump beside the castle there.'

'Good, good. More grist to the mill,' said George. 'We won't need an official disarmament process if you keep this up, Pat. Talks or no talks.'

'Ah, but,' faltered the big Garda officer, 'it was empty. Clean as a whistle but for the packaging and suchlike.'

'Gone,' said George. 'Gone and never called me mother. But who took it?'

'We're beginning to get a picture of the people who took it.' Pat put a fax on the table. 'Whoever it was had access to even more Special Forces equipment. Have any of you seen anything like that?'

The fax showed a black and white photograph of a piece of climbing equipment. Something to which a rope might have been attached for rappelling down a cliff.

'Well, sure,' said George, and then he stopped. For he realised what Pat Conroy was asking him.

It was surprisingly clear, given that the photograph had been photocopied then faxed. It was still possible to read the writing on the steel of the karabiner. Or it would have been if any of them had understood the Cyrillic alphabet.

'I've seen something like that before,' Bull said. 'Friend of mine brought it back from Africa a few years ago. Chap called Richard Mariner. He'd just finished delivering an iceberg to the African state of Mau. United Nations project. Quite a success. But my point is that he brought this thing back as a kind of a keepsake to remind himself of one of the people who helped him pull it off. Chap who owned it was killed, you see.'

He looked up. The three faces across the table were blank with incomprehension. 'That's Spetsnaz equipment,' he explained. 'Russian Special Forces issue.'

'Excuse me, Sir Justin,' said Pat. 'Are you suggesting we have a Russian invasion of Donegal here?'

'Of course not. But there's only one other realistic source of such equipment that I can think of – and it isn't terrorist. And it doesn't make very much more sense than supposing the Russian Special Forces were involved.'

The old man paused, ordering his thoughts as the others watched and waited, each probably well able to follow the train of logic to its conclusion faster than Sir Justin, but waiting for him to speak, out of simple respect.

'The long and the short of it is this,' Sir Justin concluded at last. 'If we're not dealing with current Special Forces then we must be dealing with ex-Special Forces. Mercenaries. Someone, somewhere has hired a team of Special Forces Mercenaries to take – buy, steal, whatever – a complete IRA arms dump.'

'But why?' asked Pat.

And this time it was George who answered. 'So they can start a war,' he said. 'But against who? And where?'

Chapter Five

Richard looked out across Massachusetts Bay as the flight from La Guardia swung into its final approach to Boston. He was fizzing with energy and ill-contained excitement. In spite of the nature of the mission bringing him and Bob Stark to the place, Richard felt as though he was on holiday; on an adventure. Not even the guilt of dumping the twins on Robin, and the three of them on his long-suffering parents out at Summersend, their rambling old house overlooking the North Sea in Lincolnshire, could diminish the excitement he was feeling now.

Having settled his domestic arrangements before the super-cat had got back into Dover, he and Bob were on the Virgin 747 out of Heathrow just before midnight. They had taken a twin berth on the top deck and managed to get a good night's sleep. New York had been sweltering, even at 6 a.m. local time, but all they had seen of it was a distant shimmer as they were swept across from John F. Kennedy to La Guardia on the shuttle. Then they barely had time to grab a bite and make some plans before the Boston shuttle was called. Now the tone chimed and the hostess announced that they would shortly be landing at Boston. According to Richard's lean stomach it was coming up to teatime. According to his watch it was just gone noon.

Harry Newbold waited nervously in the arrivals area. She was still in shock from the news that had greeted her on her return to the *New England* in the early hours of yesterday morning – and the obscure assumption by everyone, herself included, that she bore some kind of responsibility for the tragedy. Certainly the fact that she had been unobtainable during the first few hours of the police investigation into the accident had given weight to the accusatory glances levelled at her by the hung-over survivors. What she had been doing while she had been thus unobtainable added to the weight of responsibility.

None of this showed, however. In fact she made an unconsciously striking figure in her uniform whites, standing a head taller than most of the other women there, her slim body held rigidly erect, her shoulders thrown well back, her honey hair cut in a boyish bob and shoved under her uniform cap.

Tall as she was, she had to look up to meet the eyes of the couple she was here to greet. Masculine beauty had never interested her as anything other than a distant intellectual ideal. But she had never seen anyone as good-looking as Bob Stark in all her life. Not in the flesh anyway, and rarely on the screen. The way his wheat-gold hair tumbled across his broad, lightly lined forehead, the manner in which the planes of his high, sculpted cheekbones fell to the lower slopes of his wide jaw past perfectly defined lips simply knocked the wind out of her. She moved forward towards this god-like creature knowing instinctively that this was her new captain. And then, from behind his shoulder, stepped his opposite and equal.

Richard looked older because the silver at his temples was conspicuous in contrast with the blue-black of his hair. His face was longer, more deeply lined; it was more lived-in, wiser. But the long nose, broken slightly out of line, led down to an equally defined mouth and an equally resolute jaw. It was the eyes, however, that dominated his face, ice-blue, so bright that they seemed back-lit by a burning intelligence.

Harry, already erect, drew herself up to new heights. 'Captain Stark? Captain Mariner?' Inexplicably, simply having them here seemed to lighten the computer officer's load.

In the taxi down to *New England*'s berth, Harry filled the two men in with regard to events during the last thirty-six hours. Technically, Chief Bligh was the senior officer aboard now, O'Reilley was certainly senior to her as well, and even the second officer, Arthur Walker, might defensibly have assumed command of the bridge. But the fact was that Harry seemed to have sorted everything. She had contacted owners, families, authorities – making O'Reilley's life hell. She had dealt with the police, the mortuary, the distraught truck driver, the truck owners. And lawyers. The paperwork, too, had fallen to her – logs, accident

34

reports, letters of condolence. A large number of local businessmen had had to be warned that their glad-handing cruise was going to be cancelled and ruffled feathers had to be smoothed. The Port Authority had to be informed that *New England* would not be departing on schedule, and so did the designer and creator of *New England*, Professor Alan Miles. He decided not to travel to Boston after all but to stop off at Fall River and negotiate a couple of days' grace between now and *New England*'s final overhaul – though frankly Harry could have done with some help and support from the owners' representative here and now.

'You've done a first-rate job, by the sound of things,' rumbled Richard. 'But we're here to help. Or I am, in any case. Bob's here to assume command, as you've been informed. The documentation will be faxed over later. I'm here to represent the owners, though Heritage Mariner only has a small holding, and I'll only be aboard until you get down to Philadelphia, maybe even Fall River if they're going to hold her there for any length of time.'

'I'll take over command at once,' confirmed Bob. 'I haven't been aboard *New England* since I completed my jet-ship command course. I don't think I know any of the current crew, but I'm sure we'll rub along together fine.'

Something about his tone made Harry realise that Bob Stark was a captain who would be rubbed along with whether the crew liked it or not.

'We need a new first officer, but I can stand the watches if need be, certainly round to Fall River. So, all we've missed is the glad hand jaunt and a couple of days of the schedule. We should be able to catch up if we look sharp and there are no unforeseen hold-ups either here or at Fall River.'

'There shouldn't be any problem at Fall River, sir,' said Harry. '*New England* is ship-shape. There's nothing on my computers except green lights.'

'Good enough, Harry. But I'll want to check for myself.'

'Of course, Captain.'

Part of Richard's excitement was the thought of seeing *New England* and looking around her for himself. Heritage Mariner were very junior members of Jet-Ship Inc.'s board but they were important enough to count. They were associated with the cutting edge of technology through their pair of nuclear waste disposal ships *Atropos* and *Clotho*. More recently, their active involvement with the super-cats *Hero* and *Leander* had made them an obvious target for anyone needing experimental funds.

The range of international players who constituted the rest of the Jet-Ship board were scattered all over the globe at the moment. Those who could would assemble in Philadelphia in a week's time for the official first run. Some planned to be in Southampton for the arrival if they could. In the meantime they all had their own businesses to run and most of them were much less well supported than Richard was at Heritage Mariner, and consequently much less free to move. This was exactly the kind of situation Richard and his Crewfinders team were used to walking into at a moment's notice. And the fact was, the deaths of Stevenson and Cohen, while tragic, did not really register on the corporate seismic scale of disasters.

Richard had seen round *New England* when she was part completed at Fall River, but he had not seen her since her launch and, except for photographs, he had not seen her fitted or crewed. He craned forward to look through the window, aching for his first sight of her. And, suddenly, as the taxi swung onto the Mystic wharves, there she was.

She was bigger than he remembered. Big enough, even for a man who had commanded supertankers all his working life. She was just shy of two hundred and fifty metres from slim stem to square stern; the same size as the *Canberra*, nearly up with the *Queens*, though nowhere near as high, with only four decks of upper works. Still, she was no pygmy, even compared to *Prometheus II*, flagship of the Heritage Mariner tanker fleet. The tonnage of her cargo was less than half the massive tanker's capacity, but in almost every other area of comparison the jet-ship surpassed everything else that Richard had ever commanded. She could generate 150,000 horsepower, twice as much as *Prometheus*'s massive old screws. And she could sail nearly ten times faster.

She was white, except for a vivid blue stripe along her hull, narrowing to a point at the bow. She looked like an alp and moved like an avalanche. Her deckhouse stood midships, its front sloping back at a racy angle. There was room to stand half a dozen container lorries on the foredeck and four or so behind

36

the navigation bridge. The whole bridgehouse, four decks high, was the better part of one hundred metres in length.

She was sitting high, carrying just enough bunkerage to complete a couple of cruises and get her round to Fall River, two hundred and fifty miles distant. Three hours sailing time, if they wanted to hurry, thought Richard as he got out of the car. And as he straightened at the foot of the companionway, he was still shaking his head in wonder.

The deck where Arthur Walker, the second officer, was waiting with Chief Bligh was ten metres above the dock, nearly twenty above the water. And the bridgehouse towered another twenty and more to the top of the communications stack. When the introductions were completed Bob went straight to the bridge and Richard followed. While Bob disappeared into the captain's day room to go through all the relevant documentation, Richard lingered on the bridge. He was not used to being a mere observer in any situation, but he was prepared to enjoy the novelty here. A truculent looking young man called Stubbs appeared to be holding the watch and although he eyed the interloper suspiciously he did not actually interfere with Richard as he looked around. On the other hand he did not vouchsafe much information either. Once Richard had familiarised himself with the general layout of the bridge and satisfied himself as to the functions of all the high-tech screens in their broad arc beneath the clearview, he found himself drawn inexorably into Harry's lair.

The computer equipment here was far beyond anything available even in the superbly-equipped *Atropos*. Fascinated – and not in the least threatened – he teased an enormous amount of information out of Harry who proved as eager to answer as he was to ask. By the time Bob Stark had gone through all the records he needed to consult on paper, Richard had more or less done the same on the screen. But, somewhat to Harry's chagrin, the two old friends were not quite satisfied by second-hand information, whether delivered in print or in pixels.

'I'm going over her, stem to stern,' announced Bob. 'You want to come?'

'Can't think of anything I'd rather do,' Richard said eagerly.

'We need a guide . . .' Bob's voice trailed off.

Stubbs looked round. 'My watch finishes in half an hour – not that I'm really needed on the bridge in any case.'

'Thanks for the offer, Mr Stubbs. But I don't think I'll need to disturb you. Where's Mr Walker?'

Stubbs shrugged, and Bob crossed to the ship's tannoy. He was just about to summon the second officer when Harry poked her head out of the computer room. 'I know the ship better than most, Captain. I'll get you wherever you want to go.'

'Good man,' said Bob without thinking.

They began at the crow's-nest – or as near as this princess of high-tech could come to such an outdated idea. The communications equipment was housed in a surprisingly solid looking construct. 'Everything has to be extra solid,' said Harry, well practised in guest tours. 'Although when she's at speed *New England* sits very squarely on the surface and there isn't much pitching or tossing even in twenty-metre seas, we have to work from a fundamental assumption that even in still air she will generate winds of hurricane force. In a headwind, things can get very blowy indeed up here – anywhere on deck, as a matter of fact. It's something you must always be aware of. Inside the cross section at the top there's the ship's identity beacon which broadcasts nonstop so she can be tracked. The beacon's one of the most important pieces of equipment aboard because the hull, being made of a composite rather than metal, is more or less invisible to radar. Without the beacon it would be impossible to track us with any accuracy.' Having delivered herself of this little speech, Harry turned and looked down.

From up here the layout of the long, slim hull was perfectly presented: the narrow dagger of the bows, widening to the unexpected flare of the stern; the rounded, almost moulded smoothness of the deckhouse with its sleek leading faces. 'Again,' said Harry equably, 'it has to stand up to enormous headwinds. So it has to be designed more aerodynamically than any hull ever built. Bridge wings like you have on your tankers, Captain Mariner, are out of the question. At our normal cruising speed they would simply get ripped off. The forward mast with the Doppler radar down there on the forecastle head has to be stressed like a jet's wing or it would come in through the clearview.'

'Well,' she temporised as they went down into the bridgehouse

38

again, 'it wouldn't actually come through the clearview. It would glance off, more than likely, because of the angle of the front of the bridgehouse and the strength of the glass. The whole structure has been designed to withstand the impact of water travelling at speeds of up to one hundred and fifty miles per hour.'

As the afternoon wore into evening, Harry guided the two officers through the bridge, through the senior officers' cabins and day rooms, the visitors' suite – where Richard's bags lay on the bed awaiting his convenience – the junior officers' and seamen's quarters. 'I have one of the senior officers' cabins,' she admitted a little shyly. 'Not because my commission really merits it; it's more to do with sex than seniority, I guess.' She stopped speaking suddenly, realising that her sleeping arrangements were under the direction of the new captain now; she could end up bunking in with the crew if he so decided. But she dismissed the thought at once. Bob Stark generated trust, not the sort of sneaking unease that Herbie Stevenson and Larry Cohen had given rise to.

The crew's rest rooms, exercise areas, TV lounges and bars were standard. There were galleys and a dining room, a laundry and a surgery. It was all familiar, except that *New England*'s crew was less than half the size of the average tanker's crew so everything was smaller. And once the jet-ship was in service, the deck would be out of bounds, so it was all very solid and self-contained. The bulkhead door out onto the main deck was the most massive Richard had ever seen. 'Look what it's got to withstand,' said Harry when he remarked on it.

The deck was strange, too, now that he looked at it. It was made of a composite, almost like plastic. 'Not much wear in this, surely,' he said.

'Depends what you mean. It doesn't have to withstand the usual deck work. There'll be nothing loaded on it. All the cargo will be stowed below. Anything – or anyone – up here would simply get blown away. Even the deck rails round the sides and stern are only there for when she's at anchor or in port. Other than the cargo itself, the propulsion unit and the main lading systems are the only bits of the ship that would show up on a normal radar display. That's why the identity beacon is so important, remember.'

As she led them across the snowy expanse of the afterdeck, Harry continued with her spiel. 'Under our feet are the main holds. There is emergency access, but as you can see the hatches are unusually well-fitted. No raised covers here, they would simply be ripped off. Even the handles are flush fitted.' They reached the stern rail. 'Down there you will see the main jet propulsion system.'

Obediently, Richard and Bob looked down over a white cliff. The stern of the ship was thirty-five metres wide and nearly as high. The cliff face below them was split into two massive lateral grilles whose vertical slits were about ten metres high and two metres wide. The solid struts between them were over two metres wide. The grilles stretched from side to side of the hull and stood one on top of the other. A strange odour, a mixture of ozone and jet fuel, oozed headily upwards from them.

'Those two sections stretching right across the stern are like two drawbridges, one on top of the other,' said Harry. 'They are attached to the jet propulsion system. When the jets are at full power we get the equivalent of two jumbos on full thrust down there. And that's not counting the water jets. When we're in dock, the two sections uncouple from the jet system and swing down exactly like drawbridges, opening up the whole width of the holds.'

'Can you open the drawbridges while the jets are running?' asked Richard.

'I guess so. Except that the safety overrides would cut in. If you tried anything like that, you'd lose your cargo and God knows what else. Why would you want to do anything as foolish as that, Captain?'

'I wouldn't. I was just curious.'

'Well, I guess—'

'It's not important,' cut in Bob. 'Come on. We've still got a lot to see and the evening routine will be kicking in soon. You dog the watches, Harry?'

'In port it seems to be every man for himself, Captain. I am not a qualified watch officer, before you ask.'

'Never mind, we'll soon put that right. In the meantime, I want to talk to the crew before supper and we haven't even got below decks yet.'

'I'll take you in at once then, Captain. I wouldn't be competent to take you below in any case. The infernal regions belong to Chief Bligh and his attendant demons.'

Chapter Six

There was plenty of room for the sixteen of them in the ship's bar. As it was well after six, Bob bought them all a drink and then sat and chatted with calculated approachability. Richard could not help but be impressed by the speed with which his old friend stamped his personality on the disparate group, and yet he did not seem to be unduly overbearing about it. At the same time, Richard knew that those apparently guileless eyes would be taking the measure of every man here.

By the time the first round of drinks was finished, Bob seemed to have been accepted. Richard himself would have been tempted to keep a particularly close eye on Radio Officer O'Reilley, already two drinks ahead of everyone else, and Chief Bligh seemed less easily impressed than some of the others, but that might just have been the tension between deck and engine room.

Where Harry's tour had begun at the highest point, Bligh's began at the lowest. Having taken the lift down through two cargo decks and two engineering decks, they stepped out in the lowest space aboard. They were so far down here that, as they walked away from the lift car, they could see the shape of the hull around them as though they were in some inverted garret beneath the eaves of a house.

'I brought you down here,' began their guide with an engineer's understandable pride in a spectacular feat of engineering, 'to show you how it all works. You're both aware of Froude's drag rules?'

It was like asking an astro-physicist if he knew about Einstein.

'The hull of *New England* is designed to overcome the problem of drag from the wake. It's not just the propulsion, you see, the whole thing only works because the hull is shaped in this particular way. It's the aquatic equivalent of a whaletail on the back of an old Porsche, if you like. It overcomes the rules of drag on the hull of a large vessel and it also settles the whole structure and makes it more stable. Your super-cats, Captain Mariner, rise up and skim over the waves. The Katapults do the same. The jet-ship settles down, sits firm. It cuts through any seas up to twenty-metre waves, and any weather up to a seventy-five-knot headwind.'

Richard could see why the weather deck would be forbidden under those circumstances. Air with a closing speed of nearly 200 mph. A raindrop would bruise severely under those circumstances. Hailstones would be like bullets. Even the air would be lethal.

'And these are the babies that push her along.' Bligh led them across to a companionway and sprang up it swiftly. He had the square, long-armed, bow-legged body of an orang-utan, and he moved with ape-like ease. Bob sprang gamely after him, but Richard's knees were largely held together by steel pins and he followed at a slightly more sedate pace. The climb was long and steep. The stairway led to a bridge not unlike the galleries that reach across the sheaves of pipes which run down the middle of a tanker's decks. But here, instead of conduits, eight huge jet engines lay beneath their feet. 'Biggest mothers Rolls-Royce do,' Bligh was saying. 'These are the direct line jets. They blast pure power out of the grilles at the back. Each one delivers ten thousand horsepower at full throttle. And the Pratt and Whitneys over there deliver the same again as water jets, yet the whole lot together weighs maybe a twentieth of a standard motor.' Bligh swung round and gestured at the distant walls of the place. 'Hull's light as hell too.'

'Newbold says she's hard to spot under radar,' said Bob.

'Newbold's right. That's why the beacon's so important. Magical hull altogether. The only thing heavy about her is the cargo. Talking of which . . .'

The empty cargo holds were like cathedrals, except that they were larger and more silent. Each open space was eight metres high, more than thirty metres wide and one hundred and sixty metres long. Around the upper outer edge of each stood a galleried walkway. Here, at the front and back of each hold, sat the lifeboats, each in a strange cradle whose outer side was the hull of the ship itself. If ever they needed to be deployed, the ship's side opened, the cradle rocked outwards and automatic davits swung the solid little lifeboats free. The flooring was air-cushioned.

'We can get the equivalent of seven hundred and fifty containers in the two holds,' said Bligh. 'They'll come loaded on pallets like groceries going up a supermarket checkout. Six hours to unload; another six to load up again. We should be able to turn around completely inside one working day.'

'And cross to Europe in three. One complete turn-around within each working week,' said Bob.

'That's with weekends off,' said Bligh in an 'I don't think so' voice. 'Three complete runs in a fortnight, more like.'

The chimes sounded to announce dinner, and they made their way to the dining room. Except for the one watchkeeper, the whole crew ate together, filling four tables. The dinner was excellent but neither Bob nor Richard lingered over the food. Bob had not finished his tour of inspection below. There were control areas still to be inspected, the engine control room major among them. Then there were the ship's stores, the bunkerage and all the ancillary equipment to be checked. And that needed to be done before bedtime, for Bob was bursting to take his new toy out and play with her. The preliminary negotiations with the Port Authority were under way before ten local time. The owners were alerted with cheerful disregard for time zones and sleep patterns by Richard who prefaced his busy schedule on the phone, fax and Internet with a call to Summersend where he was very fortunate to catch a couple of extremely tired and emotional children between bath and bed, and snatch a brief word with their exhausted mother.

The next day dawned calm and clear over Boston. Richard was up by five, his internal clock still attuned to British Summer Time. Thus he was able to experience the gathering bustle of the stirring ship as she began to prepare herself for sea with all the growing excitement of a bride for her wedding day.

Still in his dressing gown, Richard wandered to the bridge. It was deserted. Monitoring systems glowed faintly, already beginning to lose their light in the gathering brightness of dawn. In Harry Newbold's den a few lights flickered, denoting systems which could not be closed down, but all the monitors were dark. Scratching his bristly chin, Richard padded off down the internal

45

companionways to the galley. Even here there was no life stirring as yet, so he made himself a cup of instant coffee – there appeared to be no tea available – and wandered on down. The engine control room was as deserted as the bridge, the engine monitors for the most part dead. The rest of the cargo and engineering decks were tomb-like and silent.

The dawn air on the deck was as bracing as it can ever be in a major dock facility. Richard wandered contentedly down to the stern and divided his attention between the fantastic drawbridges of the jet grilles and the rose-blush of the dawn. It was going to be a perfect day for a cruise, he though. And he hummed cheerfully to himself as he sipped his coffee.

When he got back to the bridgehouse he found he was no longer alone. Harry Newbold was up and about, bundled shapelessly into a grey jogging outfit and trainers.

'You're up early,' she said. 'I'm just checking my babies before I take a little exercise.'

They chatted companionably as she went through a basic check on the status of the computers, then, having nothing else to do, Richard wandered down to the ship's exercise facility with her. They were talking of nothing in particular and certainly Richard was observing her as nothing more than a valued shipmate when artlessly, apparently thoughtlessly, she stripped off the grey bundle of sweatshirt and pants and stepped aboard the jogging machine, which was set for fast. Richard's conversation faltered as the femininity of her lycra-clad form hit him. Up until now she had been dressed in clothes which made no allowance for her body. Now suddenly she was a creature of long, muscular legs, flaring hips, solid but shapely haunches outlined as though the exercise outfit was simply a thin layer of paint, slim waist and perfectly proportioned chest. Richard's eyes flicked up to her face but it was closed, her eyes distant, concentrating on making the most of the exercise.

He thought of saying something but instead simply turned away and left her to get on with her work-out unmolested, vexed with himself for having looked more closely than he ought to have.

But what was it Robin said? Men always look; they can't help it.

46

Back on the bridge, the next man up was Bob. 'You're up early,' he said, echoing Harry.

'Too excited to sleep,' admitted Richard. 'Same as you, I guess.'

'Too right,' said Bob. 'I can't wait to get this show on the road!'

'When's the pilot due aboard?'

'Ten.'

'Plenty of time.'

'Just bullshit and bumph to get sorted. Stevenson and Cohen are both being flown home so there's nothing more to do here on their behalf. Never had such an easy departure.'

'Well, you're only going for a three-hour cruise. You'll hardly have dropped the Boston pilot before you pick up the Fall River man.'

'Booked him yesterday. Twenty-four hours' notice for going into Narragansett Bay.'

'Very impressive. How did you find the time among everything else?'

'Did it between inspecting the engine control room and checking the ship's stores. Only eighteen hours' notice actually, but they forgave me.'

From 9 a.m. local time, Bob became increasingly distant as he concentrated on the process of departing for Fall River.

Harry, too, was preoccupied. Richard stood back and watched.

The pilot came aboard at ten. He was a dapper, chipper little man with narrow eyes and a dry 'don't take no bull' manner. But within five minutes it was clear that he was impressed by the jet-ship and very pleased indeed to be taking her out across his harbour.

Richard positioned himself in one of those little backwaters of quiet space which seem to exist in even the busiest of places – a corner beside the open chart area from which he could observe most of the bridge. If he looked to his left, he could see everything the pilot, captain and watch officer saw almost as clearly as they could themselves. If he looked right, he could see Harry's bank of computers and monitors.

When the order came for starboard thrusters, Richard watched on Harry's schematic as the small motors glowed through various shades of red, depending on their percentage power. Then he turned his head and saw the Mystic River wheel across the clearview as *New England* came round until she was facing across the bay.

'Slow ahead outer water jets.'

At once the great engines on Harry's screen began to glow, and the thrusters faded back towards blue. There was just the whisper of sensation as the great ship surged forward. Richard could hardly have said he felt the acceleration, though he was straining to do so, but suddenly he was leaning against the corner of the wall rather than just standing beside it.

'Steady as she goes,' said the pilot to the man at the helm.

'Yes, sir. Making five knots.'

'Hold her at that . . .'

Richard switched his attention away from the run-of-the-mill conversation on the bridge and looked at Harry's schematics again. As nothing new seemed to be happening on the diagram of the ship's disposition, he looked across to the radar. Outside, on the bridge, to Richard's left, beyond the chart table, Stubbs was looking carefully into the bright square of the head-up collision alarm radar, and there on a little screen above Harry's right hand was the information Stubbs was studying so carefully.

Harry glanced up and saw him looking. 'We get full circle graphics at this speed. As we come to full ahead we get more concentration of what's ahead of us. When the big jets kick in, she closes down all rear vision automatically – nothing from behind can do us any damage then.'

It took them nearly half an hour to pick their way through the busy port and out along the North Channel past the Graves to the B Buoy. Here they came to a near stop as the pilot departed. 'Thanks for the trip, son,' the old man said to Bob. 'That was quite an experience. She's a great lady.'

This was unprecedentedly impressive to Richard who had always found pilots taciturn. And he had seen nothing particularly memorable in the experience so far. This was a situation Bob was soon to change, however. 'Right,' he said as soon as the pilot's cutter was clear, 'let's see what she can do. Ready for full power all engines.'

'Yes, Captain.'

At once the whole rear section of Harry's diagrams sprang into life. The circle on the collision alarm screen shifted more

48

towards a wedge shape, widening the view ahead, closing down the view astern, focusing on the vessels immediately behind the great jets.

'Standard sequence straight line acceleration to fifty knots,' said Bob quietly. A ripple of excitement went around the bridge. But Bob had not finished. 'Configure radar on the assumption that we will be entering stage two at fifty knots and pushing on to full speed.'

In theory it was a standard manoeuvre, but it had never been attempted by this crew. At fifty knots the water jets would be at full stretch and the standard jets idling; stage two of the sequence would bring everything up to full power and take the sleek hull to the better part of 90 knots – 160 kph or 100 mph. Harry stirred and Richard looked down at her. She smiled, with contagious excitement.

'Warp factor eight, Mr Sulu,' she said, and beat an excited little rhythm with her knuckles on the edge of her desk.

And he thought, she's a Trekkie; but of course she is . . .

He gave her a tight but genuine smile and crossed to the empty space the pilot had occupied. Here he had a perfect view of the gleaming foredeck and the empty reach of the Gulf of Maine beyond.

'Not going down the one-way system to the South Channel?'

'She won't fit in unless we hold her speed right down,' Bob replied. 'I can take her out to Georges Bank and bring her back in easier. We'll be at South Channel more quickly that way. Then we'll see about fitting in to the system.'

The easy conversation was a technical one between old friends. There was no questioning of Bob's commands or decisions. And Richard would have done the same. They had a high-power Lamborghini here; no sense taking her through a 30 mph zone for her first spin.

'All clear aft, Captain.'

'Thank you, Mr Stubbs. Engine room?'

'Coming to optimum, Captain. Awaiting your word.'

'Thank you, Chief. Mr Stubbs?'

'All clear ahead. What are we doing? Idling still?'

'Captain!' cut in Harry urgently. 'Vessel to starboard. Coming up level now. I guess he must have crept up behind us as the

49

radar focused forward. He didn't register until he came level with the bridge.'

'Thank you, Mr Newbold. Hold it, Chief.' Bob walked to the starboard side of the bridge and looked down *New England*'s sheer white side. 'Well, I'll be damned,' he said. 'Richard, look at this.'

Obligingly, Richard crossed to his friend's square shoulder. Beside the great ship, cutting arrogantly through the dead calm of the still morning, came a massive black powerboat spewing water from four great jets.

'He wants to race,' said Richard.

'Price of having the coolest wheels on the block,' said Bob.

'It would be highly unprofessional,' said Richard equably.

'Criminal and juvenile. Ready, Chief?'

'Ready, Captain.' On Bligh's word, Bob strode back to his accustomed position, leaving Richard where he was.

'First stage, then, on my mark. What's he doing, Richard?'

'Revving . . . Off he goes!'

'Execute!' barked Bob.

This time there was a very powerful feeling of acceleration. Richard found himself walking purposefully backwards as the deck tried to tear itself out from beneath his feet. Then he caught hold of the rail beneath the window and continued to observe. The powerboat was falling behind already, the black beak of its bow rising above a welter of bow wave. *New England*, on the other hand, was settling down into the water.

'Twenty knots,' said the helmsman. Richard supposed he must have misheard; surely they could only be doing ten at most so soon after moving off.

'Thirty knots,' called Harry Newbold. Richard glanced across at her distant figure, weirdly illuminated by spectral lines of green. When he glanced back he had to look far aft to see the labouring, bouncing blob of the powerboat.

'Fifty knots,' called the helmsman.

'Mr Stubbs?'

'All clear ahead.'

'Chief?'

'All aft radar completely closed down now, Captain.'

'Thank you, Mr Newbold. Chief?'

'Optimum now, Captain.'

50

'Secure all!'

Richard took an even firmer grip of the railing under the window, though there was nothing to see now, the powerboat was long gone.

'Execute!'

A gentle hand seemed to pull Richard back against the wall. The officers and crew at the clearview all leaned forward at a well-practised angle. The deck seemed to be vibrating beneath Richard's feet with just enough power to make his soles itch unbearably but at once the sensation was gone. The great hand let him go. The men in front of him were all standing normally again. The sea and sky outside were whirling past in a hazy blur. It seemed to Richard that they should have been deafened by the thunder of jet power as the equivalent of four jumbo jets lifted them up to full speed, but the helmsman's quiet 'Seventy knots, Captain' carried easily.

Richard let go of the rail, surprised to find that his grip had been so firm. He crossed to Harry again and watched in wonder as her machines reflected *New England*'s whole experience. The after section of the ship schematic was red now and a set of figures in the corner above the engine flickered up towards 80. The radar was a long thin isosceles triangle, lying in its side, looking out miles ahead with the blip of light which was *New England* at its very point.

'How far ahead is that?' Richard asked.

'Full mag. Horizon's seventy-five kilometres. But look.' Harry's long hand flicked a switch at a companion monitor and a similar, wider triangle appeared. Harry pressed a series of buttons on the console in rapid succession and the long, narrow isosceles was ghosted up into the larger triangle above. 'That's the Magellan system, using the satellites,' said Harry. 'Gives us an over-the-horizon view. Not as accurate or detailed as the ship's generated radar and it doesn't do Doppler, but it shows us what else might be out there.'

'Fantastic.'

'And that's not all. Here.' The triangle of satellite-generated information began to tilt and widen until it opened into levels.

'This central line is the sea surface. Here's a ship well ahead. Those figures tell you he's that many degrees to starboard of our current course, but he's on the same line as us because he's on the surface, see?'

'Yes.'

'Now this blip here is something else. He's a submarine in the Fundian Channel, probably heading down to the exercise area. He's dead ahead but well below us.'

'I see. So that area below him, that solid area . . .'

'That's the sea bed. And that's a rock outcrop, here, and that's the channel the sub's heading for. That looks like a wreck. You see the figures are different, and the colour?'

'Yes, I see that.'

'OK. Now look up. This blip here is a plane. He won't be there long because he'll only register while he's directly above our course. There, he's gone. But more importantly, look here.' Harry's fingers traced patterns on the screen which only seemed to exist because the long pale digits had passed that way. 'This is a weather system. It's so faint because it's weak. These are clouds here. This is a little light rain. There will be winds there too, but this can't read wind speeds. However . . .' Again, the click of keys being touched in rapid succession, and the patterns on the weather monitor began to change. 'I can make these two compatible easily enough,' said Harry, 'so that what we see on radar down here becomes what we see from the weather sats up there. And they will predict air pressure, wind speed and direction. So if I want to bring the figures down the net . . .'

The ghostly patterns on the radar picture reaching out ahead and scanning everything from the sea bed to the cloud tops were suddenly dotted with jewel-bright figures giving wind speed and direction, precipitation levels, front line and squall lines – though these were so slight as to be negligible.

'I would normally only do this if there was something big out there,' said Harry. 'It's a waste taking apart a pussycat like that little system.'

'You prefer wrestling with tigers?'

'Have to. We need to be very careful to avoid anything that will bring very big seas. We can take twenty-metre seas but anything more and there'll be trouble so we need to know for certain.'

'I can imagine,' said Richard. But then he realised the phrase was as inaccurate as it was fatuous. He most certainly could not imagine. Everything aboard *New England* was a revelation to him.

Chapter Seven

Richard left *New England* at Fall River and flew back home full of excitement. Bob stayed aboard and oversaw the minor re-fit while Alan Miles gave the crew a five-day stint ashore which they all, except Harry Newbold, took gratefully. At the end of the five days, they re-assembled, including the new first officer John Dix whom the professor had found and appointed in the meantime. Then Bob took *New England*, sedately, down the normal shipping lanes past New York, Atlantic City and Great Egg to the north channel leading westwards past Cape May, round northwards into Delaware Bay and up to the anchorage prepared for her on the Delaware shore just south of the bay made with the confluence of the Schuylkill.

Here things became frantic, especially for Bob. After the better part of a week in a boiler suit wriggling around the darker and messier parts of his shining command with Alan Miles, Fall River engineers and maintenance men, he was now at all times expected to be in his captain's whites. The only oil which came anywhere near him was a trace of scented hair oil a Philadelphia stylist slipped unnoticed onto his handiwork. Although *New England* was the centre of attraction, Bob saw less of her than one might have expected, for there was a good deal of promotional work to be done ashore. And Bob, wry and lightly self-mocking, was happy enough to do his duty in offices and public buildings as well as the Four Seasons or the Marriott.

Jet-Ship Inc., though little more than a well-financed one-man show, had enough of a publicity machine going now to make sure that the first voyage of their revolutionary new vessel would catch public attention as well as romantic imagination. Alan Miles ensured that the tragic deaths of the captain and first officer were a sad but carefully distanced memory. The brief exposure of their serious faces in the obituary notices of local papers and TV were soon replaced by pictures of *New England* herself and, increasingly, the series of dazzling, celebrity-laden receptions being held around and aboard her.

Richard would have given anything to have been at the last of these receptions, an exclusive dinner for half a dozen VIPs, held aboard *New England* the night before she was due to sail. He would particularly have liked to have been among this select few as they would not be going ashore until the jet-ship docked in Southampton in four days' time. But he had other responsibilities, personal and financial. Instead, an old friend managed to take his place.

Richard was very much on Ann Cable's mind as she was driven through downtown Philadelphia that evening. It had been little more than a week since Bill Heritage's wedding day had come to such a dramatic ending and the journalist's senses had been set atwitch by what she had overheard then and since. Her attempts to find out what Sir Justin Bulwer-Lytton had been up to had drawn a blank. Now she had called in a favour or two – from Richard and even from Bob himself – and got herself one of the coveted berths aboard the jet-ship and there was a chair awaiting her at the captain's table tonight.

Ann was a little late, but by no means late enough to be rude. Even so, she felt pressed to hurry and when she was shown to her cabin she hardly noticed that it was a twin cabin already half occupied.

The guests were assembled in the crew's lounge and the small room seemed as crowded as a crush bar though only the officers were present, since all the GP seamen were doubling as waiters. Ann was used to turning heads. Her tall, slim, perfectly coutured body supported a strikingly beautiful head beneath apparently natural waves of brown hair. High Italian cheekbones framed a long nose which plunged to a sensual mouth. Her large, intelligent hazel eyes, edged nowadays with little lines which did nothing to detract from their impact, swept around the room, meeting one set of eyes after another. But only two pairs really registered with her. Bob Stark was an old friend but the familiar crinkling at the corners of his deep, almost sapphire-blue eyes somehow struck her anew. And, oddly, the green-flecked depths of the studious young officer's eyes, standing shyly alone at the far side of the room, stirred something in Ann's mind. Perhaps it was the involuntary widening of the pupils that registered.

But then first impressions were swept aside as she was introduced to the guests, among them Senator Charleston, a tall and angular man who looked like Lincoln in later life. He was the recently retired Speaker of the House of Representatives and on the short list for the next presidential election. Ann was more interested in Senator Charleston's quiet but intense wife who, she knew, hid within her plump Southern belle's body a razor intelligence and a coruscating wit. Professor Alan Miles, the designer of the ship and chairman of Jet-Ship Inc., struck her as very much the new type of scientist, as quick and confident as a salesman. He was all boyish enthusiasm and intelligent networking. He had, Ann suspected, taken the measure of everyone here in terms of their worth to the realisation of his master plan.

At dinner, Ann sat between Bob and Professor Miles. On Bob's right were the guests of honour, Mrs and then Senator Charleston. Beyond the Senator was the shy young officer with the brown-green eyes. And it came almost as a shock to realise, when the slim torso leaned forward for an instant and the shirt front filled with unsuspected weight, that the officer was a woman.

Bob, the perfect host, kept up a flow of sparkling conversation with Mrs Charleston, and Professor Miles worked assiduously on Ann, well aware that this cruise would make at least a feature and perhaps a bestseller in her hands. Even so, Ann and Bob managed to slip in an elliptical, allusive conversation, such as only old friends can manage. They had seen little of each other at Bill's wedding, what with her late arrival and his precipitate departure, and they had a fair amount of catching up to do.

Ann and Bob had first met at the inquiry after the loss of the *Napoli* and subsequently at the court case that followed it when Richard had been forced to fight for Heritage Mariner's future. She had been with the *Napoli*'s Italian first officer Nico Niccolo then, but Nico had a wife and children now and was happily settled in Naples. She and Bob had renewed their acquaintance, if more distantly, when they had become entangled with Richard's attempt to tow the great iceberg Manhattan to Africa. But in those days Bob had been involved with the Russian Captain Katya Borodin and she had been in pursuit of a Pulitzer prize.

For the last few years they had each followed their own careers, his as a widely experienced captain, hers as a bestselling author and investigative journalist, darling of the Worldwide news screens.

After dinner there were one or two short speeches. Then the ship returned to its accustomed routine. Ann lingered, watching the helpers from the galley leave in vans marked with the name of the most exclusive local restaurant.

'I didn't know you could order out from Le Bec-Fin,' she said a few moments later, finding Bob up on the bridge.

'I thought you'd have had enough Pennsylvania pheasant and whatnot at the Fountain. Foie gras not to your taste?'

'You must know Maître Perrier better than I do, that's all.'

'Old money, wide connections,' he said, his eyes crinkling self-deprecatingly. Her own eyes creased in response and something long forgotten fluttered in her no longer maiden breast.

'Senator Charleston certainly liked it,' she observed.

'Dan's a fine man. One of the best. Heaven knows how Alan pulled that one off. Jet-Ship are lucky to have him aboard.'

There came a sudden stirring which made Ann jump. Although the bridge was illuminated, the light was dim and it was quiet, and there had been an air of intimacy between the two of them which had made Ann feel that they were alone. It came as a surprise to find the serious-looking young officer in the computer room. Ann was suddenly aware that she was blushing, as though caught doing something wicked with Bob.

'I'm Ann Cable,' she said, recovering quickly. 'We weren't properly introduced tonight. You're Harriet Newbold, aren't you?'

'Everyone calls me Harry.' Those strange, still eyes consumed her – or maybe it was just the dimness of the coloured light.

'I hope you don't mind, but I'd really like to pick your brains during the next couple of days. I've been in and around lots of ships over the last ten years or so and I've never come across an officer like you – in responsibility rather than gender, I mean.'

'Of course. Anything about my work, equipment, responsibilities. Anything . . .' The word lingered oddly.

'You two'll have lots of opportunity for talk,' Bob cut in, perhaps sensing something in the air between the two of them. 'You're bunking together.' He held up his hands as though warding off a playful blow. 'I offered of course, but I got the short straw. The Charlestons have got the owner's suite, the professor's got mine and I'm in with John Dix. It's only for a couple of days.'

'It's fine with me if it's OK with Harry,' said Ann at once, suddenly realising how very much she would like to bunk down with Bob.

'Oh, I agreed some time ago,' said Harry lightly. 'It'll make a nice change for me. I haven't roomed with a girl since Radcliffe.'

In fact, Harry's reserve seemed to increase, if anything, when they were alone together. As they prepared for bed, Ann tried to tease out of her a human interest angle to enliven what might turn out to be a fairly arid piece of reportage.

'So, do you feel ostracised among all these men? Patronised?' she called through the bathroom door while Harry modestly washed, cleaned her teeth and climbed into her pyjamas and she herself stripped off her evening two-piece and hesitated in her black lace teddy, looking for a wardrobe. Then she started rifling through her weekend case, wishing she had brought a robe; wishing that the nightgown she pulled free had less of style and more of modesty about it. Still, all girls together, she thought.

'Well,' answered Harry, opening the door and stopping suddenly. 'Well, I don't know. Do you need the head or anything?'

'I'll wash up and see,' said Ann cheerfully.

Harry held the door wide and Ann slipped past her, the nightgown in one hand and her sponge bag in the other. Harry closed the door but Ann, fed up with shouting, opened it an inch or two. 'So,' she persisted, 'do you feel isolated? Threatened?' She had broached this same subject with Richard's wife Robin, a full ship's captain who on more than one occasion had taken command of a full crew of forty men and more. Robin was modestly reserved about her experiences, eager to point out that as owner as well as commander she was usually in a position of unapproachable power. Ann found this frustrating and unenlightening. But, as is often the case with strangers thrust into unexpectedly intimate circumstances, there was a chance that she could get this shy woman to open up to her.

'It's been better since Captain Stark came aboard,' came

59

Harry's voice from surprisingly close at hand.

'That's good. He's an old friend. But it wasn't so good under the other guy, Stevenson?'

'Well . . .'

There was a brief silence. Ann stepped out of the teddy and hesitated, naked, looking around. Various bits of her were reflected in half a dozen mirrored cupboard doors, all of which seemed to be open at different angles. At the back of the little room was a darker opening with a tiny cubicle on each side, one containing a toilet and the other a shower. Ann closed the door and stepped into the toilet. 'Stevenson?' she repeated more loudly. 'Or don't you want to speak ill of the dead?'

'Not so much Captain Stevenson,' came the muted voice. 'More the first officer. Cohen. He never gave me much—'

Abruptly, what Harry was saying became inaudible under a cascade of water as someone nearby switched on a shower. Ann finished what she was doing and flushed. Then, walking to the little basin under the mirrors, she called, 'Yes? This Cohen? What did he do?'

'Well, if you go into the shower . . .'

Ann pulled her nightgown over her head and glanced at herself in the mirror. Through the sheer material it was just possible to see a shade or two of added darkness at the points of her breasts and below the curve of her tummy. Oh well, she thought. No help for it. And modesty's for the birds in any case. 'In the shower?' she called as she went through. 'Yes?'

'Under the faucet there's a soap tray.'

Ann crouched beside this, only just able to make out what Harry was saying over the roaring of the shower next door. 'Under the soap tray there's a mark on the wall. That's where I covered up a spy hole he had drilled through . . .'

Ann pushed at the pale mark and the whole wedge, fashioned from a soap bar by the feel of things, fell away. And there, on the far side of the opening, surprisingly close at hand but mercifully unaware, was Bob. Stark.

'You ever make use of it yourself?' asked Ann a little breathlessly a couple of moments later as she stood framed in the bathroom doorway looking out into the shadowed cabin.

'No. There seemed no point,' said Harry from her shady bunk.

'You may want to re-think your options with voyeurism,' said

Ann dryly, unaware that, what with the mirrors and the nightie and the light still on in the bathroom behind her, Harry was already doing just that.

Chapter Eight

The pilot came aboard at seven the next morning and by the time Ann was up, *New England* was picking her way carefully down Delaware Bay. Ann was not a breakfast person and having greeted Senator and Mrs Charleston with their jug of coffee and slices of dry wholewheat toast and nodded distantly to Alan Miles, hoping to get away before he opened a conversation with her, she took a cup of black coffee up onto the bridge, in search of Bob.

'You must be light on your feet,' she said quietly to Harry. 'I didn't hear you leave.'

Unaccountably the computer officer blushed.

Then Ann turned and was blushing herself, for Bob's blue eyes were on her and for a heart-stopping instant she thought he must know what she had seen last night. Fortunately there was a reddish cast to the dawn and the rosy light covered the colour of her cheeks. 'You're up and about bright and early,' he said.

'I don't want to miss anything,' she said. And her mind put a double meaning on that too. Damn, she thought. This is going to be impossible.

His eyebrows arched. 'This must be small beer for you. There's no Pulitzer in this.'

'Oh, I don't know,' she countered, crossing to his side. 'It's a world first, isn't it?'

'Not yet, it's not. This is Mr Beauharnais, the pilot. Ann Cable, Mr B.'

'I believe I have seen the lady on the TV, Captain. And I have read your work, Ms Cable. It's an honour.'

'Thank you, sir. Can you tell me anything about *New England* from your point of view? Is she different from any other ship to pilot?'

'Well, now . . .'

As they went down Delaware Bay, the pilot gave Ann a detailed commentary on piloting in general, piloting the Delaware in particular, and piloting this vessel on the Delaware specifically. Partway through the disquisition Professor Miles appeared, listened for a while and then wandered off to the computer area. A few moments later the Senator and his wife arrived, also listened for a moment and then went to the far side of the bridge where the radio room was. They wanted to send some important cables and faxes ashore before they came fully under way.

Outside *New England*'s sleek white hull the day expanded into azure perfection. The earlier reddish sky, as Harry's machines showed Alan Miles, had been the last high skirts of a mild front wandering eastwards. They would catch up with it again later in the day, all things being equal, and beat it to the Western Approaches. Currently they were meandering along beneath a slowly intensifying high which was likely to give the Atlantic states a hot spell long enough to welcome them on their return in less than a week from now.

'Do you know when we'll be coming to full power?' Alan Miles asked Harry.

'Just after we get there.' She pointed to the bright outline of Cape May on her schematic. She looked up at the digital readouts on the screen above the collision alarm slave monitor. 'That will be in half an hour at most. Depends on dropping the pilot.'

They came to full speed at ten. All the guests were on the bridge and it was easy to forgive Alan Miles his glow of excited achievement, for the two-stage engagement of the twin jet system was every bit as impressive now as it had been off Boston.

New England plunged her concave keel securely into the heart of the Gulf Stream and followed the course of that great current east and north. The last time Ann had sailed these waters she had been coming the opposite way on the battered old freighter *Napoli*, following the course – and ultimately the fate – of the *Titanic*. Even in that rusting, dangerous, effluent-leaking old tub, she had felt part of the sea. She remembered every aspect of the adventure – the basis of her first great bestseller *The Leper Ship* – from the relentless pitching of the little hull to the constant battering of the wind. The peculiar aroma of the ocean lingered in her memory too, as did the vivid vistas of sea and sky which the weather decks, bridge wings and bridgehouse decks had afforded her. This experience was nothing like that at all. It was totally divorced from the ocean, more like taking a flight than a cruise. Or at least that was the effect to begin with.

Just as flying is a notoriously boring experience, the novelty of moving through the water at one hundred miles an hour soon palled, even for Alan Miles. The crew had duties to perform and old-fashioned watches to keep, even though the computer systems maintained engine pitch and power, speed and course, and even monitored the cargo seated on the air-cushioned floors of the great holds. But the passengers had little to do during the increasingly long and featureless day other than to get to know each other and rely on the old skills of society and conversation to pass the time.

By lunchtime, at one, *New England* had just crossed a time line so that outside her sleek hull it was already two o'clock. By the time they finished dinner, twelve hours after they came to speed, twelve hundred miles east of Cape Race, they had left the Grand Banks behind and were beginning to cross the Mid-Atlantic Basin, and had caught up another hour on Greenwich mean time.

The second day of the trip started late for all of them and breakfast was not completed until well after ten, by which time they were two thousand, five hundred miles east of Cape Breton, just about coming north of the Azores, one more hour back on Greenwich mean time, and swinging gently north towards the Western Approaches to the English Channel. They were due at Southampton by late lunchtime tomorrow.

While still pumping Harry for the point of view of a woman isolated in a man's world, Ann was widening her area of study, with little success so far. She had touched base with the irredeemably dull Stubbs and with Dix who was still settling into his post and had few insights to offer either on ships in general or *New England* in particular. The engineers were equally uninformative. She spent a fruitless couple of hours in ear protectors trying to make sense of what Chief Bligh was bellowing over the Niagara roar of the sixteen massive engines on full throttle. Next she turned her attention to the cavernous holds. It required all of her considerable powers of persuasion to get Bob to take her down there, for the holds were normally isolated during passage and he had to override a range of safety systems to get down to them from the sealed bridgehouse. The last of these was a great bulkhead door.

'You'd better hope there's no emergency down here requiring quick access,' Ann said, only half jokingly, as they walked along a corridor towards the door.

'There's nothing likely to happen in the holds that we can't deal with through Dix's cargo control systems, which are monitored by Harry Newbold's computers. Though Dix doesn't like it any more than Cohen did, apparently.'

She put that on hold for the moment. 'Monitored or overridden?'

'Monitored, I guess.'

'You're not sure, Captain? I'm surprised.'

'I know the theory. I'm just not sure of the full power of Harry's system. The networks are designed so that Dix has control of his own programs as lading and cargo control officer. Same as O'Reilley as communications officer and Bligh as chief engineer. But everything on their computers is accessible through Harry's system and I don't know whether she could in fact program her computers to override the smaller computers.' As he said this, he opened the great iron door. There was a hiss, as though this was an airlock on a spaceship. As the door opened wider, Ann could see a vast, dark space packed with huge cubes of solid blackness.

They hesitated inside the great portal on a piece of flooring which looked like nothing so much as an iron doormat. There was what looked like a phone on the wall just inside the door but when Bob pulled it free, Ann could see it was a tiny transceiver. It even had a screen currently showing First Officer Dix's face. 'Alarms all off, John?'

'Alarms and sensors, Captain. But walk light, talk quiet, stay cool and breathe shallow.'

'Lucky I'm not an overweight smoker,' said Ann. 'God knows what I could set off.'

'Lights on then,' said Bob, paying no attention to her lame levity. And on his word, bank by bank, the darkness jumped away.

When she was very much younger, Ann, like many of her generation, had fallen under the spell of Rubik's Cube. She had spent many hours happily twisting the sectioned cube trying to make all the faces show the same colour. Never in all the hours she had spent doing this did she imagine that in the fullness of time she would find herself inside a Rubik's Cube, moving between the planes like a micron. But that was exactly how she felt during the next half hour. In the clinical atmosphere of the hold, slightly and strangely redolent of rubber and engine oil, metal and ply, the cubes looked like massive coffins awaiting some weird kind of burial at sea. Each of the great coffins contained eighteen containers, three wide, three long and two high. The coffins were piled three high to the deck above with what looked like millimetres of clearance. It was just possible to pick a way between them on the strangely springy floor.

As Bob took Ann up to the walkway above the lower hold and showed her the lifeboats, they talked easily and increasingly familiarly. It was, perhaps, too early to say that a relationship was springing up between them, but the possibility was there.

The possibility was extended in the more social atmosphere of dinner that evening. This was a rather less formal affair than last night's and the conversation was much livelier. Bob was at the top table with the guests spread around him and Harry at the end. The other officers shared the nearby tables except for Stubbs and the third engineering officer who held watches. In the relaxed atmosphere, as the main course surrendered to a pudding of considerable weight, Mrs Charleston revealed a wealth of dry and knowing observations about the rich and famous. She began at first to talk of some of the politicians she had known, then of their associates in the worlds of entertainment and the arts. Soon the great and the good of all walks were withering slightly but amusingly in the glare of her recollections. Ann made a mental note to tax Mrs Charleston more deeply in the morning. She turned to Bob. 'What was it Eleanor Roosevelt said to your father when he first took his seat?'

Her opening for Bob to add some reminiscences of his own was interrupted by an urgent buzzing which seemed to come from all around them. Bob, Chief Bligh and Harry all reached for their personal phones at once, but the chimes of the ship's tannoy stopped them. 'Captain,' came Stubbs's voice, suddenly sounding young and a little nervous. 'We have an emergency distress call coming in. It sounds important. And dangerous.'

Ann would not be kept off the bridge and Bob indulged her, on the firm understanding that she would be out on her ear the instant she got underfoot.

'And I don't want any post-mortems, Ann. I may have to make some quick decisions. I could look as frail as one of Mrs Charleston's victims under the glare of hindsight.'

'I'll keep out of the way. And I'll write nothing without your express permission.'

'Fair enough. If you're telling the truth.'

Ann had no idea whether she was telling the truth or not; what she wrote would depend on what happened. She was not, therefore, offended.

Wisely, she positioned herself in that little quiet space Richard had discovered beside Harry's lair. The night was dark and so there was nothing to see beyond the broad clearview. The bridge lights were dim and it was hard to make out exactly what the busy men all around her were doing. They all crouched over their instruments with such concentration that she would have been unable to see any displays, even had she been in a position to interpret them, which she was not. But everything she needed to know in order to understand exactly what was happening was coming up on Harry's displays, and the computer officer was keeping up a low but clear commentary on the most salient points. Her voice was quiet but it carried easily to Ann through the disorientating babble of communication going on all around.

'Situation?' rapped Bob as he strode onto the bridge.

'One vessel, yacht *Calcutta*, on fire and sinking with all hands.'

'Got her on the Lloyds' ident CD,' said Harry. '*Calcutta*, Southampton. J-class racer. Thirty-metre. Could be as many as twenty aboard.'

'She's dead ahead,' said Dix from the collision alarm radar. Even as he said this, Ann saw Harry's radar monitor light up and a bright blip at the outer range of the ship-generation triangle appeared. Harry's finger left the keyboard for the instant it took to point this out to Ann. 'Limit of our range,' she said quietly. 'Take us just under an hour . . .'

The elongated triangle started to spread and then suddenly a larger triangle sprang into life on the screen above. 'That's the

Magellan reading,' said Harry, and pulled in her breath to call out something.

'Nothing within an hour of her,' said Dix, making his report just before she did. 'Nothing over the horizon. We're her only hope.'

'The *Nordica* is nearest,' said Harry quietly. 'A Swedish freighter. Three hours at her best speed.'

'O'Reilley, what do they say?'

Harry switched another screen to life and the message flickered up before Ann's eyes even as O'Reilley called out a potted version.

CHANNEL 16, said the top right-hand corner of the screen. MAYDAY ... MAYDAY ... MAYDAY. YACHT *CALCUTTA*, YACHT *CALCUTTA*, YACHT *CALCUTTA*. SIERRA OSCAR 4574, SIERRA OSCAR 4574, SIERRA OSCAR 4574.

'What are those figures?' asked Ann.

'Call sign.'

'And those?'

'Co-ordinates. Chart position. She should give location information but she's too far out. Co-ordinates is all she's got.'

FIRE OUT OF CONTROL. LIFEBOATS GONE. FULL CREW STILL ABOARD.

'What does he mean, gone?' wondered Ann.

'Lost?' Harry hesitated. 'Burned?'

NEED ASSISTANCE AT ONCE. DOCTOR FOR BURNS.

'Do we have a doctor?'

'Captain and Dix have got certificates.'

WILL SINK WITHIN THE HOUR. NO WAY OFF.

'I should think not. It's two miles deep out there and seven hundred miles from home.'

WE WILL BE LISTENING ON CHANNEL 16, 2182 kHz AND 2MHz.

'Well-equipped, isn't he?'

MAYDAY ... MAYDAY ... MAYDAY. YACHT *CALCUTTA* ... YACHT *CALCUTTA* ...

There came a silence as the *Calcutta*'s radio man took a breath and O'Reilley stopped calling out. Into this Bob said quietly, 'John, is there no one who can get to him?'

'Three hours soonest, Captain.'

'Do we have to alter course at all?'

'No,' whispered Harry, tracing a line across her screen to

the burning dot. 'He's dead ahead.'

'Not a whisker, Captain,' said Dix.

'OK, O'Reilley, tell him we're coming and give him an ETA. Chief,' continued Bob coolly, 'can you get a knot or two more out of her?'

'I can try, Captain.'

'Pile on a couple more dilythium crystals, Scottie,' advised Harry quietly.

Once O'Reilley established direct contact, he should have been able to elicit some details from his opposite number, but the *Calcutta* appeared to be in such a bad way that it was as much as the crew could do to keep calling for help. So it fell to Harry to employ the full wonders of her machinery at Bob's increasingly concerned command.

She confirmed the location of the yacht, then did a quick scan of sea and sky conditions, factored in the Magellan and weather sat information and so began to build up a detailed picture of the exact sea and weather conditions around the yacht. *Calcutta* seemed to be lying at the centre of a calm and she was burning sufficiently fiercely to register as a hot spot with the weather sats. There was an area of high pressure above her which the weak front they had overtaken at lunchtime would not disturb until tomorrow. She bobbed sluggishly in the big swells which ran eastwards here even in the calmest weather, but the swells were at their lowest setting, for two miles and more of ocean lay under her keel and the great submarine wheels of water which produced the relentless waves would not rise until they ran up the continental shelf and onto the cliff-backed beaches of Ireland. Between the surface and the sea floor only the Gulf Stream moved, but even that great fecund river would only push charred wreckage onto the Kerry coast in a week or so's time, judging from its speed as registered in the figures on Harry's screens.

Harry began to take humidity and visibility readings before Bob even thought to ask for them. She sucked air through her teeth in a very unladylike hiss of disgust as the figures revealed that a thick fog was forming over their target. Suddenly Bob called out 'What on earth . . .'

Ann spun round and automatically stepped across the bridge to his side. The whole of the clearview was suddenly aglitter. A dully luminous wall was rearing up out of the dead darkness ahead of them with just enough intensity to make the water droplets suddenly dewing the glass gleam like fireflies as the blast of *New England*'s passage hosed them away. The wall of vapour pounced down, and had the men on the bridge been relying on their eyes they would have slowed in confusion and disorientation. But Harry's instruments registered the thickest pea-souper merely as a set of airborne humidity figures beside the readings from equipment which could see far beyond the capability of any man – and indeed of most animals.

Harry predicted for Bob how much thicker the fog would become as they crossed the last few miles, but assured him that she and Dix could still see perfectly well. Nevertheless, he ordered the engine room to engage the slow-down sequence.

The fog was glowing because of the intensity of the moonlight beaming down on top of it, coupled with the luminosity of the phosphorescent surface beneath. As they neared the stricken *Calcutta*, however, the ghostly silver of the restless billows changed its colour. Mere human eyes began to take over from the machines which had guided *New England* so far. Dead ahead, and sweeping closer with disorientating rapidity even though the ship had slowed to a mere twenty knots, a terrifyingly vivid beacon could be seen. Such was the power of the blaze that the whole area nearby seemed to be illuminated by it. As they came within a mile of the stricken vessel, with Harry and John Dix reading off the ranges like a gun layer and his echo, the veil of the mist was suddenly plucked away.

Such was the intensity of the yacht's fire that the fog itself had been burned away. It was still there, like the storm wall round the eye of a hurricane, hesitating out at the edge of the shadows, glimmering weirdly in the light of the fire. In and out under the fog walls ran the low corrugations of the sea. The slopes of the waves facing the boat were red with reflection and their backs shone like glowing green glass. Rising and falling in a spotlight of white light from the full moon directly overhead lay *Calcutta*, still brightly ablaze. Her weather deck and upper works were a maze of red and yellow. Her masts, hung with rags of flame, stood skeletally until they were lost in the dead black plume of smoke which joined her like a birth cord to the spaces between the stars.

'Where are they? Can they see us?' asked Bob with quiet

71

intensity. Such was the power of the spectacle before him he simply could not imagine that anyone could still be alive on that hell ship.

'All aft,' answered O'Reilley. 'They're in the sail locker, they say. She's well alight fore and going down by the head, but they've a few moments' grace.'

Bob hesitated for an instant longer. Ann looked away from him, and O'Reilley's words took vivid life before her eyes. The bow section of the yacht seemed to be trying – and failing – to contain half a dozen flame throwers. Gouts of flame burst upwards, streams of flame gathered themselves into rivers and gushed through molten hawseholes to flood the burning sea. And as she burned, she was sinking, the sleek bright prow forced down into the steaming, bubbling water. The pressure of the sea geysering upwards within her sent more flames bursting upwards like mortars.

'Make ready two of the portside lifeboats,' Bob ordered. 'Automatic launch. We'll pick them up at the engineering deck door.'

Ann would have given much to see the side of the ship down on the cargo deck levels swing open by themselves and the lifeboats come out automatically, as though being launched by ghosts, but she knew better than to ask.

Overseen by Second Officer Walker and watched by Alan Miles, the boats were pulled along to the engineering deck door by the four GP seamen destined to go aboard them. Bob would command one of the boats and Dix the other. It was perhaps unusual to have both senior officers at risk at once – the shades of Stevenson and Cohen proved that – but they were the two best qualified first aiders and they needed to be there right from the word go. As O'Reilley had been unable to discover from the shocked and disorientated distress caller how many were actually aboard, they would take no more than two men each, one to steer the powerful diesels, the other to secure the boats while the two officers helped the survivors aboard. Again, Ann would have given anything to have gone but she knew it was out of the question. She had no expertise or medical training. Her presence would only mean one less seat for a survivor who, if left, could all too easily die with the blazing wreck.

Senator and Mrs Charleston were both in the ship's infirmary, quietly and efficiently preparing to receive casualties, readying beds and bandages, making certain the ship's supply of Flamzine, plastic bags and distilled water were to hand. Ann knew she should be down there with them, but she did not want to risk missing any of the action. She could not stop herself from hurrying down to Bob's side, prey to a wide range of emotions, still making mental notes of everything he said and did in case *New England* was destined to join *Napoli* on the bestseller lists. Bob accepted her presence but made no allowances for it. 'When we launch, pull back a little, Mr Stubbs,' he was saying into his radio as he made his way swiftly to the lifeboats.

'Yes, Captain.'

'Walker will wait down here with the rest of the non-watch seamen and engineers to help the wounded aboard.'

'Yes, sir.'

'O'Reilley, alert all nearby ships and the nearest coastguard authority what we're doing and tell them to stand by with help or advice when we find out what the casualty list is.'

'Yes, sir.'

'Nearest coastguards will be Bantry, Scilly and Brest, Captain,' added Harry's clear voice.

'Tell them to have helicopters on standby. Chief, can our jet fuel service helicopters if need be?'

'I guess . . .'

'Professor Miles?'

There was a surprised shuffle as Walker passed Miles the handset. 'Yes, Captain?'

'Is the foredeck stressed to take the weight of a helicopter, say a Sea King?'

'I've no idea how much a Sea King weighs but I'm sure it is, yes.'

'OK.'

They rounded a corner and went down a passage that ended in a large doorway opening out onto a section of ocean at whose heart sat the blazing yacht. Past the doorway swung a pair of lines and a rope ladder. With no hesitation, Bob stepped past Walker and Miles who were standing back against the corridor wall and slipped his foot onto the nearest rung. He caught hold of the ladder and swung himself out as though this was some natural extension of walking. Ann stopped, but not before

Professor Miles reached out a restraining hand.

Bob's dark blue gaze swept over her and the corners of his eyes crinkled. Almost, but not quite, a wink. Then he was gone down into the lifeboat bobbing on the water below.

Side by side the pair of lifeboats sped across the gleaming circle of water. Bob knelt in the sharp bow of his, straining to see past the blazing prow of the sinking yacht to the aft sail locker where the whole crew were stowed. As he peered forward, wishing that his eyes were as sharp as Harry's machines, he talked in clipped phrases into his handset.

Bob's boat went first down the flame-spewing, downward angling side of the yacht. He looked at his watch, wondering how much longer she could possibly stay afloat. It was, he noticed, midnight.

The after section of the yacht was well up out of the water and he had to stand to his full six feet two and reach until his shoulder cracked before he was able to catch at the foot of a deck stanchion. 'Ahoy, *Calcutta*!' he bellowed.

No reply. They must know we're here, he thought. He bellowed again.

'Pull back,' he ordered the helmsman. 'I'm going aboard.'

There was a space where the tilt of the stern was scaleable and which the flames had not yet reached. Onto this Bob leaped, and then, crouching, he sprinted across the angled, slippery deck towards the raised hatch aft where the sail locker and the surviving crew must be. A shadow loomed, cooling his back as it fell across him, and he jumped.

'Dix! Any sign?' He tore his throat on the question but Dix showed no sign of hearing. Instead he gestured to the open hatch and the pair of them ran towards it. Like sprinters in a dead heat they arrived at the opening side by side. Bob grasped at the open trap door and looked down.

Leaned over, looked down and froze.

Ann went dutifully to the sickbay after Bob had gone. She found, suddenly, that she had to be busy with something physical. Her mind was full of that last near-wink and the manner in which it had seemed to twist her heart and clench her womb. But sorting medicines was nowhere near enough to cure her restlessness, especially as all she seemed to be doing was disturbing stuff already better prepared by the patient Mrs Charleston. After ten minutes she went up onto the bridge again, in the faint hope that Harry's machines would give her some of the information she thirsted to know. But Harry's computers for once had nothing to say. Even the radio monitor screens were blank. There was nothing between *New England, Calcutta* and the lifeboats except dead, dark air.

'I can see them,' called Stubbs suddenly. 'They're on their way back now.'

'Do they look all right?'

'Yes. Wait, I'll get the night glasses. Oh bugger! Sorry. Forgot they were laser focused. Wait, I'll just open the . . . There. Yup. There's the captain. There's Mr Dix. Everything seems fine. They've got quite a few people with them. Four in Dix's boat and five – no, six, in the captain's. No wounded, I don't think, though I can see something bundled in the bilge there. Probably just kit. Yes. That's just kit . . .'

This last observation was addressed to Harry Newbold alone; Ann had gone down to see them come aboard.

Harry sat in a brown study, staring at her monitors. Her face settled into an indulgent smile. The girls – she thought of the machines as her girls – had done well tonight. *New England* had saved ten yachtsmen from a fiery or a watery death, by the sound of things, and she couldn't possibly have done it without her girls.

But then she froze, as her captain had done when he looked down into *Calcutta*'s sail locker. And for the same reason. Reflected, mirror-like, in the monitor screen beside her was a square figure dressed in battle fatigues and a balaclava. It was standing silently in the doorway and it was pointing a strange, skeletal handgun at the frozen figure of Stubbs.

As though in a dream, Harry turned and the war-like figure swam into her vision for real. As she turned, she rose. She stepped out into the main bridge area under the gaze of clear blue eyes framed in black knitted material. The gun did not move. Instead a black-gloved left hand rose in a terrifyingly controlled motion to tear the balaclava up and reveal a spiked glitter of short blonde hair. Harry Newbold gasped as though a fist had been driven hard into the pit of her soft belly.

And thus it was that Angela Van Der Piet, known as Pitman, came aboard *New England*.

And she did not come alone.

Chapter Nine

Richard was caught up in *New England*'s fate sixty hours later, like a salmon snatched out of a deep pool hooked on a lure he didn't even know he had taken. The summons could not have come at a more difficult time. Had it not been from Sir Justin he would never have agreed to it.

He was locked in a protracted meeting with representatives of the Dover Port Authority and associated authorities with video link to their opposite numbers in France. Everyone seemed to have got cold feet again at the idea of vessels moving at very high speeds from one side of the Channel to the other. Richard knew little more about *New England*'s situation than what was printed in the newspapers piled with discarded work papers in his hotel bedroom, half read, scarcely thought through. The newspapers told simply of an heroic rescue attempt gone slightly askew, of *New England* rescuing *Calcutta*'s crew but breaking down as a result. He had received disappointing but not particularly alarming messages from Bob Stark and Professor Miles reporting damaged engines and proposing a return to normal sailing speed which would bring them safely up the Channel in a few days' time. No further help was needed. No one from *Calcutta* was badly hurt. The small reception in Southampton would be postponed. There was a new delivery date for the cargo in Zeebrugge. No towing or aid of any kind was required. Richard had given a grim bark of laughter at that last one. Damn right they didn't want any help. They would be liable for massive salvage bills the instant a line came aboard. No, Jet-Ship would have to proceed slowly but quietly under its own steam if it was to stay afloat – in the markets as well as in fact. And in the meantime he had troubles of his own.

Then Sir Justin phoned. Thinking it must be Robin, Richard answered on the second ring.

'Richard? Bull here. This is providential. Where are you?'

'Dover.'

'How soon can you be here?'

'Where's here?'

'Town. There's a man I'm extremely keen for you to meet.'

'Look, Bull, if this is a social call—'

'It's about *New England* and you need to be up here as soon as possible.'

'What on earth are you talking about, Bull?'

'Not on the open airwaves, I'm afraid, Richard. But take my word for it, there is a man here you have to meet. He's come out of the blue a bit to me but I think you have to talk to him as soon as you possibly can. I really cannot overstress the urgency of this, Richard. It's *Prometheus II* all over again, if you catch my drift.'

Richard did. And his blood ran cold. 'You've got me, Bull. When and where?'

By teatime the problems in Dover were resolved for the time being, and the super-cats *Hero* and *Lysander* were at last being laded for sea. All things being equal, Richard would have been thinking of spending a couple of days up in Summersend. He had brought the Freelander down to Dover with him and, M25 allowing, he could have been up there by dinner time.

As things turned out, however, dinner time found him in a quiet corner of an exclusive private chamber in the Army and Navy Club on Pall Mall. On his right sat Bull, narrow-eyed and silent. On his left, square-shouldered and quietly intense, sat the old sailor's contact. His name was Merrideth and he was in the SAS, apparently. He was a tall, skeletal figure who nevertheless gave an impression of vigour and explosive energy barely held in check. He was dressed in a tweed sports jacket, Cavalry twills, a white shirt and a Special Forces Club tie. He had, no doubt, a return ticket to Hereford in his pocket. He had a strange face, a mixture of youth and age, of intensity and experience. And his eyes were as grey and cold as a brackish bog puddle in the back end of bandit country. There was something about him Richard recognised immediately; something he respected and trusted.

Bull had seen the same thing and had felt the same way, the

old man had explained during the brief time they were together alone before Merrideth showed up. The soldier had approached Sir Justin with the information he was about to show Richard and asked for his unofficial guidance. Which of them had mentioned Richard first, Bull could not quite recall, but the suggestion had been good – and typical of the manner in which things were still done in Intelligence and Security.

'*New England* is here,' said Merrideth in quiet but forceful tones, as clipped as his dark moustache. He pointed to a map of the south-westernmost section of Eire, and Richard noticed he was wearing black kid gloves. 'Up at the head of Roaringwater Bay. Been there since 06:00 Zulu – that's GMT.'

'I understand,' said Richard, stealing a 'what's going on?' glance at Bull, and getting a 'wait and see' nod in reply.

'This picture of *New England*,' said Merrideth, pulling out a fax labelled Number 1 from under the map, 'was taken at 08:00 local. The Garda were on to it quickly, but then they went into wait and see mode.'

'Man I know down there's been on the look-out for anything strange for quite a few days,' said Bull. 'He'll want to take it softly, softly, I should think.'

'Well, he found it. Standard coastguard sighting report from Mizen Head. Dated six today. That's how we can place it so accurately. See the estimated speed? Sixty knots. Rang bells from here to heaven, that did.'

'She came in past Mizen head at sixty knots?' asked Richard, frowning.

'She's been skipping up and down the bay a bit,' said Merrideth. 'Looks like she's been doing speed trials around the islands there.'

Number 3 was a section of the Admiralty Chart of the area. 'Coastguard station at Schull sent this up,' said Merrideth. 'There's a track of his observed movements. They call this area Heaven's Gate locally, I understand.'

'I don't understand any of this at all,' said Richard.

'I think the next few photographs may make things clearer,' said Merrideth.

Number 4 showed *New England* apparently at anchor.

Number 5 showed the lower cargo drawbridge down and resting on a little cliff top.

'They're discharging the cargo!' said Richard.

'Not just discharging,' answered Merrideth. He shuffled through the pictures until he reached Number 9 which showed the ship backed up to a different eminence, with a truck driving into it. Numbers 10 through to 15 showed a series of trucks going in and out of the cavernous lower hold. 'They're loading stuff as well.'

'Any idea what?'

'Semtex. Hundreds of pounds of it. Old PIRA stock.'

Richard shook his head, beyond words now.

'We can't judge or even guess much beyond that,' said Merrideth. 'We can't judge the weight through displacement because they're loading on a rising tide.'

'You couldn't judge even a thousand pounds by external observation of displacement in a hull that size anyway,' said Richard with crisp authority, prompting a narrow-eyed glare from Merrideth.

'We might be able to compute something if we could get accurate measurements and precise lading and displacement figures from the Jet-Ship people,' he said, 'but an approach to them is out of the question at the moment. We're keeping a tight lid on this, and that's how it must stay.'

'I see,' said Richard. 'What do you think this is all about?'

'We don't have enough intelligence to think anything very much. But we do have this.'

Number 16 showed the bridge of *New England* in close-up. It was a crystal-clear shot taken from a prime location with a telephoto lens. Two tiny figures could just be seen and they had been framed in broad green felt lines. Number 17 showed the framed area, enlarged and enhanced. It was possible to see that one of the figures was wearing whites and that the other was in some kind of green. The figure in green had a dark face and was pointing at the figure in white. The figure in green was framed in felt tip. Number 18, the last in the pile, showed an enlarged picture of the figure in green. The black face was a balaclava. The pointing arm was a gun.

'Are you familiar with long weaponry, Captain Mariner?' asked Merrideth quietly.

'I'm familiar with that type. That's a Russian AK74 assault rifle,' said Richard.

Abruptly a personal phone buzzed. Merrideth reached into his pocket and pulled his out. 'I've got to go,' he said, having listened for a few moments. 'Bull, can you finish this as we agreed?'

'How long is it since *Prometheus II* was taken by terrorists? Ten years?' mused Bull quietly.

Merrideth had re-packed his briefcase and gone, no doubt returning to SAS Headquarters at Hereford, and they were having a late, light dinner while Bull slowly came to the point.

'This is very different, though, isn't it?' speculated Richard.

'*Plus ça change . . .*' said Bull, unconvinced. 'It'll still be wheels within wheels. It depends what they're actually up to. We'll just have to wait and watch.' Bull abruptly fell silent, looking down at his plate where part of a trout lay like an incomplete post-mortem.

Richard frowned, certain that there was something more. Something neither Bull nor Merrideth had told him yet.

'You probably guessed Merrideth is not just a simple soldier. I understand he's part of the CRW command. Counter revolutionary warfare.'

'He looks the part, certainly.'

'He tells me he's officer commanding the current Sabre Squadron on twenty-four-hour alert for a terrorist incident. As such, he'll be in close liaison with his superiors in the Kremlin down at Stirling Lines and, I dare say, with the relevant officers liaising with the Cabinet Office. But on the ground he's his own man. He has his teams to deploy and he has the say-so about how they go in.'

'I see.'

'Normally, they don't get much warning but with this he's got a unique situation as well as a bit of extra time to deal with it.' Bull looked up. 'Sorry,' he said. 'I'm beating about the bush. It's a long time since I did anything like this. Look, when Pagoda Troop went into the Iranian Embassy twenty years ago, there was no chance of the building heading off across town at one hundred miles an hour. But if Merrideth has to go onto the *New England*, it might do just that.'

'Yes, it might.'

'If the ship moves at that speed, he could find himself in

trouble. He can't get aboard off helicopters, or Harriers. He can't parachute—'

'They can't even stand on the deck if she comes to full speed.'

'You see the problem. The Americans have some Pegasus-class hydrofoils which are pretty nippy and the Italians have something similar which is at least on the right side of the pond. But they're still too far away. And probably too slow in any case.'

'You want something quick enough to catch *New England* if she goes to full speed? Is that it?' Richard leaned forward. 'You want to borrow one of my super-cats.'

'Merrideth says there is nothing else that can get his squadron there, and I must say I agree with him. And he asked me to ask you.'

'What's the plan?'

'Get as ready as you can. Prepare to leave on his word. Pick up at his rendezvous. Go after *New England* like a bat out of hell the moment he finds out where she's headed for. The assumption being,' said Bull quietly, 'that *New England*'s crew and passengers are all still aboard and will serve as hostages if the going gets rough.'

'I see.'

'And that the players aboard may be mercenaries in the employ of some mysterious person or people; that they may even be associated with the IRA, from whom they are bartering or buying arms and explosives.'

'Indeed.'

'So that *New England* is being turned into a floating fortress or a floating bomb which could be moved almost anywhere in the world at extreme speed.'

'You don't have to spell it out.'

'Leaving the authorities in any place the ship shows up with little option other than to bargain or give in.'

'Unless they decide simply to blow her out of the water.'

'With Senator and Mrs Charleston aboard? And a Pulitzer prize-winning journalist, not to mention the son of one of the most respected senators in the House? I think even Washington would hesitate over that one. So unless they're going to attack Tripoli or Cuba, negotiation is going to be the preferred option.'

'Negotiation may be a painful process for the people in the middle.'

'This whole thing began for me with two such innocents. Shot in the back with Special Forces weapons, a Black Talon bullet from an ASP nine millimetre handgun. Very smart kit. But obviously all too easy to trace so the victims were disfigured and then shot at close range with shotguns just to cover some tracks. These are not soft people. They will stop at nothing to enforce their demands.'

'Which are?'

'What?'

'What are their demands? Neither Merrideth nor you have told me what these people want.'

'We have absolutely no idea. No one seems to know exactly who they are, where they came from or what their motivation is. Merrideth says Intelligence suggests that the first sign we'll get is when they set off.'

'Which is when he wants to hit them if he can catch up with them in time. Which brings it back to me and my super-cats.'

'It does.'

There was silence as Richard thought about it.

Then Bull said, 'It would just be a few of your best men and the faster of the cats. There would be no official sanction, no confirmation, no communication with anyone other than Merrideth and his men. There would be no fall-back. No insurance. Not for your life or your men or your hull. You can't tell anyone, not even Robin or Bill, when he gets back from honeymoon. I know it's all a bit James Bond but it's the way it has to be done.'

'But there are no orders.'

'Only requests in the Regiment.'

Sir Justin's personal phone rang just before midnight and he pulled it out of his pocket. He stopped walking while he answered it, hesitating under a streetlight on the arch of Lambeth Bridge. He needed so little sleep these days, and he had decided a stroll across to the night room at Century House would be a good idea. He was going to check up on Merrideth and his merry men. His position with regard to both Security and Intelligence – MI5 and MI6 – was nebulous, but his clearances were all as up-to-date as his contacts.

'Yes?' he said into the handset, looking away along the river as he concentrated on what he would hear. His hearing was getting as weak as his sight nowadays.

'It's Merrideth.'

'He'll do it.'

'I need to be absolutely clear about this. If I call, then he's up for it? No questions?'

'Yes. He needs almost no notice. He'll go on your word. You give the "storm" code and the rendezvous, and he'll be there. Guaranteed.'

'Thanks, I appreciate this.'

'Think nothing of it. Call it the old boys' net and forget it.'

'Out, then.'

'Night.'

Sir Justin folded the fiddly mouthpiece of the phone into the closed position and pulled open his Crombie – worn in spite of the summer heat – to slip the little machine back into his inside pocket.

He heard the taxi's diesel engine at the last moment, a slight scream as it swerved and the double bump as its tyres leaped up the kerb. He was in the act of turning, his hand still in his coat as though reaching for a gun, when the bumper and black grille took him full force down the side of his body. It cannot really be said that he felt anything except a massive shock and a mild surprise. He was hurled up and back, while the taxi's wheels squealed again as it swerved back onto the road. Then the old man's legs, insensible to any more feeling, struck the balustrade of the bridge and he flipped over.

He was dead before he hit the river's silent surface.

The taxi, stolen earlier that night in Camden Town, was found burned out in Brixton next day. Bull's body was swirled around Tower Steps in the wake of a Thames barge and was not recovered until the better part of a month later when the whole thing was over, bar the shouting.

And the knowledge which had haunted him for eighty years of sentient life proved in the end to be true: Justin Edward Charles Emmanuel Bulwer-Lytton was not born to die on land.

Chapter Ten

The code name was the first word Richard heard when Merrideth called him aboard *Hero* at 2 a.m. the next morning.

'Storm here.'

'Yes.'

'We're in business.'

'Right. We can leave in fifteen minutes. No notice, no pilot.'

'Good. Charts handy?'

'Here.'

'Portsmouth.'

'Yes . . .'

'Prison ship *Alcatraz*.'

'I have it marked out by Spitbank.'

'One hundred and fifty minutes.'

'We'll have to break the speed limit.'

'Yes or no?' There was a sudden edge of tension in Merrideth's distant voice.

'Yes.'

'Right. Our ID will be white light flashes, two short, one long. We will signal as soon as we see you.'

'You'll be on the *Alcatraz*?'

'When you see the signal, heave to. We'll come to you.'

Richard's mind was racing. The new prison ship was an inspired location for a pick-up point. They would upset the coastguards all along the coast and probably the Port Authorities here and at Portsmouth but they could get it done with no assistance. And, if *Hero* moved as fast as she was supposed to, they could get it done in time. Just.

And then the real chase would begin.

Captain Andrew Fawley and his skeleton crew came aboard fifteen minutes later. 'We need to be at Portsmouth in two and a quarter hours,' Richard said in greeting.

Andrew automatically looked at his watch. 'That's pushing it,' he said. 'I'll warn the engineers. In the meantime—'

'I've charted the optimum course, checked the coastguards and the weather service – we have flat calm and high pressure. No wind at all. Full moon setting at four. And I've told the harbourmaster's office.'

'Let's not hang about then.' The stocky, phlegmatic captain crossed to the ship's tannoy. 'Slip all shore lines,' he ordered.

While the four men, captain, chief engineer, first officer and owner, crowded tensely in the narrow room above and to the fore of the main areas, *Hero* picked her way easily and increasingly speedily across the busy port and out into the quieter roads. Andrew sat in the big seat which hissed down and in close to the console so that one man could control the craft. It was his steady hand that rested on the little wheel and his closed fist that pushed the levers controlling the engines forward into the red. The first officer stood stolidly beside the communications equipment, accepting or blocking the increasingly irate radio traffic. The waters across which they were speeding are the busiest in the world and even at this time of night, traffic was so dense that the one-way system was in full force. Richard's course for *Hero* took her over to the innermost line of the down-Channel path and here she came up to full speed, streaking past the lumbering bulks of the tankers, freighters and carriers, slicing across the paths of the late-night ferries.

Richard was tense. Standing at Andrew Fawley's side looking out at the unreeling night over the square captain's steady shoulder, he went over again in his mind the conversation he had had with Bull less than six hours ago.

The facts were inescapable. *New England* had gone to Ireland instead of Southampton. Merrideth's explanation of these facts, his pictures, maps, diagrams, faxes and print-outs, were utterly convincing. That Merrideth himself was the genuine article, Richard had little doubt. And then there was Bull. Bull was the linchpin. If Richard was convinced by Merrideth, he was compelled by Bull. Except for Sir William Heritage and his own father, there was no one capable of wielding such influence over Richard. The old man was just about the last of that generation who had been the giants he aspired to emulate as he grew to manhood.

As he stood, lost in thought, the south coast of England whirled past at speeds which would have been illegal on land. The Strait of Dover fell away behind the twin arcs of white water generated by *Hero*'s water jets. Hastings and Eastbourne sped by. Beachy Head gathered and curved away. Richard turned his eyes right then and looked across the moonlit distances to the white cliff where Ashenden stood. Had he the eyes of one of the sleepy gulls their passage was disturbing, he might have seen the moon's reflection silvering the broad reach of his bedroom windows, French windows opening onto a long balcony where the sight of just such a jet-cat as this had given birth to *Hero* and *Leander* less than two years ago. Then Seaford Head, the lights of Brighton, Worthing and Bognor before the long dark reach of Selsey came southwards towards them, and Andrew Fawley's firm hand on the wheel sent him scything north-westwards into the approaches to the Solent and Portsmouth itself.

The prison ship *Alcatraz* was one of the increasing number of such vessels anchored off the south coast. Its use as a drop-off point was exactly the sort of thing SAS planners would do, and it had that self-satisfied Cabinet Office Approved feeling of convenience and cheapness about it which reeked of Whitehall.

One hundred and fifty-four minutes after Merrideth broke contact, *Hero* came nosing almost silently across the water. The moon had set. Only the lights of Portsmouth, Gosport and Hayling served to outline the bulk of the silent floating gaol in the darkness before dawn. Her riding lights defined her position and status, but apart from that she was dark. Out on *Hero*'s forepeak, straining to see anything that looked like a signal in the dark, stood Richard.

There!

Almost at water level, halfway between *Hero* and *Alcatraz*, the white torch flashed in the agreed sequence. Richard spoke quietly into his radio link with Fawley on the bridge. The super-cat, already settled in the water and moving at hardly more than idle, came to a stop. With only her running lights and the scar of brightness on the bridge showing, she sat sinister and silent on the still water. And equally sinister, almost as silent, two big black Gemini inflatable boats moved barely visibly through the shadows to her side.

As the inflatables bumped silently against the sleek white side of the super-cat, a doorway just above water level swung open and the dim light of a dully-lit corridor spread like a stain on the water. The two inflatables moved into this and Richard, standing in the mouth of the opening, holding the heavy door wide, was suddenly almost overwhelmed by a rush of men and equipment. Among the first of the black-clad figures aboard was Merrideth himself and as soon as his thick-soled Danner boots touched the deck, the SAS commander took Richard by the arm. 'My chaps will secure things here,' he said quietly, leading Richard back along the corridor. 'I'd be grateful if you could show me where the kit can be stowed, then make yourself available for a briefing.' In his whispering black kit with assault vest and webbing bulked and laden with a range of arms and equipment, Merrideth was a disturbingly different figure from the tweedy officer who had briefed Richard at the Army and Navy Club. But any lingering unease he might have felt about the man's credentials evaporated. And there was no mistaking the men who were silently and swiftly insinuating themselves aboard *Hero*. They, like their leader, were the genuine article. Richard had come across soldiers like these before, in the Gulf and elsewhere. They were unique, in his experience. Impossible to counterfeit.

The central passenger section of *Hero*'s accommodation was the obvious place for the SAS men's equipment; the two lower areas, with their aircraft-style seats, were adequate to house the men themselves. In the rear of the starboard section was the little VIP conference area where Richard had been sleeping, and it was here that he led Merrideth to set up ops and briefing.

'Can you relay our requirements to the bridge or do I need to brief the captain?' Merrideth asked.

'Tell me what you need and I'll make it happen.'

'Good. There'll be no need for any of your crew to see any of us close to then.'

'Unless you need a hand getting onto *New England*.'

'Not likely. We expect to be completely self-sufficient. We have practised procedures.'

'I'm sure.'

'In the meantime, I want to get to the Fastnet at what do you call it? Flank speed?'

Richard raised his walkie-talkie to his mouth. 'Full ahead, please, Andrew. Back onto the course as marked.'

Hero sprang to life and slid into motion with surprising rapidity. As she did so, the curtains over the doorway of the area twitched and a huge man, dressed identically to Merrideth and carrying a massive case of equipment, skipped down the stairs.

'Set up the scaley kit here, boss?'

Scaley kit? Richard dredged his knowledge of military slang.

'On the table, Op,' said Merrideth, and the case crashed down onto it with cringe-making force.

The name 'Op' answered Richard's question for him. The scaley kit was the communications equipment.

Another massive man came in and slammed to attention as the first tore the case apart. 'Area secure, boss. Guards out.'

'Fine, Mac. O Group when ops is up. This area is out of bounds. Except to Captain Mariner.'

'Right.' The man slipped out of sight.

Merrideth turned. 'Comms, Op?'

'Coming on line now, boss. Sat com in. Everything green.'

Merrideth pulled out of one of his flak jacket pockets what Richard at first took to be a bulky little personal radio. But instead of listening to it, Merrideth started pushing buttons and a small screen lit up. Richard looked up, surprised, and found Merrideth's cold grey eyes watching him. 'High-tech,' said the officer cryptically. 'She's moved again but she hasn't come to speed. We've still got time to catch her. Can I have an ETA for Fastnet?'

Richard had been expecting the question and was quick with his reply. 'Four hours. But you're in business after two. As long as they don't run north we can catch *New England* anywhere after the Lizard.'

'Good enough. Now, if you'll excuse me, I have some plans to make with my men which you need not concern yourself with.'

Richard pushed the curtain aside and climbed the three steps up. At the top stood the second big man. The one Merrideth had called Mac. Over his shoulder Richard could see that the accommodation area had been transformed into squadron lines. Black boxes of anonymous kit were stacked everywhere, arranged into little areas so that the men could have some privacy. Mac had sergeant written all over him, so Richard wasn't surprised to hear Merrideth call, 'Teams in now, please, Mac. The rest to stand down.'

'Teams move,' ordered Mac. 'Stand down the rest of you.' His voice had hardly risen above the conversational but everyone moved on his word. Two teams of four broke ranks and began to make their way towards the briefing room. The other men settled into their selected areas and starting to sort out personal kit.

Mac fell in beside Richard as he crossed the area. 'We have a fully stocked galley, Sergeant,' he said. 'The equivalent of a pretty good cafe and bar. Please tell Mr Merrideth that the men are welcome to use it.'

'They'll brew up in their bashas if they feel the need. And they won't be getting much time to relax. After briefing there'll be kit to check for when we go out on the ground.'

'I see. But tell Mr—'

'The major will contact you on the bridge if there's anything else he wants, sir.'

This quiet speech brought the pair of them to the foot of the companionway. Richard climbed up to the bridge and crossed to the watchkeeper's chair where he sat, lost in thought.

'They're a funny bunch, by all accounts,' said Andrew Fawley.

'You can say that again,' said Richard. 'This lot certainly are.'

Twenty minutes later, Richard's personal radio buzzed. 'Yes?'

'I was wondering, Captain, if you would like to join us for a section of our briefing now,' said Merrideth.

Little or nothing seemed to have changed as Mac led Richard back towards the conference area. There were no brew-ups going on in the bashas after all. Instead, the men who did not need to attend the briefing were exercising, silently but intensively. As Richard watched, one of the men doing fierce sit-ups, his face vivid under a completely white pate, pulled out a watch and took his own pulse, then silently sprang to his feet and started checking on the others like a doctor making his rounds. Mac made no comment as the pair of them passed the panting men and the crouching, bald doctor. Neither did Richard. Not aloud, at least.

The scaley kit had been moved onto one of the smaller tables under the vibrating porthole through which the dawn could be seen fighting to outstrip *Hero*'s wild dash westward. Neat little screens glowed dully, like a small sibling of Harry Newbold's system.

Chairs had been arranged in classroom style in front of the large table which was pushed up against the bulkhead. A large schematic of *New England* was Blu-Tacked to the wall above, surrounded by photographs, diagrams and cut-aways. Some of the photographs Richard recognised from the meeting at the Army and Navy Club, while others were familiar from press coverage and publicity material. There were also meteorological print-outs from the fax on the bridge and a chart of the North Atlantic.

'Thank you, Mac, I think we're all here now.' Mac took his cue and vanished through the curtains silently. But the fabric hung at an odd angle, disturbed by the solidity of his shoulders as he stood guard immediately outside.

Merrideth was standing in front, facing his audience. Under the light his face was pale and strained, slightly puffy around the eyes. In front of him sat the two team leaders, slightly separated from their men. Each had a green military Filofax open on his lap. Richard noted a new formality and tension.

'Captain Mariner,' began Merrideth. 'You are the only man aboard who has been on *New England*. I would be very grateful if you could comment on those parts of the briefing which your experience makes relevant.'

'Certainly. Do you want me to offer observations or wait until you ask?'

'If you could let me set the scene. See if my intelligence squares with yours. Now, orders for a hostage rescue involving two moving vessels at sea.

'First, the ground – inappropriate as that might sound.' He leaned over and switched on a little laser pointer. Everyone concentrated on the progress of the red dot. 'This is a chart of the North Atlantic. We are here, marked by this blue pin. The red pin is the vessel *New England*. This is the Irish coast and this is the coast of North America. These marks show territorial limits. They will be of particular importance when we discuss the time frame for this mission. Both vessels are in this area of high pressure with good visibility, clear skies and low winds. Seas are moderate. Met will be updated hourly.'

Merrideth moved so that his audience could see the large

91

schematic. 'New England is a currently unclassified vessel capable of speeds between sixty and ninety knots, in excess of one hundred miles an hour. I want you to pay particular attention to the sections marked in yellow highlighter. These are the storage and engineering areas.

'As you all know, New England was stopped in mid-Atlantic . . .'

Richard listened to Merrideth covering the gist of their meeting at the Army and Navy Club while his mind fleshed out the schematic of New England and tried to visualise the jet-ship and Hero speeding at one hundred miles an hour across the ocean. This would not be a boarding in the traditional sense at all. It would be like leaping from a jumbo jet onto Concorde in mid-flight . . .

'Mission.' Merrideth had deliberately changed his tone to ensure complete attention. 'To take New England, neutralise the men holding her and release the hostages.' He crossed to stand between the chart of the North Atlantic and a black Nobo pad in the corner. 'Clearly, with a vessel capable of New England's speed, the time frame is a major consideration. At full speed, the ship can cross the Atlantic in thirty-six hours. If we can retake the ship immediately, in Irish territorial waters, we will return her to her port of destination, Southampton. If not, and we retake her within the first twenty-four hours, we will find ourselves in international waters and may consult the captain, the owner and the relevant authorities as to whether to bring her back to Southampton or take her to her home port, Philadelphia. If we do not take New England within the first twenty-four hours, we should count ourselves as being under American jurisdiction and we should prepare to facilitate further action from the American authorities themselves.'

Merrideth turned to the North Atlantic chart. 'American jurisdiction in this case will be effective between Cape Race and Cape Horn. Neither the Canadians nor any of the authorities in the various South American states, apparently, wish to become involved. It seems unlikely to our lords and masters that New England is bound south and east, round Good Hope, though she certainly has the range if she chooses to use it. We have supplies to last us for forty-eight hours, therefore. Any American reinforcements can be expected to re-supply us. New England cannot be expected to sail at full speed for more than four days, so that is the outer edge of our time frame.'

Richard's hand went up.

'Yes, Captain Mariner?'

'The pictures you showed me of *New England* in Heaven's Gate did not include any of her being refuelled.'

'That is correct. She was not refuelled.'

'Then sixty hours is your maximum time frame. Sixty hours at most. That's all the fuel she'll have left aboard after one crossing.'

Merrideth stood silent, his mind clearly busy.

'So you have your time frame and your theatre of operations, Major. They might technically get six thousand miles in sixty hours but it's unlikely. That means, no matter where they run, south or west, they're trapped. They can't realistically expect to get out of the Atlantic.'

'Thank you for that point, Captain. Hopefully we'll get it all sorted before we get to the limit either of the time or the ocean. Now, execution.' Merrideth cleared his throat. 'This is a three-phase operation. Phase one, board *New England*. Phase two, locate and neutralise the enemy. Phase three, re-organise, treat any casualties and arrange for *New England* to return to Southampton or Philadelphia, whichever is nearer at that time.

'Phase one. *Hero* can close with *New England* but we obviously cannot go straight aboard for the reasons of design and speed we have discussed.' He began to draw on the Nobo pad. 'This is *New England* and this is *Hero*. At night we can approach and overtake her.' He drew another *Hero* at the two o'clock position ahead of *New England*. 'We can then depart *Hero* in our Geminis into the path of *New England*. As she closes with us we make ready to secure the Geminis with magnetic anchors to her hull here, just where you see this access marked "Lifeboat Port". Once aboard, we clear these areas and begin to work our way up . . .'

Richard let the rest of Merrideth's simple plan wash over him as he focused fiercely on the crucial opening section. It wasn't going to work in a month of Sundays. Merrideth had got almost every detail back to front. These men were as good as dead.

As Richard sat lost in thought, Merrideth completed the briefing. 'Any questions? Right. Team leaders will de-brief back here in ninety minutes. We'll zero weapons in thirty. We'll have a splash target rigged and fire over the stern, if we can at this speed. Sigs brief after brief-back, then we eat.' His cold grey eyes found Richard. 'Captain Mariner. Have you anything to add?'

Richard cleared his throat, then spoke slowly, feeling very isolated here. 'I think you have a problem,' he began. 'In fact you have several. You can't put inflatables into the water at that speed. You can't get across to *New England* because once you come in front of her she'll see you and take avoiding action. You won't be able to anchor onto her side, and if by a miracle you could, then you'd just find a plain surface with "Lifeboat" stencilled on it. All the access holes are automatically covered as the ship comes to speed. I'm damned if I can see any way aboard at all if you let her come up to speed.'

'One thing at a time,' said Merrideth calmly. 'We could blow the lifeboat ports open.'

'No. The hull's far too strong. And in any case, you'll never be able to hang on. You've got to get on deck before she comes to full speed. The access points you need are the aft hold hatches of the main deck but they're only a possibility if you can get up there before she comes to speed.'

'The openings above the jets,' mused Merrideth. 'Yes, we could do that. Hold on tight with the magnetic anchors and . . .'

Richard was shaking his head again. Then he was on his feet and moving to stand beside Merrideth. 'No. The hull is carbon-fibre and composite. Non-metallic. Non-magnetic. You've got to get aboard another way.' He turned to the schematic of *New England*. 'You might be able to hook on here and there, then climb up and break in. There's a narrow well where the railings can be footed. Hooks should hold securely in that. It might be possible to bring you in astern, here, between the water jets, and give you a few moments to get your equipment and yourselves up here onto the rear of the deck. But once the main jet engines start to come up to power, you would simply be incinerated if you came anywhere near the stern of the ship. So even this plan would only work if you knew exactly when *New England* was going to sail and could get there in time to fall in behind her before she comes up to speed.'

'If we timed it carefully, would there be a window of

opportunity to get aboard and into the hold during the acceleration sequence?' asked Merrideth.

'During the early part of the sequence, perhaps.'

'Not too early, however, not if we want to maintain surprise. For, correct me if I'm wrong, doesn't the radar system have a special function which alters its range as the ship accelerates?'

'Yes, I take your point. At lower speeds, the radar has a very broad range, and a clear view aft as well as forward. But as the ship gathers speed, the focus is automatically narrowed and thrown exclusively forward.'

'So there are perhaps ten minutes when we could close and board unobserved by the ship's instruments,' said Merrideth.

'By the radar at least. But it's an awfully small window of opportunity in a very large game plan, Major.'

When Richard used his rank Merrideth looked straight at him and Richard was struck anew by the utter coldness of those steel-grey eyes. 'Not necessarily,' said Merrideth quietly.

Richard's jaw sagged as the penny suddenly dropped. 'You know,' he said. 'You know where and when they plan to go.'

'Not where, but what course they're likely to follow at first. And, yes, we know when. So phase one looks as though it will work at least.'

'But how do you know?'

'Does the phrase "green slime in the head shed" mean anything?'

'No, Major. Not a damn thing.'

Merrideth's eyes crinkled, though it could not be said that he smiled. 'Intelligence from headquarters,' he explained. 'Apparently a gentleman called Seamus O'Boyle, recently arrived from south of the border and currently in a private cell in Lisburn Barracks, has indicated that the people who currently hold *New England* have ordered the last of their armament deliveries to be on board no later than the end of the morning watch.'

Richard automatically looked at his watch. The second officer handed the watch to the third officer when the morning watch became the forenoon watch at 8 a.m. 'That's cutting it very fine,' he remarked.

'Can't be helped,' said Merrideth shortly. 'To sum up then. By 08:00 today, we expect *Hero* to be in position to settle in on *New England*'s tail. As soon as *New England* starts getting anywhere near speed, we slip in under her radar, come very close, right between the water jets, and deploy hooks and ropes onto the main deck. Our kit will be on *Hero*'s foredeck and our ropes will go directly up the middle of the jet section and hook into the railing well on the aft of *New England*'s deck. We go up as fast as we can and then down the hatches into the hold while *Hero* falls away and returns home with our thanks. Captain Mariner, are you aware of any alarm systems in the hold which we might need to take particular note of?'

'Heat sensors.'

'No one will be smoking. Are they powerful enough to detect body heat?'

'No.'

'The only other heat will come from activities designed to set off all the other alarms as well. Anything else?'

'You could find yourselves on video. All the holds have closed circuit – though it's only likely to be switched on if someone on the bridge thinks something's up.

'Right. If we take the cameras out, will that automatically ring alarm bells?'

'Shouldn't think so. Those sorts of systems are always going on the fritz.'

'Fair enough. Anything else?'

Richard shook his head.

'OK. Gentlemen, have any of you got any questions for Captain Mariner?' None had.

The teams dispersed to work out the details of their tasks, each team being given responsibility for part of the mission. Richard had seen the system work before and it impressed him, both as an efficient way of making the most of the men's ability and experience, and as a testimony to the quality of these rank and file members of the Special Forces. At the brief-back, he knew, each team leader would present his plan to Merrideth and the other troops, and expect no-holds-barred criticism, accepting it the way Merrideth himself had accepted having to rethink the first phase. The result would be a plan that everyone had had a part in making and that each man understood perfectly.

Richard was conscious that his own contribution to that process could be significant, although Merrideth had given no indication that he would be included in the brief-back. Yet it was obvious that the men's knowledge of *New England* was hopelessly inadequate. Only he himself could supply the intimate detail that the teams needed and he cudgelled his brains to remember how doors opened, how lights, alarms and a thousand other features of *New England* worked – details he had not given a moment's thought to on his guided tour with Bob and Harry. Once aboard – if they got aboard – the SAS men were going to find themselves in a bewildering and dangerous technological jungle. What they really needed, in fact, was a native guide.

In contrast to Merrideth's relentless 'need to know', and as something of a reaction to it, Richard explained the major's access of information, his proposals and his plan at length, in detail and with exhaustive openness to Andrew Fawley. Moreover, he engaged the quiet but acute captain in wide-ranging and wholly unmilitary speculation about who might be holding *New England*.

When Merrideth called Richard back for a final briefing two hours later, once again Mac came and escorted him across the accommodation area. The men were all there and the bald doctor – his white dome all the more striking above a face apparently only in its mid thirties – was again testing heart rate, reflexes and blood pressure. It looked to Richard as though he should have been testing his own. His face was a disturbing jigsaw of livid colour and deathly pallor. This struck Richard as odd; in fact the whole set-up was odd, now he came to think of it. The SAS men he had known had all been super-fit and medically trained to a high degree, so that all they needed was trauma management equipment in case someone was wounded. This fierce medical attention was unusual, to say the least.

Merrideth's first words to Richard rendered much of the speculation he and Andrew had indulged in redundant. 'We have had new information about the enemy,' he said. 'There are a dozen of them, and they are definitely professional mercenaries, not terrorists. There seems little doubt that they are very well armed and supplied. As well as what was loaded aboard at Heaven's Gate, they've got the contents of a complete PIRA arms cache from Donegal. Intelligence doesn't know if they've bought it all or stolen some – there were a couple of deaths in Donegal – but they certainly have a lot.'

'But what makes you say they're mercenaries rather than terrorists?' Richard asked. Hadn't Bull said something about mercenaries in the briefing? He couldn't quite remember.

'We think we've ID'd one,' explained Merrideth glibly. 'Some traces left in a burned-out car. Enough to allow a DNA genetic fingerprint. Ex-forces personnel – everything on file and easy enough to trace with the big new NATO security system. Name of Angela van der Piet. Dutch. Ex-BSB. They train women up to front-line combat status there. But she's got a bit footloose. Gone commercial. She's a particularly bad case, by all accounts. They call her Pitman – a pun on her name. You know about the Pitman system?'

'The American forces experimental system. Body armour extended up through robotics to a sort of personal tank. Robocop for real.'

The corners of Merrideth's strange grey eyes crinkled into the ghost of a smile. 'Indeed. Gives you an idea of the lady's, ah, potential.'

'OK. But where does that get us?'

'It explains why there have been no demands. No contact even. Not with us, anyway.'

'True. But only partially so, surely. If these are mercenaries then someone hired them. Why hasn't anyone heard from them, whoever they are?'

'Because their job's not complete,' answered Merrideth. 'We'll hear from whoever the real players are when these people have delivered their load of whatever it is to wherever it's supposed to go.'

'But your intelligence and security have to have been monitoring all incoming and outgoing. Surely the Garda have the equipment for that.'

'Their Special Branch certainly do. And the mercenaries – and their employers – know that too.'

'So, no contacts.'

'Nothing out. Nothing in.'

It struck Richard that Merrideth was being unaccustomedly voluble about what his intelligence sources knew. It was almost as if he wanted to redress the balance after his poor showing at the briefing with regard to his knowledge of *New England*. Richard's concerns about Merrideth's need for a native guide resurfaced. If he was going to do anything about it, now was the time to broach the subject.

He was about to speak when the most unexpected sound came from immediately outside. A scream.

Merrideth sprang to his feet with the same alacrity as Richard. Neither of them had moved beyond that before the curtain was pulled back and Mac stood in the doorway. His face was pale and mottled. A look of awed incomprehension slackened the square of his jaw.

'It's Doc,' he said. 'Looks like a major heart attack.'

Doc had spasmed into a foetal position, dead before his knees hit the floor, and by the time Richard and Merrideth reached his side, he had been rolled over and his expertly trained colleagues were working on him.

What had happened seemed to have shaken all of them, even Merrideth. Richard crossed to the two men labouring desperately over the body. 'Any sign of a pulse?' he asked. He received a curt shake of the head in reply. Richard saw that the last thing the doctor had been doing was writing in a little book. He picked it up without thinking. A glance at the final page showed a set of figures and instructions. As though concerned that his memory might be failing, the doctor had written a series of directions to himself to give doses of various drugs to a man called Bruce and to check the effects. The course of treatment was laid out very simply and was tied to a pattern of watches due to run for the next two days.

Richard felt someone take him gently by the arm. 'That's enough, thank you, sir,' said Mac. 'We'll deal with things from here on in. If you'll just leave us to it.'

Richard walked through the men and up the steps. Tension seemed to tremble on the air like a bass note too deep to be heard but powerful enough to be felt, and it was with great relief that Richard closed the door behind him and ran up to the bridge.

These men were sick. It did not surprise or particularly alarm him that this should be so. He had been in the Gulf and knew, long before the general public, that it was anything but the 'surgically clean' campaign it had been presented as being. Quite apart from Iraqi chemical and biological attacks that the West could not admit to, troops had been exposed to a horrendous mixture of inoculations and treatments including NAPS tablets designed to protect them against chemical attack, chemical pesticides, and a grossly polluted atmosphere. And, of course, there had been the depleted uranium ammunition, highly toxic to those who had used it as well as to their targets and those who had discovered the spent rounds.

Anyone who had been through all that would bear scars. Richard himself, though not exposed to a fraction of what was around at the time, still had regular and careful checks. The men's medical status was not going to compromise the mission, they were extremely fit – fitter than Richard had ever been – and obviously on a carefully planned medical regime. It was good to see that their experience and skill had not been wasted. But he was convinced their ignorance about *New England* could compromise their mission.

'They're going against some very dangerous professionals in a completely unknown environment,' he said to Andrew, 'and maybe I can help.'

'They won't want you. You're not one of them. You're not trained, you're not fit enough and, to be blunt, you're too old. These guys are what? Mid thirties? From what you've said, even Merrideth isn't much older than that. You can give them a lot of years, and you haven't used those years all that well from a body maintenance point of view if all I've read is true.'

'I doubt it is. But I take your point. Nevertheless, I think I must offer my services. Quite apart from any other consideration, two very good friends of mine are aboard *New England*.'

It would be going too far to say it was a different Merrideth that Richard found alone in the briefing room going through Doc's personal stuff, but it was clear that the major had been badly shaken by his colleague's death. It seemed to Richard that Merrideth was being badly served by both Lady Luck and the green slime in the head shed.

He put his offer of help quickly and concisely. The ghost of what he took to be gratitude seemed to glimmer in those cold grey eyes, but for what felt like a very long time, Merrideth was silent.

Under his unwavering stare, Richard felt the short hairs on the back of his neck begin to rise.

At last, Merrideth nodded. 'I would certainly like to load the dice a little more in our favour, and as you say, you're at home on ships, and you are familiar with this one. The only difficulty will be cross-decking but we can treat you as cargo.'

The major certainly didn't waste words, thought Richard grimly.

Merrideth went out into the main area, and Richard followed. At the dead doctor's pile of kit, Merrideth stopped. 'One other thing, Captain, minor but worth mentioning,' he said. 'Normally Corporal Smith would take over Doc's duties, but he will have his work cut out with his other tasks. As you will have noticed, no doubt, we have only two patrol teams instead of the regulation three. Perhaps you would be kind enough to see to the medical side of things for us. Doc's treatment log will tell you all you need to know.' Merrideth ran his black-gloved hand through his thin hair. 'If that's all clear, then I think it's time we moved.'

Two men came past carrying Doc's body in a black bag. Stunned, Richard looked back at where they had come from and then forward to where they were headed. 'My God,' he said, 'don't tell me you're taking him with you!'

'We didn't leave anyone in Ras Al'I,' said Merrideth, 'and we're not leaving anyone here.'

A thunderbolt of revelation hit Richard. 'Good God, of course,' he said. 'It's been at the back of my mind all the time. I don't know how or why but there it is. You're the Jellicoe Boys! You're 13 Int.! Well, I'll be damned.'

Merrideth rose to his full height. 'What do you know about 13 Int.?' he asked quietly.

'More than most, I admit. I was up your end of the Gulf at the same time as you were. I heard the gossip and I read some of the reports.'

Never had Merrideth's strange eyes looked more like a pair of gun barrels, steel-grey surrounding absolute black pointing straight at Richard.

'That was a long time ago,' Merrideth said at last, his voice a whisper, like a snake crawling over sand.

'Ten years, near as dammit.' Richard's voice was cool and calculating now.

A brief silence returned. Then Merrideth seemed to shake himself. 'Right,' he said. 'There's a couple of "ifs" if you're going to get through this with us. We've got ten minutes to sort them.'

The first 'if' was could Richard actually understand Doc's treatment notes. It took less than a minute to convince Merrideth that he could. Like all senior Heritage Mariner captains, he had an advanced first aid certificate, regularly updated.

The second 'if' was more difficult to address. With the kit stowed ready in the forward hold, Merrideth called the men back. Without expression they assembled in two groups of four and a pair. Ten pairs of eyes regarded Richard rather less indulgently even than Merrideth's did.

'This man,' said Merrideth in measured tone, 'wants to help us. He does not want to join the Regiment. He is not and never can be 13 Int. But I believe he knows enough to be a considerable asset to us. He knows *New England* in detail, which we could never hope to emulate, and he has contacts among the hostages. In addition, he understands Doc's treatment book and can oversee everyone's shots. He even knows something about the way we operate. He was *there*, on the Ras, around the time we were. He says he wants to help. I think he can help. He showed us at the briefing how well he knows *New England*. I think he'll make a first-rate scout. I think he'll give us an edge. What do you think?'

Mac spoke first. 'We're working light. We need someone who can brew up, if nothing else. If he can fit in without fucking up then he'll be worth the risk.' The others stirred in silent speculation, not really convinced.

Richard felt it was time to take a hand. He either spoke up or gave up. 'Look,' he said. 'Major Merrideth is right. I'm not up with you. But I do know the score. I am not some rear echelon motherfucker just here for a ride. Whether I can brew up is irrelevant because you can't smoke or use heat on board without setting off alarms, as I told you at the briefing. And that's the heart of it. I know *New England*. I know which way the doors open, where the security systems are, where the ducting leads, what you can stick magnetic mines to and what you can't. I know where the opposition aboard are going to be and where they're not. And I know every hostage by name. I was aboard her last week. I've been shown over her by the captain. With the exception of a couple of the passengers – and of course Pitman and her friends – I know every man and woman aboard. Take me and you've got intelligence and also doctoring, both of which,

102

it seems, you can make good use of.'

No sooner had he finished speaking than his personal radio buzzed. He pulled it out and put it to his ear. Glanced at his watch, nodded once, said, 'Thanks, Andrew,' then swept a long last look around the men.

'It's make up your mind time, gentlemen. *New England*'s on the radar and we'll be up with her in fifteen minutes.'

Merrideth rapped out, 'Bruce?'

'OK, make it a go from me, boss.'

'Tom?'

'Yup.'

'Welcome aboard, Captain Mariner. Mac?'

The big sergeant stepped forward.

'Take the captain in hand. If he looks the part, the others'll come round. In the meantime, watch his back. Put him in Doc's outfit. Brief him. He goes up with the kit.' As he said this, he was crossing to the communications case. 'You haven't time for a will form, Captain. Better pray you're insured with Equity and Law. Any last messages had better be brief, broadcastable and left with Captain Fawley before you turn your personal radio in. My group uses my kit. That's all.'

The enormity of what he was doing hit Richard then. As far as Robin was concerned, he was asleep in a hotel in Dover. She had no idea of *New England*'s true situation or of his place within it. She could be a widow and the twins fatherless within the hour and she would never know why. But there was no time for reasoned explanations. And none he could offer would really be good enough in any case.

As he followed Mac across the suddenly empty accommodation area, Richard hesitated. 'I need a couple of minutes with Captain Fawley, Mac,' he said. 'I can't just go off with you. I can't just leave my personal radio, I have to leave word; there's no way round it. Two minutes.'

'Two minutes. I'll wait,' said Mac.

Richard ran up to the bridge. 'I'm going with them, Andrew,' he said as he came in through the door.

'You don't even know who they are, Richard,' said Andrew, his open face folding into a frown.

'Yes I do! They're the Jellicoe Boys. 13 Int.'

Andrew shook his head in simple incomprehension.

103

'Come on, Andrew! You *must* remember. They were the crack Special Forces unit of the Gulf War. Inter-service, half British and half American. The undercover unit that did all the dirty work behind enemy lines. The 13th Intelligence Liaison Unit. The Jellicoe Boys!'

'Right! The group that worked out of the captured Iraqi cruiser *Tewfik*! I remember reading about them. But weren't they involved in something terrible . . . ?'

'That's right. On the Ras Al'I. There was a massive battle between the Jellicoe Boys and Saddam's Elite Guards as Desert Storm went into Kuwait behind them. Fighting withdrawal along the Ras itself under a full naval barrage.'

'Jesus!' said Andrew. 'It's a wonder any of them are still alive!'

'Well, they are,' said Richard grimly. 'And I'm making it my job during the next few days to try and keep them that way. They need my help and I think they've earned it so I'm going.'

'It's your call, Richard,' said Andrew. 'Anything you want me to do?'

'Nothing you can do except go home and keep quiet. Get *Hero* onto her cross-Channel schedule and wait to hear from me. Only, if by any chance anything should go wrong and you don't hear from me in, say, five days' time . . .' Richard handed over his personal radio then.

As he accepted it, Andrew said, 'I understand. I'll hear from you in five days or I start making calls.'

'Just one. To Sir Justin Bulwer-Lytton on this number. It'll reach him any time, day or night. He'll know what to do.'

'Right. Got it. No one you want me to contact in the meantime?'

'Why hand out a lot of sleepless nights?' asked Richard, and was gone.

The forward hold was packed and claustrophobic. The sea smell Richard had associated with such places since childhood was overwhelmed by the locker-room odour of men in close proximity. It was round about now that Richard realised he had not been to the head for a while and was not likely to get the opportunity for some time. But it was too late to worry about such mundanities now. Mac was speaking to the men, and that now included him.

'Boss'll be along with Op and the scaley kit in a minute. In the meantime he wants me to complete briefing. The first abseil hooks will go up as soon as there is a clear target. Two men will go up at once and set up a secure base on *New England*'s rear deck. That'll be you, Tom, and Danny. Scaley up next and Op to go with it, and we'll have to use the kit hook for the equipment. Then the captain here, also on the kit hook. As the equipment goes up, Bruce, you and your team should send up two more lines. Then the rest of us will come up in agreed order. I'll come up before Bruce and help the captain move the kit down the hatch on *New England*. We should all be in by the time the jets kick in. Anyone who isn't had better grow wings. Any questions?'

'What about Doc?' asked Bruce belligerently.

'It's not going to make any difference to Doc, is it, Mac?' said Tom, corporal in charge of the second four-man team. 'He'd be happy enough to slip over the side, no one any the wiser.'

'I agree, Tom,' said Merrideth as he and Op arrived, 'but I think it would be safer to bring him with us. We don't want him washing up unexpectedly. Now, are we all ready? Because we're in business!'

Chapter Eleven

An abrupt change in the disposition of the super-cat made itself obvious through both sound and feeling. It began as a vibration which built rapidly and was soon joined by a gathering rumble.

'We're coming in between the water jets,' said Richard. His voice was only just audible.

As was Merrideth's 'Ready, Bruce. Stand to, the rest.'

As the automatic hatch opened downwards, a battering of wind was added to the rumble and the thunder. Richard did not see the first two men go through the hatch, but then the man immediately in front of him, the solid Op, moved forward and swung upwards, hefting the large communications set with him through the hatch. Richard was about to follow but an anonymous hand restrained him. He looked up and saw a mountainous wall of ship's hull, reaching up and up until the afterdeck rail seemed to scrape the sky. Down this whipped two thread-thin abseiling ropes and a third, more substantial, arrangement attached to a light but strong-looking net. Into this went the communications equipment and the net went up the cliff. Beside it, hand over hand, feet running up the sheer white surface, went Op. The kit in front of him was already being heaved up onto the deck and stacked ready. Op disappeared onto *New England*'s deck and the restraining hand on Richard's arm lifted, followed almost immediately by a double tap on his shoulder. He moved forward and two sets of arms reached down from the hatch towards him. He reached up and they took him, swinging him aloft.

There was surprisingly little wind out here. *Hero* was being sucked forwards by the vacuum behind the accelerating *New England*, an effect intensified by the twin arcs of water falling terrifyingly close on either hand. Richard crouched there, next to go, as kit was piled into the cargo net. A hand tapped his shoulder and gestured. He nodded once, and stepped in.

At once the net was in motion, swinging up off *Hero*'s deck. Richard stood erect, holding on to the groaning ropes. The tension his weight put on the long line made its weave tighter, swinging him in lazy circles. One moment he was looking straight into the square throat of the jet exhausts, his face and chest filled with the stench of jet fuel and ozone, the next he was side on to the black and white bars of the massive lateral grille. Then he faced *Hero*'s clearview, perfectly level with it. He waved, and thought he saw a glimmer of answering movement. This contact with a level of humanity he felt he knew and understood, even if illusory and perhaps even imaginary, seemed to lift a great weight from his shoulders.

Next, the relentless spinning of his rapid rise swung Richard into a grandstand view over the outer water jet away across the glittering emerald of the Western Approaches as he came up onto the upper gallery of jets. And just as he did so, the air between himself and the breathtaking view was torn into a writhing, heat-distorted wall. Then the edge of the deck hit his shoulder and he flipped over onto the strange white composite deck of *New England*.

'They've started the jets!' he yelled at the top of his voice as he fought free of the clinging net. A tall, square form hopped aboard behind him and was suddenly there, crouching over him, helping him free of the net. 'They've started the jets,' he yelled again into the familiar face. Mac nodded once, his lips moving and his eyes distant, obviously in direct contact with Merrideth and the team in *Hero*'s hold via the headphone of his personal radio.

As soon as his feet were free, Richard moved inboard to where the rear hatch stood open. Keeping himself carefully under control, he moved as swiftly as the increasing headwind would allow over to the square throat of the open hatchway. But here he stopped in surprise. He had expected to find the hold full of close-packed cargo. Instead, in the full glare of the ship's lighting, two abseil ropes hung down into an empty area. This had not been in the briefing.

Swiftly he crossed back to the crouching Mac who saw him coming and gestured him down with an easy motion which seemed to hold approval for what he was doing. Beside the big Scottish sergeant two of the others were working feverishly, bringing up the next load of kit. The communications case stood ready but there was no sign of Op. He was probably with the forward team in the hold – taking out the closed circuit camera, if they had any sense. With the lights on, they were clearly at risk of discovery before they even settled in.

Down the outside of the rapidly rising cargo net the two abseil ropes were trembling with tension as the next pair came up, their black-booted heels lent wings by the gathering roar of the first jets coming to power in preparation for the firing of the second pair. Richard helped unload the kit from the cargo net and carry it over to the hatchway. Here he met Op, pulling himself up over the lip of the hatch. 'Scaley?' His lips moved, but such was the roar, only Richard's lip-reading skills told him what he said. He turned, to find Mac at his shoulder with the big communications case. Op tied the handle of the case to the end of his abseil line and lowered it towards the pair of figures waiting below.

Richard used his nautical expertise to secure box after box. He sent them down, controlling what went in what order and at what speed, pleasantly surprised that his signs and signals were understood and obeyed by these fiercely intelligent men. If push came to shove Richard reckoned he could get down the abseils, with help and a team at the bottom, so he took over as effective lading officer and kept the kit coming under Mac's approving direction until it all seemed to be down.

By this time the third of the four pairs of jets was firing. *Hero* had to pull away. Richard looked around the deck, mentally counting up the crouching black figures. Were they all up? The battering of the headwind was making it hard to stand now. Anyone still at the far end of the abseils would find themselves with the deck beneath their feet falling away and the jets above and beside them beginning to fire up. Richard allowed the wind to take him aft so that he could see why the others were lingering. As he came to Mac's side, he realised with a sickening lurch that someone was in fact in that predicament. *Hero* was falling back into invisibility beyond the bright arches of the water jets. The abseils were up but the cargo net was still down and a black form was tangled within it. As Richard watched, the black bulk of the figure seemed to leap and jump as the net jerked. The men on the deck appeared to be divided between those who were pulling the line in and those determined to shake the black figure free.

'Get him up!' screamed someone. It came to Richard as the merest whisper.

'He's tangled!'

'Pull him up!'

The rope jerked as a more concerted attempt was made to raise the last man aboard. The figure had just come level with the bottom of the upper range of jets when the last pair fired. The black figure was jerked out into the haze of blue flame. The black covering whirled away like molten tar. The abseil rope stretched and ignited along its angled length but it maintained its grip on the figure for an instant longer as the black parcel disintegrated under that terrible blast.

Red flame leaped up the length of the rope to the hands of the men holding it but such was the awesome terror of the sight that for an instant they seemed not to notice. Then Merrideth's voice cut through the moment and they let it go, crushing the flames on their thin black gloves under their armpits.

'You only die twice,' said one of them, and a fluke of the wind brought the words to Richard's ears.

Beside him Mac said, 'Full Viking funeral. Doc would have loved that.'

With all jets firing, *New England* was settling down to full speed now and the wind across her decks was pushing up steadily through severe storm force to hurricane as the final group ran across to the hatch. Richard jumped into the kit net as though it was a child's swing and dropped over the edge safe in the hands of Mac and another man on deck. The others went down almost as fast as he did. He landed half sitting, half standing, looking upwards, anchoring the rope as Mac himself, last in, slid down. Then the hatch swung closed and cut their ropes.

In the relative silence that followed, it seemed possible to hear the whisper of the braided nylon as the ropes fell through the still air to pile like sleepy pythons at their feet. Oddly, it was not until the lengths of line were completely at their ease that the sound of the massive steel door clanging shut reached them.

The noise re-galvanised the teams. Suddenly everything was

concerted, decisive, practised bustle. The communications case was open. 'Not much of a signal from outside, boss,' said Op, his soft voice surprisingly loud.

'Yes,' said Merrideth. 'We're cut off until we secure the ship's control areas. Our 349s should be fine within the hull, though. And all the intelligence we need is available aboard if we use our equipment right, and our native guide here. And the guns will still work. So kit up and spread out while we've still got the light. Op, while the comms are out I want you to establish the 349s. You're zero. And keep an eye on the captain here until we're secure. Mac, you and me buddy-buddy. Let's explore.'

Five minutes later, Richard was alone with the radio operator. On his big communications case sat a much smaller personal radio. Each of the others had them in shoulder holsters with single earphones and throat microphones. Op attached a lead from the set to the speakers in the comms set and suddenly Richard could hear the other ten, working as five two-man teams as they explored the canyons between the massive cargo pallets and sought out doors into the command, accommodation and engineering areas or traps and hatches down into the lower hold where the terrorists' mysterious cargo lay.

Piled beside Richard and Op was all the kit. Richard opened one of the medical boxes and looked through it, checking its contents. In the background the wind thundered across the upper works as *New England* came up to full speed. The whine of the jets settled to a dismissable background pitch which was only occasionally intrusive. He thought about what he might need in the foreseeable future. A place to eat, sleep and, more immediately, relieve his bladder, crossed his mind. He opened another box. At least he could see what he was doing down here, with all the lights on. He wondered briefly why they were on, and how long they would stay on.

'Where's a torch?' he asked Op.

'That's made me a packet,' said the big radio operator cheerfully. 'Had a tenner on with each one of Bruce's team that your first question wouldn't be "Where's the crapper?" Silly bastards were so confident they gave me odds. Eighty quid. Thanks very much, Captain.'

He pushed a button and said '"Where's a torch?" Bruce, you sorry little shit. Pass it on to the brick. Twenty quid each.' He turned to Richard. 'You've got a Maglite and a Betalite in the doc's vest pocket there, Captain.'

'Good,' said Richard rummaging, faintly exasperated that he had climbed into Doc's blacks without checking his pockets or combat webbing. He probably had everything he needed in here.

'And in case you're wondering,' Op went on, 'we do have a crapper.' He pointed to a large roll of plastic bags. 'And you piss in that.' He indicated a five-gallon plastic jerry can marked with a bright yellow P. 'Every day we'll put in a handful of water purification tablets to keep down the smell. Got any of this?' He fished a battered roll of Andrex from his bergen.

Richard numbly shook his head.

''S all right. I can let you have some of mine. Ten pence a sheet. Take this one on account . . .'

'They're coming back in, Captain,' said Op. 'Better get the slash jars and the latrines to hand. You were the first but you won't be the last. And you'd better get ready to go out yourself. It'll follow standard pattern. Reports. Assessment. Tactics briefing. Kerfuddle – or as near as we can get to it with no heat allowed. Then they'll need you out in the contact area.'

They all just suddenly appeared. Richard had thought the place was well-lit. All the big overhead fluorescent lights were on and they illuminated the three-dimensional jigsaw of the huge containers apparently perfectly, but between the containers lay narrow, pitch-black canyons of space and out of one of these the Jellicoe Boys poured silently, like a moving extension of the black shadows. They had all pulled their black watch caps down into balaclavas and only the whites of their eyes broke the solid black of their clothing.

They put down their weapons, a bewildering selection of them, and crouched beside Richard and Op. Then they began to pull their balaclavas off, and recognisable features joined half-familiar physiques until Richard was clear as to who was surrounding him. The scrawny but bellicose Bruce and his team were on his right. The cheerfully enormous Tom and his team were on his left.

'Five minutes,' said Merrideth. 'Then reports. Bruce, your brick's first stag. Mac and I will do assessment, then we'll call briefing and really put the captain to work. Bruce, you'll set

112

traps on the way in for O Group. I don't want to give the players an inch. We'll either have a brick out or traps out until we go in. Captain Mariner, I'll want you on the ground as soon as possible now that we've given the place a security sweep. Everyone got that?'

They all nodded.

'Right,' said Merrideth.

And on his word, as though the terse monosyllable had been a secret command, the lights went out.

Into the darkness boomed a great voice over the tannoy. 'We know you're in there! Come out at once with your hands up or you die!'

Chapter Twelve

'Hands up or you're dead,' said the strange woman in army uniform three full days before Richard and the Jellicoe Boys came aboard. Slowly, Harry Newbold obeyed, fighting to believe that the apparition before her was real. Could that square, skeletal thing really be a gun? Surely such a clichéd order came from nightmares, not reality. But Stubbs at the wheel and O'Reilley in the radio room were raising their arms obediently, so she did the same.

As she did so, her gaze automatically slid towards her computers. She had to send out an alert. Could she trigger a remote-control beacon somehow? The tension on the bridge was emanating as much from their captor as from herself, Stubbs and O'Reilley. Now was the moment to try something, before the woman with the gun felt confident she was in charge of the situation. But then again, perhaps not. The tension was such that even the suspicion that something was being tried was likely to get someone shot.

Another figure entered suddenly, with Bob Stark at his side. There was no doubting the gender of this tall, powerful figure, and when the black balaclava came off, a square face with grey stubble on chin and skull was revealed. The shape of the face was strange, however. On the left side, between the grey crown and the grey chin, the bone had collapsed inwards, as though the man's head had been crushed in a vice. Scar tissue, also disturbingly grey, spread from temple to jaw line, from nostril to earlobe.

'Bridge secure, Captain Dall,' said the woman at the door.

'I see that, Pitman. The whole ship's secure. We want the communications closed, though. That means you, Sparks. Everything off. Move it!' The grey face swung round towards Harry. 'The computers go down too. All of them. Now!'

115

Harry found she was having difficulty breathing but she fought to obey, unnerved by the sight of this man and terrified by his harsh tone and chilling eyes.

Dall's action in removing his balaclava had been as calculated as Pitman's had been thoughtless, for he was used to making use of his facial disfigurement. It showed that he had been at the sharp end. It showed that he meant business. It was, simply, frightening. He swept a glance round the bridge, took in the layout and the stunned faces of the watch officer, the radio officer and the frightened computer girl. He saw in them only confusion, compliance and fear. Even so he pushed the barrel of his AK74 into Bob Stark's ribs.

'Please do what these people tell you,' said Bob, fighting to keep his voice controlled and relaxed, even though his mind was a whirl of sickening speculation. 'They have complete control of the ship and if you try to resist they may kill you. Do what they tell you. That is a direct order.'

Dall used his weapon to push Bob back across the bridge again. At the doorway he paused, but then he left Pitman where she was and swept on.

Harry grimly worked on her computers, closing them down as the scarred man had ordered. As she worked she thought she could feel Pitman's gaze like fingers on her.

She was right. Pitman was watching her closely; she was the only one with enough presence of mind to be doing something and Pitman was weighing her up as a potential threat.

O'Reilley sat by his communications equipment, his hands idle and his shoulders slumped. Stubbs stared sightlessly out through the clearview at the blazing wreck of the yacht as she settled beneath the ocean, glittering weirdly through the luminescent surface, still burning like the reflection of a falling star as she sank into the dark. The fog began to swirl in over her, then it crept up across *New England*'s white foredeck and began to rub its faintly luminous flank across the clearview. Soon it was as difficult to see a course ahead as it was to see a course of action.

The tannoy sounded. 'Hear this.' It was the voice of Dall, distorted by the system but still familiar. 'Ship's personnel report to the dining area. My personnel oversee movement then report back to post. Move now!'

116

Harry was still struggling to close down her systems in such a way that she could get back into them quickly and easily when opportunity arose. 'You!' spat the woman by the door. 'Hurry!' Stubbs shuffled past the stocky, gold-haired figure. O'Reilley reluctantly emerged from the radio room. Harry saw them move in reflection. Her breath drew in between thin, pale lips. Her fingers danced. Her shoulders prickled. She did not know it but her cheeks were flushed and the pupils of her steady eyes were dilated.

Angela Van Der Piet crossed angrily to the computers. Her left hand took Harry's slim shoulder and swung. The seat came round swiftly on its swivel and the women's knees clashed together. Pitman found herself confronted by that vivid face, all tousled hair, pink cheeks and pupils wide enough to drown in.

'Up and out,' she rasped. 'Or I'll hose the fucking lot with this!' She brought her gun down, drawing a steady bead on the nearest computer.

Harry reached over and snapped down one final rocker switch. The last screen died. She rose, bracing her body slightly against the chair to keep her balance with the belligerent woman so close to her. The soldier smelt of smoke, wet webbing, gun oil and sweat. Her golden hair was darkened by grease.

Like Dall, Pitman used her gun as a goad, herding Harry swiftly out onto the bridge companionway after the men. At the touch of the weapon, Harry jumped, whether because she was scared of the gun or because she was scared of getting grease on her nice clean whites Pitman was not sure. It did not occur to her that Harry had felt a shock of animal electricity. Pitman herself felt nothing except tension and impatience. She pushed again and Harry stumbled down the steps, half falling onto the next deck. She regained her feet quickly enough, squared her shoulders and moved on more swiftly. Satisfied, Pitman left her alone.

As they entered the dining area, Pitman turned and ran lightly back up to the bridge. She checked the radio room carefully, ensuring with practised fingers that everything was in the required disposition. Then she crossed to the helm and stood looking out at the featureless fog, lost in thought. Because the computers were of as little interest to her as the girl who operated them, she paid them no attention.

117

The passengers and crew of *New England* sat silently in the dining area. They were grouped round the tables and four of their captors were on guard, one in each corner, weapons cocked. In the middle of the room, the focus of every pair of eyes, stood Dall. He was unarmed and stood at parade-ground ease, his feet half a metre apart and his hands clasped behind his back. Every inch the professional soldier, every inch the commanding officer in the field, he said quietly, 'I thought it was time we met up and got one or two things straight.' He paused. Rode the silence. 'My name is Peter Dall.' The way he said it in that flat, precise, almost accentless English could have made his first name Pjotr or Pieter, his last name Doll or Dahl. He could have come from anywhere between Alaska and Archangel, the long way round. 'You will become acquainted with my command, collectively and individually, as and when that becomes necessary. It is enough for you to know that we are in complete control of this ship and will remain so for as long as necessary to complete our mission. You are no part of that mission and therefore we have no reason to harm you, as long as you remain passive. If you become active, however, we shall not let you live. I hope I am making myself clear.' There was silence.

'My command and I all speak English as well as a range of other languages. We are all trained in ship-handling though we will require you all to return to your duties in due course. Except for the radio officer. We have our own communications equipment. Do nothing except what you are told to do and you will not be told to do anything beyond your capability, your moral boundaries, or your laws.' He produced a piece of paper and flourished it.

'I have drawn up a schedule of the only major changes I deem necessary to your routine. These involve sleeping arrangements which have been varied to accommodate my people and their necessary routines. There will be no appeal, discussion or debate. Except with regard to Mrs Charleston. There will be a guard posted in your quarters, ma'am. Would you prefer to remain with your husband and a strange man or would you prefer to move in with the other women?'

'I will stay with my husband, please, Captain Dall.'

'As you wish. Everyone else, please familiarise yourself with

118

these arrangements. It will be lights out and full curfew in half an hour.' He turned on his heel and walked out. The dazed crew crossed to where the piece of paper lay on the table in front of Bob Stark, but before anyone could look at it, Bob was on his feet.

'Listen, everybody, please!' He held up his hands and there was silence at once. 'When I saw each of you with Captain Dall, I told you that we must do what these people say or they will simply shoot us. I meant what I said. We are not going to outguess or outsmart these people. We do what they say and we await events. Now, look to your sleeping arrangements and move your gear as necessary. Remember, curfew in twenty-five minutes.'

Ann Cable was up on her feet at once. The daughter of a workaday Italian bit-part actor and an Irish chorus-girl mother, her volatile mixture of Kilkenny and Calabrian blood was near boiling point. 'Now just a minute,' she said, throwing her hair out of her blue eyes. 'Just a—'

'Miss Cable,' snapped Bob. 'These people have twenty minutes to move their dunnage. Don't slow them down unless it's crucial. And you've got the same time to sort out your own possessions, remember.'

She paused. It seemed petty to consider it at a time like this, but there was a lot of stuff down in those bags she did not wish to part with.

Harry was perusing the list and looked up to tell her roommate that she had nothing to worry about, but Bob caught her eye and hushed her with an infinitesimal shake of his head.

So it was that when the lights went out at 03:00 on the first day, everyone was in bed except the members of Dall's command who had taken over the watches. The watches ran to ship's time and so at four Pitman came down to the cabin shared by Harry and Ann. Dall had told Pitman to keep a particularly close eye on Ann Cable who was far too volatile a mixture of temptation and disruption for his taste. The soldier left the cabin door ajar so that she could use the security light from the corridor outside to check on the sleeping woman – she had already gone through her suitcases while Dall was giving his briefing in the dining area. Then she swung the door to, spread out her sleeping bag on the floor, stripped to her T-shirt and shreddies, and re-strapped the holsters of her combat knife and

119

her 9mm ASP to her naked thighs.

Neither Ann nor Harry was actually sleeping when Pitman came into the room, though both pretended to be. Ann lay wakeful, making and discarding a range of plans. As soon as she had realised someone had been through her cases and taken her personal phone, she had known that she was no longer capable of independent action. She found that even more disturbing than the sense of personal invasion that the detailed search engendered.

Harry's mind was a whirl of thought as well. She found herself deeply disturbed by the powerful woman lying spread within arm's reach on the floor. Even with her eyes tightly closed she could see every detail of the clinging combat cotton and the cold steel against the contoured flesh. With difficulty she turned her mind to more professional considerations, in particular Captain Stark's orders to await events and follow instructions. She had the decided impression that she had been both overlooked and greatly underestimated by Dall and Pitman. No one aboard, whether among Captain Stark's crew or Captain Dall's pirates, had any idea how easy it would be for her to fire up the computers at almost a moment's notice and take over any system aboard from the engines to the communications.

Such was Harry's exhaustion that when she did fall asleep, she slept deeply and soundly. When she woke next morning she was half inclined to believe that the previous day's events had all been a dream. Certainly the disturbing figure stirring on the floor beside her seemed better suited to fantasy than to the waking world.

Under the eyes of the two legitimate occupants of the cabin, Pitman unstrapped the holsters from each thigh, stepped into her trousers, replaced the weapons and laced up her boots. Then she caught up her jacket and belt and exited without a word.

'God,' said Ann the instant the door closed. 'Doesn't that woman need to wash or use the john? I only believe she needs to sleep because I saw her do it.'

'She's probably gone to get something to eat,' said Harry practically.

'Gone to get orders from Frankenstein's monster, more likely,' said Ann. 'We'd better pray they don't involve shooting us because I don't think she'd hesitate.'

Harry slid out of bed and began to sort out a clean uniform for the day. Everything around her felt strange and out of joint. She crossed to the small window which looked out to the port side of the bridgehouse. The ship was drifting. Part of the strangeness came from the lack of engine noise, vibration, urgent purpose. And, she admitted, another part of it came from a feeling of helplessness, almost of listlessness. What was the purpose in dressing? She had nowhere to go, nothing to do, no responsibilities to fulfil. She didn't even know whether she was allowed out yet.

The answer to that last question came at once. The ship's tannoy sounded and Captain Dall said, 'It is 08:00 local time. Curfew is suspended until 20:00 hours. Ship's watch routine is hereby re-established. Watch officers and engineers to your posts, please. Non-watch officers, crew and passengers to the dining area. That is all.'

The smells which greeted the two women as they hurried towards the dining area were unexpectedly mouth-watering, but it was the interlopers who were shovelling away the ham, eggs and hash browns. Everyone else, from Bob Stark to GP Seaman Lee, the most junior aboard, was lined up along the wall under the guns of the only two men who were not eating apart from Dall himself.

'As you will have observed, ladies and gentlemen,' Dall began, 'we have made no progress along our course during the night. I have no expectation of getting back on course before tomorrow at the earliest. My Magellan tells me to within a metre where we are and I have enough equipment to alert me to the approach of any other ship or hazard without bringing the bridge equipment on line. I am therefore content that we should drift generally eastwards, without power except what is necessary to provide light and heat. And this is why I have assembled you all here now. I shall require a certain amount of help and guidance from some of you. This help will not endanger any of your friends aboard, though refusal to co-operate may do so . . .'

The long and the short of the plan was that Dall and his men wished to establish in the minds of the concerned authorities that the ship was safe, that her crew and those they had rescued from *Calcutta* were fine; that the engines were not working well but that no help of any kind was required. Then they wanted to spend the day making use of *New England*'s officers, engineers and workshops to add to the natural fortifications of the bridgehouse.

As the day wore on, almost everyone aboard who might possess the time or the energy to pose a threat was given work to do – except for Ann Cable and Harry Newbold. Although Captain Dall continued to underestimate what damage Harry might do if she tried, he did see to it that she got nowhere near the computers.

After a light breakfast, Harry returned to her cabin. Ann was already there, and sharing the cramped quarters with her was a bit like sharing a cage with a short-tempered Siberian tiger. Harry was thinking of going somewhere else when Pitman tore through the cabin heading for the bathroom. 'It's always the fucking same coming off field rations,' she spat as she slammed into the little room. She tore her trousers down to holster level as though she was alone and unobserved. Then sat with the door open and her pistol on her lap, glaring out at them.

The voice of Harry's mother came to her aid. 'Let me show you the ship's library, Ann,' she said in tones that would have done the chilly air of Lynn Harbour proud. The two women walked along the corridors and down the companionways to the small room filled with books and video equipment. Ann went through a shelf of books. 'Does anybody actually read any of this stuff?' she asked, not really expecting a response, and not getting one. 'Still, I'm glad to get away from that Pitman bitch. Pit bull more like. Bull dyke too, probably.'

She turned to a shelf of videos and did not see the expression that last sally brought to Harry's face. But Harry was too preoccupied to pay much attention to Ann. At the back of the library, unused and unremarked, was a small computer console. It had a CD-ROM facility, a printer and an easy access word processing program. It also had network capability within the ship and if Harry could get the right codes and passwords typed in, she could access every screen and system of the massive machines on the bridge. And, if O'Reilley could be persuaded to throw the right switch unobserved, it had a modem facility through the ship's sat-com phone dish and therefore access to the Worldwide Web.

O'Reilley's help would have to be negotiated carefully. He did

122

not like her and the feeling was mutual. He did not trust her and she felt the same. He might well turn her in just for the fun of seeing whether Dall would turn his men loose on her and do some of the damage she had no doubt the twisted little communications officer lusted to do to her himself. In any case, she was a member of a crew here, not a loose cannon. O'Reilley should not even be approached until after she had cleared things with her captain.

Leaving that to one side, her next priority was to get access to her computer programs. Through them she could find out about transmissions in and out, about engine status, heading, wind and weather. In the right hands, that sort of information would be priceless. She could also, if she got into the right programs, do an incalculable amount of damage. She could reverse the mechanisms of any circuit so that switches read off when on, and vice versa. She could re-program the guidance computers to go south when they read north, to go east when they read west. She could re-program the weather monitors to read hurricane force wind when it was dead calm. Quite simply, she could do what she wanted. Or, more sensibly, what Bob Stark wanted.

'Ann,' she said, 'do you think you could get to the captain?'

'Get to him?'

'Persuade him to stop whatever he's doing at the earliest possible moment without causing suspicion and come down here with you?'

'I guess I could. We go back a long way. I could get through to him if it was really important. But where's the fire?'

'Here. This computer. I don't know how much you know about computers, but . . .'

Fifteen minutes later Ann went off in search of Bob. Her mission was relatively simple but the fact that she had one at all cheered her enormously. She had already decided to make her appeal to Bob one that held plenty of scope for repetition. She wanted people to assume that she would wish to contact Bob and maybe spirit him away on a regular basis. And there was only one way she could think of to achieve this.

As a much younger man, Bob had been caught up in a situation like this on *Prometheus II*, flagship of the Heritage Mariner tanker fleet. The difference between then and now was that he had not been in charge then. Responsibility weighed heavy now, more heavily than it had since his days in command of a small coastguard unit in Vietnam. Perhaps age had something to do with it. The future no longer seemed to rest, gleaming, in the palm of his hand. Bob was following Captain Dall through the accommodation areas. Dall wanted every access point barricaded, monitored or defended. He seemed to be preparing for invasion by a considerable force. He worked out choke points and fields of fire, closed some accesses and opened up others.

'You've got welding equipment, Chief Bligh tells me,' he said. 'I want this hatchway from the hull welded shut and then I want something heavy put behind it and welded in place. I want no direct access from the outside along this route, do you understand?'

'Yes,' Bob answered. 'We can close it off against a small charge, maybe even a fairly big one, but I guess you know better than I do that there's stuff out there that will blow it open and clear this corridor no matter what we've welded there. That's independent of artillery.'

Dall was about to respond when a voice from the far end of the passageway stopped him.

'I have someone here asking to see Captain Stark.' The voice belonged to Dall's closest associate, an American named Paul Aves. No matter where they were, Aves guarded the nearest landing or entry. Anyone looking for Dall had to come through him. Bob assumed that would also be the case in combat.

'Who is it?' asked Dall, his voice distant, still preoccupied with the problem of closing this corridor. He was giving it more attention than he had given the other areas so far, perhaps because it was the corridor along which his own men had come.

'Woman. Calls herself Cable.'

'She your piece?' asked Dall.

'No!' Bob answered with perhaps more emphasis than he meant.

'Uh-huh . . .' said Dall, obviously unconvinced. 'What's she want then?'

'I don't know. To tell me something, I guess.'

'Let her past,' called Dall.

Ann came down the corridor in a cloud of Calvin Klein and keen concern. She had paused en route to freshen her make-up and settle her beautifully tailored clothing to its best effect. She was one of those people who could turn on an extra sparkle, call it charisma, and dominate a room or turn heads at will. She was burning at full wattage now. Dall and Bob watched her coming with something akin to awe. Bob noticed that the stolid Aves leaned in round the corner for a rear view as she swept past. Whatever she was up to, thought Bob with sudden clarity, it had better be worth the risk.

'Bob!' she said, sweeping past Dall and wrapping her arms round her old friend's confused neck. Her kiss left lipstick in places only maiden aunts had left lipstick. Dall's amusement at finding Bob in such an obvious lie so soon after telling it was evident. It spread even to his chilly eyes.

'What do you want, Ann?' asked Bob, breaking away.

That was the question that had exercised Ann's mind most forcefully while her fingers had been busy in her make-up bag. She had to have a reasonable, acceptable excuse for demanding the immediate presence of the captain of a pirated ship. Something simple, innocent, something so obvious and compelling that even the leader of the terrorists holding them would allow it without a second thought.

Unable to think of anything that would fit the bill, she had returned to the library to confess failure. Harry, unexpectedly acerbic, had sent her up to the bridge to talk to the watch officer. On the bridge she had come across Stubbs who, unprompted, was showing signs of genuine concern about something.

'Lieutenant Stubbs is worried about the weather,' Ann said now. 'He can't leave his post and the gentleman guarding the bridge seems reluctant to disturb anyone so he can't contact you direct and isn't allowed to call Captain Dall here. So when I went up there he asked if I'd tell you it looks as though there might be a nasty weather system coming in from north-west. Have I got that right? Can a weather system be nasty?'

'I'd better check that out, Captain Dall,' said Bob at once. 'Anything serious catching us out here without way or power could do us a lot of damage.'

'Yes,' said Dall. 'You check it out and get back to me.'

⋆ ⋆ ⋆

125

'I need to see you in the library,' hissed Ann as they hurried towards the bridge.

'What?'

'The weather's an excuse to get you away. Check on the bridge then try to get to the library before you go back to Dall.'

'They're likely to guard me on the way back. They've only let me out of sight now because you made it sound important. What is going on, Ann?'

As they hurried up the companionways towards the bridge, she tried to explain what she understood of Harry's discovery. She understood a fair amount, in fact. She was computer literate, Net-confident, Web-wise and competent with all types of modern gadgetry. Had Pitman not taken her personal phone, the Marines would have been on the way down the funnel by now.

Halfway up the final companionway, Bob stopped as the full implications of what Ann was telling him hit home. 'If she can access all the systems . . .'

'She can do more than that. She thinks she can control them!'

'And get onto the Web . . .'

'Even the CIA has a Website. The Marines certainly do, though I don't know the address off hand. We could call in whoever we want.'

'I've got to think this through.'

'Come and talk to Harry. In the library.'

'OK. Wait for me there.' He was so excited he suddenly reached for her and held her, returning her original greeting with interest.

Bob strode onto the bridge with his mind on fire. There was no one at the helm. The ship was making no way. In theory she should be showing either riding lights or a distress signal but Dall had said to leave that for the time being. Stubbs was there, on watch, mooning about, lonely, worried and depressed. In the watchkeeper's chair on the port side of the bridge a young soldier sat idly nursing a venerable but functional-looking gun. For all his lackadaisical ease, the soldier seemed to Bob to be closely on watch, ready for anything.

'Well, Mr Stubbs,' he said cheerily. 'Where's this nasty weather system?'

Stubbs led Bob over to the weather radar. 'Picture's not too good, Captain,' he said apologetically. 'All sorts of interference, I don't know where from.'

'Never mind that. It often happens,' lied Bob, thinking of Harry breaking into the system from below. 'If you're really worried we'll see about getting permission to contact a weather station.'

'We could get the British Shipping Forecast on the World Service of the BBC, if it came to that,' said Stubbs. 'We're not so far beyond their reach.'

'Hell,' said Bob, 'we could fire up the old TV and tune into the Weather Channel. But we'd have to get Captain Dall's permission to switch on. In the meantime, what have you got on the automatic systems?'

Stubbs had only brought up the idea of the BBC as a kind of moan. It was the sort of thing he did all the time. Under pressure he was a bit of a Luddite. His captain's cheery rejoinder knocked him sideways. The idea of *New England* actually relying on the television for her weather reports was simply ridiculous. But when he looked at Bob and saw that Bob was looking at the soldier in the watch chair, even Stubbs began to suspect that his captain was up to something; at the very least he was testing the guard's knowledge of the real power of the ship's systems.

'It's a tight little low pressure system coming east out of Newfoundland about now,' said Stubbs, showing Bob the cause of his concern. 'You see the pressure gradients along the fronts here? The projected path brings the tail over us within the next twenty-four to forty-eight hours with predicted wind speeds building to severe storm in this area. Its track will bring some big seas over.'

'I'd better tell Captain Dall,' said Bob and crossed purposefully towards the door.

'Wait up, Captain,' said the guard at once. 'I'll call you an escort.'

'No, that's all right. Really. I know where he is.' The newly re-invigorated Bob kept moving as he babbled. Had the guard been standing in the doorway, Bob would have had no chance, but unless the guard was going to shoot him in the back, he could not control him. Even so Bob's shoulders did not stop prickling until he had turned the corner into the companionway. He ran down it, the sound of his feet on the deck disturbingly loud. He moderated to a jog only when he reached the A deck corridor where the library was located.

He swung the library door wide, but the room was empty and the computer was dead.

'Double stag,' fumed Pitman. 'You got me double fucking stag. I am not pleased with this so you had better do what I tell you, ladies, and keep your asses clean.'

Pitman had appeared at the door to the library in a rage. The only positive aspect of her thunderous mood was that she had made so much noise on her way up the corridor that Harry had had time to switch off the computer and pile some videos in front of it before the door slammed wide.

'There you are!' spat Pitman, shouldering her way in. 'What's this Captain Dall tells me about you fucking about on the bridge, Ms Cable?'

Ann wisely said nothing.

'The captain does not wish you ladies to be running about in command areas unescorted. He does not want you anywhere sensitive at all, in fact. So I've got to keep an eye on you at all times, thank you very fucking much. It's not enough I've got to eat with you and sleep with you. Everyone else gets an on and an off with their assignments. Not me, though. Oh no, not me! Well, I tell you this, the pair of you, if I've got to watch you then I'll watch you watching me do what I've got to do. This way! Now!'

She led the subdued women along the A deck corridor past the dining area and the galleys to those sections of the bridgehouse designed to balance the mental pursuits of the starboard with more physical pastimes on the port. She kicked open a door to a neat little gym. Two benches sat at the foot of walls hung with exercise bars. There were ropes suspended from the low metal ceiling. These old-fashioned facilities were not being used but the exercise machines in the centre of the room bustled with exercising men.

Pitman's arrival was greeted with a round of jeers and lewd comments which came to an abrupt stop when the men realised she was not alone. They all stopped exercising, and eyes and lips began to gleam as brightly as sweat-sheened muscles.

With no regard for the sensitivities of anyone, Pitman barked,

'You two, sit on that bench. Move and you suffer. Lobo, let me back on that bench. I've got to be able to see these two tarts at all times. Captain's orders.'

As she spoke, Pitman was pulling off her blouse and easing the waistband of her trousers. The reluctant Lobo gave way to her and she straddled a bench, sitting with her thighs wide, her back straight, and her arms raised to a trapeze above her head. Her skeletal automatic was on the floor, its grip beneath the instep of her right boot, its barrel pointing meaningfully at her charges. Lobo crossed and looked speculatively down at Ann who thanked God silently but fervently that she had buttoned her blouse to the throat since her assignation with Bob. Harry, in her white uniform blouse, was not so lucky and the man's lingering glance made close acquaintance with the lace of her bra. 'If either of you two ladies want some serious exercise,' he began, posing like a teenage lifeguard – but the rest of his proposal was drowned out in hoots of laughter and alternative offers, all of them imaginative, few of them physically possible. Eventually Lobo crossed to a rowing machine, sat down and got to work, and the rest of them followed suit. Like Pitman, they had to rely on their bodies the same way a parachutist has to rely on his chute. Every fold had to be in the right place, every line checked and laid out free, every aspect of the packing had to be just so. Imperfect parachutes open badly. Imperfect bodies let you down.

Not since Ann had looked through the hole in Harry's shower wall had she seen so much manhood unadorned. Pitman was the only one in trousers. The others were in shorts. She was the only one in a T-shirt. A man on the peck-deck beside Lobo wore a scoop-fronted, sleeveless vest which fitted him like a second skin and under it massive thoracic muscles moved, spreading out, front and back, from the valleys of sternum and spine to the square bulk of bicep, tricep and forearm. Ann was put forcefully in mind of Messrs Willis, Stallone, Van Damme and Schwarzenegger – until she met his eyes which were resting dreamily on her as he worked. Then she was put in mind of Jack the Ripper.

Harry didn't know where to look, but her eyes kept being dragged back to Pitman's body. Muscular and powerful though it was, it retained its femininity. The arms were strong, the thews moving smoothly beneath the pale skin were steely and the veins

129

lifting into knotted definition spoke of regular and fearsome exercise. And yet the fingers gripping the handles were long, tapering to pale, ice-clear nails. The trapezoid muscles on the shoulder blades were as bulky as most men's and yet they supported the neck of a white swan. The chest was as deep as any athlete's and the belly beneath it flat and corrugated, but where the poser on the peck-deck had square bulks of granite, Pitman had something altogether rounder and softer.

The watch changed at midday and as one set of men exited, another entered. Pitman, too, took the opportunity to move. 'Mess call in half an hour,' she said. 'I've got to freshen up. Off we go, girls.'

The three of them went up to the cabin they were sharing and Ann was ordered to join Harry on her bed. Like naughty children they sat with their hands folded in their laps. 'This isn't any more pleasant for me than it is for you,' said Pitman as she shucked off her trousers, hopping from one foot to the other in the open door to the bathroom. 'But the orders are clear. And I'm keen you understand what they can mean if we don't come to some arrangement here. My turn for a public shower now. Yours next. Unless we come to some arrangement. If you catch my drift.'

She pulled off her T-shirt and pants, placed her pistol on a chair in the corner by the shower stall door and stepped in. The water poured from side to side across the opening and Pitman washed herself quickly and practically, using Ann's Calvin Klein soap for both body and hair. At no time was she more than an arm's length away from the gun. And not for one second were the two women on the bed out of her sight.

Not for one second, either, was Pitman out of Harry's sight. That a body should attain such a perfect balance between femininity and muscularity, between hardness and softness, had occurred to Harry only in her dreams and fantasies. That such a frame should be clad in that particular Dutch porcelain perfection of skin put her ability to breathe easily at hazard once again. But it was the revelation that a honey blonde crew cut could be accompanied by body hair of so much lighter and finer a shade that threatened to undo her altogether.

During the rest of the day the tension slackened slightly but the

130

regime firmed up, and not just for Harry and Ann. Once Dall had drawn up his plans, he began to put them into effect. The whip-thin captain had an overwhelming energy and he simply carried everyone along with him. The engineers might be truculent and obstructive where they could be, the deck officers unwontedly dense and disorganised, but little by little Captain Dall began to get them to do what he wished. Their plans to get into the main computers frustrated, Ann and Harry asked to visit the Charlestons after lunch and Pitman, glad to have them out of her sight, was content to guard them from outside the door of the Senator's state room. The two women, given short-lived access to a feeling of enormous freedom, found that she was willing to do this only because the room was already guarded inside by a dark-jawed, dour young man. Conversation, therefore, was shallow and stilted, and largely a waste of time until Harry discovered that the Charlestons had known her long-dead father and corresponded with her mother still – much more regularly than Harry herself did.

And so the watches went by and the afternoon waned. The evening of that first long day gathered and *New England* drifted slowly eastward under the power of the great Gulf Stream which in time would hurl its regimented swells to die like lost legions on the black cliffs of the Irish coast. Drifted east and prepared for war.

The next day dawned fair. Stubbs' weather system spun northwards to dissipate well clear of them. By the dogwatch on the second day, Dall was satisfied with what had been done and he called a halt to the work. Ship's routine was pulled back an hour. The evening meal was served at six. After the meal, the tables were cleared from the dining area and the chairs were arranged in rows. *New England*'s passengers and crew were placed in the chairs. A guard stood, as ever, in the corner of the room. After the briefest of waits, the video player from the library was wheeled in and a video was put on. Then all the captives aboard watched *A Fish Called Wanda* which, under the circumstances, raised very few laughs. Slightly non-plussed by the unexpectedly bizarre situation, none of them questioned what was happening. When the film finished, Dall was back, sparking with excitement and energy. He dismissed them all and declared curfew from eight.

'They held some kind of briefing, I guess,' said Ann to Harry as they sat in their cabin. Because of the curfew, Pitman had been assigned to the eight to midnight bridge watch. There was little chance of them getting up to mischief isolated in their cabins, and anyone who came out, even with no mischief intended, would be shot.

'It's the only thing I can think of,' agreed Harry. 'Unless he's cracking up. God, I hope this isn't going to be part of the evening routine for long.'

'Why?'

'There's *101 Dalmatians, Chained Heat II, Erotic Intensity, Black Lust* and *Co-Eds in Bondage*.'

''Nuff said.'

'I feel sorry for poor Mrs Charleston. Fortunately I think the bit about the gorgeous ass went over her head rather.'

'Don't you bet on it, Harry, that's one sharp lady.'

'Think we ought to try and get her in with us? I'm still keen to get into the computers if I can, even if it's just to see what I can see.'

'We'll need more help. Maybe more of a plan. God! If only I could get to Bob.'

Harry made no comment on that, but it seemed to her that Ann was having no trouble at all getting to Bob. They had sat very close during *A Fish Called Wanda*.

'We tried to get some plans going during the video. But it was impossible,' added Ann.

The thunder of the shower in the next-door cabin began. Harry rose to close the door. 'I guess you could go through now and make plans with his ass,' she said, hardly thinking what she was saying.

'Harry! You little genius!' cried Ann. She was up impulsively and gave the surprised officer a hug. Then she was into the shower and down on her knees, peering through the hole beneath the tap. 'Bob! Bob, it's Ann. Put on some clothes and get back here, we have to talk and I need to keep my mind clear.'

After a few preliminary pleasantries about the habits of single women, the conversation settled down. Professor Miles was now sharing Bob's accommodation and he was reluctantly dragged into the discussions. Bob was keen for Harry to run a series of

132

checks if she could get at the library computer again. There were some systems he was particularly keen to know the status of. Equally, he was game to try to get O'Reilley to activate the switches they needed for access to the Internet, but O'Reilley had already been sounded on the question of sending secret distress signals and had proved depressingly negative. Other than routine messages and the spurious reports of failing engines and the refusal of any help, the radios were all shut down and carefully guarded.

'But who are these men?' demanded Professor Miles, not for the first time. 'What do they want with my ship? What do they want with us?' Their discussions, which went on until the stirring of watch change at midnight, kept coming back to the same question. No matter what system they thought they should test, what experiment they should attempt when Harry could get at a keyboard and screen, what message they should send to which Website, it all came back down to that. Who exactly were these people and just what in hell's name were they up to?

The answer seemed to become clearer next afternoon. Dall had spent the morning running one last series of checks on the work he had had done. In the small hours he had gone all over them himself. Then he had gone over them all again with Bob, Chief Bligh, the reluctant Professor Miles, and his second-in-command Paul Aves in tow. Every addition was tested by Dall and his disparate team for strength, defensibility, the manner in which it integrated into the structure of the ship. Dall was acutely aware that it was useless to build a defensive barricade across a corridor when between-deck ducting could allow enemies easy access above, below and to the rear. He questioned Alan Miles closely about any strengths and weaknesses not immediately obvious from the plans he seemed to know almost by heart. His explorations during the sleepless hours he had been aboard – and Dall seemed hardly to have slept at all – had enabled him to get to know the ship very well, but even so there were details which only the ship's designer could be expected to know. Which was the master switch for this corridor? Could it be secured so that the lights stayed on or off? Could this position control it? Could this companionway be compromised from beneath? If a man was on these stairs, could he be shot by someone firing upward from below? Which sections would the fire sprinklers inundate? Could one such section be shut off from others? The questions were endless.

When they got to the command areas and started speculating about the shatter-potential of the glass – at rest, at half speed, at full speed – it became obvious that this battle-readiness survey was going to take a lot more time yet. Dall summoned First Officer Dix, put him in charge on the bridge, allowed Stubbs to monitor weather and Walker the collision alarm radar, and O'Reilley to monitor, though not to use, the radio; he released First Engineer Macleod to the engine control room and he called for slow ahead, water jets only.

'I need a course,' said Dix a little huffily. 'Even if I'm only making five knots and I haven't got a destination, I need a course.'

Dall smiled at him. 'You shall have both, Mr Dix. Make five knots slow ahead. Your heading is due east. Your destination is Heaven's Gate.'

Chapter Thirteen

By 08:00 the following morning they were nosing into Roaringwater Bay. At the first sight of the Fastnet Light to the south-east, Bob ordered power to be cut and they came into the bay between Mizen Head and the island of Cape Clear under water jets alone. The broad mouth of the bay narrowed rapidly and as it did so, a series of islands rose up out of the busy foam. In the middle, a long island stretched in towards the coast, splitting the bay into two narrows. To the north of this the bay was littered with more islands and the coast gathered in low cliffs down into the twisting, riverine structure of Heaven's Gate itself. At the inward end of the Gate, another island rose suddenly, spitting the narrowing passage still further before it widened again right at the back of the bay. There was something about the lay-out of the wild, uninhabited islands and beautiful coastline which rang bells in Bob's head, but the familiarity was too vague to be of any use to him as he guided *New England* closer to Heaven's Gate.

'Incoming!' suddenly squawked O'Reilley who, with Paul Aves at his shoulder, had been monitoring certain short-wave radio frequencies and CB bands. Half the occupants of the bridge jumped as though electrified and Bob allowed himself a quiet chuckle at the sight of their captors so discomfited. But then he began to wonder why they were so tense all of a sudden, just when they were arriving at their stated destination.

'Collision alarm,' he called. 'Can you give me soundings ahead, please, John?'

'No problem, Bob,' responded John Dix. 'You've plenty of water right up to the cliff edge ahead. And you've the better part of fifty metres clear on both sides before the islands start.'

'State of seas behind us?'

'Not too bad. Nothing to throw us off course.'

'Continue slow ahead then. How far in do you want us, Captain Dall?'

Dall instructed Bob to take *New England* right to the headwaters of Heaven's Gate, then he ordered that the ship be turned round. This was an easy task to achieve using the thrusters. *New England* was designed to turn like a compass needle within a circle of her own length if she needed to. But then Dall ordered Bob to take her out through the Heaven's Gate narrows again, this time coming up towards full speed. Expostulations were met with blank stares and cocked weapons. One thing Bob did notice, however. While *New England* was performing the manoeuvres Dall required, Paul Aves, his second-in-command, was busily feeding information about speeds and headings relative to the land onto the jet-ship's guidance computers.

Ann and Harry had gone to the Charlestons' quarters as soon as curfew was lifted. Pitman saw them safely stowed then went off to do some more of her obsessive exercising. They were able to get a pretty good view of the bay and its islands, for the Charlestons' cabin had a sizeable window which looked forward down the deck.

The sudden roaring as the main propulsion unit engaged surprised them as much as the order had Bob. 'Oh my! What is happening now, Miss Newbold?' asked Mrs Charleston.

'I think we're going to go back out to sea at full speed,' said Harry.

The view of the cliffs topped by emerald fields which had seemed so attractive after the days of nothing but sea now seemed far too close for comfort as they sped by at a rapidly accelerating pace. The narrows ahead, so adequate a passage at five knots, seemed a suicidal canyon at seventy-five knots. As the shaggy shoulder of the island gathered on their left, it seemed impossible that the ship would not career wildly up onto the rocks and be dashed to pieces. For minute after minute they stood, fascinated, horrified, as *New England* achieved full speed in the narrows of Heaven's Gate and then burst out safely into the broad outer reach of Roaringwater Bay.

'Now just what in hell's name was that all about?' asked the Senator.

'I don't know.' Harry watched the distant point of the Mizen swing round to starboard. 'But I think we're going in to try it again.'

She was right. They did the run three more times that morning. And at noon the trucks arrived.

New England reversed hard up against the cliffs at the back of the bay and her shore lines were run out. As soon as she was snugly berthed, all of her complement were herded into the dining area and locked there under guard.

Ann's frustration bubbled over. 'What in God's name are they up to now? Bob, why on earth aren't we doing more to stop these people?'

'We don't know who they are, what they want and what lengths they'll go to get it,' he answered.

'We know all we need to know. We know they've broken the law and they're holding us against our will. We should be fighting back, not knuckling under!'

'You saw them place guards outside the door, Ann. You heard Dall tell them to shoot us if we made trouble. Do you doubt they would do it?'

Harry entered the discussion at this point. 'One of them's called Lobo. The other one's called Lazlo, I think. He's the big one who looks as if he'd like to do weird things to you, Ann. To you personally. You want to give him an excuse to start?'

'Well, no, but . . .' Ann's colour fluctuated. Bob's frown deepened.

'You seem to be thinking that no one will be coming in after us, Miss Cable,' said Mrs Charleston gently. 'I've never been in a position like this before but I know folks who have. And someone went in after them. Maybe not at once. Maybe they had to do some planning and negotiating first. But eventually someone always went in after them.'

'All we have to do is wait,' added the Senator.

'They're right,' said Bob. 'We may have to wait a little while but those fake messages we've been forced to send out won't fool everyone for any length of time, especially now we've come to speed and sailed in here as bold as brass. It's not as if this is war. We're not in some prison camp here. It's only a matter of time before the authorities take action.'

'Well, it feels like Colditz to me. I want to organise some kind of Great Escape. I think it's our civic duty.'

'If this was Colditz, maybe it would be,' said Mrs Charleston. 'But it's not, my dear. It's an Irish holiday resort and someone knows we are here and they will come and get us out. I'm certain of that.'

'And remember what happened in the Great Escape,' added Bob dryly. 'Three made it home. Most of the rest were shot. You'd look great on a motorbike, though,' he added, trying to lighten the atmosphere, and for some reason that made Harry Newbold blush.

Further discussion was cut short by a sudden flurry of activity outside. From the windows of the dining area it was possible to look down the port side of the ship. Bob pushed his way to the best position as was his right and looked out. The upper drawbridge had been let down to rest on the cliff edge. 'John,' he called. 'Looks like they're going to try and unload some of the cargo.'

'They'll find it hard without our help,' said the big lading officer. 'Those pallets in the upper hold are too big to handle unless they've got cranes. They'd be better starting on the smaller stuff below.'

As he spoke, a pallet came into view. It toppled outwards slowly, landing on its end, half on the drawbridge and half on the cliff side. It teetered there for an instant while the whole vessel shuddered. A sound like distant thunder accompanied the shuddering and the whole thing fell forward and sideways, tumbling free of the ship and over the cliff edge to burst asunder on the rocks below.

In the silence that followed, Harry said, 'They'll be lucky if no one was hurt by that little lot.' She paused for a moment and then added, 'They'll be down here looking for competent lading officers in about two minutes, I should think.'

She was right.

Dall himself arrived, positively sparking with rage. 'I want lading officers and engineers,' he barked.

For the rest of the afternoon, Bob, John Dix, Walker and Stubbs worked on the bridge. Bligh and Macleod worked the machinery. *New England* was secured more solidly and the lower hold was emptied. This had not been part of Dall's plans at all and his temper was short, his mood dangerous.

In the dining area, after the men had been called away, Ann

138

and Harry found themselves a quiet corner and continued to plan what Harry might do if she could get at the computer in the library. The possibility seemed increasingly remote, but Harry had seen how dangerous Ann, too, could become when frustrated and she was wise enough to recognise that sitting making plans made Ann feel more secure and in control. And that alone served a very useful purpose. The conversation had only just begun, however, when another, unexpected interruption occurred. Sam Copeland, Pitman's buddy, opened the door and crossed to the two women. So sudden and direct was his approach that they both shrank back a little, fearing that their plotting had been discovered. 'You two, come with me,' he said.

Ann began to protest at once. He levelled his gun at her. 'Come with me,' he repeated.

'What is all this about?' she asked as the three of them hurried along the corridor.

'You'll see. Shut up and hurry.'

He led them to their cabin and pushed the door wide. Inside they discovered John Dix. As soon as the door moved, he rose, turning towards them. 'I can't see anything beyond the head wound,' he said, speaking past them to Sam. 'She needs rest and nursing, I'd say. You need a second opinion, but that's out of the question, I guess, unless you've got a medic of your own.'

'If I had, I wouldn't have asked you.'

'Right. Well, I'm needed back on the bridge.'

Dix walked forward and his movement revealed Pitman lying on Harry's bed. Her shirt was open, revealing a green vest, and her head had rolled to one side on the pillow. There was a red line reaching from her temple to the outer orbit of her eye.

'What happened?' asked Ann as Harry crossed to the stricken woman.

'The crate caught her as it fell,' said Sam. 'We thought it was going to crush her but I don't think it did. More a glancing blow. I checked her and carried her down. There's nothing in the trauma management kit to help. She needs a doctor, not a battlefield medic.'

'I'll take a good look at her now,' said Harry quietly.

'Dix said—'

'I heard. But Dix doesn't know me. Dix and the captain are

139

new aboard. Neither of them know me or my record.' Harry straightened. She looked the younger soldier straight in the eye and spoke with an authority Ann had not suspected she possessed. 'My folks always wanted me to be a doctor,' Harry went on. 'I was in my second year of med school when I fell in love with the computers. I'm far better qualified than Dix. You wanted a second opinion. I can give you one. Now leave us alone and I'll examine her.'

'I'll be just outside the door,' capitulated Sam.

'Before you go.'

'Yes?'

'I need a flashlight.'

Silently, he reached into his battledress pocket and produced a penlight torch. She took it and shone it in Pitman's eye. Then she handed it back to him, saying, 'Just one more thing. I need to know her name.'

Sam hesitated.

'She's had a blow to the head. She could be in a coma, though her pupils are reacting to light, which is a good sign. Even so, she's still out and I need to call her back. I need her name.'

'Angela. Her name is Angela.'

Harry nodded. 'Now wait outside and close the door. This is not a peep show.'

He did as he was told.

Harry ran her hands down the insensible body on the bed. 'Angela,' she said forcefully, penetratingly. 'Angela, can you hear me?'

Pitman did not stir.

'Nothing obviously broken or badly out of place,' said Harry. 'I think we can proceed.' Her hands were round Pitman's throat and for a moment of prickly shock Ann thought she was strangling her.

'Her neck seems OK too. We can risk a little movement. Ann, help me undress her.'

As they unlaced the heavy black boots, Ann said, 'You know we can make good use of this situation.'

'How do you mean?'

'For as long as she's out you can say you need to look at medical books.'

'So? I don't—'

140

'The medical books *in the library*.'

The boots came off and Ann automatically went to the unconscious woman's belt.

'I'll do that,' said Harry matter-of-factly. 'There may be soiling. There often is with unconsciousness.'

Ann stood back. With her hands idle, her mind seemed to go into overdrive. 'In fact,' she said, 'you might need to look at your treatment of common ailments CD.'

'Haven't got one.'

'They don't know that. It'd give you a reason to use the computer. Don't you see?'

'I do see, yes. But let's get this woman comfortable first. I think I'll need to go to the infirmary for painkillers and sutures before I go anywhere else. Angela, can you hear me? Come here and help me get these off will you, Ann? And don't get your hopes up too high. She won't be unconscious for long. No one ever is unless they're in a very bad way.'

'Pills,' said Ann, pulling a trouser leg free. 'Give her too many painkillers. Put her to sleep for a while. I'll watch her, you check the medical information on the computer. God! I bet you could even get them to let you on the Net if they thought she was bad enough.' The trousers came free. 'Jesus! I see what you mean about the soiling business. You think they'll let you on the Net?'

'No, I don't think so,' said Harry. 'I think they'd let her die before they'd run the risk.'

'Yeah. I guess. Are you taking off her vest as well?'

'Yes, it's covered in blood. I'm going to take off her clothes and I'm going to clean her up. I'm going to close and bandage the wound and I'm going to give her some painkillers. When I'm sure she's comfortable and responding to treatment, I'll start playing Mata Hari for you. But like with the Great Escape plan, please remember what happened to Mata Hari in the end.'

'Same thing as happened to Nurse Cavell, if I remember my history right,' said Ann dryly.

'If you can't be helpful,' snapped Harry, 'then leave me to it.'

Ann, chastened, sat on her bed. Harry went through into the shower room but soon came back. She crossed to the door, opened it and rapped out, 'I need a bowl of some kind if I'm even going to start here. I'll have to go to the infirmary.'

Sam would only allow the visit if both prisoners went with

141

him. Then he stood in the open door as Harry sorted out the things she needed. Whether he noticed Ann's attempts to influence some of her choices or not, he gave no reaction. Within ten minutes they had everything that Harry wanted and one or two things that she didn't. They were on their way back down the corridor when Sam's personal radio buzzed. 'They need me outside,' he said. 'You got all you want?'

Harry nodded in reply.

'OK, you go back.' He turned to Ann. 'You come with me. I'm taking you to the dining area. You I do not trust one inch, lady.'

Harry turned to go. 'Hey!' called Sam. 'You take good care of her, you hear?'

'I hear.'

Alone with her patient, Harry called her name again. 'Angela? Angela!' She put her medical supplies on Ann's bed and looked at her watch. It must be twelve minutes since the incident. Perhaps fifteen. This was quite worrying. The woman might be badly hurt. But there was no unnatural pallor, no loss of temperature denoting major shock.

Refusing to worry, therefore, Harry sorted out what she had brought, filled the bowl and set to work.

She washed and disinfected the wound on Pitman's temple first then, working swiftly, she applied a butterfly bandage, pulled the lips of the cut closed, placed two careful sutures and covered it all with a big Band-Aid. Then she washed her charge.

As she went to empty the bowl of water for the last time, Pitman's flat voice demanded, 'What are you doing to me?'

Harry jumped, slopping some of the water.

Pitman was propped up on one elbow, her torso twisted round so that her wounded head was erect. The flare of her pelvis rested on one square hip. Her eyes seemed to contain ice and fire but Harry could read nothing precise in their depths.

'I was giving you a bed bath,' she answered matter-of-factly. 'Sam brought you down because you hit your head. You've been unconscious for nearly half an hour. You are not very well at all.'

'A bed bath,' said Pitman. There was incredulity in her voice.

'You needed one. Believe me.' Harry continued to the bathroom and emptied the bowl of water down the toilet. She kicked the pile of dirty clothing into the shower stall and went back into the cabin. 'You need rest. I have some medicine for you.' She picked up the little box of pills and syringes she had brought.

'Well, you can stick your medicine right up your . . .' Pitman swung her sturdy legs down, placed her feet squarely on the floor and stood – and promptly fell forward on top of Harry, pinning her to Ann's bed and scattering the medical kit.

Harry pushed at the dead weight on top of her and Pitman simply rolled off her and collapsed on the floor. When Harry had regained her composure and sat up to look down, Pitman was just sitting there, disbelief on her face. 'My legs don't work,' she said. 'My head hurts like fuck, and my legs don't work.'

'I'm sure it's all right,' said Harry. 'It's just a side effect of the bump on your head. Let me help you back into bed and I'll give you something. Some pills. You can have a jab if the pain gets bad.'

Pitman's hand went to her head, felt the bandage, jerked away, returned, gently exploring. Her eyes seemed to see her nurse clearly for the first time. 'This is bad,' she said.

'If you still can't walk properly tomorrow, after a good night's sleep, then you may need some more serious medical attention. I doubt it, Angela. If you get a good night's sleep tonight, you'll wake up fine, I'm sure.'

'Who told you my name?'

'Sam what's-his-name. Your buddy. I made him. I needed to be able to call to you. It's standard first aid.'

'You made Sam do something?'

'I made him tell me your name, yes.'

'Must be more to you than meets the eye, lady.'

'Well, if there is, Angela, at the moment it's all working for your benefit.'

'I'll be better in the morning, huh?'

'I'm sure. I've seen it before.'

'I'd better be. If I can't pull my weight, they'll hang me out to dry. Some of them'll have a little fun with me first, I guess. Sam won't be able to stop them. Dall won't care.'

'No sense sitting there worrying about it,' said Harry bracingly. 'Go to bed. Get some sleep. Worry about it in the morning. Here.' She reached down. Pitman reached up. They embraced, cheek to cheek. Harry heaved and deposited Pitman none too gently on the bunk.

'Aaahhh!' she said, quite loudly. 'How come a pain in the butt can hurt my head so fiercely?'

'I don't think pills will be enough. I think it'd better be something stronger.' Harry held up a syringe. 'Another pain in the butt, if you'll allow me.'

'Lady, you're going to give me back my legs. You can stick what you like where you like.'

Harry rolled Pitman on her side and slid the needle expertly into the slope of gluteus behind the swell of the hip joint. 'You'll feel sleepy,' she said. 'Just give in to it. Sleep is what you need most.'

'You going to stand stag over me for a change?' asked Pitman, rolling back and settling herself.

'Your friend Sam seems to have kept all your weapons,' said Harry, pulling the sheet out from under the supine form and arranging it with some propriety. 'But yes, I'll stand guard over you.' It was the first time she had actually lied to Pitman. And she wondered why that should worry her.

Pitman's eyelids drifted shut; she said something impenetrable in Dutch and began to snore. Harry rose to her feet, took some of the medical kit, put it in the bowl and hurried off towards the library.

With her heart in her mouth, she pulled out a pile of books from the medical section and put them on one side of the keyboard. Then she put the medical kit on the other side and sat. She was finding it hard to breathe, her heart was fluttering like a bird caged by her ribs. Her mouth was dry and her palms were clammy. 'Here goes nothing,' she said and switched on the computer.

The disk drive whirred. The printer clattered as it re-set itself. The screen began to clear, numbers spinning, programs recognising keyboard, mouse, drives. Windows came up, then the icons denoting the first levels of accessibility. She scanned these with some care. The Internet icon was not among them. So the modem was switched off still. Bob Stark would have to have another word with O'Reilley.

Using the mouse, Harry selected the Network icon and then, when that opened another layer of icons, she chose File

Organiser, and, within that, Network Manager. The screen went blue. A box appeared in the middle, a bevelled grey with a letterbox two-thirds of the way down.

You cannot proceed, it told her, without a password.

The password was 'Cleopatra'.

It had begun as yet another little game designed to irritate the late unlamented Stevenson and Cohen, and she very much hoped it still irritated the foul O'Reilley. Anyone gaining access to the inner reaches of her systems could only do so by listing the names of some of the greatest women in history and one or two particular favourites of her own. Harry had never really believed that anyone would want to break into her systems for nefarious purposes. There was nothing particularly secret in here. The codes were primarily to ensure that nothing important could be done or undone unthinkingly or accidentally. The passwords had never been meant to function as real barriers, therefore it was not particularly important that they be unbreakable or particularly illogical.

By introducing the network to Boudicca, Lucrezia Borgia, Amy Johnson, Marie Stopes, Lieutenant Uhura, and several others, Harry was able to gain access one by one to each of the systems which were displayed as a group on the wall of screens above her work area on the bridge. She had just gone through Ellen Degeneres who, with the Starship *Enterprise*'s communications officer, was guardian of *New England*'s communications system, when she was suddenly overcome by an irrational fear that she was being watched. The feeling was so strong that she swiftly cleared the screen and turned, certain that someone had entered silently and was standing inside the door.

The door stood very slightly ajar, just as she had left it. No one had entered or left. Frowning, she returned to her work.

Having checked Internet access and general systems access, according to her discussions with Ann and Bob she must now see whether it was possible for her to influence the programs from here. She had devised an innocent little test which even if it was discovered could be explained in a hundred ways. A change that only she or Bob could check swiftly and easily. It would not make much difference to Dall and his pirates but would be substantial enough to be unmistakable when checked.

Something, above all, she could do swiftly, confidently and precisely, even under these circumstances. She was going to reverse the ON/OFF to the hold lights. They had been working in the hold all day. She had no idea whether they were going to be continuing tomorrow, but even if the holds were battened shut it would take only five seconds' unobserved activity on the bridge to throw a switch and check a remote monitor. And if she had pulled it off, then the next step would be something more substantial.

Trying not to think about what she might be asked to do next if this went well – or, indeed, what would happen if she was caught doing even this – Harry worked with all the speed she could muster, placing her secret little virus at the heart of that one particular system. The lights were off at the moment, it seemed. Very well. The next time they were switched they would come on, and then go off normally. Fifteen minutes after that the virus would click in and they would come on and stay that way until someone put the switches to ON, at which point only they would go off.

When she had finished, she switched off the machine, put everything back in place around it and exited the room. Feeling that she had achieved quite a lot for one afternoon, she dropped off the medical equipment in the infirmary, then hurried back up to her cabin. She came round the corner from the companionway and froze. The door to her cabin was open, wedged by the massive shoulders of the pirate with the mad eyes. He was looking at something immediately within. 'Hey! Get away from there! What do you think you're doing?' Harry called and sprinted down the corridor without thinking how dangerous such an action might be.

The man swung back, giving Harry a view of Pitman's body uncovered on the bed, her legs sprawled wide, with Lobo standing speculatively at the bed foot looking down.

'Lobo,' she shouted. 'Get away from her, you bastard. She's hurt. Leave her.'

She hit the big man at the door in a kind of football tackle as though this was the Superbowl. He simply gathered her into his arms and held her as though she was a child. 'What d'you think, Wolfman?' he rumbled. 'Double-header?'

Harry sucked air into her lungs with every intention of

screaming the place down. Casually, her captor put a massive hand which smelt of gun oil and exercise machines over her mouth.

'Nah, Lazlo,' said Lobo. 'I prefer mine with a little more life. And yours is probably a dyke.'

'Maybe I should screw her in the ass then, huh?'

'Put her down, Lazlo, you sad bastard.'

'Put her down, Patay!' said another voice. 'And do it gently.'

Harry, faint with shock and the need to breathe, turned her head to see Dall standing halfway along the corridor. He looked perfectly relaxed, his hands in his pockets.

Lobo stepped forward and stood beside his buddy, blocking the doorway. 'Put the dyke down, Lazlo,' he said *sotto voce*.

He put Harry down with a great show of solicitude. As soon as her feet touched the ground, she fought to get away, but he held her in place, pulling her clothing straight and patting her hair tidy in a parody of paternal concern.

Then Lobo caught her and pulled her free. She wriggled past him and ran into the cabin. The unknowing cause of this lay like a sleeping centrefold. Harry busied herself arranging the sprawled limbs more decorously and covering the pale body with the discarded sheet. While she did this, a lazy conversation liberally salted with expletives took place behind her. When she had finished turning down the sheet and tucking it in like the matron at a boarding school, she turned. The would-be rapists were gone but Dall stood there looking at her. She had never seen anything as utterly cold as his eyes. 'Where were you?' he asked.

'I was in the infirmary, putting back the equipment I needed.'

'Not when I checked.'

'I looked up something in the library. She was unconscious for nearly half an hour. Her legs didn't work when she woke up.'

'Were you anywhere near any of your computers, going through the systems?'

'No!'

'Trying to break out through the communications system?'

'No! I swear . . .'

'Well, you just remember, little lady, if anything goes wrong with those machines, I'll be looking for your ass. I'm not convinced by your wide-eyed innocent expression. I think you're up to all sorts of shit.' The focus of his intense gaze shifted. 'Pitman can have tonight off duty but she'd better be one hundred per cent tomorrow. I'm not carrying dead weight.' His frightening eyes shifted back. 'Dead weight is dead meat. You got that?'

'Yes.'

'Tell that to your room mates. Both of them. And remember, you only go out of this room with an armed guard. For you it is always curfew.'

When Ann returned a few minutes later, she was confronted by a woman completely in the grip of rage. Harry had spent the interim pacing up and down the cabin, eyes spilling tears of frustrated anger, striking out at anything soft to try to get rid of some of the overpowering emotions that held her in their grip far more powerfully than the obscene and loutish Lazlo Patay. If Dall had hoped to frighten her into some kind of submission, he had achieved the exact opposite.

When Ann had helped lance the boil of temper by listening to Harry's account and offering a great deal of sympathetic support, she and Harry started plotting again. It seemed obvious to them, as it must have to the others as evening gathered magnificently over the wilderness of south-west Ireland, that there was no prospect of release or of help in the forbidding Heaven's Gate, and that *New England* was preparing to set sail again. They spent much of the evening formulating wild plans which were all too easily frustrated by the presence of Lobo and later Lazlo outside the door. Quite who was being punished most by the double stag it was difficult to tell. Pitman slept on, blissfully unaware. Eventually, exhausted both physically and emotionally, Ann and Harry joined her.

They seemed hardly to have closed their eyes before the stirring of the ship woke them again. Harry came to first and rolled stiffly off Pitman's sleeping bag, picking herself up to look at the recumbent figure in her bunk. A moment of panic seized her. What would happen if she had been wrong and Angela couldn't walk properly this morning after all? She crossed to the bunk and put a hand on the sleeping woman's shoulder. She caught her breath as her fingers touched the cool flesh, and Pitman stirred. Her eyes opened and she looked up with no recognition at all.

'You have to get up,' said Harry. 'They'll want you on duty.'

'What's the time?' asked Ann throatily from her bunk.

'Seven.' Harry did not take her eyes off Pitman. 'You're expected on duty as normal. Captain Dall said dead weight is dead meat.'

'Seven?' said Ann, never at her best in the morning. 'God give me strength . . .'

'Dall . . .' whispered Pitman, her face still blank.

'Angela! Pitman! Snap out of it, for God's sake!' In her frustration, Harry shook her patient. Pitman was out of bed in one fluid movement, panther-swift. Harry found herself standing helpless with her arms twisted behind her. There was no pain, and yet she knew that one more movement by the woman pressed so close to her would unleash a great deal of pain. Time seemed to stand still for a moment, then Ann said, 'I see your legs are working OK now, Pitman.'

Harry felt her arm being released and suddenly a cold wind seemed to sweep across her back. She turned to find Pitman slumped on Ann's bed. 'Take it slow,' she said. 'You'll be all right.'

'My head hurts like a son of a bitch.'

'I can give you some pills but you'll just have to fight through it as well as you can. Can you stand?'

'Just did.' She pulled herself up and stood, swaying slightly.

The door burst open. Lazlo shoved his head and shoulders round it. 'Nice to see you up, Pitman. Captain wants you on the bridge in five.' His hot eyes lingered on Pitman, and his gaze seemed still to be sliding intimately up and down her body after he closed the door again.

A thought struck Harry. 'You'll have to borrow underwear. Yours is not wearable.' She crossed to the drawer and pulled out a pair of her own plain white cotton briefs. 'I don't think my bra will fit you. Your vest is covered with blood but I guess you could wear it at a pinch.'

'Underwear's for wimps,' said Pitman. It was the closest she had come to sharing a joke. It was a first step. She held the briefs against herself to show they would have been too tight over the hips and too loose at the waist. Then she climbed into her uniform, eschewing the vest as well. 'My bergen's with the men's kit,' she said. 'I'll rummage about if I get a chance.' It wasn't much as girl talk went but, like the joke, it was a start. 'Now, where are my babies?' she asked as she zipped the last zip.

Harry looked blank.

'My big bowie and my ASP? Weapons.'

'Sam Copeland has them.'

Pitman straightened. Took a deep breath. 'You said pills.'

Harry gave her two. 'When these wear off, you'll just have to be a man about it,' she said.

'What?' said Pitman. 'You mean I got to sob and scream and ask for my mommie?'

'That's about it.'

And she was gone.

'Well, how'd you like that?' huffed the rumpled Ann from the depths of her bunk. 'She didn't even say thank you.'

'Oh, I think she did,' said Harry contentedly.

As the last of the mysterious additions to the cargo were made in the dull light of early dawn, Dall re-assigned his men and his woman for the next section of the passage. Then, as *New England* began to nose westwards out through Heaven's Gate, he called all the deck and engineering officers to their posts and sent all the others to their quarters. His main priority seemed to be keeping an eye on the active members of his captive crew, however, and almost all of the pirates were ordered to stand guard in the command and engineering areas. Lobo and Lazlo Patay were assigned to patrol the crew's quarters, watching the cook, the steward and two unassigned seamen. Sam Copeland was posted inside the Charlestons' suite which also housed Professor Miles. And in Pitman's absence nobody at all kept guard on Harry's door.

'Honestly!' whispered Ann, for all the world like an errant schoolgirl up after lights out. 'There's no one here. Let's risk it!'

After Dall's lecture last night, Harry was less than willing but she reluctantly gave in to Ann's insistence. They crept down the corridor to the head of the companionway, and then down to the next deck. All around them the ship was beginning to throb and bustle with the threat of gathering speed. Outside, as the day gathered to a full, bright morning, the green fields above the hamlet of Schull played hide and seek beyond the humps of the islands nearer at hand. The northern coast began to fall back as the chain of little islands petered out. By the time they reached A deck, the Mizen was visible in the far distance; to the south, the Fastnet light gleamed on the very rim of the horizon.

150

Ann reached the library door first and eased it open. Harry hurried in after her and crossed to the computer while Ann kept guard at the door. Harry went into the radar guidance system first, catching the picture Stubbs could see just as it switched to the first forward setting. 'They're definitely coming to speed,' she whispered to Ann. 'What shall I do?'

'Where are we going?'

Harry called up the course planner. Saw the threat of a storm system coming in out of Newfoundland, slightly fuzzy and ill-defined but obviously dangerous. 'West,' she said. 'But south round some kind of weather system, I think.'

'Can you get to the communications? Can you pass the information out at all?'

'I can try. Wait a minute.' She called up 'Uhura' and 'Ellen'. The screen went blank. 'Ann, there's something not right here.'

'What?'

'The screen's gone blank. I don't understand it. I—'

The door burst open, throwing Ann bodily back against the bookshelves with such force that her shoulder cracked the glass in their doors. Harry leaped to her feet and turned. Dall stood in the doorway with *New England*'s radio officer O'Reilley at his side.

'There!' snarled O'Reilley. 'I told you she would be at it again, Captain. You just can't trust tarts like her.'

'Come out here, the pair of you,' snarled Dall.

Harry, terrified, walked forward. Ann moved in beside her, all sulky resentment.

'O'Reilley,' said Harry as she came level with him, pronouncing his name correctly for once. 'What are you doing working with these people?'

'My job.'

'You traitor!'

The quisling radio operator gave a bark of derisive laughter. Dall spoke over it. 'Up to the bridge. Now!'

The atmosphere on the bridge was electric. *New England* was coming up to full speed. By the time Dall arrived with Ann and Harry, the Fastnet light was gleaming quite close by and it was possible to look round the point of the Mizen. The whole of the North Atlantic lay before them with not another ship in sight.

151

The deck officers, Bob among them, were under the guns of their captors, though the control seemed to be only just being held in place. Certainly, none of them was beside his equipment, so it was just as well that the seas ahead were empty.

'Now,' said Dall, 'we have a problem.' He looked around the others there. 'These two women seem to think they're in some kind of adventure story. I tell them what to do and what not to do. They do the opposite. You all know how dangerous that can be. We've only got another day or two together, but these two put all of you at risk because they cannot do what they've been told. I think it's time to teach them a lesson.'

The tension on the bridge became even more taut. O'Reilley stood behind Ann and Harry, blocking any chance of escape. Dall crossed to stand beside Bob, as if he felt the captain needed a particularly close guard, even though he already had the barrel of a gun pressed into his ribs.

'Pitman!' snarled Dall. 'Front and centre.'

Pitman joined O'Reilley between Harry and the door.

'Captain?'

'The computer officer. I want you to hurt her. Badly.'

'But how, Captain?'

'I don't give a fuck how you do it, Pitman, I just want them to hear her screams in Boston!'

But Harry started screaming at once. She gave the wildest, maddest scream and as she did so, she punched Pitman as hard as she could right on the wound in her temple.

Pitman went sideways like a felled tree, taking the wiry O'Reilley with her to the floor. Still screaming, Harry dashed for the door, with Ann right behind her. One of the guards fired. A bullet smashed into the lintel of the door, glanced off the metal, whined across the width of the bridge and buried itself explosively in the chart table.

'Don't shoot in here, asshole!' yelled Dall. 'Just get the bitches!'

A moment or two of confusion followed as the two women hurled down the first companionway onto the deck where the Charlestons' cabin was. Sam Copeland, disturbed by the noise, stood in the open door and they rushed on down as he hesitated. Their own cabin beckoned but both of them knew there was no chance of safety there. They ran on down to A deck, past the library and the exercise room. The weather deck was out of the question now, for the ship was near full speed.

'Down!' gasped Harry wildly. 'Keep going down!' Ann obeyed with alacrity and soon the fugitives were far below deck, with the engines astern of them and the fuel tanks to the fore. There was a work area full of storerooms here which Harry hoped to hide in. Dall had said it would be over in two days. Even without food or sanitation they could last two days hidden away down here. 'We'll need some water,' she panted. Desperately, she tried to keep her mind focused, but the look in Pitman's eyes as she had prepared to obey Dall kept intruding.

'Hide first, then plan,' gasped Ann.

Dall had assigned Paul Aves to guard the engineers and the minute the women escaped from the bridge Dall warned Aves what was going on. Aves decided against leaving the engineers to their own devices at such a crucial time, but he sent his fellow guard, Slogett, to keep an eye on the companionway. Slogett was well-trained but unimaginative, and his reaction on seeing the two women was a warning shot. As the bullet bounced lethally from one impenetrable surface to another, Ann and Harry turned and ran back upwards. Slogett didn't have orders to pursue them, so he hesitated, and reached for his personal radio.

'In here!' said Harry. 'It's our only hope. They can come in after us but maybe we can get past them.' She hit the door into the lower cargo hold and stumbled in with Ann immediately behind her.

The lights were on, as they had been ever since loading had finished. The almost solid geometric puzzle of the fully laden hold had been replaced by a much more haphazard arrangement of pallets, boxes and crates. As the ship had surged up towards full speed, some of these had shifted, and one or two had toppled and burst asunder. Ann and Harry began to pick their way forward.

On the bridge, Dall was listening to Aves' report of Slogett's failure to secure them. It was as unsatisfactory as the rest of the fiasco so far. But at least it gave him a good idea where the pair of them were. He crossed to the hold observation screens. He flicked them both into light, hitting the switches marked HOLD LIGHTS as he did so. Both screens remained dark but he paid no real attention. He depressed the tannoy switch. 'We know you're in there,' he said, hearing his voice amplified throughout the ship. 'Come out at once with your hands up or you die.'

Chapter Fourteen

Secure in the knowledge that Merrideth's men had taken care of the video surveillance, Richard switched on his torch the instant the lights went out. In the dull beam he saw Bruce's team, slick and silent as tar bubbles, disappearing back down the cracks between the pallets. Tom's brick had already gone, and so had Merrideth and Mac. Op loomed above his equipment. 'Come out with your hands up or you die,' the tannoy bellowed again.

'How on earth do they know we're here?' asked Richard in a low voice.

Op held up his hand and Richard lapsed into silence. He strained to hear the merest whisper of sound out where the SAS men were questing through the darkness, but all he could hear was the thunder of the engines pushing them like a hurricane through the booming Atlantic wind.

'Have it your own way,' said the tannoy. 'We'll come in after you. But you'll regret it if we do. Take a few minutes to think about it. You're not going anywhere. Not now.'

The lights came on.

Richard found he was panting with shock. To have got this far against such overwhelming odds only to walk straight into a fire fight before he could do the native guide job for which he was here seemed totally unacceptable. Such was his preoccupation that it did not occur to him to wonder why whoever controlled the lights was switching them on and off in such a bizarre manner.

'Look at that!' spat Dall, almost beside himself with rage. 'The cunning little bitch has fucked up the lights!' The lower cargo hold was bright although the switch said OFF. 'And she's found some way to disable the cameras in the upper hold too. So that's where they are.'

Just at that moment, Pitman began to stir. Groggily she sat up. Her face was so pale it had a green tinge. Something cut through Dall's rage. She had been willing to obey his order unhesitatingly, after all. The head wound was not her fault. She had bought herself another life. A last one.

'O'Reilley,' he called.

The turncoat shuffled forward.

'Are there any computer terminals in the holds?'

O'Reilley shrugged. 'No, I don't think so.'

'Nothing that could be patched into the network?'

'Not as far as I know, Captain.'

'No need to worry then,' decided Dall. His personal radio buzzed. It was Paul Aves calling up from the engine control room.

'We're at full speed now, Captain. You'll need to get the watch alert again.'

'Right. You stay there until I contact you but tell Slogett to watch the door into the upper cargo hold. I'll be sending a team down in three minutes.'

'I'll be sending a team down in three minutes,' the voice in Mac's ear said. He held up his hand to Merrideth with three fingers raised, then tapped his watch.

Merrideth nodded, his head ghostly in the monocle of the big Scot's night goggles. Then he pulled sensor equipment from his webbing and pressed it to the door, crouching over it, looking for all the world like a frogman planting a magnetic mine.

Even through the heavy steel the sensitive equipment picked up enough sound to identify one man climbing stairs, coming up to take position outside the door. The thunder and the vibration coming through the hull interfered with the picture and made it fuzzy, but at least the noise would cover transmission from this side. 'Bruce. Up front. Cover the door. It's the only way they'll be coming unless this is even more tricky than it looks.'

'Moving.'

'Tom. Second echelon.'

'Moving.'

'Op. You keep an eye on our guest. We're going to need him and both bags of tricks.'

'Ready.'

156

Mac held up two fingers. Merrideth nodded. The sensor equipment was registering three more men coming down the stairwell from above. They would make up a brick of four. Standard procedure. Merrideth racked his brains for another way into the hold. One brick just did not seem sufficient for a frontal assault on the hold like this. But there was no other way in that he could think of.

'Fall back and hold your fire until my order,' he instructed.

Mac held up one finger, and the lights came on.

Slogett's buddy was Canada Newby. They were a good team who had survived a range of interesting encounters all over the southern hemisphere. With Newby, Dall had sent down Gus Grillo and George Bacon, another successful partnership. All four were level-headed and, compared with the likes of Lazlo and Lobo, the epitome of controlled professionalism. Dall had made clear that they should put the fear of God into the women, but nothing else. No bullets, no knives, no personal appendages.

As Slogett and Newby went through the door, one high, one low, Grillo and Bacon covered them. But the instant all four were through, they stopped, nonplussed. The camera in this hold was not working, and none of them had been into it before. What confronted them was unlike anything they had ever seen. A pallet the size of a room stood in front of them. Another the same size sat on top of it with a gap perhaps a metre wide between them. A metre to one side sat another pair of pallets, and a metre on the other side, another. The four men were in an area which could easily have accommodated a couple of football pitches. Two unencumbered women could slip easily wherever their terror might take them. Four large and fully equipped soldiers in pursuit of them would have a problem keeping up.

Slogett gestured to the others to stand and wait.

'Captain,' he called up to the bridge.

'Yes?' came the answer over his personal radio.

'Sir, this is no job for a full patrol. Let Grillo and Bacon stand by at the door and Canada and I'll shuck down on some of this kit. They aren't armed, are they?'

'Correct, Slogett. Not armed. If that's the way you want to call it, that's fine by me. But bring them back alive.'

'They may get mussed up a little.'

'That's OK.'

Slogett gestured the others out, then he and Canada stripped off their combat webbing. They took a torch in one hand and their preferred short gun in the other. Slogett's was his old Hekler and Koch P9; Canada's was a Smith and Wesson he had bought in New York on his last furlough. Red-dot sight, state of the art. 'You use that mother and your ass is in a sling bigtime, boy,' warned Slogett.

'Couldn't hit nothing with it anyhow,' growled Grillo derisively from the door. 'You know what they say: red dot, white stick.'

'Hush up, Gus,' said Bacon. 'You know he's probably all frightened up inside in case one of the ladies takes a swing at him.'

'Right,' grunted Slogett. 'You see what that dyke did to Pitman? Dyke Tyson maybe. You think?'

'Ready?' asked Canada.

'Let's do it!'

None of this conversation made any sense to Merrideth as he lay like the ham in a sandwich between the pallets two room-sized boxes away, still using his special equipment to monitor what was going on. His lean, almost skeletal body was beginning to react badly to the stress and strain he was putting it under. He gritted his teeth – and felt them move in his jaws. His mouth flooded with blood and he swallowed feverishly, his stomach revolting. He needed his medication. Feeling his mind begin to go woolly, he fought to concentrate. The pair who were coming in were on their way, and he double-tapped his throat mike to warn the others. His sensors told him that the other two had pulled the discarded kit outside the door and swung it nearly closed. That was all he needed to know about them for the moment, though he still wondered whether this could be some kind of trap.

Slogett and Canada worked their way swiftly across the open area, then slipped into the vertical gap between the massive pallets, acutely conscious that several metres above their heads was a horizontal gap large enough to contain the two desperate women. Slogett led the way down the gaps like a weevil exploring an ancient tin of biscuits on the inside. When he was satisfied that there was nothing to be seen at deck level, he got Canada to sling him up so that he could worm his way into the horizontal gap.

It was very dark in there and his torch was of little use. It was also claustrophobically constricted. The vertical spaces had allowed him to walk upright but here even crawling resulted in him bashing his backside or his head against the upper pallet. By the time he reached the first junction, he was very much of a mind to kill the women when he found them just to make his headache feel better.

He stuck his head out into the junction and looked down into the gap which reached narrowly to the floor. He wondered which way to go next, left, right, or forward across the gap. He looked right. Then he looked left and wondered no more.

The black-clad figure of SAS Corporal Bruce Jones appeared like a magic spirit from between the set of boxes opposite and broke his neck with a silent blow.

Down below, Canada Newby was becoming convinced that the women were not here. Left to his own devices he would have called out some threats to see if that stirred any game, then he would have come out and left them to it.

'Slogett?' he said into the massive silence of the hold. They had removed their personal radios with their combat webbing – something that Canada was beginning to regret. He looked around at the disorientating maze of narrow passages at whose heart he stood. 'Slogett?'

Again, only the massive silence answered, a silence emphasised by the invasive throbbing rumble of engines and speed.

He wondered why Captain Dall had thought this search was within the capacity of a single brick. What was really needed here was the complete command to give the place a proper sweep. He decided to retrace his steps to the door and check with Dall. He turned and found a man in black immediately behind him. He jerked his gun up but the butt hit the side of a pallet. The shadowy stranger's hand flashed out towards him.

'*Don't kill them!*' came the order over Tom's headphones. But he was committed now, and the player's gun was big and dangerous. The heel of his hand took Canada under the nose and drove upwards. There was a sharp crack as the upper jaw sprang clear of the front of the skull and drove back into the brain.

159

The best Tom could do was to catch the man on his way down and swing him into a makeshift fireman's carry. Then, silently and swiftly, he carried his victim back to base.

Richard's first patient was clearly a lost cause. The damage to the front of his head was massive and Richard was almost relieved to find no pulse or heartbeat. Tom crouched silently beside him, watching him make his checks. When Richard shook his head, the big soldier shrugged, opened the holster on his thigh, took out a battered old pistol and replaced it with the Smith and Wesson the dead man had been carrying. Then, vulture-like, he sorted through the corpse's pockets, keeping much of what he found there, starting with the ammunition clips for his new gun.

Merrideth appeared, coming up over the edge of the pallet like some kind of monstrous spider. He looked down at the dead man and then up at Tom. Tom shrugged apologetically. His lips moved. 'Order came too late.'

Merrideth gave a weary nod.

'*Slogett? Canada?*' The cry from the doorway was distant and weirdly distorted by the canyons and passageways through which it had come.

Tom looked at Merrideth but Merrideth was slumped strangely, clearly at the end of his tether.

Mac heaved himself onto the pallet top. 'They're calling the bridge again. They know something's up.'

Merrideth nodded.

'We have access,' said Mac. 'We could hit the door now and spread out at once.'

'I'm ready,' whispered Richard. 'I'll guide you straight up to the command bridge. No problem.'

Merrideth shook his head. 'No. There's something going on here I don't understand. We need more intelligence before we move. Call them in. We'll sit tight.'

'Slogett? Newby? Come out of the hold at once,' boomed the tannoy.

In the echoing silence that followed, Mac persisted, 'It would be four down. How many are there? Twelve in all? It's an option.'

'It would be a bloodbath. We'd be going in blind against well-prepared foe. We'd lose most of the hostages at the very least. We need more time to prepare.'

'We'll probably get that,' said Mac. 'I don't think they'll be coming back in here in a hurry.'

'OK. Call Tom's brick back. Bruce's to watch the door.'

'Right.'

'Slogett. Newby. You have five minutes. Report within five minutes or the door will be secured. That is all.'

'That is definitely *not* all,' said Mac, and he started to call the man back in.

Merrideth's whole demeanour made it obvious that he needed attention. Richard was aware, from his study of the doc's treatment book, that Merrideth's medical regimen was the most exhaustive of all of them, though the names of the drugs involved meant nothing to him and so gave no clue as to what condition they were meant to treat. In fact, when he had looked through the medical boxes, only the generic term corticosteroid meant something to him, and the only name he recognised, and that with something of a shock, was Thalidomide. Thanks to Doc's precise notes, however, knowledge of the drugs was not necessary to administering them correctly.

As they all mentally counted down the five minutes before the nameless leader of the dead pirates secured the door and locked his unwelcome guests in the hold, Richard located Merrideth's medication. 'Major,' he said, 'I think now's the time for two of these and if you'd just roll up your sleeve . . .'

Merrideth's face, disturbingly formless behind the black balaclava, turned towards him and the red-rimmed eyes squinted at him as though he was a complete stranger. When he saw the pills in Richard's hand, however, he pulled up the balaclava. Richard gasped, but the sound was drowned by the next announcement from the tannoy.

'Two minutes and counting . . .'

Merrideth's face was dead white, but the eyelids, lips and nostrils were livid. The exhausted soldier took the pills into his black-gloved hand and tossed them into his mouth. Richard had an instant impression of bleeding gums.

Radiation! he thought, his mind seeming to jump awake. What was it he had heard about depleted uranium ammunition in the Gulf? He wished he could remember more clearly, but what he did recall was that the affected people suffered from a kind of

161

radiation sickness, like the men who had fought the fires at Chernobyl. He felt his hair stir and his neck prickle. He wondered urgently whether Doc's black combat webbing contained a Geiger counter in its capacious pockets as well as the pens, pencils, flashlights and the rest. But Merrideth was exhibiting signs of prolonged exposure to radiation. Damage to mucous membranes came only after weeks, perhaps months of exposure. No. This was something else, but Richard had no idea what.

'Your time is up!' announced the tannoy.

A metallic bang echoed through the hold. The lights went out. There was a moment's silence, then Merrideth said, 'Check the door and secure the area, Bruce. Then switch the lights back on. I'll be dammed if I'll let the captain here needle me by lamplight.'

Two minutes later, the lights were back on and Bruce reported that he had taken the switch apart to remove the main bridge override. The lights were in their control now, he said, and then added that there was a funny-looking handset on the wall by the door. Videophone maybe. Merrideth, answering with the needle still in the dead white skin of his upper arm, told Bruce to leave it alone and go back to standing guard. He would check himself as soon as he was finished here. 'I'll come and take a look at it too,' said Richard. 'There should be a couple in each hold.'

The pills and the injection worked quickly on Merrideth and soon he and Richard and Mac left the men and crossed to the doorway. They found two videophone communicators, each the size of an old-fashioned telephone, with a screen about ten centimetres by ten sitting above a standard panel of telephone buttons. 'They're like radio phones,' Richard explained. 'They communicate within the hull, with each other and with the security system. When you use it you look into the screen and a small camera lens sends the face as well as the voice to the receiver.'

'Have you any idea how to use it for our advantage without giving too much away to the enemy?'

'Not yet. But maybe Mac here can tune one into the security system. That'd be useful.'

'Probably patches into the computer network somehow,' opined Mac vaguely. 'Wouldn't need a specific receiver then. Plenty of computers and screens all over the shop.'

'But you'd need to re-tune it. Take one apart. See how it works.'

'Maybe do that later,' said Merrideth, slipping one of the videophones into a pocket in his webbing.

They went back to their base.

'What next?' asked Richard.

'We need to disable the fire-fighting equipment,' said Merrideth. 'Any ideas about that?'

'There's an inert gas system,' Richard said at once. 'Follow me. Do you think he'll try to gas us out, whoever this man is who has control?' he asked Merrideth as they began to work their way over towards the pipework.

'His name's Dall. It's an option. I don't want Dall to have it any longer than necessary.'

'How do you know his name? No, don't tell me – intelligence.'

The outer edges of the pallets were mercifully more than a metre from the hold wall and here ladders allowed access to the topmost plateau. As soon as Richard, Merrideth and Mac went up, Tom and his men followed, spreading out automatically around their superiors as though someone might be hidden up here on top of the load to spring a deadly surprise.

The tops of the pallets were two and a half metres below the ceiling. They were exactly level, and it was almost impossible to see the one-metre gaps between them as they stretched like an endless prairie to the far wall and the even further reaches of the bow. In the middle rose the enclosed stairwell whose walls contained the closed and guarded doorway.

Immediately above their heads a pattern of lights were clamped to the white-painted ceiling. Around these snaked the great silver convolutions of the ship's ducting system. Above and around those writhed the white-painted worms of the water systems – fresh water for drinking, treated water for washing, salt water for the sprinkler systems. Among the water pipes ran electricity cables which carried not only current but signals and directions to the great lading, ship-handling and cargo-protection machines lying dormant all around.

'This is it here,' said Richard, 'the inert gas roses, the equivalent of the water sprinklers over there.'

'Good,' said Merrideth. 'Any idea of the pressure generated by the IG equipment?'

'High. In a tanker it can flood an area half this size in less than five minutes. This has to be similar or better. No sense in having it if it takes a lot of time.'

'Taping the roses would be no good then.'

'No. Find the main feed pipe and block that.'

'You heard the man, Tom.'

'Yes, boss. Martin, you want to come with me? Russ, you and Mike go that way.'

While they were waiting for Tom's men to report, the three of them inspected the rest of the pipework. The ducting was particularly interesting. 'You think any of us could fit in that?' Merrideth asked Mac.

'Doubt it. None of the men anyway. You might be able to, Major, you're the slightest.'

'Not good strategy, isolating the commander. A bit too Star-Trek for me.'

The phrase made Richard think of the people trapped with the men they were here to fight. Harry Newbold would be able to fit in the ducting, and so would Ann.

'This looks like the lead pipe,' called Tom a minute or two later. It was one of a sheaf of pipes running up the central column whose square walls enclosed the stairwell which connected the accommodation and command areas above to the engineering areas below. It reached up to the ceiling then branched out into the pattern they had just been examining.

'We need to be very sure, though,' warned Richard. 'Check the other side. Often several pipes feed individual sections.'

On the other side they found another pipe. Bruce's men traced it down to the floor where it vanished, apparently through to the lower hold. 'Any sign of a central feed point?' asked Richard. 'Any way to tell which way the gas runs?'

'Nothing I can see,' answered Bruce, down on his knees on the deck.

Richard craned over the edge of the pallets, straining to see the detail more than twenty metres below. 'Bruce, that area immediately inside the door is very different to the flooring beneath the pallets. There's nothing obvious from here but can you see anything like a catch or a handle? It seems logical that there should be inspection hatches there.'

'Just a minute. Well, I'll be damned. You're right, Captain. Shall I open up, boss?'

164

'Hold it there a minute, Bruce.'

Merrideth and Mac went into a huddle, and for the first time Richard was included.

'What are the risks, Mac?' Merrideth asked.

'As long as we know the stairwell is empty, they seem low.'

'OK. I'll set up the image intensifier up here right at the head of the well. If anyone comes anywhere near the first step we'll have a warning. It'll alert us to lift use too if I place it right. Captain Mariner, where would you advise?'

'Let's see. These pallets go right in close on that side. You can reach across and set it up there. Yes. That'd do nicely.' And the major did as he advised.

'Go ahead, Bruce, have a look under the floor,' called Richard a few moments later on Merrideth's signal.

Looking over Merrideth's shoulder, he strove to make sense of what the sensor was revealing. 'What can you see?' he asked.

'Silence, inactivity, lack of body heat,' came the terse answer.

'It's looking into an empty stairwell from the level to the top stair,' said Richard as the patterns began to come clear. 'There's no one on the steps there and there's no one approaching down the corridor. This is a very impressive piece of kit. You can forget about doors here,' he went on. 'This wall is much thinner than that bloody great thing down there. And they'll be expecting you to come and go through doors rather than walls in any case. That's where they'll be watching and waiting, by the door. If you positioned your charges carefully you could come straight out into the corridor. Through the wall here.'

'I've got the pipe under the floor,' called Bruce. 'Comes in through the wall on a couple of supports then splits. One bit goes up into our system. The other goes down. Standard T junction.'

'What size pipe?' called Richard, turning away from Merrideth's monitor.

'Four centimetre.'

'But how to shut if off,' mused Merrideth.

'That'd be easy enough. I could do it for you myself,' said Richard without thinking, 'if I had a hacksaw and a fifty pence piece.'

Five minutes later he was crouching beside Bruce, a hacksaw blade gripped in his long, strong fingers. He sawed at the junction

165

of the pipe, exactly across the T-junction, as though beheading the upright. 'Where's the fifty pence piece?' he asked.

'This do?' A coin rang on the deck by his side. He gasped – something he had warned himself against doing since he was cutting through a pipe full of inert gas here. In place of a five-sided coin there was a larger, golden one. 'That's a sovereign!' he exclaimed. 'Where'd you get one of those?'

'Standard issue,' said Bruce. 'Haven't you read *Bravo Two Zero*?'

'I'd forgotten,' said Richard, as the blade went through. He wedged the sovereign across the sawn top of the upright pipe. 'Now,' he said, 'we just need to tape that securely into place. The coin will stop anything that tries to come through, and the more pressure builds, the more securely will it be held in place. Think you can do the same on the other side?'

'Yup. The world lost a great plumber when you went to sea, Captain.'

'And what did it lose when you joined up?'

'Olympic standard bouncer,' said Bruce.

'Pimp more like,' supplied the dry voice of Mac, who had been listening in.

Peter Dall and Paul Aves sat side by side on the bridge looking at the blank screens which should have revealed what was happening in the holds below. Around them, the men of *New England*'s crew went about their duties grudgingly and mutinously under the guns of the guards. Dall's gruff order to Pitman to hurt Harry had in an instant destroyed the growing co-operation between the mariners and their captors. All they offered now was the basic minimum required to make the ship secure and be passage safe – except for O'Reilley, who was openly with Dall's men now, though even he was still watched by one of the guards.

'Those women couldn't have taken out Slogett and Newby,' Dall said again. 'That's simply not possible. There is simply no way two unarmed tarts could have taken out those two. With a gun maybe. With grenades sure. But there were no shots. There was no explosion.'

'Grillo and Bacon heard nothing,' supplied Aves. 'Traps?'

'They didn't have time.'

'Could they have set it up? They fucked up the lights. They screwed the surveillance.'

166

'They did those things from outside, through the computer. They couldn't have got into the holds themselves. Jesus, we were only in there ourselves this morning.'

'So. No traps.'

'Looks that way.'

'So they could not have taken care of Slogett and Newby. They were a very fine team, Captain.'

'Agreed. And we assume that Grillo and Bacon were reporting truly and accurately what they saw.' Dall dropped his voice slightly as he said this.

'We don't assume it, we know it. We were monitoring them.'

'Then either Slogett and Newby changed sides . . .'

'Not possible. They're one hundred and ten per cent, you know that, Captain.'

'Or . . .'

'Or what?'

'Or we are no longer alone.'

Merrideth and his men were well aware that they were operating on borrowed time. There was bound to be some sort of recognition soon that they were aboard.

As far as the SAS men were concerned, the correct way to deal with such a potential threat was to pre-empt it. The preferred method of doing this was to mount an unexpected and preferably overwhelming attack. But at the moment they could only hope to break out into an isolated and certainly guarded stairwell. The passages leading to and from the stairwell would also be defended, perhaps even fortified. Hope of surprise was nil, the chances of casualties among the unit high and any hope of rescuing the hostages before they, too, started dying zero.

On the other hand, Dall had found that sending men into the hold was fatal. He would realise that the hold as a battleground was unthinkable, for all the advantages he held in the rest of the ship were held by the men in here. Further, it seemed highly unlikely that Dall could have any idea of the number or disposition of his enemy. With any luck, he was still in some doubt as to what exactly had happened to his patrol and was, therefore, in two minds how to proceed. It might suit him to sit tight and play a waiting game. Certainly, unless there was something like the inert gas system that could get rid of them with little collateral

167

damage to hull or cargo, then they were effectively unassailable in here. Even replacing the water in the sprinkler system with something more toxic, if it could be done, seemed fraught with more difficulties than advantages, for the only toxic agent likely to be aboard in sufficient quantities was jet fuel. And spraying the highly volatile fuel in here would be an invitation for all aboard to undergo a Viking funeral.

But the SAS men had no intention of throwing up a defensive perimeter and sitting tight. Merrideth took Richard's suggestion that, with the explosives available to them, the walls were as much an option as doors for access to other parts of the ship, and he extended the idea vertically. Sections of the ceiling above them were removed, and the pipes, lines and ducts up there pushed aside where possible. Image enhancing equipment was pressed to the metal flooring above and slowly the floor of A deck was charted. Possible access points were noted but none of them seemed promising. Such was the size and disposition of the upper hold that the line between the footing of the bridgehouse itself and the open foredeck could be charted as well. When they traced the outer edge of the rear bridge sections, they discovered that the weather deck immediately behind the upper works appeared to be in a wind shadow similar to that which had protected *Hero*. This might allow a team to get up the back of the bridgehouse and break in unexpectedly from outside after all. But the only way of testing this was to do it, and risk potentially disastrous results.

The flooring was examined too, though as Richard had warned them, its composition made a way down through it unlikely. Instead he advised them to look near the central tower of the companionway, and there they discovered four hatches. The possibility of exploration in the lower hold was balanced against the possibility of infiltration and attack from the same quarter.

Next they turned their attention to the pallets. They had trap doors as well as ladders built into them. The containers inside the pallets had trap doors also. All those opened and inspected contained Federal Motors off-road vehicles, and not even the most imaginative among them could think of a use to which such a squadron of vehicles could be put at the moment.

In the meantime, Op had been inspecting the videophone that Merrideth had pocketed earlier. Having completed a sweep of all the wavelengths in the nearby ether, he had tagged those being used by all the equipment aboard and was preparing to listen to everything broadcast in the ship, not just on the battle band of the personal radios carried by Dall's men. And he flicked it on and off in short bursts to explore the areas it might observe, hopefully without alerting anybody as to its use.

All in all, a great deal of exploration was completed in a little under two hours and a range of possible actions was on the table for consideration when the next move in the game was made.

In sharp contrast the all the brightly-lit, highly organised activity in the upper hold, things in the lower hold were sadly antediluvian. Ann and Harry elected to leave the lights off, especially after the disturbing announcements over the tannoy. Once Dall had worked out the reversal in the light switching mechanism, the only illumination in the lower hold was a series of bright red dots high in the Stygian gloom which denoted the position and activity of the surveillance cameras. The women had neither the training nor the equipment to disable the cameras and so they preferred to remain in darkness.

As soon as it became clear that, whatever had been threatened in the tannoy message, they were not about to be pursued or re-captured, they began to explore.

Beside the door into the hold, just beneath the videophone, they found torches and decided to make use of them. The risk of detection as a result seemed preferable to sitting in the dark doing nothing.

'We can't just hide away down here for ever,' said Ann.

'Perhaps we should look for somewhere we can defend,' said Harry. 'That means looking for weapons.'

'That shouldn't be too difficult here, should it? I mean, what else is this stuff they loaded in Ireland likely to be?'

'What, you mean it isn't a toy set from the top of the beanstalk?'

'Was that dry humour under extreme stress or incipient hysteria?'

'Is there a difference?'

'Depends on your gender, as I understand it.'

'Think of me as Bruce Willis then.'

'You look more like Demi Moore.'

'Think of me as GI Jane then.'

169

'I thought it was GI Jane you laid out flat earlier!'

Harry was silent. She half believed her wild blow must have killed Pitman, and the thought troubled her. She might even have felt guilty, but once again the blood lust she had seen in Pitman's eyes rose to haunt her. The memory sickened her.

'Look at this, Harry,' said Ann.

They were in the aftermost section of the new cargo pile now and Ann's torch beam played over several crates that had burst open on the floor. There were no clear identifying marks on the crates; the wood showed pale scoring where such markings had been largely erased. One large crate had disgorged four green fibreglass boxes and one of these, too, had burst open. A gleaming tube lay half exposed among its foam packing. Ann crouched down beside it and eased it out of the box. It was more than a metre long, with an obvious handle and an inconspicuous trigger among the folded sections of metal. Ann handled it with experienced fingers, but she did not open out any of the sections. Instead, she carefully put it down again and sat back on her heels.

'What is it?' asked Harry.

'It's a Stinger.'

'What's a Stinger?'

'A guided missile.'

'What?' Harry picked it up. It was solid but well balanced. Surprisingly easy to handle.

'Put that down!' said Ann sharply. 'Do it gently and don't touch any of the catches or switches. You might arm it by accident.'

Harry did as she was told with an obedience her parents would never have recognised. 'What is all this stuff?' she asked, suddenly uneasy.

'It's one of the better stories of the nineties,' said Ann. 'The CIA lost a complete consignment of these things in Afghanistan when the Taliban militia took over. They'd apparently smuggled them into Kabul to help the Afghans fight the Red Army but when the Soviet Union collapsed, the Afghans simply took them and started offering them for sale. There were nearly three hundred of them and at least one hundred are still out there. I cannot believe the IRA had them but didn't use them. And to have sold them on, even now . . .'

'Maybe things are looking better for Ireland.'

'Maybe.' Ann didn't sound convinced. 'Depends who actually sold this stuff, what else they've got in stock and what they buy with the money they get for it. But that is of academic interest. What I'd like to know is what is it all doing here?'

'And what is going to be done with it when we get where we're going?'

'Only one thing can be done with a Stinger. You use it to shoot down aeroplanes. That's all it does. They're still wondering about TWA Flight 800 . . .'

'How do you know all this stuff, Ann?'

'I'm a reporter.'

'I know but—'

'What? You thought I did social stuff? Articles for *Hello!* and *Cosmo*? At Home with Hilary Clinton and How To Keep Your Lover Through The Menopause? That sort of thing?'

'Well . . .'

'You ever read any of my stuff?'

'I'm afraid not.'

'My first big story was about the illegal transport of nuclear and chemical waste. I actually have registered radiation sickness from that one. I could smoke forty cigarettes a day for the rest of my life and it would hardly matter. The best one was my report on the illegal sale of arms and materiel to the warring factions of an African civil war right under the noses of the UN. I went into the bush and met the people. I actually got some of the illegal arms used on my own fair person. I have had blackwater fever, beri-beri and God knows what else besides. I do not do "Tea With The Queen" articles, all right?'

'I see. So you're an authority on this sort of stuff, are you?'

'Not exactly, no. But I know it when I see it, and I know what this is.'

'And how to use it?'

'If push comes to shove, yes.'

'Good,' said Harry. 'Then we're just a little more secure.' She stroked the Stinger almost lovingly. 'No one messes with Harry unless Harry wants to be messed,' she said.

Ann gaped at her. 'Do you know what you're saying? This isn't an anti-personnel weapon. You try and use that in here and we'll all be toast.'

171

'Makes you think, though, doesn't it? It'll make them stop and think as well, won't it?'

'Talking of thinking . . .'

'What?'

'What on earth is actually going on here? I mean we've been sailing the Atlantic for days, loading and unloading in Ireland, chucking away Federal Motors' finest and apparently gearing up for World War III. For what? Why?'

'You only gear up for war if you're going to fight.'

Ann nodded. 'Who? Where?'

'From what I saw before we exited the bridge, we are taking our war machine westwards. So we may be fighting American aircraft.'

'Who may be attacking us.'

'Trying to stop us doing something.'

'Something on water.'

'Being done at one hundred miles per hour . . .'

They fell silent then and Ann turned off her torch. And each became prey to disturbing speculation.

When the tannoy came on again it made them both jump. 'We need to talk,' it said. 'Pick up the handset by the doorway and dial 01 for the bridge.'

'What do you think?' asked Ann.

'What can it harm?' answered Harry. 'They know where we are. If they want to come and get us, they can. Maybe it would be a good idea to warn them we're armed.'

'And then some,' added Ann to herself.

'Could be a trap, though.'

'How?'

'To get at least one of us over by the door.'

'I see your point. Worth the risk, do you think?'

'Probably. I'll go. Why don't you cover me with the Stinger.'

Ann picked up the missile and hefted it to her shoulder. With expert fingers she snapped the fold-down sections into place. Her knowledgeable eye told her this was the later model with the POST system, the ultraviolet as well as the infra-red, the heat and movement seekers. She did not switch it on.

Harry approached the door like a kitten stealing from a watchdog's bowl. Her feet made less noise than her heart and every sense she possessed was focused on discovering whether

172

or not someone was waiting to grab her as she got near enough. Her torch beam showed her that the door was securely closed – but in revealing this information it also told potential watchers how close to it she was. She put the torch down and sneaked off to the side, hoping she was invisible to the surveillance cameras. She crept up to the videophone, grabbed the handset and hit the buttons with shaking fingers. As chance would have it, she pressed 02 instead of 01. The little screen flashed on and Harry was confronted by a head thrust right up close to the screen. The head wore a black covering with a helmet on top. Where the face should have been there was a gas mask with black fittings, huge round eyepieces and a great flat filter sticking out of the side. Harry gave a cry of fright and dropped the handset altogether. It skidded away across the floor.

'What is it?' called Ann, shocked by her friend's reaction.

Harry sank to her knees, striving to control her breathing. Ann called again but Harry simply could not answer her. She scrabbled round until her back was hard up against the side of a friendly crate. Ann called for the third time. 'All right!' answered Harry. 'Just got a shock.'

'An electric shock?' Ann could not imagine anything less having such an effect.

'Surprise . . . There's something . . . Someone . . .' Harry's right hand fumbled on the deck, searching for the handset. When she found it, she lifted it slowly to her face. She dialled 01. The busy signal came up.

She dialled 01 again.

Busy.

Now she tried 02.

Busy.

Comprehension began to dawn. Stations 01, the Bridge, and 02, the Upper Hold, were talking to each other. The creature with the fearsome mask was in the hold immediately above their heads. Mind racing, Harry did what she did best. She hacked. The videophone handsets had a conference facility to allow a third party monitoring rights in another conversation. Swiftly she dialled the sequence and finished with 01.

Dall's face filled the handset screen. '. . . need to get this situation sorted out,' he was saying. 'Before any more lives are lost.'

173

She dialled 02. The monstrous face reappeared. 'Your call,' came the laconic, inhuman reply. Breath hissed eerily in and out.

She dialled 01, then continued dialling in the breaks, trying feverishly to follow the conversation.

'It's a stand-off. You're not going anywhere and if you try to come in here, the passengers and crew go first, you know that.' There was no room to doubt the threat in Dall's cold voice.

'We'll be coming in there sometime soon,' said the man in the mask with equal certainty. 'What you do, you answer for. One way or another. You and your people.'

'Maybe,' said Dall. 'In the meantime, you think about what I said.'

'I'll think.'

Connection broke.

'But what did you say, Dall, you son of a bitch?' said Harry, flicking the off switch on her handset before her eavesdropping was discovered.

'What was that all about?' asked Ann when Harry pulled herself back to her.

Harry explained the new situation as she saw it and Ann's eyes grew wide with speculation. 'We have to make contact with these people,' she said.

'I'm not so sure,' said Harry, her mind still full of that terrifying, inhuman face. 'They don't look all that user-friendly to me. And anyway, what do you want to do? Try and make it up the stairs to the top hold before Dall sets the dogs of war on us again?'

'The handset. Give them a call.'

'They've got it switched off. Anyway, they don't look the sort of people you call up just for a chat.'

'Dall did.'

'Yes. He did, didn't he?' There was a little pause. 'But he had to get their attention on the tannoy first.'

'Yeah,' Ann conceded. 'So what do you reckon we should do?'

'Keep the Stinger handy.'

'Yup.'

'And go through this lot in more detail. Maybe the guys upstairs would trade a full inventory for a little protection. Though I have to say, they look more like something I'd want to be protected *from*. Now, how many of these Stinger things are there, precisely?'

They spent the next hour or so going through the pile of arms and equipment. And wherever they went, the trusty Stinger went with them.

So that when, all of a sudden and shockingly close at hand, two hatches burst open and two figures dressed in black abseiled rapidly to the floor, Harry was able to grab the missile and swing it up to her shoulder, looking every inch the twenty-first-century soldier.

'Freeze,' she bellowed, her only experience of situations like this having come from Arnold Schwarzenegger movies. 'Keep your hands where I can see them. Ann, shine the torch on these two. I don't want to miss anything important if I have to pull the trigger here.'

And, with his hands obediently above his head so that his shoulder could depress the on switch to his throat mike, Lance Corporal Bruce Jones said, very quietly, 'Bloody hell, boss, we're in deep shit here. There's a couple of tarts down here and one of them's kitted out like Tank Girl. I kid you not. And she has a Stinger pointed at my bollocks.'

Thus it was that representatives of the security forces first made contact with representatives of the *New England*'s resistance fighters just as the jet-ship came up towards twenty degrees west longitude, somewhere south of Iceland, somewhere north of Madeira, less than forty-eight hours from the eastern seaboard of the United States of America.

Chapter Fifteen

Merrideth turned to Richard who was crouching at his side when Bruce's message came through. 'Friends of yours?' he whispered.

Richard had been close enough to his side to hear what the corporal was saying. Now he gave a tight nod, his mind racing. Of the three women he knew to be aboard the only one likely to be able to recognise, let alone handle a Stinger was Ann Cable. Any women brought aboard by the pirates were unlikely to be running around in the lower hold – unless of course this was some obscure flanking manoeuvre or attack from the rear. 'I'll go down,' he said. He was in action before Merrideth could agree or demur.

Richard did not use the abseils. He swung himself onto the rungs of the ladder reaching down the wall of the stairwell. Like a diver descending into a sea of darkness, he swarmed down into the lower hold. His first movement attracted a torch beam and as soon as he could do so with safety, he swung round so that the light could play on his face. 'Ann?' he said quietly into the dazzle. 'Ann, is that you?'

'Richard?' There was total disbelief in Ann's familiar voice. 'What on earth are you doing with these guys?'

'Looking for you. Don't you recognise a bunch of knights in shining armour when you see them?'

'Well, I'll be damned. OK, Harry, I guess we can lower our guard a little now.'

'Thanks, Captain,' said Bruce in a whisper as Richard stepped down beside him. 'I owe you one.'

'Forget it, Bruce.' He looked around the hold, noting the array of red dots. 'I think we need to take out the surveillance equipment as you did in the upper hold and then we can switch on the lights and have a good look around in here. Stinger missiles are not on the original manifest.'

Bruce hesitated. 'I'll just check with the boss,' he said.

Merrideth agreed but he drew the line sooner. 'I'm not having people getting sidetracked into going through a terrorist arms cache,' he said to Mac later when the cameras were off and the lights on. It was the first time Richard had heard the terse commander go through his reasoning at such length and he even glanced at his watch to see whether Merrideth was due for more medication. 'There'll be nothing there we can use,' he went on. 'Our equipment is the best suited for the job in hand there is. Anything else would be irrelevant. I don't want the men going magpie on me and loading themselves down with lots of shiny new kit when their own is totally adequate. When we have control of the ship, we may think again. For now we'll just close it off.'

'But you'll want to do a list of what's there, won't you?' Richard said.

'Maybe later. In the meantime we have some debriefing to do.'

Ann had been on the point of telling Merrideth that she had completed a pretty thorough examination of what was there. Perhaps it was his tone, perhaps it was the way he dismissed the cache as a whole; whatever the reason, she changed her mind and kept quiet. So did Harry.

Merrideth's questions focused on the pirates to begin with, then he widened his view to include an assessment of their motivation, their relationship with their captives and the position – and willingness – of the captives to take action for themselves. Ann made some perceptive observations but it was Harry who could furnish most detail about her erstwhile colleagues. The interrogation moved onto a completely new track when Harry described some of the defensive work done by the pirates, apparently in preparation for just such company as Merrideth and his men.

The debrief continued until Ann acerbically pointed out that she and Harry had bodily needs as well as duties; a cup of coffee or tea would go down well about now. Lunch for the men had been a substantial but unappetising affair of cold sausages and beans scooped out of foil packages just a little before the expedition into the lower hold. Even during this excuse for a meal, none of the men removed their black gloves. The women were given tea and then their debriefing continued, but soon after that Mac approached Merrideth and the two went into a huddle.

Richard had no idea what they could be discussing now but he was happy at this stage to have his own, low-key debriefing with Ann and Harry. The information was not all one way, however. Ann particularly was fascinated by Merrideth and his men. She was aware that she was in the middle of an excellent story here, and she was keen to pursue it, but she knew that trying to interview any of the SAS men as they went about their work was out of the question. And it was obvious that whether they were preparing to go into battle with Dall and his men or simply patrolling the holds, these men were always at work.

The attitude of Merrideth's men towards the women was simply that they were members of the hostage group who had been rescued and whose debriefing might be useful as part of the stratagem to rescue the others. In different circumstances, once they had yielded the information they possessed, they would have been passed onwards and upwards. The SAS team were not equipped to nursemaid women or civilians and their existence here, like the pile of IRA arms, was a distracting and therefore dangerous irrelevance.

Ann observed that in the simple world the SAS men seemed to inhabit, men were either for killing or bonding with, women either for pinning up or pinning down.

'That's not fair,' said Richard quietly, aware that he was, in fact, being distracted himself by the requirement simply to deal with their presence here. 'They have to be focused all the time. They rely on each other absolutely. There can be no unknown quantities. This is a battleground, after all. Really, we have no place in it. We're innocent bystanders trying not to become collateral damage.'

'When is the battle due to start?'

'As soon as they can find a way into the bridge without endangering the captives.'

'They won't be able to, though, will they?' said Harry. 'Dall and his men have got everything rigged so tight that even these men won't be able to break in anywhere without starting a war, no matter how much help and advice you can give them.'

'It certainly looks that way,' agreed Richard. 'The only route out of here seems to be through the ducting and none of

Merrideth's men is slight enough to fit. And anyway, one soldier would not be able to do much, even if he could go somewhere sensitive.'

The conversation between the three of them ended there, for Richard was called away, but an idea from it remained in Harry's head, and then began to expand, especially when it became obvious that her estimation of the situation was accurate and the SAS men found themselves in a stalemate.

The change came slowly but noticeably. It was a feeling at first. The tempo of the activity died back. The disposition of the men became genuinely defensive rather than defensive through offence. Teams stopped reconnoitring and checking. The ducting was all laid bare. The ceiling and the floor were stripped and sectioned. Areas which might make excellent attack launch points were marked. It was when the crates were moved against the doors so that they would give good warning if Dall should try a full attack, however, that everything really began to slow. This happened at 20:00 hours. They had been aboard twelve hours exactly, and it was clear not only that they were going nowhere but that they had accepted the fact. Once the doors were secure, Merrideth ordered the men to stand down and allowed them to brew up, and even to warm up their bangers and beans. There was no risk that the heat would trigger the fire alarms, because they had disabled the sprinkler system as effectively as they had closed off the inert gas equipment.

Out of brew kits and zipped pockets and all sorts of secret places came the various condiments by which each man made his food less bland and more individual. Blueys fired up like the camping gas cookers used on family picnics, tea was made, beans began to boil and the racing spoons came out as each man not already cooking went to check out the culinary expertise of his friends. The relaxation was only surface deep, however. They might be having a fuddle, but they were doing so in the middle of a battlefield.

The differing characters of the two patrols began to show now. Bruce, Danny and Smell went up to the upper hold where Pain was still on guard. They set up their bashas with Op, Merrideth and Mac among the equipment on top of the pallet. Here they shared their tea, bangers and beans.

Tom, on the other hand, seemingly possessed of more social

skills to go with his open, boyish face and jug-handled ears, allowed Martin and Russ to pull their bashas together down where Mike stood stag and where Richard, Ann and Harry preferred to stay. Tom and his men seemed happy enough to share their food with the three guests – and then to explain how the five-gallon 'personal relief' jerry can might best be adapted to the peculiar requirements of women. The bags of course would work the same for everyone. Richard gallantly saved them both a fortune in Andrex by sharing Doc's supply which he had found earlier.

The medical equipment Richard was in charge of remained up beside Op's great communications case and last thing that evening he picked his way through the pallets to make sure his charges all had their medication. This meant he heard the final briefing of the day. Except for the two guards, everybody was there and it seemed natural enough to Richard that he should be included. It did not occur to him that at least part of what was said was for his benefit alone.

'Overview,' said Merrideth, drawing his black-gloved hand back over the dome of his head. Thin black hair almost indistinguishable from his knitted balaclava failed to stir beneath the weary gesture. Grey eyes in their strange swollen sockets stared round at the men whose slight listlessness betrayed the bone-deep weariness of having stood battle-ready for so long for so little result. 'We have achieved our first objective and have secured all available areas not held by the players. We have completed full recce and have marked off all possible attack points. Further progress is halted for the time being by the lack of surprise, the unexpected level of player preparation and by the danger to the hostages. To our advantage remain the following. One, two players down. Two, Dall and his people can have no idea of our actual number or disposition, though they must know by now that we control both holds and, therefore, the equipment in the IRA's cache. They can also assume that we have made contact with the women. But, and this is very important, they do not know we have the co-operation and expertise of Captain Mariner. Four, they do not yet know of the contingency plans we and others have in place. If we cannot make this area the ground for an attack within the next twenty-four hours then we can make it a beachhead where we can welcome reinforcements.

181

And that depends on the damage we can do to the propulsion systems and to the hull if necessary. Mac and Op will have more to say on that front later in the briefing. I want you all to try and rest tonight. We still have a lot to achieve. Stags change at two. That is all from me. Captain Mariner, if I might just have a word while Mac and Op finish things off?'

The word was simply about the sleeping and toilet arrangements. Richard was surprised by Merrideth's solicitude – and was too tired to see that the main objective was to stop him overhearing what Mac and Op were saying to the rest of them.

Tom's four-man brick possessed two sleeping bags and these he offered to the ladies. With a combination of exhaustion and disorientation making her unusually nervous, Harry begged permission for herself and Ann to set up their own little basha far from prying eyes away over by the port side. Ann, who in fact had no intention of removing anything intimate or displaying anything more arousing than her knees, nevertheless agreed to the demands of the exhausted Harry. They put their sleeping bags side by side beside a stand of pipes where one of the pallets had been positioned at a slight angle. On hearing that the lights would be extinguished at twelve thirty, Harry begged Richard's little penlight torch and he was happy to give it to her in spite of the smirks of Tom's men. The massive pallet gave such good cover that, greatly daring, Harry stripped off her uniform to reveal a heavy-duty sports bra and support knickers stretching from waist to mid thigh like bicycle shorts. Ann persisted in her decision to keep everything she was wearing designed by Janet Reger covered and soon they were bedded down comfortably.

At twelve thirty the lights went off. The muted thunder of the engines swelled with the dark, overwhelming all other sounds, but the vibration all around and on the air itself was soporific and soon everyone was asleep. Richard, who had had very little sleep aboard *Hero* last night, was particularly pleased to slip into a deep slumber disturbed only by the realisation that he had not phoned Robin as he always did in the evenings when they were apart. She would definitely know that something was up now and he was going to be in very severe trouble when he got home. It never once occurred to him that he might never be going home.

The inspection panels on the square air ducts clipped in and out. Even with short fingernails it was easy enough to free them. They were strong but light, and they made no noise either coming out or going in, so Harry was able to open the panel on the duct beside her head without disturbing Ann or alerting Mike on stag by the blocked door. It was going to be a tight fit, even wearing only her underwear. She would have liked to have replaced the grille behind her, but it was as much as she could do to slither into the square metal tube; bending down to recover the grille was out of the question. This section of the pipe reached vertically through nearly two decks. It had a set of tiny rungs in it, just big enough to take the toes of an engineer's boots during an inspection. After stripping off her uniform, Harry had put her deck shoes back on; no one's toes could have taken the strain of carrying a body's weight up that sharp-edged little ladder for long.

Step by step, Harry went up, breathing silently through her mouth, acutely conscious of every sound she was making, every squeak of rubber, every slither of skin or stretch fabric, every rumble of her starving tummy. She wore the torch jammed uncomfortably but safely down the back of her underpants in the valley between her buttocks. She did not reach for it until the vertical section of the pipe bent suddenly away to her right. This shift in direction was not unexpected but it was abrupt enough to cause her a bump on the head. She froze, in case the sound of her head striking the covering should have alerted the sentry in the upper hold.

When nothing had happened after a slow count of one hundred, she rummaged in her drawers and withdrew Richard's torch. Its unsteady beam revealed a long, square tunnel. It was clear of dust and gleamingly clean. She hoped fervently it was also as strong and well-secured as it looked. She wanted no panels banging in and out under the weight of her knees. She wanted no sections tearing free from wall or deck to pitch her down onto the pallets below. God alone knew what the terrifying black-clad invaders would do if they caught her crawling about in the dark like this. Shoot her as a spy, probably. And she could hardly blame them. It was probably insane of her to set out on such an adventure without either consultation or warning. But she had

183

known from the first that they would never agree to her doing anything like this. She squeezed round the bend, went onto all fours, wedged the torch in her cleavage so that it shone ahead of her, took a deep, silent breath and proceeded.

The horizontal section held up beneath her weight well enough and she made it to the next vertical section with little trouble. Here she liberated the warm torch and flashed it around herself. The tunnel of the air ducting bifurcated here, and split several times again off each new tunnel almost at once. This was where the air-conditioning system reached the accommodation areas. Harry closed her eyes and her nearly photographic memory recalled the layout of the ducts through the rooms and quarters on A deck below her. Then, slowly, pausing every now and then to think again, she worked her way through the system.

At last she stopped. Her face was pressed up against a grille exactly as wide as her shoulders, held in place with nylon clips as easy to release from this side as the other. She was looking into a silent, darkened room. Before she did anything else, she flashed the torch around the room to make sure she had reached the correct destination. The legs of chairs. The bases of shelf units. Rows and rows of books.

Harry pushed the panel out silently and it toppled to the carpet like a feather landing on a duvet. With the torch still on, she pushed her right arm and shoulder through the opening, eased her head out next and followed that with her left shoulder, bust and torso. When she was half out, a swift wriggle of the hips allowed her to roll safely and silently into the room.

She knelt, flashing the torch towards the door, which was thankfully closed. Then she pulled herself to her feet and followed the pale beam over to the piles of books and videos still half concealing the computer. Oh God, let it still be working, she prayed as she moved the chair closer and sat before it.

Harry switched the rocker and the screen jumped into life. With the speed of a striking snake she hit the volume on the speakers, silencing them before they could sound the chord of connection. Directions and connection codes scrolled up the screen.

WINDOWS it said.

Harry took the mouse, her heart thumping, her mouth wide. The icons came up. She was in!

Her plan was simple from here on. She was going to override the propulsion control programs if she could. She would reverse some, put viruses in any she could infect and smash up as many of the others as she could. By the time she had finished, it would be easier and quicker to row this tub wherever they were taking it.

PASSWORD.

Cleopatra, she typed.

As she did so, the door behind her swung silently open. Harry had no inkling. There was no sound beyond the insistent thunder of the distant engines she was trying to emasculate. There was no light, no stirring of the air discernible even to the sweat-slick surfaces of her bare back. Such was her concentration she had no idea that a tall figure was moving up behind her as silently as any of the super-trained Special Forces men below.

PASSWORD.

She hesitated. Some sixth sense warned her, perhaps. But too late. There was a whisper of movement and a solid *thud* as a blackjack hit her head. She slumped forward onto the keyboard.

PASSWORD NOT ACCEPTABLE said the screen and died.

A long thin hand came forward and snapped the rocker off. Then the same hand took Harry by the shoulder and lifted the unconscious head up off the table.

'Now that,' said Pitman quietly, 'makes us even. Almost.'

Harry regained consciousness to find herself in a workroom in one of the engineering sections. She was sitting in a low-backed swivel chair. She glanced down first, not around. And she was relieved to see, through the swirl of dizziness the movement caused, that her clothing, what there was of it, was still in place. Her next instinct was to move and she discovered that she was secured to the body of the chair. She looked at her right arm and saw it had been taped to the arm. There was a loud bang. She looked up.

Pitman had made the sound by thumping a black moulded plastic case on a metal table just off to Harry's right. As Harry watched, Pitman pulled out various pieces of equipment. The first was a hand-held drill. Pitman pointed it at the ceiling as though it was a gun. It resembled a gun with its square black body, long moulded stock and bright red trigger, though it was a far bulkier weapon than Pitman's beloved ASP. The chuck, which looked like a squat black barrel, spun when Pitman pulled the trigger and the powerful little motor whined.

Harry's flesh clenched into goose bumps all over her body.

Pitman inserted the drill's key into the side of the chuck and turned it. Three claws pushed up out of the body of the chuck and spread, as sinister as the claws of a vulture. When the claws had spread sufficiently, she took a long drill bit, the longest Harry had ever seen, and inserted it between the claws. A flick of the wrist tightened the claws, leaving the better part of twenty centimetres of drill exposed. She reached into the depths of the case again and pulled out a handful of 25 centimetre screws. Then she came round the table and put the whole grim set close by Harry's securely-taped arm. Pitman pulled up a second swivel chair and sat on it, facing Harry, her knees between Harry's knees. She leaned forward so close that when she spoke Harry could feel her breath against her cheeks. 'Now,' said Pitman gently, 'I'm going to ask you some questions and if I don't like the answers I'm going to screw you to that chair. Do you understand?'

Harry, beyond speech, simply nodded. There was a lump the size of an Easter egg in her throat and she needed to pee so badly.

'ANSWER ME!' screamed Pitman.

'Yes,' said Harry. 'Anything. I'll tell you anything. Don't hurt me. Please.' Her voice quivered, and her eyes overflowed.

'So many questions, so little time,' said Pitman to herself. 'Where to begin?'

Harry watched her, her pupils huge with terror.

'How many of the crew are in on it?'

'I don't understand. What?'

'Like O'Reilley. In on the deal? Dix, Bligh, the captain?'

Harry shook her head. She could not bring herself to speak. Pitman leaned forward again, looking deep into her eyes. She raised her hand, wiped away a tear almost solicitously. Harry's head slammed away from the soft caress as though from a vicious blow. Pitman frowned. 'You really don't know, do you? You have no idea what is going on here at all.'

She sat back. Harry's eyes remained riveted to hers. There was nothing going through Harry's mind at all. She was focused on each succeeding moment so fiercely that there was no room for speculation or much rational thought. Pitman asked, she answered. That was all she understood. Except that if she answered incorrectly then this woman was going to drill holes in her and screw her to the chair. She understood that all too well. The only time her eyes shifted was when Pitman lowered the drill into her lap. Harry registered that she was in a clean green T-shirt and fatigue trousers. She had found her bergen then.

Pitman left the drill sitting in her lap looking incongruously like a black kitten. With very long claws. She raised her left hand to her head and caressed the bandage at her temple. Harry was clearly not the only person in that strange little room who had a headache. 'Tell me about your new friends, then.'

'I don't understand. Who—'

'The men who killed Slogett and Newby. The men in black.'

'I don't know much about them. I think they're British. They seem to be soldiers of some sort.'

'SAS,' said Pitman quietly.

'There are maybe ten of them and Richard Mariner's with them. He's advising them, seems like, but he also seems to be giving them pills and whatever . . .'

'Unit medic. But why would they need one?'

'I don't know. I guess some of them are sick maybe.'

'What do they plan to do next?'

The knot of fear in Harry's chest tightened and she gasped. Her ignorance threatened her. 'I don't know,' she said, praying that Pitman would believe her. 'They've all gone to bed. They had a briefing at about midnight but they wouldn't let Ann or me up there.'

Pitman gazed at her victim. Of course the SAS men wouldn't include some unknown girl in a major briefing. But it was a pretty unusual SAS team that had guest medics.

Dall hadn't said anything about the SAS. As far as Pitman was aware, no one aboard had any idea exactly who Dall had arranged to meet up with, but no one had mentioned SAS. If they had, she suspected Dall's last command would have been even smaller than it was. She hated to be so ignorant – hated the fact that her careful watch on the library had got her such a promising source of information. Hated the fact that her source turned out to be as ignorant as she was herself.

Without really thinking, as much to busy her fingers while her mind raced, Pitman raised the drill and placed the point of the bit on the swell of the chair seat between her prisoner's thighs. She pulled the trigger and the electric motor whined. The bit spun, its steel point ate into the cloth, shredding it in an instant. It sliced through the foam-rubber padding, spraying tiny grains of it onto Harry's thighs. Suddenly threads of grey plastic whirled up as though being pulled out of the body of the chair by invisible threads. The bit sank through the chair completely and the chuck thumped meatily into the seat, its blur of grey steel mere millimetres from the pale curves of Harry's body. She was trembling so much the chair was wobbling.

'Please,' she whispered. 'Don't! How could you? When I . . . When I . . .'

Pitman snapped out of her reverie. Shock that she should have done something so dangerous in such an utterly unconsidered fashion made her tear the drill out of the chair in apparent rage. Harry flinched so powerfully that the chair sprang back on its castors.

'Tell me more!' spat Pitman.

Harry concentrated on what little she knew about the SAS men. She did not articulate her thoughts and suspicions about her shipmates. She did not describe the Stinger missile she and Ann had found in the hold. She did not admit what her own plans for the computers were or how nearly she had been able to carry them out. She focused on Merrideth and his men and gave every detail she had observed, been told, guessed or overheard. And it was a word that Richard had used while he was talking to Ann that brought Pitman up short. And that word was Jellicoe.

'What?' she hissed. 'Are you telling me that these are the Jellicoe Boys? Are you serious? But I thought—' She froze. 'Jesus Christ!' she said, but Harry didn't hear her because of the explosions.

Merrideth's men came out of the hold at 2 a.m. They came through the walls at the foot of the stairwell, blowing open the steel panels with shaped charges of P4, as Richard had suggested. As they came through, the two bricks split into pairs and whirled away through the undefended engineering sections. Merrideth

188

and Mac stayed with Op to direct and monitor the operation with the aid of a map of the engineering decks. Bruce and Danny were the A team, at least by their own estimation, and so they ran the furthest and did the dirtiest. They slithered like penetrating oil down the passageways to the engine control room. They arrived there only instants after the sound of the explosion. Paul Aves had been on duty here until Dall called him up to consider the communications with their unwelcome guests. He had left Lazlo on watch. Lazlo was slow. The first thing he knew after the roar of the explosion was the thump of a stun grenade landing. Then he knew nothing.

Smell and Pain went through the corridors behind Bruce, securing empty and undefended areas. They arrived at the engine control room in time to help the other two tidy up.

Russ and Mike went on down a deck and into the massive engine room itself. The place was utterly deserted.

Tom and Martin were the real A team. They were faster, quieter and better organised than Bruce and Danny. They whirled along the corridors as though surfing on the sound wave of the explosion, checking in doorways, one high, one low, scanning lengthy fields of fire, moving like shadows, never still, never appearing at full height, never exposing anything other than body armour and armaments, always covering each other.

It was Tom who came through the door of the makeshift interrogation room first. The sight of the apparently naked form of a woman he had last seen bedded safely under his own guard, taped to a chair with silver ducting tape, brought him up short. He registered the black DIY box on the table, and caught the look on the face of the woman whirling to confront him, raising a massive, but unfamiliar, black gun.

'NO!' screamed Harry, fighting to tear herself out of the chair. It spun, teetered dangerously, and crashed into the table.

Pitman whirled, years of training taking over, raising the weapon in her hands and pointing it straight at the head of the first man in. She pulled the trigger. The drill whirred.

Tom fired. The shot went in under Pitman's uselessly spinning drill and hit her exactly between the breasts. As Merrideth had given strict instructions that no one should be killed if humanly possible, the bullet was a lightweight plastic training round. It smashed into Pitman's breastbone, lifting her off her feet and knocking her backwards over the table. The drill went one way and the black box another. Pitman slewed wildly across the table and slithered into the lap of the still screaming Harry. This time the chair toppled over. Harry's shoulder and arm hit the floor, and the muscles down one side of her neck tore painfully. Pitman's body rolled away from her and, as though in one final insult, Pitman's left boot smashed into Harry's ear and everything went black.

When Harry came to a short time later, the chair was upright but she was still secured to it. Pitman was lying on the table, her vest and underclothing torn, with one man standing between her straddled legs doing something sickeningly rhythmic to her naked torso while the other crouched over her head, balaclava cast aside, pressing his mouth obscenely to her slack blue lips.

For the last time that night, Harry sucked in her breath to scream, fighting against her bonds. But as she did so, familiar words began to seep into her consciousness.

'. . . three, four, five. BREATHE . . .'

Harry realised what they were doing and called, 'Angela! Her name is Angela!'

The one doing the chest massage continue to count. The one giving the kiss of life glanced up and winked at her, his face ridiculously boyish with its freckles and jug-handle ears. 'Come on, Angela,' he said. 'Come on back to us, my old lovely. Here's Harriet waiting to talk to you . . .'

And Pitman coughed, stirred.

As though they were face to face, head to head across a negotiating table, Merrideth and Dall faced each other over the videophone link. 'I underestimated you,' grated Dall, his voice tinny through the little speaker.

Merrideth looked straight into his opponent's eyes. 'We've taken a small step,' he said calmly. 'We hold a little more ground and a couple of your people. You still have control. You still have the power and the hostages. We are no threat to you here. Don't do anything precipitate.'

'Precipitate,' grated Dall. 'What d'you mean precipitate, you pompous, patronising Limey bastard?'

'There is no need for anyone to die.'

'Just what the fuck are you doing here if nobody has to die?' snarled Dall.

'We're trying to retrieve the situation.'

Dall lapsed into silence, glaring into the camera. Merrideth tried to see behind the iron gaze in that flat little picture. He had gambled on Dall reacting sensibly. The SAS were in control of the engineering sections as well as the holds now. Nothing Dall could do would alter that. He had control of the command and accommodation areas. And there was not much Merrideth could do to alter that. The heart of his gamble lay in Dall's reaction to the new situation. Would he start killing hostages out of frustration or spite? Merrideth hoped not. He had two hostages from among Dall's personnel and he didn't want to get into the game of trading body bags – or body parts, come to that. Surely Dall could see that nothing he could do – no one he could execute – would make things any better for him. The balance had shifted slightly. The stand-off was still the same.

'Short of sabotaging all the engines, there's nothing we can do down here. You know that. You still have all the control up there,' Merrideth said again. A massive weariness suddenly swept over him. It seemed to him that he had spent all his life dealing with men like this, untrustworthy, self-serving, lazy and vicious. From Whitehall to Washington, from Colombia to Kuwait, from Belfast to Belize, one side or the other, it made no difference. 'It's your move, Dall,' he said. 'Put up or shut up. When you've made up your mind, give me a call. Out.' He snapped the connection button to OFF.

Mac, beside him, said quietly, 'Shall I get something from Doc – from the captain?'

'No. I'm just tired. Dall won't do anything. He's a cheap whore in a big game. In over his head and he doesn't know it. Playing for time, trying to up the ante, trying not to get screwed. No chance on any front, I'd say. Especially when Marshall comes aboard. What's the time?'

'Rising four on ship's time. Three local. We've moved time zones.'

'More than two thousand miles out. Over the Newfoundland Basin. Over the edge of the Grand Banks by morning. Then we'll have to start preparing for the next set of guests.'

191

'Yup,' said Mac. 'But in the meantime we really can get some rest.'

'Leaving out some solid stag, if you'd be so kind. If Dall's having trouble handling this, then he's only got two ways to go. Kill hostages or attack us.'

'OK, boss. What about the prisoners?'

'I don't want to deal with them now. What sort of state are they in?'

'Alive. Just. Carefully restrained. The ship's computer officer's pretty competent as a nurse. She's keeping an eye on them. Stag could keep a distant eye on her.'

'Fine. Let's do it.'

'Consider it done.'

Angela Van Der Piet awoke slowly with an ache in her head and a pain in her chest. It was a sharp pain and so precisely placed that it felt as though her heart was breaking. Half-conscious memories fed disturbingly into her confused and aching head. She felt as if she was coming to after a lengthy session of physical and sexual abuse. This supposition was compounded by the fact that she was firmly secured to the bed.

She raised her head, trying to look down in the dim light. A sheet failed to cover her torso and she knew at once she was naked to the waist at least. The bruise along her sternum deepened the shadow between her breasts, seeming to make them fuller, and she felt terribly defenceless and at risk. Even more than most women, Pitman feared rape. She had taken the physical prowess of her girlhood ultimately into the Dutch army where she had forced her way into the special forces regiments by sheer strength of will. But once there she had found herself surrounded by men who saw women mostly as sex objects or good-luck charms. The whole of her gender, it seemed sometimes, were divided into mothers or faithful girlfriends far away, or good cheap whores nearby. As well as being physically at risk, she found herself sexually at risk as well, and the only way she could deal with it was by becoming almost nun-like. Asexual. And as butch as the most masculine of the men.

But the men Pitman worked with kept going into situations where the physical danger escalated and, with it, the sexual danger for her when she accompanied them. Even had she been safe

192

from the attentions of her own squad, there was usually the rest of the army to contend with. And always the enemy. In war situations, the rest of her squad feared capture, torture and death. She feared capture, rape, torture and death. It had, in fact, never happened. And she had thought she had come to terms with the fear of it.

The simple pirating of a ship, the loading of some illicit cargo and its delivery to a prearranged location known only to Dall and Aves had seemed the least risky of all the assignments she had ever been on. Even the unfortunate need to dispatch the PIRA watchkeeper and his American girlfriend had hardly ruffled the surface of her calm. Nothing on this job had. Until that strange girl with her intense, intelligent eyes had appeared out of the woodwork to watch her the way certain men had watched her all her life. Until the S A bloody S had arrived on the scene so unexpectedly.

A figure suddenly loomed out of the shadows at her bedside. It was not that of the big rough corporal with hot bristly lips. It was that of the dangerous girl called Harry. What little light there was seemed to have been captured by her eyes and multiplied until they shone. She moved strangely, stiffly. Pitman suddenly, poignantly, regretted hurting, humiliating and scaring her so badly. It seemed for a wild instant that the pain in her heart was there because of that.

But then things took an unexpected twist.

'You're awake,' said Harry quietly, and she sat on the bed with her hip snugly in the hollow of Pitman's slim waist. She reached over for something Pitman could not see. She brought it into the light and it was Pitman's turn to gasp.

Harry put the point of a drill bit exactly in the middle of the bruise on Pitman's breastbone and raised her strangely shining eyes. 'Now,' she breathed. 'Where were we, Angela?'

Chapter Sixteen

During the next eighteen hours, while the stand-off persisted, *New England* continued along the old Great Circle route from Fastnet to Cape Race. She might be everything of the twenty-first century encapsulated in one vessel, but the timeless laws of physics and navigation dictated that the route followed by Brendan in his coracle, almost by Columbus in his caravels and by all the great ships from the *Titanic* to the *Queens* should be the course beneath her revolutionary keel.

As she sped westwards, at one hundred miles an hour, the Porcupine Bank gathered and fell away beneath her. The edge of the continental shelf tumbled vertiginously into the West European Basin. For the better part of a thousand miles this great abyss reached down before rising up into the North Atlantic ridge which in time fell away into the Newfoundland Basin, the northern arm of the North-West Atlantic Basin, joining the icy deeps of the North American Basin with those of the Labrador Basin. Beyond the Newfoundland Basin, the Grand Banks thrust out past Flemish Cap and the Newfoundland Rise. Here the North American continental shelf heaved itself up into the shallows which would in time fall back to become the rocky coastlines of Newfoundland, Nova Scotia, New England and New York.

Out across these mountainous ridges and abyssal deeps, like a great submarine wind blowing ever eastwards, the enormous wash of the Gulf Stream came. In the ancient days of sail when a ship might move at speeds of half a dozen knots on average, the eastward surge, travelling counter at a knot or two, was worthy of consideration. Beneath *New England,* the Gulf Stream was reduced to insignificance. But great forces of nature have been belittled and dismissed before. Never for long.

Above the steady thrust of the Gulf Stream whirled unquiet

air. The heavy atmosphere of the cold polar cap sat uneasily on the Arctic. The weight of its chilly density pulled it southwards while the buoyant warmth of the southern continental or maritime winds made them push up over their slow and heavy cousin. To the interface of warm air seeking to rise above cold, the physics dictated by the spin of the earth added a constant variety. The westward passage of the sun reflects the eastward tumble of the earth, and the air above the spinning continents and seas is disturbed, twisted and ultimately embroiled by the power of its passage.

So it is that the straight and steady line which would define the interface between polar and temperate air becomes a series of ripples, and the ripples become whorls and the whorls become depressions with warm, light wind trapped in toils of cold, heavy atmosphere. Where the airs intertwine – they hesitate to mix – pressure gradients build. In time, these stabilise to become warm fronts and cold fronts striving to contain the unquiet airs. Invisible, but as real as ski slopes, the fronts form in the air and sweep eastwards, while up and down their glacial slopes move columns of water vapour coalescing into clouds.

The winds which would blow contentedly westwards over the east-tumbling earth become embroiled in this system also, rushing out of high pressure towards low pressure, pushing the clouds they carry up and down the slopes of air. The speed of the winds is dictated by the intensity of the depression and the steepness of the pressure gradient around which they are proceeding. Further south, in the equatorial regions of the North Atlantic, storms sent westwards out of Africa tighten the gyre so fiercely that the winds whirling round them can travel at speeds close to 200 miles per hour. In the central and northern regions, such hurricane winds are rarer but they are by no means unknown. And they bring with them mountainous seas. Seas big enough, according to one record, to drive back the complete bridgehouse of the first *Queen Elizabeth* by more than a foot one stormy night in the Second World War.

Above the whirling air, mankind has hung necklaces of weather satellites which originally broadcast to forecasters and coastguards, though later to every properly equipped vessel.

The warnings from the weather sats kept *New England* on the southern edge of the great circle route as a series of unseasonable weather systems did much to spoil the first summer of the brave new century in northern Europe. She had been sailing at full speed for nearly forty hours when she skimmed over the banks south of Cape Race and set her head southwards, keeping along the line of the coast well east of Avalon, St-Pierre and Cape Breton, down towards Sable Island.

Things had deteriorated on the bridge. Dall had executed no one in retaliation for the loss of the engineering sections but it had been a close call and everyone knew it. The team he had brought aboard with him were confused, defensive, under great strain. They had lost two of their close-knit number, dead at the hands of the SAS, and two more whose fate remained unknown. The fact that each of the second couple was half of a particularly close buddy pair made things worse. The depressed Sam Copeland could think nothing but good of the trusty Pitman, and little but evil of what must be happening to her. Even Lazlo seemed to have gained a range of positive attributes in the eyes of Lobo and his friends.

While the strain on the pirates mounted, the strain on the crew of *New England* reached breaking point. There seemed no doubt now that they were heading for North America and the best-defended, most closely guarded coasts in the world. Dall's plan as far as anyone could penetrate it seemed to rely on the jet-ship outrunning anything sent after or against her until she could make a secret landfall or rendezvous. Ahead lay more unknown, incalculable danger from without and the increasing certainty of execution during some forced and botched negotiation within. If push came to shove, the SAS might well be more interested in regaining control of the ship than in preserving the lives of the hostages. But the gloomy restlessness of the imprisoned men and woman was kept on a tight rein by the threat of their eight captors – nine, counting the turncoat O'Reilley. If the SAS wanted him they would have to be very quick indeed to get to him before his muttering ex-shipmates did.

'Don't you see?' Bob Stark was saying, much more loudly and forcefully than was absolutely necessary, almost shouting across the bridge at Dall. 'We'll be in United States territorial waters any time now. And if the government thinks we pose any

197

kind of a threat, *New England*'s speed won't matter a damn. They'll just blow us out of the water!'

'Like fuck they will,' snarled Dall, goaded. 'With the Senator and his wife, the professor, you, and a Pulitzer prizewinner aboard? Will they hell! They'll do what they do best. They'll hesitate. Shit, look at Desert Storm. Look how that turned out after all the huffing and puffing. We had Saddam over a barrel with a grenade shoved up his nose and nobody had the balls to pull the pin!'

O'Reilley shoved his ferret face onto the bridge. 'They're sending again,' he said. 'Same message, same wavelength.'

'Still no idea?' Dall turned his back on Bob, concentrating on the radio operator. Every hour for the last six hours O'Reilley had picked up a transmission coming out of the communications system Op had set up below.

'Nah. Short burst, encrypted signal. Could be going anywhere between here and Jupiter just about.'

'Best guess?'

'American Special Forces. If the SAS can't slow us down, then maybe the SEALs will.'

'Yeah. That's right. So we've got to watch for incoming encrypted. And Dix, we've got to look out for incoming fast craft. You keep your eyes peeled or you lose them. Paul, have you any idea at all as yet how those sucking SAS men got aboard?'

'Not one, Captain,' answered Paul Aves. 'But they've been light-footed and light-fingered so far, even though they haven't managed to slow us yet.'

'Don't be so stupid,' snapped Bob. 'The SAS could slow us or stop us any time they wanted to. All they have to do is pull the plugs or blow the fuses.'

'Who's being stupid?' snarled Dall. 'It obviously escaped your notice that we spent all of that first day setting this place up to be a fortress that can double as a firework display. They've worked it out, even if you haven't. They touch one thing on this fucking boat they should not and the whole shitload, including us, goes up like the Fourth of July.'

Although neither of the women was included in the next briefing, Richard was. If pressed, he would have admitted that his inclusion seemed a little casual, almost accidental, given that his advice had made all the difference so far.

'Mac,' began Merrideth, his voice little more than a whisper, 'you and Op have checked all the hands-off and the surprises. Summation?'

'Tricky. They've put a range of systems and devices in place. But they seem to have placed overrides in parallel with them. If we try to power down the engines either directly or from the engine control room, then the whole lot goes up in our faces. If they decide to do it from the bridge then that'll be AOK.'

'Op?'

'Mac's got it in one, boss. Take a specific. If we tried to override the controls and open the rear cargo hatches from here, we'd trigger God knows what. If Dall decides to open the whole shooting match from up on the bridge then that'll be fine. The systems we've checked have all been rigged like that. Signal from the bridge, fine. Signal from down here and it's goodnight Vienna.'

'But why would you want to open the cargo hatches?' asked Richard, intrigued.

Op looked at Mac first and then at Merrideth. The major shrugged wearily and infinitesimally – the way he did everything at the moment. 'To let the Friends in,' he answered. The way he said it made it clear Friends had a capital F. Richard guessed that they must be American Special Forces. A little spring of excitement began to well up in him at the thought.

'What's the plan?' he asked eagerly.

'Well,' wheezed Merrideth, 'it's simple enough really. They're reckoning on coming aboard in the same way we did, except that we're already here to signal time and location.'

'But you said you were planning to open the cargo hatches.'

'Right. On an agreed signal at a prepared rendezvous, they'll place themselves like we did on their own super-cat or hovercraft. At the correct moment, we were to open the rear hatch to the lower cargo hold and they would come aboard.'

'God! They'd have to be quick! The safety override will kill the jets and the hatch would go down all right, but the people on the bridge would press their own overrides and the thing would swing shut again almost immediately and power up again as soon as it did so!'

'We'd calculated a window of ten minutes in all. They don't

need to wait for the hatch to open fully and they can still come in while it's closing if they're fast. Ten minutes is all they'll need, with luck. But it's all academic now. We can't get on the bridge and we can't override the cargo hatch controls, or anything else, from down here without setting off booby traps. Can you?'

'Well, no,' admitted Richard. 'But I know a man who can. Well, not a man, actually . . .'

'Of course! I hadn't thought!' said Harry.

'You've been preoccupied with the wounded,' said Richard.

Harry dropped her gaze. Her preoccupation had not arisen out of humanitarian considerations at all.

'But now that it's under discussion,' pursued Richard, unaware, 'could you patch through from one of the terminals within our control to your own system on the bridge and then make the systems down here think the programs they are running have come from the command areas?'

'Well, if my experience with the terminal in the library is anything to go by,' she answered slowly, 'there certainly seems to be reason to hope.'

'I get the impression we'll need to be pretty certain,' said Richard. 'If anything goes wrong then the whole ship is rigged to explode, so Merrideth says.'

'Now that is nasty,' whispered Harry. 'I tell you what,' her wide eyes rose to his face, their gaze troubled but earnest. 'You leave this with me for a while and I'll check.'

'Check?' he asked, a little taken aback. 'What do you mean?'

'I'll ask Angela if the major's information is true. Then I'll see about setting up a test or two. In my head at first, but on the engine control room computer later. Don't worry,' she added, noting his expression, 'I'll be sure to check with you at each important step.'

'With me or with the major.'

'With *you*,' she said emphatically, squaring her jaw suddenly. 'I don't think I entirely trust the major.'

Richard nodded and he returned to the cargo hold while Harry went back to the sickbay to carry out the first part of her scheme.

Pitman and Lazlo were having a hard time of it. The SAS men expected no quarter and offered none. All of them had spent hours, days even, in the most acute physical discomfort merely as a part of their training. As a result, the two captives were permanently handcuffed to the bed. They were allowed no freedom of movement at all, and the cuffs themselves were only loosened occasionally and sufficiently to maintain circulation. As Merrideth observed, the only thing worse than a prisoner is a sick prisoner. They were fed, watered and passed the bedpan by hand. Harry doctored them, Ann nursed them as necessary, the SAS men guarded them, and that was all. Harry had suggested a bed bath but the suggestion was vetoed as being too dangerous.

Lazlo grunted as Harry entered but he hardly registered her presence; she had been keeping him semi-comatose with drugs. Ann was away in the lower hold, ferreting around in the IRA armaments – with Merrideth's grudging permission. So Harry and Pitman were effectively alone. They had forged a strange bond which had begun, oddly enough, when Harry had put the drill down, unable to do more with it than offer the most illusory of threats.

Pitman had naturally assumed spineless weakness in her enemy and had been moved to no gratitude whatsoever. But Harry's continued care and attention, selfless and apparently so artless, had begun to wear her down. They communicated now with some directness across the barricades of their armed truce. But, as with Harry's apparent guilelessness, Pitman's gruff honesty hid more than it revealed.

'Merrideth says Dall's got this place all wired ready to blow,' said Harry softly. 'Richard Mariner's just told me about it and I'd trust him with my life.'

'Yes. As far as I know, Dall's got systems in place to destroy anything your friends handle wrong.'

'Not just the bits and pieces. The whole ship.'

'Maybe. Seems logical.'

'No. It doesn't. If this was a desperate stand-off and he really had his back to the wall, do or die, then I could maybe see a reason. But to risk the whole ship on the off chance that the SAS might want to slow her or even stop her – I just don't see it. Not unless there's a hell of a lot you're not telling me. Or a hell of a lot he hasn't told you.'

'Very likely. Either one. I've told you, I'm not going to give you much more than the big four, even if you bring the drill back in. And even if I did spill my guts, you can bet all Dall's briefings are "need to know". Only Dall and maybe Paul Aves know the whole story. I only know what I need to know in order to do my job and collect my pay.'

'Then I hope you've invested some of that pay in good insurance, because I'm off to do some serious tinkering with Captain Dall's booby-trap systems.'

The engine control room still stank of flash powder. The floor, walls, and some of the equipment bore clear evidence of the stun grenades which had overcome Lazlo. The main force of the blast had been absorbed by the central bank of instruments but even so, one of the monitors which stood in the rank along the left-hand wall was weirdly distorted.

Harry crossed to the machines with a barely-controlled skip of excitement, Richard close behind her. They sat down and Harry flicked switches and pressed buttons, bringing the machines to life. Like many of his generation, Richard had taken to computers with rather less ease than video players, so the speed and mastery shown by his slim companion fascinated him.

As the screens awoke to her bidding, they demonstrated the programs for which they had been prepared, primarily the status and disposition of the engines. Like many an expert being observed, Harry kept up a running commentary as she worked. 'This pre-programming is simple surface stuff,' she said. 'Suitable for heathen engineers who have little idea of the subtleties. Let's see what happens if we close this engine monitoring program down and get deeper into the file management system.'

'Is anyone on the bridge likely to be monitoring this?' asked Richard as the screen went blank and then re-awoke covered with a bewildering range of linked icons.

'Not unless they've started up my computers. Still, let's see . . .'

Harry's voice was full of a strange mixture of breathless tension and ill-controlled excitement. She had missed the machines almost as though they were friends – or lovers, thought Richard. As he entertained this strange fancy, Harry was changing the display on another screen from measurements, stresses and load factors to a completely new series of icons. This was the blast-damaged screen nearest to the door, and its image was disturbingly askew. Richard was surprised it was still working at all. As he watched, the screen suddenly went red, as if it had flooded with blood. SECURITY said a glaring word in blue against the shocking background. PASSWORD.

Harry typed so rapidly that Richard could not follow her fingers and a series of asterisks came up onto the screen. He counted eight of them before the security system, satisfied, allowed them onto the next level. The screen cleared and then produced a weirdly twisted monochrome image of the bridge.

'Sound?' asked Richard, leaning forward.

''Fraid not. Can you lip-read?'

'No. I couldn't on this screen anyway. It's so twisted that these people don't look human. It looks like a Quasimodo convention up there.'

'It's the best I can do. Still, you can see that no one's paying any attention to my equipment. There's the captain and Dall up by the helm. That looks like Stubbs by the radar display and John Dix, for some reason, by the weather monitor. And there's the foul O'Reilley coming out of his pit. Can't see who the guard is but that looks like the lot. They don't seem to have noticed the security camera coming on. As long as we don't move it about, there's no reason to suppose they will ever work out they're being watched. Now, on with the show.'

Lacking Harry's youthful confidence, Richard kept one eye firmly on the collection of dumb dwarves and silent trolls currently manning the bridge. Because of this he missed some of the finer points of Harry's mouse-handling and keyboard technique, but her running commentary kept him up with what she was planning and what she was doing. 'There are levels which we want to go down here,' she said. 'It's not quite *Tomb Raider* but it'll do. First we want to make sure we can ferret around in here without anyone catching us at it. After setting up our bridge watch we've got to check for traps and alarms. Can we disable the whole system security program without setting something off? Lucrezia, you look after security, what do you think? Lucrezia thinks not. So . . .'

The second level of Harry's game was to plan ahead what systems she would want to consult and disable their security programs one by one.

'Now, let's follow lovely Lara down the next set of passages. Where can we actually *go*, now that the traps and gates have all been disabled and opened to us?'

All of this would have been gibberish to Richard had not both William and Mary introduced him to the intrepid animated virtual explorer in their own junior versions of the best-selling computer games. How typical of Harry, he thought, that she should identify with such a strongly twenty-first-century woman. Indeed, the whole system seemed to be guarded by women. Lucrezia Borgia, Boudicca, Joan of Arc, Marie Stopes. Because they were exploring the control areas, not the communications, Ellen Degeneres and one or two others who might have raised Richard's eyebrows and alerted him to Harry's orientation remained secret still.

'And here we are on the lowest level. We can go where we like through the command systems with nobody any the wiser. But what can we actually do?'

Harry's flying fingers paused. Hovered like hawks above the keyboard. Her eyes, slowly clearing of their concentration and reminding Richard disturbingly of Robin's eyes awakening in the morning, swept up to his face. 'This is the most dangerous level,' she said. 'I've given it all the thought I can but it may be good to talk. What can I do to test our access without alerting them?' Harry gestured to the trolls on the bridge monitor with her chin.

'It has to be something in this area,' mused Richard. 'It's this area that we have to control if we're going to make Merrideth's plan work.'

'And this area is outside their control and observation,' she agreed. 'But if anything goes wrong, it'll be this area that blows up.'

'But haven't they wired everything so that the whole ship goes up no matter where security is breached?'

'That's what Merrideth says. That's what Angela says. I wouldn't trust either of them as far as I could throw them.'

'That's as maybe. But so what?'

'Well, I was thinking, what about a little anchor malfunction? Two seconds. Maybe light up a monitor on the bridge but switch it off again at once. Shake them up a bit, maybe. And if anything local is set off, we're well away.'

'And if Merrideth is right and it all goes up?'

'Well, we're no worse off than we would have been in any case.'

Richard thought it through. She was right. He was beginning to question Merrideth himself now, and obviously only a fool would trust either of the captives. It would be worth trying the anchors – a localised explosion away in the chain locker wouldn't do them any harm back here.

'Right,' he said, unconsciously tensing the whole of his great body as though to ward off the half-expected cataclysm. 'Anchors away.'

Ship-handling was part of Cleopatra's province – in Harry's system as in life. As soon as the Egyptian queen got them through the last security check, Harry only had to click on an icon to open the anchor control system.

STATUS, said the screen. *Anchors stowed.*

DIRECTION, typed in Harry. *Lower port anchor.*

SAFETY ALERT, said the screen. *Anchors may not be lowered while vessel under way.*

'Ready?' said Harry. Her voice was quiet, her tone gentle. 'Want to alert Merrideth's merry men?'

'No point. If nothing happens we can tell him later. If something does happen he'll notice.'

'I guess,' said Harry, and sucked in a lingering hiss of breath.

DIRECTION, she typed. *Systems manager override.*

The seven dwarves on the bridge monitor all swung round as though Snow White had just arrived. They began to gesture at the console, at each other. A light was flashing insistently. No doubt an alarm was ringing.

Most importantly, however, nothing seemed to be blowing up.

Richard sucked in his breath at the sight of the furore on the bridge. But the light abruptly stopped flashing. The figures stopped shouting and gesticulating. Turned away, puzzled. The hunched homunculus of Dall crossed towards the console. Hit it like a man exasperated with a malfunctioning television.

Richard's eyes flicked across. The words DIRECTION: *Override* were jumping up towards the top of the screen. Below them stood STATUS: *Anchors stowed.* His gaze moved round to

Harry sitting at his side, her face flushed and her eyes sparkling. 'Bingo,' she breathed.

'We seem to be in business,' he agreed.

But then the twisted figure of Dall tore itself out of its seat, rushed across to Lobo and ripped the guard's gun from his hands. Shouting obscurely and silently, the distorted figure rushed out of picture, firing wildly as he did so.

'God!' wailed Harry. 'Oh my God, what have I done?'

'Just a minute,' urged Richard as though the people on the ruined monitor could hear and might obey. 'Just hang on one minute here . . .'

On the bridge all hell was loose. As though the sudden malfunction of the anchor alarm had been a kind of trigger, the communications room exploded into frenetic activity the instant after it stopped shrieking.

'Jesus! What the fuck is it now?' screamed Dall, unnerved by the lights and the sound.

'I'd guess we just entered US territorial waters,' answered Bob, still frowning with concern over the anchor alarm.

'O'Reilley, get your idle little ass into the communications room!' snarled Dall.

'Sure, Captain. But what in hell's name am I supposed to say?'

'Keep your hands the fuck off or it's Armageddon in here.'

'Think they'll buy it, Captain?' whined O'Reilley, obviously worried.

'I do not give one good God-damn. It's part of the plan and it's an order. Now just fucking do it, will you?'

'Aye aye, Captain,' muttered O'Reilley and sidled away.

Dall swung round, hurling his whole body about as though he was paraplegic. 'What was it with that alarm?' he demanded, following the direction of Bob's distracted gaze.

'I don't know. Just a glitch, I expect,' said Bob dismissively, giving himself a very vigorous mental shake. It was one of three things, he calculated, and all of them could do him good. The machine was malfunctioning, which might somehow give them an edge if it continued or worsened. Or the anchors were actually loose and slipping, which would sure as hell slow them down at any moment now. Or someone was tinkering with the systems.

206

There was no telling where things would end if that was the case. Given inspiration by the train of thought, he stole a secret glance up to the security camera in the corner. The red light was on. Curiouser and curiouser. He hoped it was Harry and Ann. More especially, vividly, he hoped it was Ann, safe and sound and sexy as ever . . .

'Captain.' O'Reilley came out of the radio room quite pale and obviously shaken. 'I got the Coastguard. I got the Civil Defence. I got the Navy and I got Strategic Air Command. One and all say they are getting ready to blow us straight out of the water unless we explain ourselves pretty fucking quick. I kid you not. What do I do?'

'I'll show you what the fuck to do!' snarled Dall, hurling himself to his feet. He strode across the bridge, tearing the semi-automatic rifle out of Lobo's hand as he passed him.

As though in slow motion, Bob turned, looking after the madman in stark disbelief. Lobo, too, turned, spun by the force of having his gun wrenched from his hands. O'Reilley took two steps away from the door and then literally dived for cover behind the watchkeeper's chair. Dix, his eyes fastened on the collision alarm radar, began to straighten and his movement summoned Stubbs's attention down out of the clouds.

As he moved, Dall flicked a switch on the side of the gun and brought it up to his shoulder. Sighting down the barrel as he walked, he pulled the trigger and automatic fire blasted into the air. Hot shell cases arced across the bridge in a bright brass rainbow. A wall of smoke and sound came out of the little radio room, shot through with flashes of fire and shards of flying debris.

''Nuff said?' snarled Dall at the cowering O'Reilley in the instant of quiet before the fire alarms came on.

Bob swept past Dall carrying the fire extinguisher and sprayed the little room. Every machine, every display, every dial was dead. No, not just dead. Destroyed. Black plastic lay shattered and smouldering. Glass lay strewn on the floor or stuck like quills into every surface. Wires lolled like eviscerated entrails, their bright plastic coatings giving disturbing impressions of blood and bodily fluids. It was the radiophonic equivalent of Golgotha in there. Golgotha burning. Bob sprayed the inert-gas electrical-safe foam in carefully practised swathes, burying the hissing obscenity. Dall might not be sane but he certainly wasn't joking.

207

The Coastguards and SAC could whistle after this. They could send the *Nimitz* out and no one aboard *New England* would know a thing about it until the first wave of F18s hit.

But then, he thought, maybe Dall wasn't all that mad after all. 'Turn off the alarms, please, Mr Dix,' he called. Maybe it was all part of what was going on here, whatever the hell *that* was. He passed the empty extinguisher to Stubbs and said, calculatedly, to Dall, 'Lucky that lot wasn't wired to explode like the rest of the equipment, huh?'

'Screw you!' spat Dall, chucking the empty gun at Lobo. But Bob got the impression that the pirate captain was more relaxed now, perhaps even grimly cheerful about the result of his outburst.

When the pair of them were back at their accustomed places before the main command console, O'Reilley wormed his way out from under the watchkeeper's chair and sneaked off the bridge. The moment he was out of sight, Dall said to Lobo, 'I want him watched. The Devil finds work for idle hands.'

As he finished speaking, Senator Charleston strode onto the bridge. His nose twitched at the telltale odour of powder and burning. 'What were those shots?' he rasped. 'Captain Dall—'

'It's all right, Senator,' said Dall, unexpectedly placatory. 'I lost my rag and shot the radio. No big deal. No one dead but the air. Lot of dead air now, though. Lot of deeply pissed people. Let's see what they'll do when we start playing hardball. Helmsman, let's head five more degrees west, if you please.'

The helmsman, GP Seaman Lee, looked at Bob as he always did when anyone else gave an order. As he did so, Lobo snapped a new clip into his gun with a crisp, threatening sound. Bob nodded, depression washing over him in reaction to the last few minutes' action.

New England's sleek head swung obediently five more degrees west of south and she ploughed at a sharper angle towards the rocky coast of the United States, cutting down and in at one hundred miles an hour.

It began to register on Harry that Richard was telling her to hang on and not to jump to conclusions. And when she began to understand that Dall had been shooting at the radios and not at people, she returned to her accustomed calm and suggested they try one more test.

Richard agreed. He raised the little hand-held radio he carried to his mouth and pressed the button to contact Merrideth.

The machine spat in his ear – there was a strict radio regimen based on the SAS men's assumption that O'Reilley and Dall would be monitoring them.

'Listen. I've just seen Dall blowing up the radio shack,' said Richard.

Silence.

'He's probably got equipment like this aboard and can still monitor us, I suppose, but the big stuff must all be gone. That's why the fire alarms are going off. They're hosing it out with the fire extinguisher now.'

'Right. I hear you. Is that all? Over.'

'No. Expect the hold-lights to flash in a while. We have to run one more test on equipment down your end before we risk overriding the rear door mechanism from here. Out.'

The alarm stopped. Eventually the hold-lights flashed. Nothing blew up. All was right with the world.

Richard left Harry calmly fiddling with the systems and went back to the holds. It was time to dole out the second to last dose of the medicines. As soon as he arrived in the pallet-sized bivouac, Merrideth said, 'We've changed course.' He gestured with a black-gloved hand at the Magellan equipment. Richard could see at once that *New England* was moving significantly inwards. Before, they had been on a southerly heading. Now there was a decided western bias. The list of positions and the current reading formed charts in his mind: the looming coast of Nova Scotia; behind it, Maine. 'You'd better get organised,' he observed dryly. 'Your Friends will be calling soon, I should imagine.' As he spoke, the lights flickered again. Off . . . two . . . three . . . four . . . On.

Merrideth's pale, gaunt face turned up to the glare of the lighting. 'We're ready,' he said. 'If she is.'

'She's as ready as she'll ever be,' said Richard. 'If she can make the lights flash she can open the rear doors.'

'Then all we need is the word.'

The word came through as the first wave of jets came in over the top of them at zero feet three hours to the minute later, just as they passed south of Cape Sable, still at sixty-five degrees west, 350 miles out from Portland, Maine. Even had Dall been as cunning as Richard supposed and set one of his own radios to monitor the SAS wavelengths, the speed of the encrypted transmission combined with the sound of the jet fighters scant metres above the deck would have confounded him. Merrideth's plan proceeded.

Ann had spent much of the interim re-examining the armaments loaded in Ireland as a way to stop herself worrying about Bob. Her activity became hampered when Merrideth's men began moving it back along the cargo deck. Whatever Dall might have booby-trapped out in the accommodation and command areas, he had not thought to set any traps down here, though much of the Semtex seemed to have radio-controlled detonators attached to it. The IRA, or their representatives, had been careful, orderly packers. Apart from the boxes which had fallen at the first acceleration, everything else remained shipshape and easy to handle. Ann lingered, watching the soldiers. The weapons they were clearing had been loaded aboard in lorries and on fork-lift trucks and so much of what was there had to be unpacked before it could be moved by hand. When they had cleared a sizeable space in front of the stern wall of the hold, they started to set up lynch points on the ceiling of the hold, almost as though they proposed to hang someone up there. Several people, in fact, for the rope-work stretched from one side of the hold to the other. Ann watched with the same slightly sickened fascination with which she had watched ants devouring the rotting corpse of a dead bird as a girl. The soldiers looked like black ants, swarming everywhere in silent indefatigable industry. Ann was rather relieved when Richard turned up. 'What are they doing?' she demanded.

'Hanged if I know,' he answered breezily, and involuntarily Ann's eyes were drawn up to the strange series of lynch points again.

Merrideth arrived then, with Mac at his side. He looked coldly at Ann and hesitated, clearly wanting to say something to Richard which he did not want her to hear. She looked him straight in the eye, smiled and waited.

'We must be ready in one half-hour,' he said at last.

'Ready for what?' asked Ann.

How exactly like gun barrels his eyes look in this light, thought Richard as Merrideth stared at Ann.

'Guests,' he said, articulating the word carefully, like an amateur auditioning for a part in *Who's Afraid of Virginia Woolf?* The effect was so theatrical that Ann looked questioningly at Richard.

'Friends,' he confirmed, a little over-seriously.

'You're joking!' said Ann.

'Why don't you go and check on the prisoners, Ms Cable,' ordered Merrideth. 'Newbold is busy and I think they need tending.'

'Now just one goddam—'

'Ann,' said Richard gently, 'I think it'd be for the best. Honestly. I really don't think you can stay here. And our patients haven't had anyone anywhere near them for hours.'

Perhaps only Richard or Bob could have got away with it. The heady combination of Kilkenny and Calabria in her blood gave her the most volatile of tempers, but it also made her particularly susceptible to charm. 'Well,' she temporised. 'If you say so, Richard.'

She went.

Merrideth watched her striding across the hold and the minute she was beyond earshot he tapped the tab of his personal radio. 'Bruce,' he spat. 'Watch the tart.'

The SAS corporal's black figure casually detached itself from the bustle of the welcome preparations and drifted after Ann. Abruptly, Richard looked squarely into those gun-metal grey pupils. 'What do you need now?' he demanded.

Merrideth did not answer at once but met his gaze with silent calculation. 'We've got to risk a radio message to Newbold,' he said at last. 'Even if Dall is listening on his own 319s or 349s now that he's blown the big stuff away, we still have to send one signal to Newbold. Something simple. One word. The equivalent of "Open sesame". We've only got ten minutes – we have to time it exactly.' He checked his watch. Even though the face was upside down, Richard could see that he had set the minute counter to 'countdown' and there were less than twenty minutes left.

'It could be anything,' said Mac. '*Sausages* . . .'

'How about just opening the channel like this?' suggested Merrideth.

The radio by Richard's ear hissed. 'It'd only work if I had one of those 349s with an earpiece like yours,' he said. 'And even then, only if there was dead silence.'

'Which is too much to ask,' acknowledged Merrideth. 'OK. Choose a word. Any word.'

'*Gate*,' said Richard without thinking. Heaven's Gate lurked at the back of his mind. The association seemed appropriate. The unease he felt about the place matched the current atmosphere aboard *New England*.

Merrideth flinched, as though he had been struck. 'What?' he spat.

'I just thought *Gate* would do,' said Richard, surprised. 'It means nothing. It's an easy word to hear. Easier than *Sausages*. But if you don't like it, choose your own.'

'No,' said Mac gently. 'It's cool. *Gate* should be fine. What do you say, boss?'

'Fine,' said Merrideth, as though he had never demurred. '*Gate* is fine.'

'Right,' said Richard. 'We'd better get weaving then. We've less than fifteen minutes, by the look of it.'

'So,' said Harry five minutes later, 'I have about seven minutes to get into the cargo hatch program. Then when someone says *Gate*, I press OPEN LOWER and pray.'

'That's right,' said Richard. 'Except that we all pray.'

'Oh well, *that's* all right then,' she said, busy already.

The seven minutes passed in a flash. Richard had vaguely supposed that they would stretch out as though he was waiting for a kettle to boil or a tedious watch to end. But as Harry worked her way through the last of the password codes to gain control of the required programs, the situation became a race against time. 'Delilah' had no sooner yielded than the call came in.

'Why Delilah?' Richard was inquiring, intrigued.

'She controlled Samson, didn't she?'

Then the radio spat: 'Gate!'

'Gate,' said Richard at once.

Harry punched in the directive. 'Right,' she said. 'That's it. Do you send an acknowledgement?'

'No need,' said Richard. 'Delilah should be letting Samson's hair down even as we speak.' Suddenly filled with excitement, he got to his feet. 'You want to see what's happening?' he asked. 'I mean, since we don't seem to have blown up, you might like to take a look at what's going on in the hold.'

'No, I don't think so,' said Harry. 'It'll be more boys with more toys. I think I'll go and see how Angela's doing. I haven't been taking care of her . . .'

Richard arrived in the lower hold at a dead run. He burst through the door – though he could have come straight through the wall – and was pitched straight into a constricted tempest. The rear hatch, right across the width of the hold, was opening. As soon as the great drawbridge started to swing downwards, the jets immediately behind it cut off, but the jets above were still roaring at full blast and the ship was still surging forward at one hundred miles per hour. There was a hurricane of back draught washing in over the top of the slowly opening drawbridge, bringing with it a torrent of spray from the water jets to either side. The thick, wet wind set everything in the hold dancing and flapping. It seemed to thicken the atmosphere into ancient bottle glass, whorled, impenetrable and green. It battered against Richard's eardrums like drumsticks in his head, and fluttered in his heaving lungs like a flock of starlings taking flight. The atmosphere closed around him like a wild typhoon – but such storms, of course, were familiar to him. As bone-deep familiar as battle conditions were to the SAS men all around.

Richard saw the hooked lines being shot in over the top of the lowering drawbridge to catch among the lynch points suspended from the decking above. As the rear wall continued to fall outwards and downwards, he saw the lines tauten and begin to bear weight as the first great packages of equipment streaked down the lines to break away and fall onto the foam-washed spaces cleared by the soldiers earlier.

As the lines flexed and heaved and load after load thundered aboard, the SAS men in the hold struggled against that bottled hurricane to secure the equipment.

And then, as the great bridge slammed down flat, the forward section of a great hovercraft travelling at jet speed appeared, terrifyingly close behind. Its forward deck, magically in still air just beyond the maelstrom of *New England*'s wash, was swarming with black figures. The lines coming into the high points were

213

supplemented by lower lines which carried men. The soldiers in the hold all ran forward into the blast and gathered in dense groups around the landing sights where the men from the hovercraft would finish their wild ride aboard.

Just how many Friends came aboard in those few frenetic moments Richard could not calculate. But he saw them in over the drawbridge as it reached the horizontal and he saw them come in over the top of it as it began to shut again, directed by the command bridge override. He saw the welcoming committees of SAS men collect them and hurry them away out of the blast until the drawbridge was too high for any more to make it in. Two men came towards him. Both were dressed in the black uniforms, gloves and balaclavas of the Special Forces. Both were running with water, battered breathless by the blast. One he recognised as Merrideth. The other, taller, gaunter, was a stranger.

The ill-matched pair stopped directly in front of Richard, close enough for him to study the few details of face and eye visible behind the balaclava. He saw mottled black skin, the wide bridge of a thick nose, deep, thick-edged eye sockets surrounded by lined and mottled black skin. The eyeballs were the colour of pale egg yolk, the eyes so black it was hard to distinguish between pupil and iris. 'So you're Richard Mariner, are you? I hear you've been of some help here and I thank you. But we won't need your help any more now. And when the action starts, stand well back out of it.'

Richard's teeth went on edge. He had not been addressed like this since his earliest days at Fettes College. But he held his peace and returned the black stare without flinching.

The new man said, 'You understand me?'

Richard still did not answer. There was a silence behind which bustled the sounds of unpacking and the whine of the jets re-starting.

Merrideth said, 'He understands, Marshall. Come on.'

As the two men turned away, Richard allowed himself to relax a little, his mind racing. Merrideth and Marshall. The names went together in popular legend like Bonnie and Clyde, Robin Hood and Little John, Pat Garrett and Billy the Kid.

If Merrideth and Marshall were here, then doubtless all the legendary men from the British and American sections of 13

Int. were here as well – all who were still alive, at any rate. The Jellicoe Boys were back to full force.

Chapter Seventeen

Andrew Fawley, captain of the Heritage-Mariner super-cat *Hero*, met Robin Mariner, his boss and the wife of his boss, partway through the worst day of his life, about two and a half hours after he was placed under arrest. In the intervening time he had been hauled away from the breakfast table in the Dover hotel he usually patronised and read his rights at Dover central police station. He had been bundled, dazed and compliant, into the back of a police Rover and driven at speed to London. Two young men in dark suits and pale raincoats, who had flashed their warrant cards far too publicly for Andrew's taste in the hotel dining room, remained with him through the initial process and the car ride. But they refused to clarify the charges, to explain his position or to reveal their destination to him. So he settled back and watched the road unreel past the windows, with no idea what on earth was going on, though he had a bone-deep, sick-making suspicion that it had something to do with Richard and the SAS men.

The young policemen took him to New Street police station. All Andrew knew was that it was somewhere in London, over the river, north of the City, beyond St Paul's, beside a huge, half-familiar railway station. His arrival was registered with the gaunt sergeant behind the reception desk. The sergeant took his watch, keys and tie; noted the fact that he wore no braces and had slip-on shoes. Andrew signed a docket to this effect. Then he was hurried to the holding area at the back of the police station, but not before he noticed a tall, tweedy man, startlingly out of place behind the desk, who glanced at him coldly and began to punch in numbers on a telephone as he was hurried away.

At the end of a cream-painted corridor, Andrew found himself confronted by a large iron door. One of the young plainclothes

officers inserted a key into its lock. Andrew assumed, almost
with panic, that he was about to be secured in a cell, but when
the door was opened he saw there was a table with a recording
machine bolted securely to it and a range of chairs. An interview
room, then. That was better, he thought. They ushered him in
and left him there.

At first, Andrew sank gratefully into one of the battered chairs,
exhausted by the shock of what was happening to him. But he
was an active man of generally forceful and commanding
disposition. Soon restlessness began to fizz in him, and the
beginnings of outrage. He rose and began to pace the room, not
really taking in any details of the place, aware that he needed to
order his thoughts. But as he paced, he became aware of a
whining sound. It took a little while to cut through the blanket
of his preoccupation but when it did, he looked up to find himself
under the chilly scrutiny of a security camera. For some reason
he found this particularly offensive and the passive machine
formed a channel for his growing rage.

'Now just you look here,' he began, bellowing up at the glassy
eye of the lens, assuming there must be some kind of microphone
behind it. 'I don't know who you think you are or what the hell
you think you're up to, but I—'

The door opened. A man and a woman entered, a couple
Andrew was ever to remember as the bulldog and the Siamese
cat. He was square, squat, deep-chested and many-jowled with
an underslung jaw and a belligerent roll to his walk. She was
taller, slighter, dressed in a business suit coloured somewhere
between beige and cream with the faintest plain-chocolate
stripe. Her hair, tights and shoes were one shade of brown away
from black. Her eyes were the most extraordinary greeny-blue
he had ever seen. She did not walk, she moved with something
between a slither and a glide. When she sat – the bulldog
remained bouncing on the balls of his feet – she placed a leather
briefcase on the table, opened it and removed a folder of notes.
Her movements were deft and precise. The tacky little room
filled with the aroma of leather. She extracted a gold fountain
pen and unscrewed the top. She slid a cassette tape out of a
little pocket in the briefcase and slipped it into the machine.
She looked up at Andrew, the light shimmering in those
extraordinary eyes, then she snapped the cassette holder shut,

glanced at a slim gold watch, and pressed Record.

'Interview commenced at ten thirteen precisely,' she said in the accents of Cheltenham Ladies' College. 'Sergeant Bates and DCI Tracey in attendance. Captain Fawley, you were read your rights at Dover central at eight oh four this morning?'

'Well, yes, but—'

'And you understand the nature of the charge?'

'Well, actually . . .'

'Yes, Captain?'

'I was charged with barratry! It's like piracy. Something out of the age of sail. I didn't know an offence with that name even existed any more.'

'Oh, sections of it still exist, Captain, though the offence itself was abolished by the Criminal Law Act of 1967. But that doesn't stop people doing it. Like mutiny and piracy, it is still very current.'

'Barratry of the master and mariners,' intoned Bates. 'Any wrongful act willingly committed by the captain or crew to the prejudice of the owner—'

'Oh, come on, Inspector Tracey! What exactly am I supposed to have done?'

'In that you did,' said Sergeant Bates formally, 'on the sixteenth day of this month take the super-cat *Hero*, property of the Heritage Mariner Shipping Company, and, without due recourse to required company procedure, or to required pilotage customs, or to registered shipping directions in force for the Channel and the Western Approaches, take the said vessel at maximum speed into international waters, having taken aboard person or persons unknown for purposes deemed to be detrimental to the interests of the owners.'

'That's pompous bullshit. I did what I did, in contravention of whatever procedures, customs, directions or whatever, under the direct and personal orders of the owner, Captain Richard Mariner. Who, I might add, was transferred out of *Hero* safe and sound with the others.'

'Captain Fawley,' purred Tracey's voice with gentle insistence, 'we have in our possession records from the Dover Port Authority and a range of other authorities along the coast which establish what *Hero* did, and we have witnesses who say that she did it while under your command. The ship's movement records and log books, however, make no mention of the mysterious little trip you took, or of the presence aboard of Captain Mariner or of anybody else.'

'The master must keep an official log,' observed Bates. 'And this, with the ship's papers, he must guard and show to the proper officers when required to do so.'

'Yes, Sergeant, I am aware of that, but under the circumstances—'

'And what circumstances are those, Captain Fawley?' demanded DCI Tracey.

'This is ridiculous! I was assured by Captain Mariner that this situation could not arise, that using *Hero* to help the SAS . . .'

Two pairs of eyes seemed to pierce Andrew as he said this. The red-rimmed bulldog brown ones were bad enough but the icy Siamese ones were really unnerving. He stopped speaking, a dull, formless dread filling him. This must be even worse than he had supposed. He took a deep breath. 'I'm not saying one more word without my solicitor, a representative of my professional association or of the owners here with me,' he said.

A minute later he made the acquaintance of Robin Mariner. She slammed the heavy metal door open as though it had no weight at all, then slammed it shut and leaned back against it. Her eyes were the most unnerving of all.

DCI Tracey leaned towards the cassette recorder. 'Owners' representative Captain Robin Mariner entered the room at ten twenty-four,' she said.

Robin was slighter than Andrew had pictured her. But she was burning with an energy jarringly at odds with her physical appearance. In a manner not even the Siamese cat could emulate, she dominated the room. Sparks seemed to fly from the busy gold ringlets of her hair and the long, grey-blue eyes. Her jaw was square, and right now her lips were thin. She paid no attention whatsoever to the two other people in the room and came at Andrew all guns blazing.

'Right!' she snapped. 'Let's get on with this. You'd better have some pretty good explanations for all this, Captain, or I'll charge you with a damn sight more than barratry. My husband was aboard, you say? And you were acting directly under his orders?'

'Well, yes. You see . . .' Andrew explained about the midnight summons, the tense briefing, the secret preparations, the mad dash westwards.

'Typical,' she fumed. 'This is just flaming typical! Bloody man!'

Andrew explained about the clandestine assignation by the prison ship *Alcatraz*, about the mysterious strangers, and their Special Forces kit.

'It's like Ian bloody Fleming!' said Robin.

'More like Andy McNab!' corrected Bates, earning himself a withering look from both the women and a rather more grateful one from Andrew.

'Can you describe this so-called Special Forces team?' asked DCI Tracey, her tone making clear her scepticism.

'No. I never saw them up close. But I know who they were.'

'Who?'

'They were the Jellicoe Boys.'

'Who?' demanded the young inspector.

Andrew looked across at Bates, seeking some understanding, some sharing of the revelation. 'The Jellicoe Boys. The Special Forces team from the Gulf War. You must have heard of them! They were almost as famous as Bravo Two Zero!'

'How do you know this?' demanded Bates, his voice dry.

'Richard told me. Then he went off with them. Asked me to wait five days before I told anyone . . . Still a while to go, you see.'

'Richard went off with a bunch of strangers? Out of the blue? Just like that? That's inconceivable, even for him!' said Robin caustically.

'No, he had met one of them at a briefing in London. What was his name? Merrideth, I think.'

This revelation gave Andrew's interrogators pause. This was something of a relief to him, until his active imagination presented his mind with a couple of extremely disturbing possibilities. Either Merrideth was someone else disguised well enough to fool even Richard, or Merrideth was not the powerful official he had presented himself as being. Andrew's fear for Richard increased, and it jolted his memory. 'Richard mentioned someone else,' he added, inspired. 'The person I was to contact. He was a wedding guest at Sir William's reception aboard. The one who was called off to Ireland – something about Black Talons?'

'Bull?' said Robin, more than a little off balance herself now.

'*Bull* got him into this?' She slapped her forehead – hard enough to be audible. Andrew had heard of the gesture but he had never seen it done. 'Of course!' she said. 'Who else could? It had to be. We've got to—'

'Sir Justin has vanished,' said DCI Tracey quietly, and Andrew at once began to suspect that, like Merrideth apparently, she was something other than she seemed to be. 'He disappeared on the night this phase of the incident began. There's been no word. No sign.'

This phase? thought Andrew. This *phase*? 'And what incident is this?' he demanded. 'Something rather larger than bloody barratry, I imagine.'

Tracey reached over towards the cassette recorder. Her long, slim fingers hovered over the Off switch. 'Interview terminated at ten forty,' she said.

They left Andrew there for another hour during which time his temperature rose and his self-control diminished. He was an outdoor sort. A captain. A man with a lively sense of justice, which he exercised to the benefit of his commands and expected to have equal benefit of himself. And yet here he was, confined in a small interview room, being bossed about by jobsworth officials, undergoing a very unjust experience at the hands of the woman from whom he should have been able to expect maximum help and support but who, it now seemed, had had him arrested and brought here instead. He had mentally rehearsed several increasingly acrimonious letters of resignation and was just adding a postscript to the last threatening extensive legal action of his own when the door opened again.

It was a different Robin who came in this time. He had met the high-powered, ruthless and decisive business executive. Now he was to be introduced to the gentle, kindly, understanding wife and mother. She came in with a large tray laden with an electric kettle, a teapot, a jar of excellent instant coffee, milk, cream, sugar, a packet of ginger nuts and another of chocolate digestives. 'I know it's well past coffee time,' she said, 'but I thought you could probably do with a little something.'

'What I could do with,' he grated with unaccustomed rudeness, 'is an explanation followed by some kind of apology.'

Robin pulled out the cassette recorder's plug and replaced it with the kettle's. It began to grumble as the water heated. 'Of course I apologise,' said Robin. 'I am very sorry for several things. I am sorry Richard got you mixed up in this, whatever *this* actually is. I am sorry that you were summarily arrested. And I am sorry that I was not more supportive when I arrived. Coffee or tea?'

'Tea. Strong. Please.'

'A man after my own heart.' She busied herself with the tea things, her eyes lowered as she continued, 'I cannot tell you exactly what is going on, however, because no one in authority seems to know.'

Andrew digested this nugget while she poured hot water into the pot and let it heat through. 'How could they not know about the pirating of a ship, the kidnapping of crew and guests, contacts with the IRA or whoever and heaven knows what else besides?'

'Oh, they seem to know about all that,' she said, pouring the hot water back out of the pot carefully down the spout of the kettle, and reaching for the tea caddy as the water came back up to the boil. 'But they say it all happened in international or foreign waters. The only thing that has happened within British jurisdiction is that a couple of corpses have washed up somewhere in Ulster. They have consulted the authorities in the Republic of Ireland.' She measured three heaped spoonfuls of black tealeaves into the gently fuming pot. 'And they are in contact with the authorities in America, where *New England* seems to be headed.'

The kettle boiled again and Robin poured the bubbling water over the leaves in the teapot.

'But the problem is, no one in authority here seems to have been asked for official help of any sort by anyone. Intelligence and Security have monitored the situation. The Cabinet Office has received reports. But no action has been deemed appropriate. Milk?'

Andrew nodded.

Robin poured. 'Stirling Lines has not been contacted. The SAS has not sent anyone out.'

The tea, Andrew noted approvingly, was slightly lighter in colour and liquidity than creosote. Even when mixed with the milk, it remained the colour of teak. He reached for a ginger nut and dunked it thoughtfully. 'But Merrideth,' he said. 'The Jellicoe Boys.'

Robin looked up, her eyes luminous, fathomless, full of worry.

223

'The British contingent of the Sabre Squadron was apparently disbanded soon after the end of the Gulf War,' she said quietly. 'Something terrible happened during the final days of the conflict. Something very secret so I have no details. But something so bad that it has affected them all. Physically. Mentally. All of them, including Major Merrideth. They've been invalided out for years. Institutionalised, some of them. They are very sick men indeed. They may have managed to keep enough contacts and get access to enough information to fool Sir Justin and Richard. But they're nothing to do with the British authorities. And no one seems to have any idea what they're up to.'

Chapter Eighteen

As the great drawbridge closed behind them, Merrideth and Marshall, without apparently exchanging a word, moved off. They stepped through the wreckage of the wall and went to the foot of the main companionway up into the accommodation and command areas. Intrigued, though still fuming at Marshall's patronising orders, Richard followed them and no one tried to stop him. At the foot of the half-ruined stairway he joined the two soldiers who were still deep in their apparently communicative silence.

'You any idea what the son of a bitch is up to?' grated Marshall at last.

Merrideth shook his head.

'I guess it's time to go ask him.'

Merrideth nodded.

'Your boys armoured?'

Again, the infinitesimal nod.

'Fully kitted?'

'Yup.'

'You know where he is?'

'Command bridge. Closing the back door.'

'Let's call the bastard's bluff.' As he spoke, the American gave a shrug, easing his own black body armour across his massive torso.

The pair of them started up the stairs, walking steadily, making no attempt to use anti-personnel tactics. The only gesture they made towards the seriousness of their situation was the fact that they both pulled out their side arms. Marshall held his in his left hand while he carefully fed the gloved fingers of his right into the trigger guard and round the grip.

At the top of the stairway they stopped. Marshall's left hand moved, fingers pressing the button of his personal radio. 'To me all A teams,' he ordered quietly. 'Comms and medic sit tight.'

'Communications, as you were,' added Merrideth. 'Sit tight, please, Op. Stay with him, Mac.'

Still at the bottom of the stairs, Richard suddenly found himself at the heart of a crowd as black-clad men moved silently through the rents on the hold walls. They carried a disquieting array of arms: bulky, unfamiliar shotguns, skeletal AK 47s, M16s, Berettas, Minimis, Heckler & Kochs and at least one Steyr which looked as though it had strayed out of a science fiction movie. Richard had never seen such a weird range of guns all in one place and he found it disturbing.

Suddenly Mac's familiar brogue sounded in his headset. 'Door closed,' he said, and the surge beneath their feet told of full power re-engaged. As it did so, Marshall's black-gloved left hand gave the old US cavalry signal for 'Forward'.

The teams of men moved off, except for one anonymous American who held himself squarely in Richard's way to prevent him following the others. After a moment's silence, Richard turned away, apparently defeated, apparently obeying Marshall's arrogant order to stay well clear of the action.

The American also turned, whispering away upwards as rearguard to the rest, satisfied by Richard's capitulation. But he did not know the ship, or the Englishman. Richard was bound for the engine control room, and the video monitor, via the makeshift sickbay.

'What is it?' demanded Ann as soon as she saw him at the door. She was standing at the foot of Lazlo's bed checking the cuffs which secured his ankles to the frame.

Ann's tone made Harry look up from her position beside the securely restrained Pitman.

'They're on their way up to the bridge. All of them except four in the hold.'

Pitman's frame gave a lurch at the news and the cuffs securing her to the bed rattled.

'They're well armed,' Richard said. 'But I don't think they're expecting a fight somehow. I'm listening in on the radio and there's nothing doing. Not even orders.'

'Let's follow them,' said Ann at once.

'No need. We can monitor them,' answered Richard swiftly, all too well aware that Ann was mad enough to do what she said

– and that he himself wasn't a hell of a lot saner than she was.

'Yes,' said Harry feelingly. 'That's much safer. Let's go.'

'Let me come too,' said Pitman. The three of them froze. Exchanged looks.

'You? Why?' demanded Richard.

'I need to know what's going on as much as the rest of you. More. They're my buddies. It's my life . . .'

'Pitman, for Christ's sake,' said Lazlo from the neighbouring bed. 'What are you up to, you crazy bitch.'

'Cuff me. Hobble me. I won't try anything. It's just . . . I've got to know.'

'Let her come,' said Harry decisively. 'I've got her gun and if she tries anything I'll shoot her. I will,' she added, looking deep into Pitman's eyes. 'You know that.'

'Crazy fucking bitches, both of you,' snarled Lazlo.

That and Harry's request swayed it in Richard's mind. Not that he was particularly in charge here. He knew Ann would make up her own mind in all things even though she would listen to him as a good friend. And Harry, too, was her own woman. In fact she was already busy releasing Pitman's left hand. She re-secured it to Pitman's right wrist before releasing that one and allowing Pitman to sit up with her hands bound behind her back.

The four of them arrived in the engine control room at the same time as the figures of the SAS men and the SEALs arrived on the damaged monitor screen observing the bridge. Four of the strangely distorted figures were gesturing at each other while around them stood their fiercely armed soldiers. Beyond the central figures stood the hostages, wary and tense.

Then, suddenly, there was sound. Someone on the bridge had switched their 349 personal radio to general broadcast. The shouting brought the twisted pictures to horrifying life.

'Clear the bridge!' Marshall yelled. 'Get all non-coms out of here!'

'Sure,' capitulated Dall. 'Non-coms to their own quarters. My men, stand. Captain, you lead the way. This is all over now. All you've got to do is sit and wait in any case.'

A stir of reluctant movement.

'In your own quarters. Out of the line of fire. Just in case,' emphasised Marshall more quietly. The threat in his words sent a current of fear through the bridgehouse that was almost tangible.

'Who will take the helm?' demanded Bob, hesitating. 'We're still at full—'

'Later, please, Captain,' snapped Merrideth. 'One situation at a time.'

Bob capitulated. This, more than anything, told Richard how stressful things on the bridge must be. Nothing but the most extreme circumstances would make Bob Stark leave the bridge of a ship sailing at 100 miles per hour through crowded waters.

Richard glanced at his companions to see how they were reacting. Ann was riveted, her face pale, her eyes fastened on Bob, tears of tension trembling on her lower lashes. So was Pitman, except that the object of her scrutiny was Dall, and her eyes were very dry. Harry was torn between the desire to watch the screen and the need to keep Pitman's strange, square, skeletal gun firmly to the side of its owner's neck.

There was a brief as the crew left. Into this, urgently, came Mac's voice, reporting from the hold with a warning. 'Major! Someone has their radio on general broadcast.'

'Thanks, Mac. All of you—'

'Right, Dall,' broke in Marshall, 'just what the fuck do you think you're playing at?'

'We want more. We took all the risks. We got you the Stingers. We delivered the goods. We got the whole thing sewn up tight. But you never told us about any Stingers. We want more and that's—'

The general broadcast ceased abruptly. As it did so, Marshall's right hand flashed upwards like a black snake striking. The black fist put the pistol to Dall's head and pulled the trigger. It was so quick and so unexpected that they were all stunned. One second the pirate was shouting at Marshall, the next he was dead on the floor. The silent figures on the bridge spun in a strange kind of dance, guns up and pointing. Spun, danced, but did not fire. Then a figure stepped forward slowly, unarmed, with his hands raised and his lips moving. It was Paul Aves, the dead man's second-in-command.

'Bastard!' shouted Pitman at the top of her lungs. The sound was so loud and unexpected that Harry jumped. So did Pitman.

She jumped a metre off the floor, bunching her body into a solid ball and swinging her bound wrists beneath her feet like a skipping rope. As her feet hit the deck again her arms rose in a blur as quick as Marshall's and she snatched the gun from Harry and jammed it directly to her heart.

Stasis. Both here and on the bridge there was no movement at all. On the silent monitor, Aves was still talking but there was no sound in the engine control room except panting. Pitman stood looking straight into Harry's eyes. Her bound hands held the gun between Harry's breasts without a tremor.

Sound came again. The tannoy this time. 'Situation resolved,' came Marshall's voice. 'Lieutenant Aves' men will lay down their arms. We are in charge now. Report to the ship's exercise facility. Captain and watch return to the bridge. I have a new heading for you to follow.'

There was a stirring on the ether. It was as though the very air relaxed a little – everywhere but in the engine control room.

'Pitman,' said Richard in his gentlest tone. 'Look . . .'

On the monitor, the pirates, led by Paul Aves, were laying down their arms.

'Shit,' said Pitman quietly and lifted the gun until it was pointed at the deckhead above. Carefully, Harry reached over and took it back. 'Assholes!' said Pitman.

'I'm going to have to edit some of this language if I ever get to write this book,' said Ann.

New England turned a degree or two further west and headed down the coast towards her home port of Philadelphia. On the face of it, the situation was resolved. The pirates were disarmed. All of them, including Lazlo and the uncuffed Pitman, were under guard in the ship's gym. The forces of law and order were in control. *New England* was heading home.

And yet Richard was not the only one aboard who believed the apparently cosy situation was entirely illusory. The men in charge of the ship were not representatives of law and order now, even if they had been once. They had been in some way associated with Dall all along. Indeed, the more Richard thought the situation through, the more it became obvious to him that everything that had happened since *New England* had gone to the aid of *Calcutta* had been simply a lengthy scheme to get these men aboard under the eyes of the American authorities in such a manner that the arrest or destruction of the jet-ship would be at the least stalled. His own involvement had begun with the strange messages that had interrupted Bill and Helen's wedding reception – or, more specifically, the message for Bull, which had led to that first meeting with Merrideth in London. It followed, therefore, that the story in fact began with what had happened before that message was sent – with what had caused it to be sent . . .

What, will the line stretch out to the crack of doom? Richard wondered wryly, ready as ever with an apposite quotation.

But there were still one or two elements of the situation Richard could not work out. If the surviving Jellicoe Boys had re-assembled themselves from far-flung corners of the world, organised financing and armaments and gone through all this in order to take *New England*, what did they want her for? The fastest gun-runner in history? They were certainly well enough stocked with guns, rockets and God knew what else, courtesy of the IRA. And where were they taking her? Back to Philadelphia seemed so very unlikely in the circumstances but on their current heading down the coast, unless they were going to turn sharp right suddenly and head into Boston or New York, nowhere else sprang to mind. They could go on down the coast and swing into Delaware Bay or Chesapeake Bay, he supposed, and scare the hell out of everyone in Washington, but what was the point in that?

He had seen these men at work. They did absolutely nothing without a clear, defined objective. This was all part of a three-point plan agreed between Marshall, Merrideth and, he guessed, Dall. Dall had let them down, double-crossed them, demanded more money before he would agree to fit back into the original plan. So they had come aboard and taken *New England* back. And they had killed him. Stepped on him like an ant. The shock of it lingered, deeply disturbing. And the question still remained – what plans did these mysterious, driven, conscienceless butchers have for the rest of the people aboard? Richard hesitated uncharacteristically. He really had to have a complete mental picture of what was going on here before he took any sort of action.

The American medic Bone appeared suddenly at Richard's

230

side to break into these dark thoughts and remind him he had medical responsibilities still. The Americans had brought new supplies. 'Come on, Captain,' said Bone. 'Time to do our rounds.'

'These doses seem to be much higher than the ones I was giving,' said Richard as he looked at Bone's case full of pill bottles and syrettes. 'Why is that?' It was an innocent question, arising from nothing more than a well-trained first-aider's interest in medicine. But Bone's answer was to give him the next important piece in the puzzle he had been working on.

'The bulk of the medication is simply designed to stop the disease,' said Bone. 'Once it's in place, of course, the degeneration it causes can't be reversed. None of this stuff can regenerate the tissues damaged by the bacillus. Not even the Thalidomide. Even with Hansen's original strain that would have been impossible. With this new mutant it's out of the question. Thank God it's non-infectious, eh? Not like that new plague virus they discovered last year. Or Hong Kong Chicken Flu. So it's just a question of containment. Doubling the doses of steroids will build up strength in the undamaged tissue.'

'But that's very short-term, surely,' said Richard. 'Steroids themselves will begin to damage the tissue with doses as massive as this.'

Bone was at the ruined wall, half in and half out of the hold. He turned to give Richard the strangest look. 'Short term is all we've got,' he said. 'All we've got either way. I thought you knew that.'

Richard stopped dead in his tracks. Like a sleepwalker awoken by a punch in the solar plexus, he stood there gaping at Bone's white face.

The drugs. The syrettes. The sunken yellow eyes, the deformed bone structures, the gloves, the care they took even with holding their guns. The apparently illogical decision to bring a dead body with them out of *Hero*. The burning gloves extinguished thoughtlessly – painlessly – under armpits. The bleeding gums and pallid skin which had made him think of radiation poisoning and depleted uranium bullets. But the Ras Al'I. That was the key to it all.

The mutant variety, Bone had said. Short term was all they had.

And Hansen. Hansen's *disease*.

231

Dear God, thought Richard. Oh dear God. The Jellicoe Boys were dying of leprosy.

Chapter Nineteen

Right up to the late seventies there had been a thriving little port facility at the outer point of Great Egg Head. It had picked up the coastal trade plying between Atlantic City and Norfolk, Virginia, and some of the deep-water work in too much of a rush to swing round into Delaware Bay and up to Philadelphia. But after the oil crisis and the grinding reduction of ship-borne trade which characterised the eighties and the nineties, it had slid inexorably to the wall. All that stood there now, on the long, lonely thrust of land looking out across the Atlantic, was a derelict factory complex and a ruined little hamlet around it. It was a ghost port, too lost and lonely even for vagrants to bother with. The local turnpike wound lazily in from Wilmington but for more than a decade nobody had followed it.

Until now. During the last few weeks there had been a gathering of surreptitious activity here. The long-dead leaves on the turnpike had been stirred by great tyres. The long dark windows of the houses and the factories had gleamed with lights far into the night. The still air of the place had been enlivened by something more purposeful than the voice of the east wind and the scurrying of local vermin. The quay had been strengthened enough to accept shipping and bear weight. The chandlering and maintenance facilities were almost up to spec. The warehouses contained wares – petrol for the most part, in great tankers labelled Amoco, Shell, Texaco, which had been hijacked further inland and driven here secretly at night, their original crews dropped far away and their destination one of the many unsolved mysteries on the files of the FBI. Among them, more carefully secured and also counted as lost at Federal level, stood an armoured vehicle brightly painted with the words 'First National Bank of Idaho'.

★ ★ ★

233

New England eased into the half-ruined quay at Great Egg Head at sunset. The westering light threw long shadows from the derelict facility towards her as though gathering her into its secret heart. And out of that shadowy heart came men to greet her.

Since 13 Int. had taken command, everything had changed. In their presence and even behind their backs the hated tabloid name the Jellicoe Boys was never used. Unlike the late Captain Dall's mercenaries, caught between an unstable commander about an unexplained double-cross and a group of desperate, deadly adversaries, Merrideth and Marshall had gone to work with a will. New England had an immediate purpose and a tight schedule. If Richard and his friends aboard remained ignorant as yet as to what these were, no one could doubt that they existed.

13 Int. had gone over *New England* with a fine-tooth comb. The automatic tracking aids and the ship's identity beacon had been removed from the aerodynamic communications mast. Her ruined communications facilities had been replaced with specialised narrow-band equipment. The lower hold had been closed. Tom and his patrol had been mysteriously busy down there with Mac and Op, and some of the Americans too, but the ability of Bob's crew to observe this action was increasingly circumscribed during the day as their liberty, too, was increasingly curtailed and finally cancelled altogether.

Richard's position was now very much changed; trust was no longer a feature of it. Nevertheless, he decided to confront Merrideth and Marshall with what he now knew about them at the earliest opportunity. No other course occurred to him. He knew as much about Hansen's disease as most, especially as his first aid training had been carried out with work in the Gulf in mind. He knew the bacillus passed from one victim to another in breath droplets and that it lodged first behind the nose before spreading through the body, damaging tissue and killing nerves. He knew that there were two forms, tubercular and general. He knew that it could be held in remission with the very treatments he had been administering. He knew that it was incurable. He had never heard of a whole group of men being infected with it like this but he was one of the few who could begin to imagine the circumstances in which such a disaster might occur, because he knew about the Ras Al'I.

Richard knew that leprosy was not easily spread and was

reassured by Bone's revelation that this mutant variety was entirely non-infectious. But he was sharply aware that up to thirty per cent of a random selection of people could be susceptible to the ordinary variety and would be very much at risk if Bone had got his facts wrong; and the longer they stayed in the company of what was left of Merrideth, Marshall and 13 Int., the more likely it was that someone else would catch it. To tell the others what he knew at this stage might be very dangerous. The group of crew members and guests who were still effectively prisoners might panic or begin to confront their captors, and Marshall's method of negotiating with the double-crossing Dall showed all too clearly what the outcome of such a confrontation was likely to be. But doing nothing was out of the question and it seemed to Richard that the only course of action possible for him was to confront the two commanders himself, man to man. So, having completed his medical rounds with Bone, he made his way swiftly to the bridge before it occurred to somebody to confine his movements.

Merrideth seemed to know the instant Richard arrived on the bridge and he touched Marshall's arm. The three of them went into the radio room as the nearest relatively private place. Merrideth pulled off his balaclava, and with the wisdom of knowledge, Richard looked at his face closely. As well as the livid skin colour and flesh tones around the eyes, lips and nostrils that he had noticed earlier, he could see that the delicate bone of the eye sockets and at the bridge of that aquiline nose showed a strange thickening. A close inspection would no doubt reveal the same of cheekbones and temples – the onset of the disfigurement called *leonine faces*, lion's face. Marshall, too, pulled off his balaclava and on his face Richard saw the full flower of the disease. Marshall's nose was almost nonexistent, his mouth was swollen, the mottled black ballooning stretching up towards the thick-edged hollows of his yellow eyes. It was hardly a human face any longer. It looked like something out of a horror movie instead; animal, monstrous. It took all of Richard's fortitude not to step back or flinch away. It was only when he drew breath to talk that he realised he had not breathed since entering the room.

Both men were watching him quizzically, uncertainly, as though awaiting his reaction. 'I'm the first outsider who knows,' he said.

'First one other'n family,' agreed Marshall.

'And the odd quack,' added Merrideth.

'Have all of you got it? All of 13 Int.?'

'Even the dead ones. That's why we tried to bring the doc. Ex-Special Forces men with advanced mutant Hansen's disease. A bit of a give-away, wouldn't you say?'

'But how did you all become infected?'

'It's a long story,' said Merrideth.

'It was the Ras, wasn't it?' prompted Richard. 'Some lunatic sent you in along the Ras Al'I without warning you that it had been a leper colony for the better part of five hundred years.'

'It was right at the end,' said Merrideth. 'Twenty-third of February, nineteen ninety-one. The day before Desert Storm was launched. We got a request to do some charity work. Protect a food shipment for UNICEF. They told us the Iraqis would let us through like they had the others. It was just *charity*, for God's sake.'

'Charity and a smooth-talking s.o.b. called Hoover,' added Marshall bleakly.

'He convinced us it was a simple watch job. No worries. We went in along the Ras with no trouble at all and set up to watch the road, the main supply route from Mina Al Ahmadi to Kuwait City. But no one told us there was some kind of double bluff going on. The Iraqis had no intention of letting the UNICEF convoy through and Hoover knew it. Saddam's elite guard units came down on it like wasps on a jam pot – and down on us as well, clearing the way for the whole Desert Storm invasion. We ended up in a fighting retreat all through that afternoon and night, forcing our way out along the way we'd come in, back along the Ras Al'I, through a full barrage, followed by every crack unit in the area. Inch by inch through a leper colony's graveyard nearly five kilometres long while the whole lot went to hell in a handcart around us.'

'And the invasion of Kuwait started for real just along the road behind you,' said Richard, 'with even Stormin' Norman wondering why there were so few crack front-line troops standing against him . . .'

'And every mine, grenade, shot and shell threw up a kind of cold soup made of mud and blood and lepers' dust. We were drenched in it; we drank it, breathed it, hour after hour after hour. We had no idea. Thirty-six of us went in. Sixteen of us came out and we thought we were the lucky ones. Until we came home. Found out. It's a hell of a way to die, leprosy. The worst way there is, believe you me.'

'Let's cut to the chase here,' snapped Marshall. 'Time's awasting and we don't have a lot. We've all got it. There's no cure. No one else has it. No one else will. It's unique to us and our experience. A non-communicable form. You could only get it if you went through what we went through in the Gulf. You didn't, so you're safe. Same for the rest.'

'OK. But I still need to know what you think you're—'

'No you don't,' interrupted Merrideth gently. 'You already know more than you ought. We had an arrangement with Captain Dall. He got greedy and tried to double-cross us. We needed you to get aboard and we needed you once we got aboard. Your help's been much appreciated but we can handle it all ourselves from here on in.'

This told Richard what he needed to know and confirmed his darkest speculations. They were not making this up as they went along. They had always planned to come aboard. Dall had pirated *New England* for them. He himself had only been pulled into the situation because Dall's double-cross had necessitated some improvisation. But when Dall's command failed to avenge his death, 13 Int.'s plan, whatever it was, had come back on track.

Richard looked from one man to the other. 'May I tell the others?' he asked. 'I assume I will be joining them now.'

'Oh, I think not,' said Merrideth. 'There's still far too much mischief a man like you could make. I shall invest one secure room and two guards in your good behaviour during the next few hours at least. Bruce,' he called. 'Take the captain down, please.'

Merrideth was correct about the amount of mischief Richard might do if allowed to mix freely with the others. He had failed to calculate, however, the amount of ruthlessly clear thinking Richard could do when locked away alone, and the extent of the planning which could be based on that speculation. Much of Richard's incarceration, therefore, was spent in bitter reflection on the absolute manner in which he had been fooled, in an unflinching examination of incident after incident in which

Merrideth had succeeded in pulling the wool over his eyes, and in trying to work out a method of striking back.

With the benefit of hindsight, Richard was able to trace the pattern of Merrideth's actions. Dall had collected the arms in Ireland at 13 Int.'s instigation and put them on *Calcutta* as planned, always with the intention of pirating *New England* and delivering her, fully armed, into the hands of the embittered Special Forces men either in Ireland or in America, perhaps even at the destination they were bound for now. But something – the Stingers, perhaps, which had featured in that bitter exchange between Dall and his killers – had prompted Dall's double-cross. This was a double-cross about which Dall, for reasons of security, paranoia, greed, had not warned his command. Certainly, he had not warned Pitman at least; and she was different from the others only in gender and intelligence. But the double-cross – typically, Richard now realised – prompted pre-emptive action from Merrideth himself.

Dall, Pitman, whoever, had left the dead bodies and other clues behind in Ireland. These had rung genuine alarm bells and Bull had been called in. Merrideth, on the old school net, perhaps, had heard a hint and found himself the perfect springboard for an improvisation. Getting Bull's co-operation had gained access to Richard – or, more importantly, at that stage, to *Hero*.

Merrideth's briefing at the Army and Navy Club had been inspired and yet, looking back on it, Richard saw all too clearly that the maps, faxes and so forth which had so impressed him could actually have come from other members of 13 Int., waiting, thwarted and beginning to recognise the double-cross, in Eire – and not from the authorities in either country at all. Leaving the briefing early and getting Bull himself to put the final proposition was inspired. How perfectly effective it had been! Richard would have lengthy words with Bull when he got home.

But to be fair, Richard could understand all too well how his old friend had been hoodwinked, for ever since he had heard the code-word 'storm', he had been completely fooled himself. How could he have delivered his ships, officers and crew, good name and expertise to these men? It seemed incredible now that he should have been so foolhardy and yet there had

238

been something about Merrideth, Mac, Op, Tom and the rest which had simply swept him along with them. Little by little, with details apparently fed in by 'Green Slime' and 'Intelligence' adding their weight, he had come to believe in them without a second thought. Nuggets calculatedly slipped past Merrideth's spurious 'need to know' which established a completely fictional but all too convincing official network behind them all the way up to the Kremlin at Stirling Lines and the Cabinet Office itself. Nuggets of apparently genuine intelligence like details of the PIRA arms cache, Pitman's identity, and, later, Dall's.

But they had genuinely come to need him; Richard was sure of that. His continued survival was probably proof positive. In the end, Merrideth had been lucky as well as inspired in his choice of patsy. Unless the major had seen all the little news-snippets of information about Heritage Mariner's pre-eminence in the fields of advanced shipping on both sides of the Atlantic and had targeted Richard specifically because he knew he had access to *Hero* and experience of *New England* herself . . . But the supposition that such a man as Merrideth might have been watching his every move so closely made such speculation too uncomfortable even for Richard Mariner.

Sufficient to say then that Merrideth had got him hooked and decided to take him along – particularly after he revealed so artlessly that he knew who the ex-Special Forces team really were. That one slip – Ras Al'I – had been enough. It really had shaken Merrideth – perhaps more than Doc's death. Richard could see now all too clearly that they would have been no more willing to leave him behind after that unthinking revelation than they had been willing to leave Doc's body; and yet to kill him as they had snuffed out Dall would have been impossible on *Hero* before the transfer – and after the transfer he had proved all too invaluable all too quickly. Now, however, things were different. 13 Int. had no need of him now at all; no need of any of them, in fact. Another avenue too unpleasant to explore for the time being. But, even so, Richard felt that these men were not conscienceless. They reserved their full, lethal anger for those they thought had betrayed them. Men like Dall, and the other man they had mentioned, the man who had duped them into going onto the Ras in the first place, this man Hoover . . .

But that line of thought led to a dead-end, too. As did all

reflection which focused so clear-sightedly on the past. The only line of speculation Richard was really interested in following was one which guided him into the much more murky waters of the future. One which would build on the past with the founded certainty of an Egyptian pyramid and point unerringly to the answer to the most important questions of all. Why had 13 Int. caused the IRA arms to be appropriated? What did they need *New England* for? Why were the Stingers so important? Just what, exactly, were the Jellicoe Boys up to?

Always more able to think better on his feet, Richard pulled himself erect, clasped his hands behind his back, thrust his chin a little forward in an unconsciously bellicose expression, and began to pace, going over his thoughts again, looking for answers to the fundamental questions, and ways to extend those answers into action – any action which would stop whatever 13 Int. were up to without putting himself or anyone else aboard at further risk, if it could be helped.

While Richard was locked in the captain's cabin with a guard beside him and another at the door, the rest of *New England*'s complement sat in another kind of close confinement.

Twenty-five people could easily fit in the officers' lounge, which had the conveniences of comfortable chairs, toilets adjoining, and plenty of alcohol. The tables had been pushed together to form two large tables. Round one sat *New England*'s crew, and round the other her officers and passengers. The Charlestons sat close together, almost as close as Ann and Bob Stark. Between the couples was Harry. Professor Miles sat between First Officer Dix and Chief Bligh. O'Reilley was conspicuously some distance from the others, though seated at the same table.

They all wondered what was keeping Richard, but since there was no way of finding out, the talk moved on to speculation about why the ship had not been stopped by the American authorities. O'Reilley unexpectedly revealed, albeit grudgingly, that the SAS men had used their own communications to convince the Coastguard and other interested authorities that the ship was now back about legitimate business and in the hands of its lawful crew. The emergency was past, they had announced, and all would be revealed when she docked in Philadelphia. As

240

the Coastguard could not catch her and therefore could not board her and the only other option was to attack her, the authorities had apparently declared themselves satisfied, for the time being at least.

'So that's where we're bound,' said Senator Charleston. 'Philadelphia.'

'That doesn't seem likely,' said Bob. 'I don't think these men intend to hand her over. I mean, the lawful crew is all here, isn't it? So we are clearly not in charge, contrary to what 13 Int. want the Coastguard to believe.'

'So we only have until the authorities' patience runs out,' said Senator Charleston.

'And that will be pretty soon after we don't show up in Philadelphia,' concluded Ann.

'We could be in Philadelphia within six hours from our position when I was last on the bridge,' said Bob.

'Doesn't give them much time,' observed Dix uneasily. 'But wait.' He held up his hand and there was silence. 'Aren't they cutting speed?'

'Yes! You're right! They are,' said Bob.

And Ann of course asked the sixty-four thousand dollar question: 'What in God's name are they up to?'

The door opened and Bruce and one of his men entered. 'O'Reilley and Newbold, come with us,' said Bruce quietly, his voice somehow managing to drip with threat.

'Why?' snapped Senator Charleston at once. 'What do you want them for?'

'Major wants them on the bridge. Couple of questions, that's all. They'll be fine. You all will. Unless you disobey.'

'It's all right,' said Harry, sensing the others squaring up dangerously. 'I expect it's just a question about the computer or something. Come on, Oh Really. You should be safe as houses up there. Any problems and you can just change sides again. If you can remember which side you're actually on, of course.'

Harry came back alone an hour later. 'No sign of Captain Mariner, I'm afraid, but we're almost down to normal cruising speed for coastal shipping,' she announced as she joined the others. 'Though I have to say there's precious little shipping actually about. I sneaked a look at your radar, Mr Dix. We're not far off Atlantic City and still heading south, Captain. Maybe we are bound for Philadelphia. Who knows?'

'What did they want you for?' asked Bob.

'Nothing much. They wanted access to some navigation program and I showed them the way in. Didn't seem all that important. Though it's funny, I've never seen it before. You remember a ship-handling program called HG, Captain? Mr Dix?'

Both men shook their heads.

'When was it put on the system?' asked Ann.

'A few days ago. In Ireland, probably.' Her brow furrowed in thought.

'What does it do?' asked Ann.

'Handles the ship. It's in among the docking programs. Handles the ship in restricted waterways, ports and harbours, I guess.'

'Maybe you'll get a chance for a closer look later,' suggested Bob.

'Maybe,' said Harry doubtfully.

'Could be something to do with where we're going,' suggested Senator Charleston.

O'Reilley returned, big with news. They would be arriving at their destination within half an hour and they were all due to be put ashore there.

They spent the intervening time at the windows, straining for the first view of land, Bob particularly keen to try to regain some initiative, some element of control in this strange situation. Both he and Richard carried in their memories charts covering half the world. And Bob particularly was familiar with the East Coast since he had trained there.

It could hardly be said that there was a line of armed guards to shepherd them out of *New England* and into the cell which had been prepared for them in one of Great Egg Head's derelict facilities, but the ex-Special Forces men were positioned at every tactical point and oversaw the line of silent prisoners out of one confinement and into the next. They came out of a door in the side of *New England*, down a short gangplank onto the quay and along to a brick extension to a cavernous corrugated-iron warehouse. Within the warehouse, lights burned and vehicles stood, and shadows moved about industriously. As they reached the iron-bound door of the brick building with its faded lettering 'Port Authority. In Bond. Secure Area. No Entry', the first big petrol tanker began to grind down the quayside behind them.

Their new place of confinement had basic toilet facilities but no running water. There was electric light and the bedding was thick and soft. A table held cold food and a range of drink. Twenty-five or thirty people could stay here relatively comfortably and very securely for a couple of days. It was only when they had all arrived and the door was closed behind them that they realised Richard was still missing and O'Reilley was no longer with them.

'I guess this is where mercenaries and assorted turncoats get their pay-off,' said Ann from her position close beside Bob, a position she had assumed and maintained since the moment of their reunion. It was clear to everyone that the only thing keeping their hands off each other was their audience.

'I guess it is,' said Harry. 'Did anyone else see a bank truck out there? That must be their money.'

Bob's mind was on something else. 'That looked like Cape May in the distance to me,' he said.

'Yup. Mouth of Delaware Bay without a doubt,' agreed Dix.

'So we're south of Atlantic City, round about Great Egg. But why? What is there here?' asked Senator Charleston.

'Just the docking facility?'

'So they want to load and unload something more?'

'They did enough of that in Ireland, surely.'

'Maybe they need more supplies of something easier to get here than in Ireland.'

'That could be anything from doughnuts to drugs,' said Ann.

'I thought I saw a gas bowser start up the deck on our way in here,' volunteered Harry, whose eyes had been busy.

'Yes, I saw one too,' said Bob. 'What would they want petrol for? Did anyone else notice this?'

A couple of the others thought they had, then Mrs Charleston ventured, 'I think Harry's right about the bank truck too. I certainly saw some kind of armoured car.'

'Well, there you go,' said the Senator. 'Gas and dollars. Two things which are definitely in greater supply here than in Ireland.'

'They're not going to like that,' said Harry suddenly.

It was such an unexpected observation that it brought the other speculation to a halt.

'Who's not going to like what?' asked Ann.

'Well, the only reason a bank truck could be in a place like this is if someone hijacked it.'

'That seems likely,' said Ann. 'They've had no qualms about hijacking a whole great ship, after all. So?'

'Well, if the Special Forces men are staying aboard *New England* the money in the bank truck must be for the mercenaries – for Pitman and the others. I bet they'll just pull them off *New England*, hand them their cash and wave them bye bye. But they're not going to like being paid in stolen money. That's all I meant. They're not going to like it at all.'

'Right,' agreed Bob. 'But they won't be able to do anything about it, will they? Really only Dall had the forethought to organise any comebacks. Which may be another reason Marshall killed him out of hand like that.'

The others nodded in silent agreement. Except for Harry. 'Oh no,' she said quietly. 'Dall wasn't the only one who could organise a little comeback.'

The door slammed open and two guards ushered Richard in at gunpoint to join the others at last. There was a general movement of relief and welcome. Richard was eager to tell them what he had discovered about their captors, and as soon as he had their attention, he began. 'Right. The situation is this. In the latter stages of the Gulf War, the Jellicoe Boys were tricked by some sort of smooth operator pretending to work for UNICEF. The outcome was that they spent the whole night of the invasion of Kuwait fighting a bloody retreat along a long spit of land called the Ras Al'I.'

'No wonder they're bitter,' mused Ann.

'It gets worse,' warned Richard. 'The Ras Al'I has been a leper colony since the Middle Ages. It was only closed in the nineteen twenties. Their retreat has infected them with a mutant bacillus. They aren't infectious. They're absolutely clear about that and I believe them. But they've all got it and they're all dying.'

'Oh my Lord!' said Mrs Charleston, her ready sympathy engaged far more swiftly than her senses of horror, disgust or self-preservation. 'Those poor boys . . .'

'But don't you see?' spat Dix in outrage. 'They're lepers! *Lepers.*'

'Lepers with a mission,' said Richard quietly. 'And whatever that mission is, I am personally very keen to screw it up if I possibly can. I've been made to look a fool by these people and I don't like it. I've been lied to and used. And you've all been put through a thoroughly unpleasant experience. What's more, there's a fair chance most of your careers will be ruined with this lot on your references. Jet-Ship Inc. will be lucky if it doesn't face a massive lawsuit from Federal Motors for the loss of those cars, and what the insurance boys are going to make of this I hesitate to think. All of our lives are going to be greatly complicated courtesy of this little lot and I personally would be happy to get some retaliation in if I can.'

'The problem is,' said Mrs Charleston, 'even if you could break out of here – which looks impossible to me – you'd probably only succeed in getting yourself killed, wouldn't you, Captain Mariner? And what sort of revenge would that be?'

'You're right, Mrs Charleston. If I do manage to formulate a plan, I'd be very careful indeed about how I put it into action. I would like to know what Merrideth and Marshall are up to and I would go to most lengths short of death to stop them if I could.'

'Well, it seems to me,' said Senator Charleston slowly, 'that they're getting ready to take *New England* into battle. Why else would they have taken aboard all those arms in Ireland?'

'And not just arms,' added Ann who had explored the lower hold most thoroughly. 'Some of those containers contain explosives. It all looks to be the same and the bits of it I managed to get closest to seem to be Semtex.'

'If you're right,' said Bob, 'there must be a thousand pounds of the stuff, maybe more.'

'That'd make a big bang,' said Richard. 'But even that much Semtex isn't going to amount to a hell of a lot unless it's set off in a special place or in a certain way.'

'Or unless it's used as an accelerator of some sort,' said Bob. 'I mean, if Harry's right and they've a warehouse full of petrol bowsers out there, they could turn *New England* into one heck of a Molotov cocktail.'

'Big enough to take out a couple of city blocks,' agreed Richard.

'A couple of city blocks in Atlantis maybe,' said Dix. 'I mean, where else would they be able to take it?'

'Anywhere with an inland waterway, of course,' said Harry rather fiercely. 'We were supposed to be on our way into Philadelphia. If they actually took her in there, they could blow away a good piece of Wilmington, Gloucester City or Camden if they wanted.'

'Would anybody notice?' sneered Dix dismissively.

'Harry's right,' said Richard. 'If they filled the upper hold full of petrol and sailed her into a waterway at the heart of a big city they could do an enormous amount of damage.'

'It wouldn't work,' said Dix. 'What city has a waterway wide enough to allow them to move at anything like full speed? A city that counts, I mean? If they're not going to go at full speed, why take *New England* in the first place? And what's to stop the Coastguard boarding them? And even if they are going at full speed up this big waterway through this big important city, what's to stop Strategic Air Command from blowing the crap out of them?'

'Well,' said Ann, 'they've a fair number of Stinger rocket systems in the lower hold. A Stinger would make most things think twice, even jets out of SAC I should imagine.'

'Oh, this is just fucking fantasy!' said Dix. 'I mean you haven't even answered my first point! Where are they going to go at one hundred miles an hour? The Hudson fucking river? Niagara, for Christ's sake?'

'Where they were practising for in Ireland. Wherever Heaven's Gate was standing in for,' said Harry.

'Oh, for God's sake, woman,' bellowed Dix. 'That was a different set of people!'

'But it was the same ship,' she shouted back. 'It was the same guidance system. The same computers. Dall programmed them at Heaven's Gate for these people! Don't you see? He programmed my computers to take *New England* somewhere with millimetre precision at one hundred miles an hour whether there's someone at the helm or not. Somewhere that has the same layout, the same structure, the same conditions, islands, the same—'

'The same name,' said Richard remembering suddenly

246

Merrideth's strange reaction to the code-name 'Gate'. 'The same name or near as dammit. My God, I think I know where they're going.'

Chapter Twenty

'Hell Gate is here,' Richard said, pointing to a section of a rough map drawn on the cleared table top. 'Where the East River narrows down at Ward's Island. The Triborough Bridge goes over it, stepping onto the island and running up to the expressway and St Mary's Park. There's a point which pushes out into the river quite a way, here, making it narrow and fast-running. Almost like rapids when the tide's moving. Hence the name. Then immediately to the south there's the north-eastern end of Roosevelt Island. What's the road that runs down the east coast of Manhattan Island here?'

'Franklin D. Roosevelt Drive,' supplied Senator Charleston. 'It sits a couple of metres above the high-water mark. Some of it's pretty open on the river side. It has eight lanes. Backed by high-rises. The odd park.'

Even Dix was paying attention now, peering at the makeshift map of New York City.

'And here?' asked Richard. 'On the Brooklyn side, south of the point?'

'Vernon Boulevard,' answered Ann. Richard glanced up, alerted by something in her voice. Raised in the Hollywood Hills, she had adopted New York as her home and workplace, and she loved the vibrant city with all the fervour of an immigrant.

'OK,' he proceeded. 'The Queensborough Bridge comes over here, steps over Roosevelt Island and then on westwards over Roosevelt Drive.'

'It joins Second Avenue, just north of 57th Street,' said Ann.

'Right. Then on south we get the end of Roosevelt Island, and the next hazard for shipping as I remember it is the Queens Midtown Tunnel which joins the Long Island Expressway with 34th Street here.'

'I'm due to be here tomorrow,' said Senator Charleston

suddenly, apparently apropos of nothing. His long finger indicated a point just north of the angle made by the tunnel and Roosevelt Drive, on what was effectively the eastern coast of Manhattan Island.

'Why is that?' asked Richard.

'Big reception at the United Nations. They're swearing in the first ever American Secretary General tomorrow night. Great big fireworks party, the lot. Everyone who is anyone in the UN will be there, plus invited guests. Biggest occasion in the UN's history, so I'm told. Though I think they could have got a better man for the job than Hiram Hoover. Still—'

'Wait!' said Richard. 'Who did you say, Senator?'

'Hiram Hoover,' repeated the Senator, mildly surprised. 'You've heard of him surely. He must know where the body's buried with a vengeance. I can't say I've ever warmed to the man but he must have *something* to have been accepted as the first American Secretary General . . .'

'Let me get this quite clear,' said Richard slowly. 'This is the same Hoover who came up through UNESCO?'

'Yes, that's right,' confirmed the Senator. 'How did the *Post* put it? "Out of total obscurity and into the brightest spotlight on earth . . ." Something of the sort. He did good work in the Gulf, I understand.'

'That's it,' said Richard. 'That has to be the trigger. And he's the target.' He looked around the assembled faces. 'It was Hoover,' he said. 'He was the man from UNESCO who sent the Jellicoe Boys onto the Ras Al'I. The UN building's not far from Hell Gate and *New England* has been programmed to take them in through Hell Gate at full speed, so they must be planning to go in there. And maybe come out again, but I doubt it.'

They looked at each other, stunned by the enormity of their conclusions.

'So, what are we going to do about it?' asked Ann.

'What can we do?' demanded Dix. 'We can't get out of this room. Look at it, it's a bond store. Thick brick walls, concrete floor, iron-bound door. Solid roof. No windows. We might as well be gold bricks in Fort Knox. Even if we could find some way out, we'd like as not get shot like Captain Dall. The only way we're likely to survive out there is if these SEALs and their Limey leper buddies have gone. No disrespect, Captain Mariner.'

Then what do we do anyway? We're in the back of beyond, by the look of things. We walk out to civilisation and try and raise the alarm. Like maybe in a week's time or so.'

'Yes,' said Richard. 'They must reckon it'll take us too long to get out of here to be in time to raise the alarm. The only other course of action guaranteeing absolute security would be to kill us all, and they could have done that more easily and efficiently long ago.'

'What about Dall's men?' said Bob. 'They'll presumably be sent on their way once they've been paid, but that seems a bit risky.'

'Particularly if they're paid off in hot money, like Harry said,' observed Ann. 'The minute they try to spend it they're liable to be picked up. And if they are arrested they'll tell everything they know.'

'So if Merrideth and Marshall aren't worried about that then they expect whatever they're doing to be over by the time that happens, or at least too far advanced to stop,' said Richard. 'That sounds like a twenty-four-hour time frame to me.'

'But I still don't get it,' said Dix. 'I mean, how can they let us go? We can identify them. Especially you, Captain Mariner. You can identify almost all of them.'

'But that doesn't matter, does it? The men I can identify aren't coming back alive. Hiram Hoover's adventure for the Jellicoe Boys in the Gulf has turned them into a bunch of terminal lepers. They've nothing to live for. But it seems they've found something to die for.'

'But their friends, family . . .'

'Someone related probably works pretty high up either in Jet-Ship Inc. or in the Massachusetts Institute of Technology. Professor Miles, can you remember anyone mentioning to you that they were related to a Gulf War veteran? Especially, I should think, someone who's just left your employ and maybe even dropped out of sight.'

The professor shook his head and continued to stare at Richard's roughly sketched map. 'What you're saying,' he said, in the voice of a man contemplating the death of a loved one, 'is that these lunatics are turning *New England* into a huge bomb and tomorrow night they plan to go charging at full speed into the middle of New York City where they are going to blow the hell out of themselves, the United Nations and anyone nearby.'

'That's about the size of it,' said Richard.

'Then you have to stop them.'

'Excuse me?' said Ann, taken aback by the childlike demand in the professor's voice.

'Captain Mariner brought them aboard. He helped them gain control of my ship. Now that they have control they're going to destroy it and maybe kill hundreds of people and it's his fault. He's responsible. He's got to stop them. You've got to stop them, Captain Mariner.'

Ann and Bob gaped at him, shocked by the accusation in his voice and by his selfish twisting of the facts.

'Like I said, I was thinking the same thing myself,' responded Richard quietly. 'What sort of people are we if we sit here and do nothing? In two days' time there'll be reports in the newspapers and on the news channels about all the people killed by this bunch of madmen in *New England* and we'll go through the rest of our lives thinking that we might have done something to slow them down or stop them. And we did nothing. I couldn't live with a thought like that.'

'Better be ready to die with it, then,' said Dix soberly. 'If they catch you trying anything, they'll kill you out of hand.'

'We can cross that bridge when we come to it,' said Richard. 'We start our own game in safe waters and see how far we can get. They won't kill us just for speculating and planning. If we can settle on a course of action which has a chance of succeeding at relatively low risk, we can weigh the odds and think about moving past the planning stage. For now let's just organise what we know, assess what we can do and start to make a plan.'

Most of the crew were shocked and apathetic, active only in their fierce wish to remain inactive. They slowly withdrew to the piles of bedding, taking food and drink with them. The rest gathered round the table, discussing alternatives and examining possibilities. Dix, with Stubbs in tow, crossed to the door to keep an ear, if not an eye, on what was happening outside.

As the evening wore on, some sort of plan did begin to emerge. Like one of Merrideth's classic military stratagems, it had three parts. Get out of the bond store. Get aboard *New England* unobserved. Stop the attack. So elegant. So simple. And absolutely impossible to carry out. There was no way out of the store. A thorough check was undertaken by Bligh's engineers under Engineering Officer Macleod. They were trapped and that was that. Dix observed, through a crack in the rusting though still solid door, that there was so much activity on the quayside between them and the ship that they would stand no chance of getting across to her unnoticed.

If they could overcome these obstacles, getting aboard might be feasible. The doors in the side were open. The upper tailgate was down. Pallets of Federal Motors four by fours were being replaced by petrol tankers in the holds. And, observed Professor Miles, even had these access points been secured, there were other ways into the hull if *New England* was tied up at the dock. The deck hatches Merrideth's men had used with Richard could be reached from the main or after decks. There were doors and more hatches in the bridgehouse, though access to some of them was complicated by the absence of external companionways. The big cradles in the side containing the lifeboats were also accessible from outside, but, again, only if the ship was at rest against a dock or platform at the correct height, for there was no way up and down the sleek composite hull. If all else failed, a couple of people could conceivably climb the anchor chain and sneak into the chain locker through the hawseholes, which was how rats traditionally came aboard.

Once aboard, there were only a limited number of ways to stop *New England*. Both the engine room and the engine control room would doubtless be manned and guarded, so they considered the possibility of breaking into the lower hold and making use of some of the explosives. They discussed the idea at some length before they realised that no one had the faintest notion how to make a bomb. Breaking into the communications somehow and signalling for help was not an option either because Dall had blown the radio shack away. And in any case, like all the major equipment aboard not secured in the engineering areas, the remaining radio equipment was on the bridge where the bulk of the soldiers was bound to be. So if they couldn't switch off the engines or blow them up or send for help, what was left?

Computers. Harry, for reasons of her own, had already said that if anyone else was going to go aboard, she wanted to go with them. Gaining access to the computers would be even more difficult than climbing like a rat through a hawsehole into the chain locker, but the fact was, only Harry's computers, the web of machines accessible from any point by any strand, seemed to offer any possibility of hope. This brought them right back to square one, for of course there was no hope at all if they could not get out of the building they were in and across to the ship.

At this point Dix, still on look-out by the door, noticed an abrupt change in the tempo of work outside, as though a close deadline had suddenly been moved much nearer. Then, over the dockside noise of machines and orders came a massively amplified voice followed by a vicious fusillade of shots. Out of the night sky a helicopter swooped downwards, searchlight ablaze. The men on the dockside froze, then their activity became frenetic. Another fusillade of shots rang out and the helicopter soared upwards and away.

'Well, I'll be damned!' yelled Dix. 'I think the FBI just arrived!'

Richard was at his side in an instant and straining to see through the crack in the door. 'But they're too late to stop *New England*!'

'Looks like it.'

'Christ, I wish there was some way through this door. They're far too busy to bother with us now. We could maybe make a difference if—'

'Someone's coming!' hissed Dix.

A pair of legs in black Danner boots and camouflage trousers filled the crack they were looking through. Two bolts slammed back and the door burst inwards. A square, solid, familiar figure filled the doorway. Blonde hair glinted in the light. Blue eyes raked across their incredulous faces. 'MOVE!' yelled Pitman. 'It's going to hell in a handcart out here and you really do not want to be caught in the middle!'

The better part of twenty people ran out of the building and headed inland. Pitman was already moving in the opposite direction when she noticed that a group of people led by Richard were also heading out towards the ship.

New England was obviously preparing for a rapid exit from Great Egg Head. Her tailgate was closing, the gangplank fell just as the party arrived, and the door in *New England*'s side slammed shut. The after line was a pile of cable on the quayside as they leaped over it, sprinting down the ship's side, Richard's knees beginning to complain for all that he kept himself generally fit and active. Then Professor Miles was out in front, reaching up to grab a handhold in the sleek side of his brainchild. *New England* was not moving forward yet, but her side was no longer snugly up against the buffers. Her fore lines were still attached, seven hundred metres further down the quay, but her hull was swinging outwards onto the tide. Alan Miles was swung upwards and outwards over the water as his grip twisted the handle he had caught. And as it did so, a panel in the ship's side swung out and down, dropping him back onto the quay. There in a great cradle, her davits automatically swinging out over the dockside, lay one of the lifeboats. 'Up!' gasped the professor. 'Up and in!'

Pitman needed no second bidding. The FBI helicopter was on its way back behind them, the accusing finger of its searchlight rapidly approaching. She was into the boat in a second. With no hesitation she swarmed forward to grab at the handle which would close the cradle again. Bob Stark swung up into the little craft and turned automatically to catch at the next arm behind him. By the time Pitman had the lever in her hand, Richard was aboard and both men were reaching back.

The soldier releasing the fore line turned and loosed a stream of bullets at the FBI helicopter, making it pull upwards. *New England* began to gather way. The shoulders of the two men in the lifeboat threatened to pop with the strain as they hauled Ann Cable and Harry Newbold aboard. Then *New England* was moving too fast for human legs to follow and Pitman had pulled the handle. Wind thundered over the closing cradle and the five boarders huddled down into the bilge of the lifeboat.

On the quayside, Alan Miles fell gasping to his knees. It was fortunate he did so, for as he fell forward, the air immediately above his head was blasted into a writhing inferno by *New England*'s outer jets. A horrific thundering came and went in the professor's reeling consciousness and he found it difficult to breathe. Then the outwash of *New England*'s water jets came pouring down upon him like the wrath of a tropical storm. After that was silence, largely because the professor had been temporarily deafened.

After a while he stirred and rolled into a sitting position. Then he began to pull himself erect, but as he did so a hurricane wind battered him to the ground again as the FBI helicopter landed not far from him. Doggedly, indomitably, Professor Miles began to haul himself into the blast. 'Help!' he called. 'You must help. I know exactly where they're going and I know what they're planning to do!'

Hiram Hoover's office in the United Nations building sat on the north-east corner of the fortieth floor. Its windows looked down across the plaza and Franklin D. Roosevelt Drive to the East River. The view east was spectacular. In the middle distance Southpoint, the southern tip of Roosevelt Island, parted the slow mahogany water, and the sprawling ruins of the old sanatoriums, hospitals and laboratories that had stood there for a century mouldered picturesequely in ten acres or so of weeds and wisteria. Here the men from Macey's fireworks department were busy preparing the display they would set off tonight at midnight, a display set to outdo any they had ever presented for New Year's Day or the Fourth of July. Beyond lay the bustling heave of Queens, and beyond that the rest of Long Island. The view north was striking also, the perspectives of FDR Drive, the long, slim island and the narrow, busy river seeming to pull the arch of the Triborough Bridge closer as though the very geography of New York wanted to bring Hell Gate a little closer too.

The windowed corner framed Hoover's shoulders as he faced the room. The decade since the Gulf War had added to his stature and his consequence. He had become fat and pompous. 'So what you're saying,' he said to the men from FBI and UN security, 'is that I have to tell the President, the ex-President of South Africa, seven premiers and a dozen prime ministers, their parties and their families that the reception and inauguration tonight are cancelled. I have to call up the Mayor, the City Council, the fire service and the police and tell them there will be no party tonight, take down all the bollards, pack up the bunting, and cancel the overtime. I have to contact every celebrity invited from Tom Hanks to Elton John and say sorry, guys, we have to take a raincheck on this. I have to call up every fucking news network from here to Ho Chi Minh City and explain that the fireworks are off after all. And all of this because half a dozen Gulf War vets have hijacked a boat down in Great Gatsby country. Is that what you're telling me?'

'There's more to it than that, sir. The ship is full of explosives.

256

It's incredibly advanced, fast and dangerous. They're well armed and apparently they have nothing to lose. And they're coming here, sir. To Hell Gate, at least. And to be fair, sir, the Jellicoe Boys are more than just a bunch of vets.'

Hoover's eyes narrowed. 'They were good ten years ago,' he said. 'In the winter of ninety-one, 13 Int. were the best. Now they're has-beens. Sick has-beens. You stop them. Or you kill them. I'll be damned if I'm going to cancel my party.'

'He'll be damned if he doesn't,' said the security man in the elevator on the way back down. 'What've you actually got that'll stop these guys if push comes to shove?'

'The Coastguard, the Navy and the Strategic Air Command, if we can get the clearances in time.'

'You're keeping a close eye on them and all your options open?' The UN security chief was responsible for what happened in the secretariat building, the General Assembly building, the conference building, the Hammarskjöld library, and that was it. His power and authority did not stretch to First Avenue and certainly not to the East River. His ass was on the line here, he knew; and his power was absolutely zero.

'Close eye,' said the FBI man with unexpected sympathy.

Unexpected sympathy but not a lot of veracity. The FBI were being fed information from SAC and the Coastguard. SAC had the ship on its satellite-generated map of the East Coast area, but *New England*'s signal moved erratically and flickered wilfully as her automatic identification beacon struggled to function – presumably because 13 Int. had attempted to deactivate it but with only partial success. It wasn't much, thought the FBI man, but any sign of a mistake or weakness in what appeared to be a faultless operation so far had to be encouraging. The Coastguard had *New England* on their long-wave radar, but again only sporadically. Because of the composition of the ship's hull, it treated radar waves much as it treated magnetic force – in a strange and unpredictable manner. The FBI man's director, who had been in charge of the assault on Great Egg Head, had attended a short briefing by the Coastguard and had been told that should *New England* come anywhere near full speed, she might effectively become a Stealth ship as far as coastal defences were concerned. Indeed, she had dropped off their charts and disappeared altogether once so far, only to turn up again at Great Egg Head, providentially before anything too disastrous had happened – and having the ship placed there, apparently immobile, had prompted immediate FBI action. It had seemed like over-kill at the time. Now it looked like too little too late.

The FBI man was not happy about the current situation or Hoover's reaction to it. He felt that he had been too lightweight a messenger. But he knew that the next few men up the pecking order were briefing more senior dignitaries. The United States may have paid the UN all its outstanding contributions and the organisation might have reacted by proposing an American Secretary General, but there was still something fundamentally un-American and suspicious about it, and not just in the FBI man's mind either. Still and all, Hoover was going ahead with his party, so the FBI's duty was clear.

As he stepped out of the elevator, the FBI man tapped the pressel on his personal radio. 'He's going ahead,' he said to the team parked outside on the corner of First and 42nd.

'You can't use that in here,' said the UN security man, without thinking.

The FBI man stopped in the middle of the concourse and turned. He looked like what he was, very Brooks Brothers, very *Men in Black*. He turned heads among the bustling crowd. 'Do tell,' he said.

There was a moment of silence. Then the security man asked, 'What about the civilians? The ones who went back aboard?'

Again, the FBI man seemed to react with unexpected humanity. 'We'll do our best, of course,' he said. 'If we send in the SEALs, they'll be briefed. They'll be careful and we'll have to hope none of the bystanders get into the line of fire. It's all we can do.' That's what he said. What he thought was, unfortunately they don't make smart bombs smart enough to tell the difference . . .

Hoover made the decision to proceed at noon. *New England* had been moving in a generally north-eastwards direction during the morning, shying away from any near-approach by ship or aircraft, well out towards international waters. Had the ship not been in the hands of rogue and dangerous men, she would hardly have attracted any official interest, but the fact that she was being

258

held illegally by well-armed professionals with a target, a grudge and, apparently, a plan, changed things radically. But the problems which had faced the Irish authorities – and the British ones when they became involved – remained. The ship could outrun anything waterborne sent against her and the chances of transferring any kind of law-enforcement unit aboard from anything airborne were zero. The FBI advised that for the moment the situation should be treated as a hostage negotiation and everyone should stay calm and inactive – though there was no negotiation actually going on because *New England* and the men aboard remained stubbornly silent. Only Professor Miles, the other ex-hostages and one surviving, severely wounded, pirate had anything to say. Senator and Mrs Charleston were on their way up to New York by limousine, being debriefed on the way. In spite of everything, they proposed to be at the United Nations building tonight.

'There were more mercenaries than the five you have,' the Senator was saying. 'And the wounded man, O'Reilley, seems to have been a member of the original crew who changed sides. I see no mention on your lists, for instance, of anyone called Copeland or Aves, and they were both there. You'll have to check with First Officer Dix. Or wait until you can speak to Captain Mariner or Captain Stark, of course.'

The likelihood of that receded as noon passed and Hoover made his decision. The situation was simple, as far as the authorities saw it. The inauguration and reception would proceed tonight between eight and midnight Eastern Standard Time. The men on *New England* would know all about it simply by tuning to any commercial radio or TV station. If the men on the ship were going to carry out their assumed threat, they would have to move at that time. And the closer they got, the more limited the options became. If they couldn't be boarded, they would have to be stopped. If they couldn't be stopped then they would have to be destroyed.

There was some discussion about the possibility of disabling *New England*, but no one could see any way of doing it – not the man who had designed her, or the USAF colonel liaising from SAC. The precision of fire needed to hit the engine with no collateral damage was simply not available, especially if she started to move at speed, and precision was essential given that she herself seemed to be one big bomb. As far as anyone could see, they would simply have to wait until the last safe moment, allow the lunatics aboard as many chances to give themselves up as possible, and then just blow the sucker away.

At no time did anyone seriously entertain the idea that the ship might actually get through into the East River and complete her explosive mission, in spite of the fact that 13 Int. had out-guessed and out-gunned everyone who had come against them so far.

Chapter Twenty-One

Time in Great Egg Head had been well spent. The later than anticipated arrival of the FBI had allowed one or two more embellishments than Marshall had planned for. It had also meant that Dall's mercenaries had got in the way of the FBI and slowed them down. Richard and Harry's speculations had been quite correct. Dall's men had been less than happy at being paid off in stolen money fresh out of the back of a hijacked bank truck, but under the guns of 13 Int., even the well-armed amongst them – including Pitman – had accepted their wages and faded into the night. Less than a mile inland the first of them had stumbled onto the approaching FBI and someone had opened fire.

Twenty minutes later the original crew of *New England* had added to the confusion and only the quick-thinking leadership and stentorian voice of Senator Charleston had averted a bloodbath as the unarmed ex-hostages strayed into the crossfire. In the confusion, most of Dall's men had managed to vanish inland.

In the event, only the helicopter among the FBI contingent had got anywhere near *New England,* and even that useful vehicle had been damaged by a riff of automatic fire and then side-tracked by the importunities of Alan Miles. So that, by the time the authorities arrived in any force at the quayside itself, there was no one there for them to talk to, and nothing left for them to see except empty, night-bound sea.

New England spent the last hours of darkness that night picking her way carefully out of the busy coastal waters to an area where, unobserved, 13 Int. could practise their run a couple more times before they did it for real.

They had attained that unit-wide focus again, as they had on the Ras Al'I. They were one machine, like a colony of ants; defined by objective, function and relationship within the group. There was no speculation, no doubt, no second thoughts. No one mattered but the men of 13 Int. Nothing else existed but the mission.

It was well for the five interlopers in the hold that no one else aboard had the slightest idea that they were there.

If Bob Stark had been on the command bridge, he would have been astonished by how much had been achieved in so short a time by such a small group of apparently unskilled men. For a start, the foredeck, over which the clearviews looked, was no longer empty. Secured upon it was a powerful-looking matt black powerboat; a wedge of shadow perhaps eight metres in length from needle to bow to square stern. It was designed to take two people, a driver and his passenger, somewhere very fast indeed. Like the petrol tankers and the First National armoured van, the powerboat had been collected in the last couple of weeks by Marshall's men in one of a series of carefully planned but apparently unrelated robberies up and down the coast and inland as far as Ohio. Over the powerboat crouched a makeshift davit obviously designed to swing it overboard easily and quickly. The passenger seat had been removed and in its place was a big black box which had been secured to the body of the boat as close to the centre of gravity as possible, but not too near the stubby speed controls or the thickly-padded little steering wheel. The remaining seat had as many webbing straps and buckles as an old Martin Baker Zero-Zero ejector seat in a jet.

The forward section of the command bridge was untouched, but the windows on either side of it had been removed and scoops of light, strong steel had been bolted and welded onto the solid metal frames. These open ports gave an unrivalled view, and an overlapping field of fire, down either side of the bridge, to port and starboard. The first two might, at a pinch, also give some possibility of forward fire too, and the prospect of firing at full speed was supported by the fact that there were heavy harnesses secured to the floor, as though the men destined to stand there might be fishing for monster sharks.

Through the wreckage of the radio room on the port side and through Harry's domain to the captain's bridge day room on the starboard, tracks along the deck told of heavy equipment swiftly and carelessly moved. Here the stern-facing walls had had openings cut into them, which gave fields of fire from the front and sides towards the stern. Between these two openings, the rear bridgehouse divided the field of fire and created a blind spot on the afterdeck and down towards the water immediately behind the massive jets. Clearly, the architect of these fortifications had been concerned to protect the bridgehouse against attack from above rather than below.

As the morning passed, Marshall and Merrideth checked all of these new facilities and prowled further afield. Standing on the afterdeck, right in the blind spot, they luxuriated in the sensation – what they could feel of it – of sun on unmasked faces and discussed the feasibility of setting up one final little foxhole here where a couple of men could sit secure against the hurricane wind of full speed. But there was no realistic way of doing it. Even an open hatchway, with carefully-prepared support immediately beneath it, would not really offer sufficient protection.

'And besides,' said Merrideth, closing the hatchway, 'it's the one position that we simply cannot be attacked from.'

'You got aboard here,' Marshall reminded him. 'And so did we. It's the Achilles heel.'

'They're not going to send boarding parties when we make our run. They'll send F18s with smart rockets and maybe cruise missiles,' observed Merrideth quietly. 'They're finished fucking around with Special Forces teams. Not that they ever actually started. Too slow even for that.'

'And I guess it's a dollar to a dime that a heat-seeker up the ass'll do for us whether we've got some poor son of a bitch sitting on top of it or not. We'll just have to rely on the Stingers like we planned and hope none of the jet jocks get a chance to squeeze one off.'

'It's a good plan, Ira. It'll work. Even if it doesn't go one hundred per cent as planned, we'll still frighten the sorry bastards shitless and go down in glory.'

'I hope so, Merrideth, I surely do. But either way's OK with me. Mamma Marshall didn't birth no boy to die a broken leper in some chickenshit sanatorium. Same's true for all my men.'

'Mine too.'

'OK. Let's do the drill one more time.'

They returned to the command bridge. Neither of them

thought to call for the hold lights to be extinguished now that they had finished with them.

The five who had leaped into the lifeboat as *New England* sailed out of Great Egg Head were much less focused than Marshall, Merrideth and their men. They had no immediate plan and only the vaguest of long-term objectives. They were unarmed, except for Pitman, and hugely outnumbered. And they were all too well aware that there was no way back and very little chance of survival. They were quite comfortably ensconced in the lifeboat. They had easy access to the lower hold when they chose to step out. In the meantime, they had a well-supplied, very well-equipped little redoubt which might prove an effective hiding place. At a push it might even prove defensible – for as long as the flares and Pitman's ASP held out against 13 Int.'s 203s.

There was nothing to see over the lifeboat's gunwale except a great plastic-wrapped pile in the centre of the hold. Richard wondered whether they should inspect it more closely, and that brought to mind the security cameras. Were they switched on? he wondered, straining his eyes to see the telltale red dots. He began to feel about, trying to locate the lifeboat's binoculars. The first thing his hand encountered was soft, warm and rounded.

'Apologise or die,' came a gruff whisper.

'What are you doing here, Pitman?' he asked, moving his hand carefully away.

'Damned if I know. Same as you, I should think. Beginning to regret it now?'

'No!' came Ann's voice, a little more loudly than Richard would have liked. 'We have to stop these people.'

'Shhhhh,' said Bob. 'You're right, Ann, we have to stop them before a lot of folk get hurt. But we won't stand a chance if they find us. So let's not alert them too soon, huh, honey?'

There was an instant of silence during which Richard fully expected Ann to snap, 'Don't you *honey* me!' But the words never came. Son of a gun, he thought. Bob's mellowing her!

'But what are we actually going to do?' asked Harry.

'Work out exactly what their plan is, then work out some way to stop it and walk away,' said Richard. 'If we feel we've made a terrible mistake we can still back off if we have to, but we've got to be certain, we all have to agree and we've got to time it right.'

'Back off how?' demanded Pitman. 'This looks like a one-way ticket to me.'

'The lifeboat,' Richard explained. 'It got us in, it can get us out whenever we want.'

'As long as *New England*'s not at full speed,' cautioned Bob.

'And as long as we all agree. We can't have just a couple going out and leaving the rest in the lurch.'

'Perish the thought,' said Pitman. But she sounded more cheerful now that she had her escape route clear if it all went pear-shaped – which was, in her view, the most likely outcome. But there was something about these two men which put them above the common run. And it was more than their looks. If anyone could pull them through this, it would like as not be them. Richard in particular, she thought. She looked no further into who else was here or why she was here herself. One step at a time, she thought. One step at a time.

'So, what were you looking for when you got on my tits, Captain?' she asked companionably.

'Binoculars. We've really got to play this one carefully. Check the lie of the land before we put a foot out of here.'

'Good thinking. D'you suppose they've got the surveillance cameras on?'

'No red dots that I can see. We'd see them easily right across the hold, I think, but the binoculars will let me check more closely. Anyway, I doubt they had time, or reason, to fix them at wherever it was they held us, no matter what else they may have done.'

'I'm sure it was Great Egg,' said Bob.

'I agree, but I don't think it's important,' said Richard. 'It's where we are now and where we're going that counts.'

'We're going to Hell Gate,' said Harry decidedly.

'Right, Harry, but via where?'

'You mean are we going past Staten Island and Liberty or are we skipping round Montauk and coming in through Long Island Sound?' asked Ann.

'Yup. It'll make a lot of difference, I should think.'

'To what?' inquired Pitman as she explored, leisurely, looking for the binoculars too.

'To their chances of pulling it off. And therefore to our chances of walking away.'

'Can we be clear about that?' said Ann. 'I mean, now that we are here, in another fine mess, so to speak, *walking away* is our highest priority. I mean, when the going gets tough, we all get going. Yes?'

'Yes,' said Richard at once. 'If these men want to kill themselves, that's fine by me. I'd like to try and stop them destroying *New England* in the process and I certainly want to stop them killing anyone else while they're at it, but the bottom line is just what you say, Ann. If anything hits the fan we pull the ripcord and that is that. You've all got lives to lead. I've got a wife and a family.'

'As long as we're all aboard when the lifeboat goes over the side, like you said, Captain Mariner,' said Harry.

'Yes. It's musketeer time, I suppose.'

'All for one and one for all?' inquired Pitman.

'That goes for us,' said Bob. 'If it goes for you.'

'I guess,' said Pitman.

'Meaning?' There was a distinct threat in Bob's voice.

'Meaning I'm still trying to work out what in hell's name tempted me aboard. And what I'm going to do now that I'm here.'

'You came aboard to save your ass,' said Harry. 'And working with us is your best bet for keeping it safe.'

'Keeping it safe for what? That's the question. Like as not you good folks will hand me over to the authorities the minute we're out of this mess and I'll spend the rest of my natural fighting off dykes in the prison showers. Am I right or am I right?'

'Well, of course . . .' began Bob, who had every intention of seeing her rot in jail with the rest of Dall's command if ever he got the chance.

'No,' said Richard quietly but firmly. 'This cancels all debts. It has to. We're in this together and we get out together. It's the only chance we have. The past is dead. Bury it.'

'Wish these guys took that viewpoint,' said Pitman, her voice showing she was unconvinced.

'They are the past,' said Ann. 'And they're dead, poor bastards. Dead men walking. They just want to be cold before they're buried. That's all.'

266

'There's more to it than that,' said Richard. 'And this is more than their own peculiar style of cremation. They're going to do a lot of damage and take a lot of people down with them unless we can stop it.'

'You don't trust the authorities to do that?' asked Ann, as though she was interviewing him.

'Ultimately, no, I don't. It's not that I think the Coastguard, the Navy and the rest are incompetent. I just think these men have a plan more clever than the authorities have calculated. I think they'll carry it through no matter what the cost and I think if we can't stop them, no one will.'

'This is getting a little circular,' observed Pitman. 'Here.'

Richard felt a cool rubberised column being pushed into his hand and he pressed the binoculars to his eyes without further words.

'Can one camera be turned on and the others left off?' he asked at the end of his careful survey.

'No,' answered Harry.

'Right then. All the cameras I can see are off, so they must all be off. We're safe for the time being.'

'Relatively speaking, of course,' observed Pitman.

Richard gave a quiet bark of laughter. He liked the gentle pressure coming from this mercenary. He had no doubt that, no matter what, Pitman would keep him up to scratch. He lowered the binoculars, squirmed down and round, and faced the others.

They made a fairly motley crew. Three women and one other man, each in their own way widely experienced and capable. Each one, with the exception of Ann, brought something invaluable to the situation they were in. He could hardly have chosen better if he had had infinities of time and co-operation. Bob was the only man who knew the ship and her general capabilities better than he did himself. Harry was the only one who knew specific and vital areas better than both of them. Pitman understood the military implications of anything they might undertake and could assess better than anyone the likely reaction of the soldiers ranged against them. All four of them were also fit and strong. But he must not underestimate Ann Cable. She was much more than she appeared. Intrepid, intelligent, cool under fire. She had come through wars like the ones fought by Pitman in Africa. She had come through

267

shipwreck and bomb attack and the first day of the Macey's sale unscathed. No, Ann should never be underestimated.

'So,' Richard said quietly, 'how d'you think we're going to pull this thing off then?'

They spent the morning in quiet discussion, safe in their little eyrie, careful to think everything through to the finest detail.

Richard established that the plastic-covered bundle in the hold was Semtex, and Pitman, who knew more about explosives than the rest of them, confirmed that it was designed to blow the upper deck and its contents into airborne droplets. Chained to the deck of the upper hold was a carefully placed series of massive petrol tankers. These would become a huge cloud of lethal mist which would in turn explode into a firestorm triggered by the first explosion. The second explosion would take out a whole city block with ease. If the explosion went off in Hell Gate, everything on either side of the East River from the Triborough Bridge to the Queens Tunnel would be flattened as far as 21st Street on the Queens shore and Second Avenue on Manhattan. Everything from Astoria Park to the Empire State Building would be at risk.

'And if they pull it off tonight,' emphasised Ann, 'it'll all go up in the middle of the United Nations inauguration party. The UN building is right in the middle of the blast area. I can't tell you how many people will die at the reception, but Tom Hanks will be one of them and that's enough for me.'

'Yeah, but they have to know the UN building's at risk,' said Pitman. 'They'll cancel the reception or they'll close the river up tight. Or both.'

'I agree,' said Richard, 'except I'm certain these men have thought of a way round anything the authorities have planned so far. They'll have thought this through as well.'

'Something to do with the speed of the ship perhaps,' hazarded Bob. 'I don't think they've finished using that facility.'

'Something to do with my computers,' said Harry. 'Remember, they only went through Heaven's Gate in Ireland so that they could set the automatic navigation system.'

'And they stayed there just that bit longer so they could do so, in spite of the added risk of the Garda arriving on the scene,' added Pitman. 'So I guess it was really important.'

'And something else,' said Richard. 'I can't help thinking there's something else we haven't thought of yet. An extra edge they've got for themselves.'

They never worked out the extra edge, or rather two edges, that the soldiers had, for they knew nothing of the powerboat and its black box; and only Professor Miles really knew just how invisible his ship could become to radar when the automatic beacon was out. All they could do was make the best possible plan, but as Pitman pointed out, effective action required intelligence as well as planning. Unless they knew the critical moment at which to take action, everything else would be pointless. So the first thing they had to do was break into the ship's security and communications systems. Either physically or electronically, they had to be able to observe what was going on on the bridge and, if possible, influence it.

Harry and Pitman went out of the lifeboat first to search the hold for anything that might allow access to the ship's computer network. If there was nothing in the hold, they would report back and discuss their options before proceeding through the damaged walls into the stairwell.

As he watched them move along the access balcony, Richard frowned. He did not trust Pitman at all and there was something disturbing going on between her and Harry which put Harry's motives under serious question. But they were definitely the men for the job.

New England, her exercises complete for the time being, turned and began to move purposefully west and north. As she gathered speed, following the slow decline of the sun, three figures came out of the A deck bulkhead door and onto the forward weather deck. They walked towards the powerboat and climbed up onto the edges which stood out on either side of her sleek black frame like the running boards of an old-fashioned car. Corporal Tom Smith stepped into the boat and lowered himself into the vacant seat next to the black box. While Merrideth and Marshall watched, Tom adjusted the webbing straps so they fitted him perfectly.

'You confident about handling this thing?' asked Marshall.

'Yes, sir, I am,' said Tom. 'It's been my hobby for years. I was coming up to championship level when the disease became a problem. I may be a bit rusty but I'm well qualified for what we want.'

'You want another dry run, Tom?' asked Merrideth quietly.

'No thanks, boss. I know what I'll be doing. There's no need.' Satisfied that the straps were correctly adjusted, he unbuckled them and stepped out of the powerboat again.

'Right,' said Merrideth. 'Let's put the cover in place now.' With an ease which belied the damage to their nerves and muscles, the three men pulled a white cover off the deck and slid it over the black boat and davits. When they had finished securing it to the deck, there was nothing but a white hump visible, and that would be distinguishable only from here or from the bridge. Any further away than that and it would merge indistinguishably with the hull.

'That's it, then,' said Marshall. 'Nothing else to do until dark. I guess we can stand the men down. Let them have a bit of a rest.'

'Except for the obvious ones, yes,' concurred Merrideth. 'It'll be their last chance.'

'That it will,' said Marshall looking up at the bright warm sun whose heat he could no longer really feel. 'That it will.'

Harry and Pitman sat side by side looking down at the little videophone handset they had taken from its clip by the door. It had escaped the blast damage that had affected the screens in the engine control room.

'This would do to spy on the bridge,' said Harry quietly. 'We did that all right when Dall was in charge. We can do it again. But we want to be able to do more than that.'

'What do you want to do?' asked Pitman.

'Access the computer through it.'

'Like a portable phone going in through a modem?'

'Exactly. So I need to get to a terminal and open it up in some way so it can communicate with this.'

'But this is just a videophone. It has a ten-digit dialling pad. Surely you need a keyboard to control a computer.'

'Not necessarily.'

'So, do you need access to a modem? Your own computer up on the bridge? A substation? The engine control room? The library? What?'

'The library computer is linked to the Internet so it has a modem. All I have to do is tune this handset to the wavelength of the satellite phone link and then make sure the computer is on and controllable from here.'

'Yeah, but that's like saying to get moon rocks, all I've got to do is go to the moon.'

'Not quite. I've an idea which might make everything we want to do quite feasible. But I will need to get to a terminal.'

'The nearest one's in the engine control room,' said Pitman.

'Do you think they'll be guarding it?'

'They don't know we're aboard or they would have taken some action against us before now. So they have no need to guard it against anything as far as they know. Is there any reason why they would need to man it? Like to control the engines or anything?'

'All engine control can be done from the bridge. The systems down here are maintenance and breakdown diagnosis mostly. They'll need them if anything goes wrong but not until then, as far as I can see.'

'Probably safe to assume there won't be anyone watching them then. And there's been no sign of anyone going past on patrol while we've been down here. And again, why bother? They think they're secure.'

'Right then. Let's do it.'

Pitman moved forward towards the bomb hole in the metal wall. As she did so, she reached in under her blouson and slid her hand up to the waistband of her combat trousers. When her fist reappeared it was holding the skeletal form of her beloved stripped-down 9mm ASP.

'Hell, I wish I knew where they were and what's taking them so long,' said Bob.

'It can't be anything too bad,' said Ann. 'They said they'd report in if they were thinking of leaving the hold, didn't they?'

They looked across to the column of the stairwell in the distance. The hole where Merrideth had blasted into the engineering areas was hidden behind the hill of Semtex. It was the Semtex, rather than Harry and Pitman's whereabouts, that was preoccupying Richard, however. Even if Harry found a way to spy on the bridge, it would not do any of them much good if

271

the Semtex remained armed. And even if they managed to disconnect all the fuses and get away, 13 Int. could just re-arm the explosive if they wanted. Their only option was to remove the hill of Semtex altogether. Over the plastic sheeting covering it, a cargo net secured the mound to the deck. If they could release or cut the cables holding the net to the floor and re-attach them to act as a tow line, the whole pallet on which the Semtex was sitting might be moved – if they could find the power to do it.

They had one source of power immediately at their disposal, if Harry's tinkering with the computer could be made to harness it for them. If they could attach lines tightly and securely to the rear doors and then activate the opening mechanism, the whole pallet might be pulled aft and out of the ship. And if the lifeboat they were occupying could be positioned to take advantage of the opening doors as well, then maybe they could do what they had come aboard to do and walk away after all. To do this, they would have to move the lifeboat out of its cradle. Thanks to 13 Int. themselves, this ought to be possible, for the strong lines that had brought Marshall and his men aboard were still secured to the deck head just above them. Various slings and pulleys dangled there ready and waiting to take the weight of the boat. If the SEALs' lines could be run through the pulleys above and then re-attached to the lifeboat's lowering winches, it ought to be possible to swing the boat into the middle of the hold instead of out over the side. Then they could attach it by a long line to the Semtex and by a much shorter one to the tailgate. Once all these lines were secure they might indeed be in business.

SAC kept the FBI informed of *New England*'s movements with hourly pictures, taken by satellite and aircraft, giving latitude and longitude readings. The ship's flickering identity beacon allowed her progress to be plotted only erratically, but they kept track of her this way as well, knowing that all too soon the satellites and aircraft would be effectively blinded by the darkness.

The FBI passed the information to the Coastguard and the New York Harbour Authority, as well as to UN security and the White House. No one had any real doubt that *New England* was going to try to get to Hell Gate tonight, but they were confident they could stop her. Once they were sure of her preferred route, whether up past Staten Island or down Long Island Sound, the shipping nearest the first choke point in the channel would simply be directed to form an impenetrable barrier.

But, as the senior harbourmaster pointed out to Professor Miles and the FBI, they would have to be careful how they called it because high tide would be running fast tonight. And the harbour was likely to furnish only enough ships to close one choke point. They could close the river at the Triborough Bridge or they could close it at the Brooklyn Bridge. But not both. So they had better be sure. And did they actually *know* this was a suicide mission? The Hell Gate programme might after all be an *escape* route . . .

Unknown to mere mortals at Professor Miles or the harbourmaster's level of clearance, the plan was to blow the ship out of the water if it came anywhere near New York Harbour, long before it even got a glimpse of the Statue of Liberty or the Manhattan skyline, let alone attained the choke points of Brooklyn or Triborough Bridges. And that was just as well, for Hiram Hoover's guests, including Senator and Mrs Charleston, were already getting ready, the UN hospitality staff were busy in their hundreds setting up the reception areas, and the cooks were preparing mountains of refreshments. The police, firemen, ambulancemen and paramedics were all on alert and overtime. The local hospitals had all been briefed for huge crowds were expected. The first sightseers were assembling behind the barriers along Second Avenue, hoping to catch a glimpse of the powerful and famous from all over the world; the first police helicopters buzzed noisily just above them. And the men from Macey's were finalising the sequences for the tens of thousands of dollars' worth of fireworks they proposed to set off at midnight from Southpoint on Roosevelt Island opposite the UN building, halfway across the East River.

The computer in the engine control room was up and running. The twisted monitor showed the strangely misshapen men coming and going on the bridge. Pitman watched the monitor as Harry worked on the computer, going in through her female passwords, deeper and deeper into the control areas.

'What are you doing?' asked Pitman after a while.

'I've tried to get to the modem via the library computer but it's switched off. So I'm putting some quick releases in place for when I get up there. It won't be as safe or as quiet there as it is down here.'

'I guess not. I wish I could see into the minds of those guys up there. Find out exactly what they plan to do.'

'Nice dream. Or maybe not so nice, all things considered. I can't get into the Hell Gate program from down here. It's the only one that's still closed. But I imagine it's just a series of directions and measurements. It'll all come down to turn a bit left or turn a bit right in the end.'

'I guess. So you're going to have to go up to the library?'

'If I can. It's the only way I can link the whole system to this handset.'

'Well, if these guys don't know we're aboard, then sneaking through the air ducts like you did last time can't be much more dangerous than what we're doing now.'

Famous last words, thought Harry.

The engines immediately outside suddenly began to whine with new deep-throated urgency; Harry felt the surge beneath her feet and one of the automatic read-outs on a screen to her right began to wind up. *New England* was coming up towards full speed.

It was sunset, and as soon as the light began to change, Merrideth called for more speed. Full speed was out of the question for the time being. They had to be very careful not to go too fast too soon or the powerboat would leave the foredeck and come in through the clearview. But the surge of speed sent a kind of electricity through the whole command. Although it was too early for them to be needed yet, many of the men came to their positions and began to sort their weapons. Marshall and Merrideth did not stop them. There were no more commands for them to give. Everyone was fully briefed. Each man knew what he had to do and was well able to improvise according to circumstance. Such was the nature of Special Forces. The objective was agreed. The plan was set. The final briefing had been held. The action would either follow its predicted course within parameters they could handle, or they would fail. That was all there was to it. And failure was not something any of them was contemplating as the sun set upon them for the last time and *New England* came towards forty knots, cutting in along the sun's blood-red track westwards.

'You see how it will work?' Richard asked. Harry and Pitman both nodded, both of them impressed by the ingenuity of his plan to use the lifeboat and the long lines. 'But we'll have to be quick to pull it off. We'll have to activate everything at the critical moment. Is that possible, Harry?'

'Yes. As long as I can set up the library computer.'

'But how can you control the computer without a keyboard?'

'I can set it up to read from the numbered keypad as though it was a mouse. Use the numbers two, eight, four and six to go up, down, left and right. Zero to activate. If I can get the screen on the videophone handset to show the computer screen, I can move the cursor anywhere I want, pull down any list of commands I need and get the programs to do what I tell them. I've set up some quick releases that will cut in past my security walls so I won't have to type in the codes. If I can just get the modem in the library switched on and adjust this thing to the correct frequency . . .'

'We'll be in business,' supplied Pitman. 'And none too soon, judging by the way *New England*'s moving now.'

Just as she said this, the great grumble of the jets behind the drawbridge aft of them lessened and the hull stopped vibrating as *New England* began to slow again.

There was almost total darkness now. Low cloud obscured the stars and the moon. The three men walked down the deck under a glimmer of light from the bridge and pulled the cover off the powerboat. Tom swung himself up into the cockpit and while Marshall opened the black box at his side, Merrideth strapped him in. 'You still fit for this, old man?' Merrideth asked quietly.

Tom nodded, his face the slightest doughy smudge in the darkness.

'You know where you're bound?'

'Same place as all of us, boss,' Tom said, but as he spoke, his black-gloved finger flicked a switch and a navigation screen lit up, its green display marked with his route.

'Good man,' Merrideth said almost silently.

Marshall raised his arm and the gesture was just visible enough to call forth a squad of men from the bridge. In a matter of moments, the powerboat was swung up and over the side. As soon as it sat safely in the water, Tom fired up the motors and the almost invisible shape began to move away south and west, bearing *New England*'s identification beacon down towards Cholera Bank and Coney Island, powering up towards speeds which only the jet-ship was apparently capable of.

Marshall and Merrideth ran back up to the bridge and *New England* began to come back up to speed, turning away north towards Montauk Point and Long Island Sound.

Pitman followed Harry into the air duct. The soldier hated confined spaces but, as with so much else in her life, she had learned to overcome her fears. The battle between her iron will and her psyche filled her blood with a dangerous cocktail of hormonal drugs, however, the most plentiful of which was adrenalin. Within moments her face was burning and her breath was short. And her nipples were hard and her loins were burning. Every time she looked up, there was Harry, slim and sinuous, slithering away from her with the merest sibilance of crisp cotton over slick steel.

By good chance the women had started their sortie just at the right moment. The powering-up of the great engines had summoned all the men of 13 Int. to arms. There was no one at all in the accommodation areas now. Everyone was at his post, and all the posts were up on the command bridge. The engines would hold up or they would not; no guarding or nursing could change that now. There was no more food to be eaten; no more coffee to be drunk. And if anyone got caught short, the water bottles and the plastic bags were to hand. Even the communications kit was closed down now and Op was standing at his steel-guarded window with the rest of them, for there was no one left that they would listen to and nothing left to say. The men were in full battle dress – or as close to it as they could manage now. They were four hours at most from the climax of their mission and all the way in they would standing to and waiting.

Harry eased the cover off the air duct and lowered it silently to the floor. Lithe as a constrictor, she wound her way out into the dark room. She pulled a torch from her pocket and flashed it around. The computer was sitting dark and dead and she crossed to it at once. Pitman eased herself stiffly out as the screen lit up and the library was flooded with flickering light. Harry tapped the keys and patched the monitor into the security net, revealing the bridge at once.

'Shit!' whispered Pitman, running an experienced eye over the picture. 'These guys have been busy, and they're loaded for bear with a vengeance! You see what they've done? Each of those embrasures has a pair of men and at least one Stinger. Looks like the ones at the front have all got two Stingers and one man strapped in tight. Jesus! This is something to tell the grandchildren about.'

'If we live to have any,' said Harry.

'Can you traverse that thing so I can see the full disposition?'

'No chance, Angela. If they even dream they see the security camera move they'll be down here like gangbusters. You know that. Anyway,' the picture died and the screen filled with icons, 'we're not here to sightsee. Let's get this modem connected to the ether and then set the videophone.'

But like many an apparently simple plan it was easier said than done and as Harry worked and Pitman watched, their time was running away.

'There she is!' exclaimed Professor Miles, looking at the little screen in the harbourmaster's office which was video-linked to SAC for the evening. The screen showed a schematic of the waters off New York Harbour and there, moving unmistakably down towards Cholera Bank, was the bright display emitted by *New England*'s automatic identity beacon. 'She's making what? Fifty knots?'

'Dangerously fast for those waters, ship that size,' said the harbourmaster.

'But you know which way she's coming in,' enthused Miles, carried away by the fact that they had found her, too excited to see the implications.

'Too late to change her heading now,' said the harbourmaster, speaking more loudly so that his voice carried into the conferencing facility. 'She'll have to come in through the main harbour entrance. We'll stop her at Brooklyn Bridge if not before.'

'Please arrange to do that, sir,' came a distant, anonymous

voice. 'In the meantime, gentlemen—' Whatever else was said died as the sound and then the picture vanished.

The silence and the shadows washed into the office, then the harbourmaster was up and reaching for the phone. 'That's it,' he said. 'He's coming in past Staten Island. The hogwash about Hell Gate was a bluff after all.'

Only the straps held Tom in the powerboat as it hurled forward towards the shipping lanes at full throttle. No one had bothered him so far and he was mildly surprised that there had been so little shipping, military or civilian; and no air traffic to talk of at all. He knew this state of affairs could not last very much longer. He lifted his hand from the steering wheel and twisted his thick, unhandy, insensitive wrist until he could see the illuminated display of his watch. It was after ten. If they didn't stop him soon, he thought, he would be up with Lady Liberty herself, under the lights, out in the open, as exposed as the Staten Island Ferry, and that would never do. His mind and spirit as carefully insensitive as his body, he pushed the throttle forward and hammered onwards at the better part of sixty knots towards the bright horizon.

The F18s came out in a squadron of four. During the day they had dropped out of a clear blue sky onto a discreetly isolated runway of John F. Kennedy Airport overlooking Jamaica Bay on the south side of Long Island. Here they had refuelled and sat waiting as helicopters buzzed around them delivering and removing maintenance personnel and equipment. By the time they were called to action it was well after ten at night and the weather had closed in. Still they went up through the low, drizzling cloud, confident that they would have no trouble locating their prey, led by the strong signal from its identity beacon. And so it proved. They slipped away over the incoming shipping along the Fairway from the Great South Channel, dropped to zero feet and skimmed in through the low overcast over the outbound fairway, the telltale signal in their sights. Neither fairway was particularly busy. None of the pilots – nor the men at SAC they were reporting to – were of maritime background. SAC was not communicating this down the 'need to know' chain anywhere near as low as the New York

278

harbourmaster now they had closed the conference facility down, so no one saw anything unusual in a ship the size and speed of *New England* passing through these waters unremarked and in the wrong lane.

The jet jocks armed their smart seekers, watching the head-up bifurcate as the upper quadrants displayed what the rocket's onboard guidance system could see while the lower continued to show the signature of the radio beacon. As the beacon settled brightly and unmistakably into the centre of the target area, the lead fighter pilot fired, and watched the picture in the upper quadrant unroll as a haze of cloud, spray and water whirled towards him.

Tom heard the fighter aircraft and a kind of madness overtook him at the sound. It was not any desire to spoil the boss's plan, or even the faintest dream of survival. It was, if anything, a desire for one more gesture. A wish to go out laughing. Tom began to jink the powerboat to the limits of what it, and he, could handle. As the missile, designed to target on the heat from *New England*'s jet motors, came screaming down towards him, Tom had just a fleeting chance to whirl the boat out of the way. The rocket sensed no heat. The powerboat had not been illuminated. It was moving, suddenly erratic, at nearly sixty knots, and the man at the wheel was still smarter than the bomb. The missile plunged into the water harmlessly. 'One up to me, you arrogant son of a bitch,' yelled Tom, then hurled the powerboat hard over, knowing there would be another on its way.

And as luck would have it, he turned exactly into the path of the second one, so that even had he been able to, he would not have felt a thing.

The powerboat's hull and the black box itself, under the beacon, had been packed with explosive. The leader of the squadron forgot his perplexity at the failure of his first rocket to hit and triumphantly reported the total destruction of the target and all who sailed in her as he pulled his F18 up over the fireball on Cholera Bank.

It was 10.30 local time. Ninety minutes to midnight. As Tom was enjoying his last laugh, *New England*, invisible, unremarked and unsuspected, was swinging round Montauk Point, turning south at a little over sixty knots, exactly ninety minutes north of Hell Gate.

Chapter Twenty-Two

The north shore of Long Island Sound is low and marshy for three miles or so before it gathers into the hills and bluffs of Connecticut and Massachusetts. The southern shore has no low plain but rises in cliffs and headlands straight from the water. On that night, the northern bluffs were shrouded in mist and the beginnings of rain. The southern cliffs, too, lost their heads in low clouds and their feet in the beginning of a sluggish fog which had begun to curl off the water soon after ten. Shipping in the three channels joining the Race to Throgs Neck was sparse, slow and careful. The pilots who had come aboard foreign vessels out at No. 2 Lightbuoy and who would give place to East River pilots down at Execution Rocks peered warily westwards through the gathering murk, feeling beneath their wise feet the surging of a spring tide which would crest in Hell Gate with a surge of more than four metres around midnight. It was lucky there was a calm this evening, they thought, or folks on FDR Drive might be getting their feet wet at the flood.

New England swung onto her heading at 22:30 on the dot. The backwash of her wake spread across the Race and added further complications to the Plumb Gut before crashing onto the New London shore. In the near-dark of her command bridge, Merrideth and Marshall stood side by side, their bodies indistinguishable from the shadows and their faces made even more weird by the light from the illuminated displays. The Differential Shipmaster program had been carefully set with the route between here and the Throgs Neck Bridge and the on-board computer systems honed its accuracy from ten metres to less than three. The echo-sounder and the radar equipment were all factored in as well so that all the American Dick King at the helm had to do was to stand there watching in wonder while the ship swept down the Main Channel, heading south and west, directly towards the heart of New York City.

Dick King knew these waters well; before the disease hit, he had been as keen a seaman as the late lamented Tom. Indeed, a neat little 30-metre ocean-going yacht was nestled in his berth on the Mystic River not very far north of here now. And she would remain there, unclaimed, for some time to come. But he had never dreamed of coming in past Rocky Point and the Six-mile Reef through East Long Island Sound at anything like this speed. The radar picked up the threat of a slow barge in the gathering fog ahead and adjusted the course slightly to sweep past her on the northern line, where the water was deepest. Then the echo-sounder called a discreet warning. The two commanders stepped forward. There beneath them, powering out towards the sea, was a submarine. But even as they registered it, they had passed it.

Had it only been the barge captain who reported the passage of a huge vessel running at more than fifty knots in the Main Channel of East Long Island Sound, the report might well have gone unnoticed. But when confirmation came from the commander of USS *Flatfish* as well, interest was stirred. Unfortunately, the messages did not arrive until well after eleven and so rang alarm bells in offices recently vacated by men assured that the danger they had feared was past. By that time, *New England* had swept past Horton Point and Falkner Point, and the waves of her passage were washing over Stratford Shoal as she entered West Long Island Sound, less than sixty miles north-east of her goal.

'Jesus, girl,' whispered Pitman in a flurry of tension. 'Will you shift that pretty ass of yours!'

The ass in question was all that was visible of Harry Newbold as she knelt under the table making some final adjustments to the modem and the little handset which was linked to it trying to tune the one to the other. The bright screen above showed a maze of icons and in the middle of them sat the white arrow of the cursor. During the last hour and more Pitman had watched Harry's nimble fingers tap in directions which complemented the shortcuts she had programmed into the computer in the engine control room. Now, each icon represented a whole program which would open under the cursor when the zero button on the handset was pressed. One wrong move on the keyboard, indeed any move at all on it, would trigger alarms on the bridge. Rather than think about this, Pitman watched Harry's ass, literally as well as figuratively. It was, in fact, a distractingly well-shaped piece. And the combination of tight cotton, blue light and mysterious shadow presented it to disturbingly attractive effect.

'There,' whispered Harry at last. 'All done, I think.' The curves and concavities under Pitman's eyes began to wiggle seductively as Harry backed carefully out from under the table. Bubbling with girlish glee which was seriously out of place in a whole range of ways, she held up the videophone for Pitman to see. The little screen showed exactly and clearly what was on the monitor in front of them. 'I won't move the cursor again,' said Harry breathlessly. 'But I could and it would work. As long as this is in range, I can control the whole system. Well,' she temporised with that occasionally devastating honesty of hers, 'I can for a couple of minutes until they break the connection or override me.'

'But it's the best you can do? It's all we've got?'

'Yup.'

'OK. Let's go.' Pitman knelt down and insinuated herself swiftly into the ventilation duct. Harry knelt to follow, automatically glancing around the room as she did so. Everything was exactly as they had found it.

'Hurry!' hissed Pitman.

Except for the computer! 'You go on,' breathed Harry. 'I'll just . . .' She crossed to the computer and reached behind the monitor. She snapped the rocker to OFF and watched the screen die. Then she glanced down at her handset. It was still bright. In the same way that a video player attached to a TV aerial can record programmes whether the television is on or off, Harry's handset was picking up signals direct from the computer via the modem to which it was now tuned. The monitor in here was incidental now. All that showed the machine was working was the red light on the computer box itself and the quietest of hums.

In the sudden darkness Harry groped after Pitman and slid into the duct behind her. And just in time. As she picked up the grille to snap it back in place behind her, the library door was thrown open. A pair of black Danner-booted legs strode in.

Stopped. Turned. The light came on. Harry remained where she was, frozen. 'No,' said a harsh voice. Merrideth's voice. 'Nothing in here.'

The relief made her begin to shake even before he turned. The grille, unsecured, trembled dangerously in its clips. But suddenly, unexpectedly and blessedly, an arm snaked round her waist and Pitman gave her a powerful, reassuring hug.

The moment of danger passed. The light snapped off. The door clicked closed.

'They know something's up,' whispered Harry.

'But do they have time to do anything much about it?' wondered Pitman.

New England surged past the Stratford Point light at nearly seventy knots and pounced towards the two Captain Islands while, all unknown to the two captains hiding aboard her, Merrideth continued his search. He had nothing to go on except a gut feeling and a firm belief in Murphy's Law. On this mission more than on any other, if anything could go wrong it would. It had been some unregistered stirring of the bridge programs that had alerted him and he checked all the computers first. But Harry was a neat worker as well as a very careful spy. Everything she had used she had returned to the state she had found it in – on the surface at least. So there was nothing to reveal her passing except perhaps some mingled odours on the ether – the ozone scent of freshly used equipment, a hint of her perfume, the musk of Pitman's body. In the engine control room these would have been lost beneath engine smells in any case; in the library Merrideth had sensed nothing of them because the nerves in his nose, like those in much of the rest of his face, were dead.

But still, with the disgruntled Bruce in tow, with Danny, Smell and Pain behind, he prowled onward and downward relentlessly.

Pitman and Harry dropped down onto the gantry on the wall of the lower hold. Apparently nothing had changed down here. The lifeboat's falls among the hangings and anchorage points of the upper deckhead were difficult to see, but Harry knew what she was looking for and made straight for it. She met up with the other three outside the boat and told them what she had done. Pitman's warnings cut through any congratulatory air, however.

'Merrideth's on the prowl,' she said as soon as she could get a word in. 'My advice would be to get back in the lifeboat and hunker down. He can't have time for a detailed search. This mother has to be coming down the Sound like a bat out of hell. And he can't afford to be hanging around here with a brick of men behind him once we get into the East River, can he?'

'No,' said Richard decisively. 'You're right. We'll still have Throgs Neck and Hell Gate to get ready in. *New England* will have to slow a little there. Harry, can you call up some kind of navigational information on that thing without ringing all the alarm bells?'

'That's what it's for.'

'Right. Into the lifeboat and let's have a look. Now is the time for a final briefing in any case. Pitman?'

'Sir?'

'You've got the best eyes. You've got stag. OK?'

'Sir.'

Things got very snug in the lifeboat. The three sailors lay side by side squashed along the keel. Ann squeezed in beside Bob so she could look over his shoulder at the tiny screen of the handset. Side by side, their flanks burned together from her knee to her breast. It was very distracting. Her body felt naked against Bob. Pitman crouched in the stern among their legs, her head almost invisible, using the lifeboat's gunwale as a parapet. Every now and then she would glance down or move her fingers, repeatedly re-checking the disposition of her ASP, though what use even Black Talon bullets would be here she could not imagine.

As *New England* surged past the Great and Little Captain Islands, Merrideth swung into the lower hold. His eyes were beginning to go, he knew, just as his ears and nose were, but the lights were bright enough to show him all the details he needed to see. The Semtex was piled, netted and secured. The hold was empty and, apart from the muted thunder of the engines, it was silent. He glanced up at the maze of hangings on the deckhead above and frowned. He was a meticulous man and he would have preferred to go down with everything squared away shipshape. But sorting that lot out was out of the question now. Even doing this patrol was a dangerous indulgence. If the SAC jet jockeys showed up now, there would be an appreciable gap in their defences. But from the sound of things, Tom's final ruse had worked well enough. SAC were too budget-bound to send more than one squadron of F18s. And now that they had been out, it would take someone very quick-thinking indeed, someone confident enough to break all the rules, to get them out again. Even so, that was one worry.

Another was the possibility that the tide would not reach its critical surge at midnight. Or that they might somehow miss it. They wanted to blow away as little of FDR Drive as possible. Not because they cared about it but because the sea wall on its outer side was their last real barrier, so the higher the water was when they tried to sail across it, the less they would have to destroy to make a slipway.

But everything would be rolling forward at the better part of one hundred miles an hour by that time anyway, so even if *New England* blew up on the Drive itself, everything ahead of it would be toast in any case, everything from the General Assembly building to the Empire State.

Merrideth turned. 'That's it, Bruce,' he said quietly. 'Back to the bridge.'

And, tidy-minded man that he was, he switched off the lights as he left.

The clouds were low. The weather over the Atlantic was terrible, as it had been on and off for weeks. The weather over the Pole was worse. The flight from London was late and those from Moscow, Tokyo and Beijing later still. There was a stack of airliners building up above JFK which barred even the four F18 jet jocks, spoilt as prom queens though they were, from landing. The fighters were curtly told to circle over the submarine exercise area out over the Great South Channel – which they did for nearly half and hour at little more than stalling speed while their increasingly irate pilots sent increasingly urgent messages to their superiors at SAC. SAC checked with all the local airports, civil and military, up and down the East Coast and as far inland as Chicago, but it was a bad night for air traffic and the jets were better off where they were. It was a bad situation, for three of the F18s were still fully armed and the danger of an accident rose exponentially with every minute that the fighters sat out there, waiting for a chance to land. This point was made to the

Eastern Region senior flight controller and to the Director of the Federal Airports Authority. The net result of all this was that just after eleven twenty the fighter pilots were told there would be a place for them at La Guardia. They would be given approach headings and finals in fifteen minutes' time or so. In the meantime they should hang tight, stay calm, double-check the safeties on their weapons and burn a bit more fuel because they were more than likely going to take the big loop up over New York City before dropping in over Paterson, Paramus and Hackensack down beside the Triborough Bridge low over Riker's Island on the northern approach across the East River near midnight. And with that they had to be content.

The five in the lifeboat had to be content with the darkness. At first this was no great burden; with the exception of Pitman, they were all glued to the bright screen of Harry's videophone handset. This was currently alight with a bright schematic of the channel which they were following and the shores on either side of it. *New England* herself featured as a bright dot hurling at incredible speed along the channel. The Captain Islands were falling astern now and the Stratford Point light was scrolling inexorably towards the bottom of the tiny screen as well. The Old Fields Point lay up ahead and, near it, Cable and Anchor Reef over whose back the flood was making rapidly now, adding another four knots or so to the hectic progress of that bright green dot down the last few miles towards Execution Rocks. Up at the top of the screen sat a neat little tool bar and beside it the pointer of the cursor which would open any of the other programs.

Richard began to stir. 'We can't hang about here watching videos,' he said in the paternally disapproving tones he usually reserved for the twins. 'It's time to swing the lifeboat out into the hold. Anyone seen the torch?'

Working in the dark slowed them down dangerously, but turning on the lights was too risky. So by the light of the lifeboat's two torches they disengaged the gears of the lifeboat winch and took as many turns round the drums as the falls would make, then one man and one woman each took the remaining rope in hand and strained. Bob and Ann pulled at one end, Richard and Pitman at the other, their plan simply to lift the lifeboat up out of its cradle, then swing it across the floor of the hold to the rear-facing slope behind the hill of Semtex.

Harry stood back, her fingers busy as she guided the cursor over the icons to open the mysterious HG program – if she could find a way into it. She glanced at her watch. If she hadn't broken into it within the next twenty minutes, she wouldn't need to; it would be running for real.

Richard and Pitman lifted the stern out of the cradle before Bob and Ann could lift the bow, but then the first two had to stop and hold their section still until the others caught up. As the bow came up out of the cradle, the boat swung out onto the falls – and the long cables groaned. Both teams staggered as the weight of the boat came onto the winch drums – but it was halved by each turn, according to the laws of physics, so the four pairs of hands and the four pairs of feet held firm.

'Harry!' hissed Richard. 'Get the light on the boat. Quickly, please. We need to see where we're lowering it!'

Harry put the handset down, picked up a torch and pointed it at the boat which was swinging like a pendulum above the Semtex hill.

'Right,' said Richard, 'when I say "now", I want us to lower the boat very, very gently.'

With Harry illuminating the lifeboat as though it was a trapeze artist at a circus, the four of them moved the boat out over the middle of the hold and lowered it onto the rear-facing slope of the Semtex hill. The keel made contact with the netting, then settled sideways until the Semtex nudged its port side. The net tightened over the grey plastic slope and that was all.

'She seems firm enough,' said Harry. 'Yes. She's settled fine.'

'Right,' said Richard. 'Stage two. And let's be quick about it.'

'Execution Rocks,' said Merrideth. 'We have to cut speed here.'

'Pull back,' called Marshall to the man at the helm. 'We go through here slow and easy or we lose control down in Hell Gate.' As he spoke, he glanced around the shadowy tomb of the command bridge. Sixteen men were at the wide, scooped windows, eight each side in pairs; Dick King was at the helm, Mac and Op at the opening into the dark, silent radio room, their last duty completed with Tom's last laugh on the radio. Merrideth stood at the clearview, watching over the sleek white dagger of the foredeck as the bright arch of the first bridge on the East River came down upon them like the blade of a guillotine.

'Slow and easy,' Marshall repeated, a break in the rumble of his voice.

New England's version of 'slow and easy' was unique. She came down towards Throgs Neck and the East River at more than forty knots, her scanners and read-outs feeding straight into her control systems. The massive surge she created in the narrowing waterway lifted her high on top of the flooding tide and, fifty metres above, the upper reaches of her radio mast smashed into splinters against the central span of the Throgs Neck Bridge.

'This is it,' sang out Marshall a little wildly as the whole bridgehouse lurched at the impact. 'Welcome to the Big Apple!'

The shuddering impact made the lifeboat stir, but it did not begin to slide. They were as busy as ants around it, using the two torches to light their work as best they could. One team was detaching the lines from the net and gathering them together like a vast spider's web to be attached to the lifeboat's stern by a strong line, thirty metres long. The bow was being attached to *New England*'s lower drawbridge. The touch of a button on Harry's handset would trigger the drawbridge's opening mechanism. The lowering of the drawbridge would launch the lifeboat and pull the Semtex hill forward. The launching of the lifeboat into *New England*'s wake would tip the Semtex to which it was carefully but distantly tied over the edge and into the East River where it could explode with relative safety, under water and well away from the petrol in the upper hold – thirty metres away from the lifeboat as well. That was the plan. It would work well enough if Harry could throw the right switch at the right time, if the force of the lowering door was enough to do the job, if *New England* was moving fast enough to propel the lifeboat forward when it went into her wake, and if the long lines held.

The second team was bringing down the strong, moulded plastic top to the lifeboat which they reckoned on securing in place so that even should the little vessel be totally submerged by the powerful forces they were hoping to unleash, they all stood a fighting chance of being cocooned in warmth, dryness and breathable air, for a while at least. How everything would hold up when the Semtex detonated, or if it sank without exploding and pulled the boat to the bottom of the East River with it, was anybody's guess.

'Bob,' called Richard as he worked. 'That impact must have been the first bridge. They're coming down on the flood. If they hit the first, they'll hit the others too, I guess. Can you remember the sequence of the bridges?'

'I can,' called Ann at once. 'Throgs Neck, Bronx Whitestone, Hell Gate, Triborough, Queensborough, Williamsburg, Manhattan and the Brooklyn.'

'Yes,' said Bob. 'They get lower and lower. Triborough may be a metre higher than Hell Gate, but if we hit Throgs Neck, we'll hit them all, like as not.'

'Then we've got a countdown. We can orientate ourselves pretty accurately without using the handset. Harry, keep trying to get into the HG program. But if you simply can't, you'll have to try something else.'

'Like mixing up the guidance? I could do that.'

'OK. But remember, the minute we come out of Hell Gate we've got to override everything and lower the drawbridge here.'

'That's factored in, but you know it'll ring alarm bells on the bridge.'

'With any luck it'll be too late to do much about it then.'

Richard and Bob were sorting and measuring lines. Then Bob and Pitman, fit, fast and without steel pins in their knees, went swarming up the SEALs lines on the aft drawbridge and fed them through the fastenings there according to Richard's instructions.

Two minutes after the impact with Throgs Neck Bridge, the bridgehouse shook again. Bob and Ann called out together, 'That's the Bronx Whitestone Bridge . . .'

'We'll be passing La Guardia Airport next, won't we?' asked Richard.

'Yes,' said Bob. 'They'll have to slow down past Riker's Island. Then it's the Hell Gate rail bridge.'

'Then it's Hell Gate,' said Richard almost to himself. Automatically he looked at his watch, flashing the torch down to see the battered old Rolex analogue face. It was 11:45.

The F18s were on short finals now, coming down through the

thinning murk over Hackensack, heading south-east at stalling speed, which was still far faster than normal approach speed for a commercial aircraft. The squadron leader was first, his wings empty. Immediately behind him, his second-in-command, a young man called Decker, burned with frustration that he had not been given the chance to demonstrate his prowess. As with most high-efficiency battle teams, fierce rivalry was used to give that extra sharpness to the battle edge, and there was no rivalry keener than that between Decker and his commanding officer.

Decker eased his F18 into that strange upside-down world immediately below the cloud base. The flat, greyish plain of vapour whipped past immediately above his cockpit as though he was scuba-diving beneath an iceberg. His eyes flicked up then down from the head-up displays to observe the jewelled brightness of Interstate 80 winding down towards the Hudson River and the George Washington Bridge. The voice of the air control officer at La Guardia droned in his headphones, giving the non-military version of final approach instructions – elevation, wind speed . . .

Precisely who cut into the monotonous instructions, and with what authority, was never really clear to Decker, but suddenly, just after 23:45, an urgent voice came onto the airwaves: 'It's still out there! *New England*'s still out there!'

Decker's commanding officer answered, cool as ever: 'Say again? We have destroyed *New England*.'

'No! She's coming down the East River. Jesus! She's just hit the Throgs Neck Bridge and the Bronx Whitestone. She's off La Guardia now, going at one hell of a . . .'

Decker knew his moment had come. He eased the control column slightly to his right and began to slide away. His headphones went mad at once as the men behind him called out, as his commanding officer barked orders, as the air controller at La Guardia started warning him he was deviating from the prescribed flight path. But Decker didn't care. He was in the grip of fate. The amount of collateral damage which might arise from hitting a ship full of explosives with a high-explosive warhead in the middle of New York City simply beggared imagination, but Decker didn't care. History was calling. It was him and *New England*, head to head – or rather, head to tail. Nothing could stop him now.

With her engines idling, the high arches of her water jets little more than a trickle, and all of her manoeuvring jets pointing forward and full on to slow her, *New England* came past the end of La Guardia's main runway and out round Riker's Island. She was completely under the control of the computer now and the moment she passed under the Hell Gate rail bridge, the HG program would click in. The only manual instruction would come when Marshall hit the red button on the console behind the helm to execute a hard turn to starboard.

As the power of the wind past the steel-scooped windows lessened, the roaring noise on the bridge diminished and it became possible to hold conversations. But no one had anything left to say. Those at the windows watched the lights of New York passing but their dead eyes saw nothing of worth or beauty there. They saw only enemy positions, possible attack points. They thought of no one in particular – of not one individual among the bustling masses up there. They thought only of the enemy who might at the last moment thwart their plans. They were in the grip of the kind of group hysteria that can take hold of religious sects, united in this instance by a sentence of death through the slow, irreversible, inevitable rotting away of living tissue by a mutant strain of Hansen's bacillus. Each and every one of them was all too well aware that no one could stop it, that no one cared. There was one man responsible: Hiram Hoover III. And the organisation for which he worked, the organisation which had allowed him to do this unspeakable thing to them, had no intention of punishing him; on the contrary, it was honouring him with the most prestigious post it could offer. Right now he was on the fortieth floor of the United Nations building less than ten minutes downriver, waiting for the fireworks to begin.

'Secure here!' called Bob.

'And here,' sang out Pitman.

The bridgehouse gave another lurch. This one was longer and more severe, shaking the hull like a rat being killed by a terrier. Bob and Pitman half jumped, half fell onto the deck. Pitman rolled expertly, trained in parachute drops; Bob landed less well but picked himself up with hardly a wince.

'That was the Hell Gate rail bridge,' said Ann.

'Triborough will be next,' panted Bob. 'Five hundred yards between them. Two cables.'

'We're in Hell Gate,' sang out Harry. 'The Hell Gate program's running. I can't stop it now.'

'Do what you can,' said Richard. 'We'll finish getting the lifeboat ready. We've got what, five minutes?'

'Six,' said Bob. But the word was lost in the shuddering as they scraped beneath Triborough Bridge.

New England came out from under Triborough Bridge and into the narrows south of Wards Island at thirty knots. Immediately the program kicked in full power. The water jets thundered and the jet engines fired, hurling the massive ship down towards Randalls Island with the sort of acceleration normally only seen in powerboats. The air battered past the open windows on the bridge where the men of 13 Int. stood ready, their concentration fine-honed to a higher plane of existence, far removed from the rotting corpses they were trapped within.

Then, with less than five minutes to go, things started to go wrong. The warning lights on the control panel began to flash and Mac, at the rear of the ruined radio room, lifted his Stinger to his shoulder and called, 'We've got company!'

Decker dropped his F18 so low he nearly blew the traffic off Triborough Bridge with his exhaust. *New England*'s stern filled the whole of his attack display at once and he hurriedly armed his heat-seeking missiles. The heat generated by *New England*'s jets would make this easier than shooting fish in a barrel. He tensed himself to fire.

But suddenly the heat register on the lower bank of jets began to fade. They were cutting power. His eyes flicked up from the read-outs. Scarcely able to credit what he could see, he realised they were opening the lower cargo drawbridge. At full speed, in the middle of the East River, they were opening their back door. The realisation was instantaneous. As was the decision to disregard it. The part-completed command to his right thumb went on. But in that micron of hesitation all his alarms came on. The F18 was being targeted by a ground-to-air missile. Automatically, Decker disengaged and pulled away, the speed of his reaction testimony to the training that qualified him to be in the cockpit of an F18. His eyes flicked wildly over his

293

instrument displays and then out into the sky, looking for the telltale of bright rocket exhaust. But all he could see were the lights of Manhattan and against these no exhaust would show up. Screaming with a combination of fear and frustration, he put the F18's nose straight up and broke the sound barrier in a perfectly vertical climb which, like the scream, did not ease until he was more than twenty thousand feet above the city.

Senator Charleston looked up, frowning at the sound of the F18 going through the sound barrier immediately above his head, and caught a glimpse of its improperly armed heat-seeking missile heading uselessly out over Liberty Island. He did not know what the sound was, but he had been on edge all evening. Only his dear wife's determination and excitement could have got him here tonight, after all that had happened. But she had so wanted to come. The authorities had been alerted, she argued. It was inconceivable that they would have allowed the party to go ahead if there was any danger. So he had steeled himself and agreed.

But there had been more than simple marital indulgence in the Senator's decision to come. The actions of 13 Int. in pirating *New England*, holding them all to ransom and planning their terrible revenge filled him with utter loathing. But so did all the actions of the man which had prompted them. Senator Charleston had an agenda of his own here at this reception; an agenda in direct opposition to the dreams of his beloved wife, but one he had been working on with increasing determination since the debriefing. For the Senator had arrived with every intention of confronting Secretary General Hoover and putting to him, face to face and man to man, in the most public manner possible, the terrible accusations of Merrideth, Marshall and their dying men.

But the Jellicoe Boys had managed to thwart him even in this. Such was the security surrounding Hoover as a result of their escapade so far, that he had found himself unable to get anywhere near his host at all. And now, at midnight, he found his own plans being subsumed beneath fatigue, hopelessness, old age, and a growing desire to be satisfied with his wife's simple pleasure at being here after all. And he was glad he had done nothing, for her sake. She positively glowed with pleasure as she mingled with the glittering array of celebrities. But the flat detonation which rattled the windows of the fortieth floor of the UN building and hushed the cheerful chatter of the Secretary General's reception chilled the Senator's blood. He could not get it out of his head that the men from 13 Int. would somehow manage to gatecrash the party. But then, he reckoned grimly, with a thought darker than any he normally entertained, it might be as well to go out like this, now, together, with his wife so happy. God knew what the succeeding years would bring but the Charlestons would probably never be at a party like this again.

Gloomily introspective, the Senator turned and looked out of the window, along the length of Roosevelt Island up towards Triborough Bridge. And as he did so, the terrifyingly familiar shape of *New England* came charging into the North Channel round the island, filling the narrow waterway, seemingly heading straight for him. And in that instant of stunning shock, the Senator was revitalised. There was, in fact, so much to look forward to – so much to do. Into his mind whirled a prayer for more time – a prayer it was already too late to pray.

Merrideth pounded down the internal companionways at a dead run, with Bruce and his brick close behind him. Merrideth held his 203, Bruce carried his Stinger missile, and the others were equipped with an assortment of weapons.

As soon as Mac had seen off the F18, the group of SAS men had sprung into action, Merrideth grimly certain that his earlier unease, so painstakingly examined and dismissed, was well-founded after all. Someone was down in the lower hold monkeying around with the equipment and a penny would get you a pound it was that arrogant bastard Richard Mariner. Whether they managed to blow away Hiram bloody Hoover or not, if Mariner was down here then he was personally going to settle his hash. It was little enough to ask of the last four minutes of life. He slammed through the door into the lower hold and hit the lights.

The rear drawbridge was half open and with a mixture of frustration, horror and simple awe, Merrideth saw that the untidy mass of ropes and pulleys which they had had no time to clear away since Marshall's arrival had all been put to shockingly good use. As the massive drawbridge door wound inexorably down, it was pulling the whole pallet piled with Semtex smoothly towards the opening. And slipping out across the hold deck itself, waiting to be launched, moved the lifeboat, sealed and shut tight, behind it trailing loop after loop of line attaching it to the Semtex.

Bruce, Pain and the rest crowded in. Merrideth's mind was racing. What could he do to stop what was happening? The answer was swift in coming.

'Bruce,' he bellowed, staggering forward into the gathering storm to position himself, 'give me the Stinger! Now!'

'They're trying to override the open door command!' called Harry, her eyes fixed on the little handset's bright screen.

'They'll be trying a damn sight more than that!' said Richard. 'Leave it now. We know they can't override it until the door is fully open. What can you do with the guidance program, Harry?'

'Like I said—'

The boat gave a lurch and all of them wedged tightly in the bottom flinched. They knew this was going to be a rough ride and they had emptied out everything that wasn't screwed down and then they had tried to pack themselves in with padding to protect them. They all wore lifebelts with wedges of polystyrene round their waists and inflated lifebelts round their necks, shoulders and chests. Even so, when the lifeboat moved, they were hurled forward down the tiny space towards the bow with threatening power.

Richard and Bob had laid down a series of lines calculated to tighten at different times and at different rates as the rear drawbridge swung down. The first series, which unknown to them Merrideth had already seen, was designed to move the Semtex towards the opening in the cargo bay. The second set, which had just engaged, was designed to ease the lifeboat forward and launch her down the slope of the drawbridge into the East River. The third set, thirty metres long, would tighten as the water pulled the boat away at nearly seventy-five miles per hour and would drag the Semtex over the edge and out of *New England* altogether. The instant they hit the water, Harry was going to screw up the guidance system so that *New England* would not go where she was directed. This interference could last for only a minute or two, but if the ship could not be handled at the critical moment and they passed their target, Marshall, Merrideth and their men would surely have no reason

296

to continue their wild dash to doom.

Merrideth had the Stinger on his shoulder and was peering through slitted eyes at the side of the lifeboat as it slid away. He pressed the button to start up the targeting. He pressed it twice, in fact, unable to feel anything through his dead fingers. He heard the hiss of the cooling system switch in. He prayed that Bruce and the others had had the good sense to keep well behind him. He closed the talon of his hand round the firing mechanism. The target jerked forward out of his view.

Screaming with frustrated rage, he hurled himself forward until he could see the boat teetering on the lip of the drawbridge. All he saw was the target, a dead black bulk against the shining, light-spangled water. He did not see the grandeur of Hell Gate behind with the shoulder of Roosevelt Island rising to the light at its far north point. He did not see the suspended tramway on his right hand high above the Roosevelt Island condos. He did not see the distant span of Triborough Bridge crossing to the Manhattan shore. He did not see the skyline rising brightly above the low, black sea wall, along the top of which ran FDR Drive.

He closed his fist and launched the rocket. It flashed forward faster than his eyes could measure and slammed into the solid side of the lifeboat.

Slammed in and cannoned off. In his mad desire to get close to the target, he had miscalculated – the missile had not travelled far enough to arm itself.

Its impact seemed to tip the balance of the lifeboat and as the rocket soared away along *New England*'s massive wake, the boat vanished down into the turmoil of the East River.

The lines between the lifeboat and the hill of Semtex wound out to their full length and tautened at once and the great pile of explosive was jerked onto the lip of the drawbridge. The lines gathered the cargo net into a massive bundle as they moved and the toils of woven plastic fibre gathered the screaming soldier to themselves. Like Ahab riding the back of Moby Dick, Merrideth disappeared out of the ship fastened to the pale mountain of Semtex.

In the lifeboat more than thirty metres away, things were even worse than they had imagined. *New England* had accelerated to the better part of seventy miles an hour down the straight section of the East River and at that speed, the water was only a little less solid than the sea walls on either side of it. But the game little craft held together and the fastenings kept the watertight top safely in place. Its occupants rattled around inside it like dice being shaken by an energetic craps player. Only the care with which they had padded themselves kept ribs, backs and necks from being broken, though there was some very painful damage being done to, and by, feet, knees and elbows. Bob and Ann were wrapped tightly round each other, and Pitman had wrapped herself round Harry and was somehow managing to hold her and the handset safe. Richard yelled, 'Now, Harry! Now!' and Harry obeyed. With her hands and her eyes fixed on the little instrument as though nothing else existed in the whole world, Harry punched in the final order to the modem in the rapidly departing ship's library.

'NOW!' screamed Marshall, and he hit the red button so hard he shattered his right fist. He felt no pain.

He had imagined this moment and had assumed Merrideth would be at his shoulder if and when it came. But there was no sense of loss or disappointment that the major hadn't made it in the end. He was somewhere aboard, Marshall knew. Fighting to the last to make this thing happen. And it was happening now. It was midnight, the tide was at the flood. Little more than a metre of wall stood above the surface and a couple of Stingers armed to explode on impact would clear that out of the way. All they needed was the roughest of slopes – perhaps not even that – and they were through. *New England* and everyone aboard her would be one massive fireball rolling across the black wilderness which had once been the United Nations building.

It towered like a bright blade just ahead and to the right, and behind it rose the other Manhattan giants. The low clouds were breaking and the moon hung behind the Empire State, magnified by some trick of the atmosphere.

Their lives could be counted in breaths now, in breaths and heartbeats.

'NOW!' called Marshall again. The men along the starboard side armed their Stingers and zeroed on the wall, waiting for the ship to swing in under the dictates of Marshall's broken hand upon the emergency right turn button.

And deep within the ship's guidance system Harry's little virus threw a switch, so that when the command came TURN RIGHT, the system read TURN LEFT. That was all. It was as simple as that. And it was enough.

Marshall stood, riven with disbelief as the skyscape of towers swung away on his right. The men at the windows lowered their Stingers, turning towards him. He raised the ruin of his fist. Drove it hard down upon the red button once more. His black glove burst. Pieces of his hand spattered across the console as though he had been shot. He felt nothing. Nothing but an instant of utter defeat.

New England was travelling at seventy-five miles an hour when her left side swung into the Southpoint seawall on Roosevelt Island. The power of her jets drove the under-loaded hull up onto the blade of land. There, amid a wasteland of wild overgrowth, untouched except by the men from Macey's and their fireworks, untended in nearly a century, stood the ruins of the old City Hospital, the Strecker Laboratory and the Smallpox Hospital. Into them *New England* tore with incalculable force. The petrol tankers in the hold ignited, detonated by the impact-sensitive device in the bow. The blast flattened the ruins of the ancient hospitals and rattled the windows of Manhattan, and a massive balloon of fire mushroomed into the sky. It rolled sinuously over the fireworks, setting them all off in one incandescent show.

Like Sir Justin Bulwer-Lytton, whom he had hoodwinked so effectively and whose death he had personally arranged, Merredith had thought of his own death and had assumed, especially recently, that it would be by fire, not water. And yet as he struggled ineffectually against ropes he could not even feel, let alone unloose, he found the chilly strangulation of the East River flooding into his nose and mouth as the Semtex to which he was secured plunged downwards. He was forbidden even a final sight of his men. Instead he was dragged swiftly and inexorably into the cold black depths and death became an icy hand pushing its fingers deeper and deeper down his throat. Almost the last thing he felt was the cold. And that in itself was a kind of victory, for it was so long since he had actually *felt* anything.

But then *New England* ploughed over the sea wall into the ruins on Southpoint and the impact detonator in her bow sent its brief message to the slave detonators in the Semtex and the explosive erupted. So that it could be said that Merrideth had foreseen his death accurately after all.

The lifeboat was tethered to the Semtex by a tangle of netting more than ten metres long and by Richard's thirty metre line. The explosion blew it free. Having dragged it into the depths of the river, the dead weight of the explosive now reversed the process with some force so that the buoyant little vessel, its watertight top still in place and its occupants battered and bruised but by no means beaten, exploded out of the river like a champagne cork.

Mrs Charleston joined her husband at the window just a moment after midnight, vaguely wondering how a wind had sprung up strong enough to rattle the windows. She nestled up beside him, full of excitement, life and love. She looked down onto the southernmost point of Roosevelt Island.

'Oh look,' she said, her evening rendered perfect, 'they've lit a bonfire and set off all the fireworks! How beautiful!'

And the Senator turned with more forcefulness and decisiveness than she had seen in him in over a decade. 'No, my darling,' he said with quiet but terrible authority. 'The fireworks are only just about to begin.'

Epilogue

The big black Jaguar E Type cruised down the suburban street like a shark on land. Abruptly its indicator flashed and it turned left between two unremarkable suburban houses. As soon as it had done so it slowed, coming to a stop with its sleek snout within a couple of centimetres of the bright security barrier. A uniformed corporal came out of a hut at one end of the barrier and crossed to the car as its window wound down.

The corporal found himself looking down into two pairs of the brightest blue eyes he had ever encountered. 'Sir?' he enquired.

'Captain Richard Mariner and son. Here for the ceremony.'

'Right, sir. When I raise the gate, please drive directly to the guardhouse. Do you know where that is?'

'We got a map with the invitation.'

'Fine. They'll give you the necessary ID and direct you on.'

'Thank you, Corporal.'

'Sir.'

The barrier swung up. The E Type rolled forward. Richard Mariner and son entered Stirling Lines, headquarters of the SAS.

It was mid-August and ferociously hot. Robin and Mary were currently cruising up the M6 in the Freelander, bound for Carlisle where Richard and William would meet them at Cold Fell this evening. Then they were all bound for Skye and for their summer holiday. Two weeks of rest, relaxation and relationship building.

This sidetrack to Stirling Lines wasn't helping matters but Richard felt that he simply had to go in spite of the fact that it added yet another grievance to the wall which was all too rapidly growing between Robin and himself. As far as she was concerned, he had gone too far this time. Throughout all the years of their marriage, he had often pushed her to the brink. He saw this as unavoidable circumstance. He always seemed to be where things

301

happened. He always seemed to be the one expected to pick up the pieces.

But of course Robin was the one who had to pick up the pieces after him when he was picking up someone else's pieces. And as far as she was concerned she had to do it once too often. He had put his life, their company and their marriage on the line again without even warning her, let alone consulting her. It was thoughtless, juvenile and selfish and she was not going to bloody put up with it any longer. Further than that she had not thought. Yet. As far as she knew.

'Are you and Mummy going to get divorced?' asked William now, his wide bright gaze seeming to shine across the sultry gloom of the E Type's interior.

'Of course not! Why do you think that?'

'Mummy called you "that bloody man". Mummy only uses bloody when she's very angry. Andrew Motion's mum and dad got divorced when his mummy got angry with his daddy. But that was something to do with the au pair. We haven't got an au pair.'

'Well, there you are, then,' said Richard, inspired. 'Look at that map, will you, old chap? Do we turn right here or left?'

'Starboard your helm,' ordered William. At the age of ten he was really beginning to explore the adult world around him, and to look more deeply into his father's and his mother's professions, prompted by his apparently more intelligent and mature twin sister. Richard obeyed without hesitation; William was a solid little navigator and seemed to have known port from starboard since before he understood left and right.

'Remember,' said Richard quietly, 'this will be a very sad and formal occasion. We are very honoured to have been invited. We must call everybody by their rank – just listen out for me. If in doubt, call them "Sir".'

'Even the girls,' asked William as a squad of mixed gender ran past in fatigues and white T-shirts.

'You may call any woman there "Ma'am".'

'Same as the Queen,' William informed him. 'Miss Featherstone says we must call the Queen "Ma'am" if we ever meet her.'

'Miss Featherstone is quite right, and I'm glad to see all that expensive education isn't being wasted,' said Richard. 'Knowing what to call the Queen is an important life skill. Here we are.'

'Andrew Motion says the most important life skill of all is to keep your parents together,' observed William seriously and thoughtfully as they walked towards the red-brick guardhouse.

The ceremony in the Regiment's cemetery was brief and quiet. None of the men of 13 Int. whose names adorned the simple grey-white stones beneath the winged daggers were actually lying under the turf. None of them had any serving colleagues in attendance. The Regiment had sent representatives as well as the burial detail, but no one else was there. For all of them, even for Merrideth, the SAS had supplied all the friends and family they had. All of the dead men had come from other regiments originally and had transferred to the SAS twelve years earlier. The regimental culture is that men who apply to go to Hereford consider themselves too good for their original squads. But the SAS looks after its own.

After the service, the men who had been detailed to mourn Bruce, Danny, Smell and Pain, Tom, Martin, Russ and Mike, Op, Mac and Doc went back to the club. Richard, William and the brigadier went to the mess with the men who mourned Merrideth. It was ever thus – though not in the cemetery, Richard had noticed. The gravestones stood side by side, officer and men all in a row. Marshall and his men would be commemorated, equally democratically, somewhere on the other side of the Atlantic, wherever they buried SEALs, no matter where they had died, or how or why.

At the subdued little reception in the mess, Richard sat with a wine glass full of sparkling Malvern water, talking quietly to the brigadier. William paid scant attention.

'We've given our evidence to the Committee of Inquiry in Washington,' Richard was saying. 'They'll publish a report, I know. No one in London seems to want to do one here.'

'We've been told to hang fire,' said the brigadier. 'It's not actually a Regiment matter apparently. Though that's not what the papers think, or the news services. The Jellicoe Boys ride again, I'm afraid.' He winced as he said the name.

'If you need me, just ask,' said Richard. 'I'm the only one who can give chapter and verse from beginning to end.'

'Even with the reports in the papers,' said one of the young officers, leaning forward and forgetting his funereal air in the intensity of his interest, 'it's almost impossible to tell what actually went on. Could you fill us in on the detail, sir? Off the record, so to speak? If that's all right with you, Dan.'

'Well, yes, Peter,' said the brigadier. 'I must admit there are details I would like to have a firm grasp of. I simply cannot seem to get their basic motivation clear.'

All the young faces round the table – and even the brigadier was a good ten years his junior – turned towards Richard. Something about the intensity, the respect in them, caught William's attention then. He looked across the crisp white linen to where his father's long, familiar fingers toyed with the stem of his water-filled wine glass.

'Well, obviously,' said Richard slowly, sorting things out swiftly in his mind, 'obviously it all began in the Gulf. But perhaps a little further back in time than you might think . . . Have any of you heard of Ras Al'I? No? What about Hansen's disease?'

'Miss Featherstone,' said William at once, 'says that's another name for leprosy.' Then, seeing that everyone was looking at him, he shyly added, 'Sir.'

'Look at this,' said Robin, coming across the sitting room at Cold Fell later that day. 'I brought it up from Ashenden specially to show you.'

Sir William looked up from his *Daily Telegraph* and the new Lady Heritage put down her well-thumbed copy of *Manon des Sources*. 'This' was a postcard. 'It's from Bob and Ann,' said Robin. 'They're on holiday too.'

'Really? Somewhere exciting?' asked her father.

'Somewhere romantic?' inquired her stepmother.

'Neither. Somewhere isolated. They're in a place called Valentine, Nebraska.'

'It sounds romantic,' observed Helen. 'Well, more romantic than some places. I once met a Swiss girl in Sainte Maxime who had honeymooned in East Grinstead and considered that *extremely* romantic.'

'No, they haven't gone there for adventure or romance. Well, they have, I expect, but you know what I mean. Or for a honeymoon. Yet. No. Ann took Bob there because it is the furthest you can get away from the sea in the whole of the United States.

She got a map and ruler and she measured it. There's nothing particular there, but it's over fifteen hundred miles away from the coast in every direction! Isn't that a scream?'

'Very amusing, dear,' said Sir William, picking up his paper again. The headline on the front said, 'FIRST AMERICAN SECRETARY GENERAL RESIGNS BECAUSE OF GULF WAR SCANDAL'. In smaller writing it added, 'UNITED NATIONS IN TURMOIL AS SENATOR CHARLESTON LEVELS CHARGES'.

Helen pushed her book further away and held out her hand for the postcard. Her placid Provençal face was folded into a frown, for she had seen far more than her bluff husband in the words and tone of her stepdaughter. 'Where is Mary?' she asked quietly.

'Up on the landing looking out for Richard. William phoned on the mobile when they came through Carlisle. They had one of their chats.' Since going off to boarding school together, the twins had become close companions with their own impenetrable, almost psychic, conversational codes.

Helen patted the seat beside her. 'It will be very difficult for Ann and Bob,' she said as Robin sat. 'But I know they will make a go of it.'

'Depends how much actual romance there is in Valentine, Nebraska.'

'Enough for those two, I should think. I will have to start looking out for a wedding outfit. But it will be hard for them. She will not give up her career. And Bob will not give up the sea. He will find it difficult enough to be that far away from it, in Valentine.'

'That's why she took him there.'

'A high-risk strategy, *mon ange*.'

'He's worth the risk.'

'He always will be,' agreed Helen companionably. 'It is hard, but men such as him are always worth it.'

Both of them knew they were not simply talking about Bob and Ann. Robin herself had for some years mentally been keeping Richard in Valentine, Nebraska, asking him to stay as far away from the sea as he could, fearing that it would be the death of him. A fully qualified ship's captain herself, she never gave a second thought to it when she herself went off in a boat, but for

305

him she had begun to see blue water as The Widow-maker of legend. But with the able assistance of a perverse fate, he had answered her loving requirements by getting lost in the storm of the century, being marooned on Tiger Island in the China Seas, dashing off after *New England* in *Hero* and becoming closely acquainted with death at Hell Gate. But he came back. Time after time. And this time, too. He would be here soon, bright-eyed, aglow with enthusiasm, irresistible. And they would be off to Skye in the morning.

And Heaven knew where after that.

Helen was right. It was hard. But was he worth it? That was the sixty-four thousand dollar question. Was he worth it? *Bloody man* . . .

Mary erupted into the room, all flying elbows and knees and blonde curls. 'He's here,' she shouted. 'Daddy's here! Oh, this is going to be the best holiday ever!'

Whether this was the elegant timing of fate once again or her twins' simple genius with poor Andrew Motion's life skills, Robin never knew.

In Friesland also it was hot that August; hotter in fact than in Hereford or Skye. The little resort of Harlingen sweltered under tropical skies. The Waddenzee wavered under a heat haze like boiling mercury and a couple of kilometres south the Ijsselmeer seethed and steamed. All along the inland edge of Harlingen's North Sea beaches stood little beach huts extended into summer residences. Here one-room chalets boasted twin bunks with sliding doors and great swansdown pillows, bright-curtained windows, clean pine furniture, peace, privacy and free clogs. Here Harry Newbold and Angela van der Piet had come to rest, together, for a while. Harry remained beside Angela because to part from her would simply hurt too much. Like the rest of *New England*'s crew, she had been paid off after the loss, but well paid, by a grateful company taking much of the credit – and free publicity – for saving every major head of state alive; and Tom Hanks. She had been ready, willing and able to take a long holiday in Europe.

Why Pitman allowed Harry to accompany her home to Holland she never said; perhaps as insurance should the false papers or the hot money be called into question. But even when she had reached Holland safely Angela had not waved good-bye to Harry, so perhaps there was more to it than simple insurance.

They had been here for ten days so far and nothing had come of their easy intimacy. But time was running out and Harry was getting desperate. She lay now on one of the beds in the tightest of her high-cut bathing suits, one leg folded, thigh calculatedly akimbo, like the trunk of a fallen tree. Over the top of an English language newspaper she watched Angela as she finished her exercise routine, the green T-shirt and Calvin Klein shorts she favoured darkened intimately with perspiration. They would go for a swim later, when the fierce heat went off the golden sand. And take their bikes out in the cool of the evening, riding out to a little inn near Leeuwarden, further inland.

Harry's eyes were blind to the newsprint. Even had she actually been interested in British news, the story of an Essex fisherman who had hoped to catch a bass in the mouth of the River Thames but who had actually pulled ashore the late Sir Justine Bulwer-Lytton, missing since his mysterious disappearance some weeks ago, would hardly have held her love-smitten attention, since she had no idea how intimately that strange event was bound up with her own recent experience.

Angela had brought the paper back from Leeuwarden with her yesterday when she had returned from a mysterious little foray alone, which had terrified Harry with the thought that she might not return at all. The fact that she had done so at once gave Harry renewed hope and had spurred her to consider more positive action. The revealing costume had been donned – and had apparently gone unnoticed. The gestures had become franker – as unmistakable as she dared make them, in fact. The looks more lingering and, she prayed, seductive. But she had balked at making physical advances for there had not been the slightest intimation of response from the woman she loved. And the risk of alienating her through precipitate action was more than Harry dared face.

And yet the sight of Angela exercising, the uncalculated, intimate glimpses their proximity afforded, robbed Harry of breath and sleep. She accompanied Angela to the restaurants and snack bars where Angela consumed wide varieties of local fare, fries and mayonnaise, but Harry herself had no appetite.

About the only thing that passed her lips apart from breath was her fingers as she chewed her nails. She was doing this now, holding the paper one-handed, while Angela, her feet wedged under the bed foot, her legs slightly parted, finished fifty sit-ups, fingers laced in the sweat-darkened curls of her nape, elbows to knees, T-shirt gaping at the neck as she curled.

Then, having completed the final series, she leaped to her feet and turned, still fizzing with energy. Lifting the hem of her vest distractingly high, she mopped her face with it, then she threw herself down in a chair by the pine table. She reached down into a kitbag which had gone with her to Leeuwarden yesterday and had come back with more than an English-language newspaper in it. It made a disturbingly solid thump as it landed on the plain pine boards. Angela delved into it while Harry laid the useless paper aside.

'Here,' announced Angela unexpectedly. 'I got you something else.' She pulled out a book and lobbed it. Harry caught it easily and looked at it. *The Poems: Sappho of Lesbos*, said the cover.

Frowning, Harry looked up. Angela was deep in the kitbag again. Only the blonde spikes of her hair were visible above its woven black sides.

'Poetry?' said Harry quietly. 'From you, Angela?'

'We got to meet halfway, Harriet,' said Angela, her voice deadpan. 'Read me some.' Harry opened the book at random and obediently began:

> He is more than a hero
> he is a god in my eyes
> the man who is allowed
> to sit beside you . . .

There was a strange sound which made her look up.

Angela was sitting watching her; her eyes were almost black, the pupils were so wide. She was breathing through flared nostrils and slightly parted lips. Her hands were busy with something wrapped in cloth on the table, but all of her attention, suddenly and breathtakingly, was on Harry.

'Go on, Harriet,' said Angela quietly.

Harry's eyes went down to the page.

> If I meet
> you suddenly, I can't
> speak – my tongue is broken;
> a thin flame runs under
> my skin . . .

She stopped, simply unable to read any more. The words of the poem were coming true for her. Her tongue was broken. Her skin was on fire under Angela's unwavering, all-engulfing gaze. She could feel the blood drumming in her ears and she was running with perspiration as though she had been exercising side by side with Angela. She began to shake, her head whirling, faint as death.

Angela's hands stopped moving. The pale cloth was unwound and tossed aside. The last of yesterday's purchases lay naked and wicked in the afternoon sun. Steely, skeletal; familiar. 'Come over here,' she said, her voice low, seductive, irresistibly tempting. 'Come over here and I'll show you how to field strip a nine millimetre ASP . . .'

Acknowledgements

I read more than sixty books in researching HELL GATE but it would hardly be of use or interest to list them all. The most important in the story should prove enough for even the most intrepid armchair adventurer or soldier, and to each and all of the men and women who wrote them or who stood at their centres I extend my deepest respect. Except, perhaps, for some of those about the IRA.

Because of Harry and Pitman, who were always the way they were almost without conscious design on my part and certainly well before their chosen style and orientation became so fashionable, books about women in the Forces were of the first importance. I most strongly recommend Sarah Ford's fascinating ONE UP (HarperCollins, 1997) and Kate Muir's ARMS AND THE WOMAN (Sinclair-Stevenson, 1992); Jenni Atkinson's A GIRL IN SQUARE RIG and Dea Birkett's JELLA also detail the lot of women afloat. Of the books about the SAS, I can do no better than to recommend, alongside ONE UP, Andy McNabb's BRAVO TWO ZERO (Corgi, 1993) and Chris Ryan's THE ONE THAT GOT AWAY. All soldiering buffs will also be up to their armpits with books about the SAS: its formation, history and so forth. Every library and bookshop I have visited during the last few years has been packed with them. This is also the case with books about the Gulf War though I relied most strongly on the books named above (and Ms Muir's), Stanwood, Allen & Peacock's THE GULF WAR: A DAY BY DAY CHRONICLE (Heinemann, 1991) and, of course, General Sir Peter de la Billiere's STORM COMMAND (HarperCollins, 1992). The names of Dall's mercenary group were taken from Peter McAleese's NO MEAN SOLDIER (London, 1993), which is also a fascinating read. The ending of the book would simply not have been possible to write without the help of Kelvin Hughes who, as always, discussed my research requirement in patient detail and then supplied charts and Pilots of the East Coast, New York harbour and the East River. What *New England* passes in her last wild dash is there, cable for cable, bridge for bridge.

In fact, HELL GATE began with a pair of newspaper stories, one by Sean Ryan, *The Sunday Times*'s science correspondent, published on 5 March, 1995, under the self-explanatory title JET-SHIP POISED TO SHATTER SPEED BARRIER; the other by *The Times* foreign correspondent Daniel McGrory, published on 3 November, 1996, under the title CIA STUNG BY ITS STINGERS. The relevance of both of these to the overall shape of the plot should I hope, be obvious. I contacted neither of these journalists and my story is a fantasy entirely independent of their fine reporting. The same is true of the wealth of video-TV- and radio-generated material I used, from the excellent series about the Gulf War in its totality, to the individual programmes about Gulf War Syndrome and – more disturbingly still – about the effect of depleted uranium ammunition on the soldiers involved. It was the striking similarity in some of the symptoms described to those of Hansen's disease or leprosy which gave me the final piece in my narrative jigsaw.

As is often the case with my work, all the research is far outweighed by the kind support and guidance given by a range of friends and experts whom I am pleased to acknowledge here. I must thank Geoff Corkish of the Isle of Man Steam Packet Company, Captain Dermot O'Toole and First Officer Dominic Bell for showing me around the bridge of the SEACAT I.O.M., and explaining to me how much of the equipment there is used now – and how the next generation of this equipment might be expected to function in the near future. I must thank John Murr for his advice about shipping matters and, through John's good offices, Zarina Bhesania of Richards Butler for some direction as to the current standing of barratry in the statutes.

As always, I must extend a wealth of thanks to friends on the Isle of Man, not least the librarians in Port Erin, Castletown and Douglas, who help me with research and are unfailingly generous with their advice and their time. The list of friends on the Island who listen, discuss and offer their advice and experience is endless, but special place must go to Alec and Joan Rodden who gave me free use of their spare rooms and computer systems. A special thanks to David Taylor for a range of advice – from computing to sailing. But especially to Alec again for retrieving some unaccountably missing files from the depths of his machine memory. It would have been a much shorter book without you Alec.

I owe an enduring debt of thanks to the staff at the Sevenoaks Library who have left no stone unturned in helping with my research. Full time and part time, they have been more like friends than public servants. And good luck at university, Amy.

I owe a debt of thanks to Max Frost for finding out the last few details I simply could not get hold of about the current state of Southpoint, on Roosevelt Island, straight off the Internet. Research just doesn't come any more current. Thanks, Max.

Although my writing is carefully calculated never to interfere with my 'day job', I must as ever thank colleagues at The Wildernesse School for their help and advice, from John Wright and Paul Clark with information about weather sats, the North Atlantic and New York, to Ron Herbert the headmaster and law tutor for his thoughts about barratry, piracy and suchlike in the early twenty-first century, and to Roger Hood (and his sister-in-law Rosemary Hood) for priceless, and extremely current, information about exactly what it is possible to do with a phone, a modem and a computer network.

I could not have written HELL GATE in its present form without the commentary of my most active critics, Juliet Evans and my wife Charmaine, who went through the early drafts re-balancing soldiering with storytelling, reckless adventure with adult relationship. And without Charmaine's forbearance as she (yet again) took the boys off and amused them for ten hours a day during the long vacation – followed by one complete week in the autumn while I wrote, edited and printed from dawn to dusk uninterrupted. So much of Robin is in Cham – even as I vanish annually into fantasy as Richard vanishes into his adventures. The domestic effect is much the same, I have to say. And, needless to say, Guy and Mark are the backbone of William and Mary in all sorts of ways.

Finally, HELL GATE would not have been as authentic without the selfless and time-consuming help of Dale Clarke, who wishes simply to be known as my armaments officer – in spite of the fact that for some parts of the military sections he was almost co-author. Much of what is wrong with those sections is down to me. Most of what is right is down to Dale.

Peter Tonkin, Sevenoaks and Port Erin, 1997.